the HOUSE
of HENSHAW

a Love Story *at the* Dawn
of the American Revolution

H. M. MAST

ISBN-13: 979-8-218-43503-5

For those who escape into stories to heal.

the SPRING SOLSTICE REVEL

March 14th, 1773

Barrels roll like thunder through the Boston Port, pushed to the weary chant of sea-shanty voices. Rising over working men's breath, the songs still in the air like water tossed on a frozen day. Yet, shatter the salt-worn wood, and give birth to a gilded life, tumbling through folds of foreign silk.

Spices and teas and rich spirits will thaw the heart of New England winter.

I am a merchant.

I live for the loss, I die for the gain. I rise in the morning drunk on the bliss of discovery.

B oston's harshest winter, not yet officially passed, could take on the guise of spring, if the situation were correct. Which, to Martha Ann Gracey, this situation decidedly was. New ships at the port always meant a thrill. New cloths, eager to be stitched into the next piece of finery. New trinkets—pretty tins, letterboxes, and tea caddies; and William Gracey would let her take what she wanted, without slight to the record books. He had better things to do, hunched in the counting room under the shadow of a towering pallet of blackstrap molasses, scribbling in his diary, drunk on something more potent than his usual port.

Spring, perhaps.

Martha was accustomed to seeing oddities ebb and flow from the doors of *General Store, William D. Gracey, Proprietor,* but even if she thought a pallet of blackstrap was an odd choice of investment, she said nothing. A flash of green caught her eye. For someone with a newfound appreciation for the glamour of textiles, there was nothing better than being the daughter of a "general" proprietor. She saw all the finest things first, from all facets of trade. A bolt of green silk, catching the sun like scales on an iridescent fish, was more than enough to distract her.

"Papa!" She snatched it up. "How beautiful. For the Solstice party?"

"My dear." Mr. Gracey eyed her soulfully. "It's an exotic piece. One of the ladies of Beacon Hill might pay a pretty penny for it."

"Who, Mrs. Henshaw-Dunaway? She'd dribble sherry on it!"

Mr. Gracey flinched at the name. "Well, perhaps I could deflect her. But surely, we've an abundance of cloths off Lord Tucker's sloop this morning. Go and see. I saw a blue satin. You can have it with no slight, I'll mark it as damaged at the dockyards. There, there, please don't pout!"

Martha did pout, but dropped the silk with a sigh. Mr. Gracey rarely pulled a win, and besides, he was right; the silk was far too costly to write off in the record books, so balanced they were in the direction of marked gains. Anything that came from Lord Tucker's sloops was sure to be fancy enough for the Henshaw-Dunaways' Spring Solstice party, mere days away. She made her way to the shop floor and fingered through the rolls of cloth. Yellow: decidedly not her color. Brown: too boring. A white with floral print: too homely, like a cottage girl (never mind that home was a cottage outside of the city).

At last, she found the blue satin, accepting it as satisfactory. Richard, Mr. Gracey's apprentice, hissed at her from the gap between his teeth, but nevertheless wrapped the cloth in paper and tied it sloppily with twine.

"Thief," he muttered, flicking the brim of his hat.

"You've been nipping from the snifters," she shot back. "I can smell it."

Richard grunted, settling onto his customary stool and doing nothing to hide the damp glass just beneath the lip of the counter.

"Papa?" Martha rounded the door of the counting room.

The counting room…where her childhood brimmed from open windows, catching snowy dust in beams of sunlight. Where so many times, she'd laid on the floor in front of the grate, pitting corn-husk dolls against each other while Mr. Gracey mused over his poetry. It was a wide open room, low-ceilinged, the bare joists clinging with bark and years of grime, pungent with the smell of must masked with myrrh—William Gracey's attempt at cleanliness, which was to sprinkle oils to hide any offense. Stacks of books piled high in all corners. There were no shelves except one, high above the mantel, from which Mrs. Caroline Gracey was memorialized in egg tempera and glass. Against one wall stood Mr. Gracey's cherry bureau plat, stained with years of ink fingerprints and pock-marked with burn holes. Only that, and a high-backed leather chair, furnished the room. Otherwise, the expanse of groaning floorboards was merely a place to put "things" that wouldn't fit on the burgeoning shelves in the shop. Sometimes cloth. Sometimes millet, or nuts, or tea. And sometimes, as it seemed, blackstrap molasses.

"He'll be pleased," Mr. Gracey was muttering. A white afternoon sun bounced off the bald dome of his head. "Half a pallet to Sanders, yes, half a pallet to the distillery–"

"I've taken the blue satin." She frowned, tucking the parcel under her arm. "Don't forget to mark it down." It crossed her mind to ask, but asking was opening a door to Mr. Gracey, one that she preferred remained firmly shut. He was a rambler when it came to things that interested him (and bored Martha), mostly tricks of the trade. She brushed past the pallet, her skin prickling with cut rope, and kissed him on the back of the head. From the corner of her eye, she caught a sealed crest at the top of a letterhead, clutched in his nervous hands. A scripted, simple *W.E*

"New merchant?" she asked, forgetting that the door needed to remain shut. She had a gown to sew, after all.

"What's that, my dear? Ah yes, yes." Mr. Gracey straightened his spectacles. "Wet goods, spirits and spices…"

But Martha was already gone, slipping out the door and skipping through the alley behind Ann Street.

❀

The gown was beautiful, even if it wasn't green silk. Trimmed with white lace and ribbon, every stitch was deliberate. Blue *was* her color. White was the perfect contrast, to compliment the bends of her wrists. Earrings would brush the angle of her jaw, just so. Her scent would be roses; her hair would be high, studded with pearl pins.

On the day of the party, she rose and took a cup of Hyson tea and a pathetic spoonful of hasty pudding. Nothing else would be eaten until she arrived at the Henshaw-Dunaways; she'd sewn that gown with her smallest corset in mind. Besides, she was far too nervous to eat. Who would she meet at this party? It was possible to meet very exciting people–pretentious people, but the sorts that could nevertheless wonder how a cottage girl could present herself so well. At least, she hoped that was what they wondered; she assumed it, or she wouldn't have been invited to revels like that in the first place. And she certainly wouldn't be giddy with the idea that she might dance with Robert Henshaw.

She squinted, following the form of Judith Beecher, (the hired Mrs. Gracey) as she bustled here and there, pinching the curtains and shuffling coals. Hawkish Judith had tended to Martha since the day of her birth, yet still, after twenty years, never ceased to be appalled by her behavior. She was a round woman with a rolling gate, testy and annoyingly Puritan; since Mr. Gracey had never found it in him to remarry, Judith had been fair enough a substitute. She plodded, her weight upsetting the groaning stairs, scrubbing just enough clothes and spending just enough time in the kitchen to keep her pay in the pocket of her apron.

As Judith brushed her hair with quick fingers, Martha watched herself in the mirror. Her hair was copper red, her skin fair; her beauty was definite, though not conventional. She was too thin (having grown on her own curated regime of quick bites and long hours, wandering outdoors) and her rosebud mouth didn't smile often. Her blue eyes were unreadable, sea-glass above a button of a nose. Yet, as Judith sculpted and curled her hair into a sunset tower, she was confident.

"Your dress is cut too low," muttered Judith, patting powder.

Martha glanced at her fingers. They were trembling. The room was cold; despite the white glare of the sun it was only March, but she knew it was pent anticipation.

"At least I know you'll be dancing with Mr. Henshaw." Judith poked Martha's shoulder in warning. "No nameless reprobates, I don't care how much you like drooling over new men."

Judith liked Robert Henshaw because he was a gentleman.

"I'll dance with many men, I'm sure." She spoke pertly, but for once, Judith was right. Anyone who saw Martha and Robert Henshaw together just—*knew*. Her cheeks warmed, and she turned to Judith to receive a brush of rouge. "Thank you," she added grudgingly. "You've done a fine job with my hair."

"At least Mr. Henshaw has you wearing your stockings and busk, like a real lady." Judith circled, a pestering crow, pulling and pinching her masterpiece to faultlessness. Stockings were pulled over slim white legs, silk garters tied, corset strings reeled like a fishing line.

Martha bit her tongue.

Her mind wandered to Robert. Revels were pivotal moments when it came to him; it was fine and one thing to walk with him to the city, or meet him at the cottage for tea. But to slip her hand through his arm, at a party, where everyone could see—it spoke. Frances and Hannah, (his stepsisters by Mrs. Henshaw's late marriage) were her closest friends, and both would be sure to confirm his interest. She needed it; something delicate craved the assurance. Robert Henshaw was, after all, gentry. Head of the House of Henshaw. Not the most prominent mercantile house in Boston, but it was a name spoken with pride and grandeur.

She frowned at her hands. If she thought about it too hard, the familiar irritation rose, of trying to make sense of something that didn't have an answer. Why Martha Ann, shopkeeper's daughter? There were other ladies, born in the houses that had not long ago been shut doors to her. Ladies who would've suited him much better. But Robert—Robert was different. Robert had opened those doors; he'd led her beneath crystal chandeliers, down halls with marble floors. He'd watched her fingers brush damasks and satins from rich, exotic places. Perhaps it was how simply she fell into those things that induced her craving for them. Besides, Robert was easy; if she didn't curtsey quite low enough or accidentally let out a squeal of excitement, it was effortless for him to quietly correct her. Even if his ease and buoyancy faintly annoyed her at times, she still woke in the mornings with an elated heartache, and the wild desire to know what would happen next.

When Judith was done, she considered herself in the mirror. She picked up her fan, slid it open, shut, then open again, and held it against the satin. The blue pulled out the white lace as fresh as new snow, and her hair gleamed in the high afternoon light. Fighting the urge to bounce on her heels, she snapped the fan shut once more.

"All right then," she said brightly, ignoring Judith's scowl. "I'm ready for the wagon."

This revel, being the Henshaw-Dunaways', lent an extravagance rivaled only by the Tuckers (of Beacon Hill). It wasn't a small cottage party like the Graceys may've had, with close friends around the rough table, and her father sawing badly at the violin. No; this was the sort of party where she met people and wondered where they were from. Merchant friends of the late Mr. Henshaw and Mr. Dunaway, and all the ladies who pretended to be friends with Mrs. Henshaw-Dunaway (though she was loud, and drank too much sherry). It was the sort of revel that Martha preferred. She wouldn't be bound to close conversations; she would know few names.

For that reason, she was disappointed when Hannah and Frances sought her out, and suggested that she come upstairs to freshen up. She reluctantly agreed and kissed William on the head, turning in time to catch his watery smile; his dislike for Henshaws in general was hard to hide. Rounding the banister, she caught him drifting to the refreshments for a port.

"Martha, you look stunning tonight." Upstairs, Hannah sat at the dressing table, pulling out a powder tin. "Come here and let me touch you up. You've a little dampness on your forehead."

Hannah's cool fingers grazed her skin, calming her heartbeat. *She's so used to these sorts of revels, and I'm trying too hard!* She took a deep breath, loosening her shoulders. Hannah was an uncontested beauty; not interesting, but blushing and sensually tender. Her tone was loud, her trilling laugh like a bird song with a sly connotation, and it always meant good fun.

She dropped her eyes, squeezing her pinched toes in her dancing slippers, and wished she wasn't so quiet.

"Robert was asking after you," said Frances. Frances was a variety of Hannah washed out and wrung of color. She was pretty, but she wasn't threatening; without the blush of her cheeks and her round pink mouth, she might've been considered plain. Besides, her character was meek; she was nearly thirty and still Hannah's shadow. Martha felt briefly sorry for her.

"You can't be silly, Frances." She dropped her lashes.

"Don't act so demure." Hannah regarded herself in the mirror, adding a spot of rouge. "We both know that he walked you to the city last week. You and Robert would be a fine match. That face! You could stare at him all day and never get bored. The two of you together, it's like a fine painting in my head."

"I wonder if he'll ask me to dance," said Martha, shyly, though she was only pretending. There was a lot of pretending that must happen around the Dunaway girls, in order to be proper. A part of her hated it; it felt like betrayal, though she wasn't entirely sure why. She didn't want to be a cottage girl anymore.

"I suppose he will." Frances was breathless. "He asked whether you were coming."

"He's invited a fancy friend from New York." Hannah opened her fan with a flick of her wrist. "His cousin. I met him, many years ago. He's been living in New York as a bachelor. How fun!"

Frances blushed.

"Is he reputable?" asked Martha, though she was thinking about Robert. How fine he would look, in the best satin frock coat, the whitest cravat, gleaming buckled shoes. She pictured his face, and her heart flipped. Hannah was right; he was beautiful, and she loved to look at beautiful things. And how it had felt when she'd slipped her fingers through the bend of his arm! The soft velvet of his coat teasing her skin, how she'd fought to keep the smile from her face.

She frowned at the floor, the girl's voices muddled behind her thoughts. Now that she thought about it, she didn't remember saying a word, and–well, was she that uninteresting? Or had she simply been too thrilled to be with a man so pretty, she'd forgotten how to speak?

"I don't think him so reputable," Hannah was saying in a clipped tone. "I've heard a funny thing or two about the way he does business."

"What sort of business?" asked Martha, throwing off the vision of Robert.

"Trade," replied Hannah. "And law. Robert is jealous of him, for he won't agree to a partnership. What a shame. Robert says he has quite the talent, though he suspects he makes fast money. And to be a lawyer! How interesting."

"Can fast money, be decent money?" Martha asked, thinking it was a very good question.

"Well." Hannah was pert. "I do say, we can forgive it if he shows us a handsome face and a fat pocketbook. The handsome face not quite so important." She threw back her head and laughed; Frances gasped, but Hannah brushed her off and called for more port.

Martha was glad. The knots in her back eased, and the faint headache of worry faded under the haze of drink. She was ready to face the bursting room when she entered it a few moments later, newly powdered, smelling softly of roses. She kept her arm looped loosely through Frances's, saying their names to guests, lingering at walls. Her feet and hands were warm. *Heavens,* she thought, *I'm smiling. I wonder where Robert is? I hope he hasn't forgotten.*

But he hadn't forgotten, and in a manner very sure of herself, she felt that he was waiting for the proper time to approach. She caught his figure in a group of men, exquisite in a dark blue satin suit. Oh, she'd known that he was going to be wearing something blue! It was the perfect color for his full-blooded complexion, the gleaming gold of his hair.

"Let's say hello." Hannah tugged at her arm. "Come now, we all know why you're here."

Martha hesitated long enough to take him in. The structure of his bones, the way he stood tall and straight, hands behind his back. The squareness of his shoulders, and the breadth of his chest. She narrowed her eyes, watching as he recognized her. He smiled widely, and her belly curled; there was a light-heartedness in his expression that seemed almost forced. Was that a flicker of anticipation, or merely the luster of candlelight?

Oh dear. What a silly thought. She pulled away from the girls and smiled in return, her face flushing.

He was followed by a man who stood taller–remarkably taller–than Robert, who was a large man. The fancy friend from New York, she supposed, only he wasn't very fancy at all. He was a lean man, waist slim, shoulders broad, with a warm-toned complexion, as if he spent too much time by the water. In one hand he held a glass of brandy; his fingers were spotted at the tips with faded ink.

She could always afford a man a glance. But when she met the eyes of this one, her heart quickened, and she dropped her lashes. She'd never seen such eyes–large, burnished brown, with an expression of such irritated reserve it was nearly scolding. Dark brows drew close in a frown, and his mouth was set. Chestnut hair curled thick and unruly over his head, shorter than was fashionable, and around his ears, it was laced with soft gray.

"Miss Gracey." Robert bowed and kissed her hand. She flushed harder. "My cousin, Asahel Wyeth. Wyeth, Miss Martha Gracey, and you know Hannah, Frances."

"Asa." It was a clipped correction; the man's voice was low, coming from a deep place within his chest, and he frowned, dipping his head. His frock coat was dull grey, undecorated, and–*good heavens,* she thought. *What sort of fellow wears riding boots to a revel?*

"Welcome back to Boston, Mr. Wyeth," said Hannah, smiling warmly. The pocketbook must have won; she threaded her hand through the bend of his arm, not seeming to notice that he startled at the gesture. "We shan't be rude. This is our party. Let Frances and I introduce you to everyone, and you'll tell us about New York."

11

"Very well," replied Asa, though he still frowned. Then he added, "I wouldn't want to be any sort of trouble. I can manage on my own, all right." His accent was clipped, thick with a blunt tongue that she knew, having heard enough wily merchants in the counting room, was particular to New York.

"Don't be a fool, Wyeth," snorted Robert. "Go with the girls. I can't have you ruining a good time skulking about the walls."

"Robert, don't be rude." Frances's tone was soft, and she was blushing. Something in Martha's gut squirmed, and she caught Frances looking Wyeth up and down with her dull eyes. Briefly, she wondered why; though a good-looking man she couldn't deny, he was snuffed by the peacock that was Robert Henshaw. At any rate, a different sort of handsome, but a moody man was a waste of time.

Wyeth gave in, stepping away with a lady on each arm as if it were his solemn duty. Robert put out his hand to Martha, when Asa turned abruptly, pulling the girls with him.

"Miss Gracey. Your father. He's here?"

She started at the question. She didn't know anyone by Wyeth, though it was possible with Mr. Gracey's rambling, it had gone in one ear and out the other. Quickly, she answered, "Yes, sir. Over there, by the port."

She hated that she reddened. To those who knew the Gracey's, it wouldn't have given her a pause; but to those who didn't, the fact that her father relished parties, and often took to drinking more than was decent, could slight her own carefully maintained reserve. But in a moment he was gone, and her shoulders eased. How satisfying to have everything turn out so perfectly! To look so well as she glided with her hand on Robert's arm, feeling his eyes on her face.

She couldn't forget the day she had first seen him, standing between Hannah and Frances in the doorway of *General Store,*

William D. Gracey, Proprietor. How the brawny angles of his figure drew a stark shadow against the light of the outdoors, how struck she'd been by the sky blue of his eyes! Back at the cottage, she'd stared at the ceiling above her bed, thinking *God, I think I'm in love. I've never seen such a man.* It nearly made her silly, just to rouse that image in her head.

Yet, she'd considered herself, wondering what it meant to be in love with someone. What being in love felt like, or if perhaps she really wasn't in love, merely taken aback by his handsome face. But she was listless, and the things that used to occupy her time were boring and wasteful.

It didn't particularly matter, as she'd continued to wake with an ache in the pit of her gut, that she began to apply changes to herself for Robert's sake. As quiet as she could be on the outside, her mind roared with wild ideas; she was a cottage girl at heart, and Robert was gentry. If he came by to see her in his fancy frock and stiff cravat, he certainly couldn't catch her, feet bare and hair loose, coming in from the Common astride one of Mr. Gracey's boney mares. Oh, dear–no! It was a small sacrifice to make, and now, there was nobody else in the room. In bending candlelight, he watched her from across the dinner table. Everything about him spoke of strength; the strong angles of his jaw, the rise of his cheekbones, the ruddy glow that followed him everywhere he went. The very air around him was good-humored, unbroken by concern of opinion; he could have whatever he wanted, with that face, and such a laugh!

She blushed, twisting her hands in her lap, and forgot her inhibitions.

There was a period of repose before dancing. Clusters of skirts, low laughter, and clinking glasses scattered from the ballroom to the parlor, where the tables were brought out for cards. This fascinated her, so she stayed, lingering close to

Robert. Frances and Hannah followed suit; Hannah didn't seem keen to leave the sight of Asahel Wyeth, who was sitting at the card table smoking a pipe.

The table was four; Wyeth, Robert, and two of Lord Tucker's sons, brawny men with bright faces, James and Hiram Tucker. Martha considered them. *I haven't cared to look at the Tucker boys before, they're handsome fellows.* Yet, with bewildering haste, her attention pulled back to Robert.

"Dealer's bet." Robert shuffled the cards for whist. "Let's deal for the finest dance. The winner gets the prettiest lady."

"How can you be so cruel," said Hiram Tucker, laughing. "All the ladies are the prettiest!"

"It's not a ranking." Robert smiled brightly. "Whist is a game of luck, so there'll be no partiality. Four games. Winner of the first gets Hannah, the second Frances, and the third Miss Martha." As he said her name, he met her eyes and smiled. "The fourth, I'm afraid, will have to dance with my mother. May the best man win the most ladies."

He threw back his head and laughed. Hiram and James laughed too, and Hannah tittered.

Martha couldn't help but notice that Asahel Wyeth didn't laugh. In fact, his expression proved rather blank, and when he looked up at the present ladies (as if considering if they were worth his time) his eyes ran over Hannah and Frances (pausing at Frances, who blushed), then languidly considered Martha.

It was instinctual for her to measure her beauty sensibly; she knew how to turn her throat to catch the light or lift a hand just so to display the bends of her tiny wrists. The instinct wasn't lost. She turned her head, knowing exactly the way the lowlight caught her earrings–*Oh, whatever's the matter with me!* She flushed, dropping her eyes just as Wyeth's dark brows lifted in a faint show of awareness. When she regained herself, he was regarding the toe of one ridiculous riding boot.

Robert dealt and the men laid down their cards. Here and there, as the first hand ran out, Robert smiled at her, and she smiled back.

"Ha," cried James Tucker, "Hannah Dunaway, I'm a lucky man!" He gathered the cards.

"And I, a very lucky lady," replied Hannah. There was something distinctly perfect about the way that she dipped her head as she laughed. Martha felt herself dissipate, but she knotted her shoulders against the feeling. Hannah was not a competition. Besides, Robert was the only one who mattered—she dared to look at Asa Wyeth once more. Lean fingers toyed with the lid of a pocket tobacco caddy as if he were bored.

James dealt the second hand for Frances. *Surely, she wants to dance with Wyeth, since he has a fat pocketbook.* Plain Frances would do well to marry for money; she'd never have any complaints, content to be with any man as long as she was fed and entertained. Or perhaps, noting Frances's gentle enthusiasm, she would adore him too much, and stifle him to hatred. *Goodness!* She shook her head. *My thoughts are very bad today.*

Frances's round was won victoriously by Hiram, and Martha watched in silence as her own was dealt. Her heart picked up pace, warmth spreading to her fingertips. She would win Robert. She had to; it was fate—but then, Wyeth gathered up the cards, and her heart sank as her round was wasted. She fought her disappointment, yet, somehow the regret of not being "won" by Robert was a blow enough that she felt suddenly stupid, watching them play games over her time. She dipped into the shadows as James Tucker took the last round, and the unique opportunity of dancing with Mrs. Henshaw-Dunaway, by then quite silly with sherry.

"Everyone has won but me," sighed Robert, as the tables were cleared. "After round three, I consider myself lucky. Don't tire yourself, I'll be waiting."

"I as well," replied Martha shyly.

"And Martha." Robert paused, dropping her hand. "Don't let Wyeth ruin your mood."

Martha nodded, though an odd bewilderment pinched her heart. She watched his form, steps assured and shoulders back, fading into the throng. Then she started, quickly following.

The banter moved through the mouth of the ballroom. Martha was a practiced dancer; she was light on her feet, and she was sure (even through the gentle muddling of port), that she wouldn't make a fool of herself in front of Wyeth. She hoped that Robert would have the grace to leave until the misfortune was over–but then, she reconsidered. Perhaps it was best for him to be jealous.

"Your body is in the room, but your head isn't." Wyeth's tone was irritated as he led her to the floor.

"Please forgive me, sir, I assure you my attention is here."

"It's all right." He faced her haughtily, chin out. "I won't be dancing at a revel again. Suppose I'm lucky I won a pretty girl."

It sounded like a compliment, but it was also rude. "Don't you enjoy dancing, Mr. Wyeth?" she asked.

"If dancing is a duty of your time, it rather takes the gaiety out of it. Don't you reckon?"

"I enjoy a revel." An unwelcome defensiveness stiffened her shoulders. "The music makes me want to dance."

"You're young," he replied drily. "Wait a while. The racket of a revel, and the hounds of war baying in the trees, it's all the same."

16

"I'm sure I don't understand, sir," she responded with a clenched jaw. Men who spoke in riddles were an exasperation, and Robert's barefaced buoyancy was all the more desirable.

Mouth pressed, he extended his hand. "This is a business meeting, Miss Gracey," he said tersely. "Nothing more."

She placed her fingers in his palm, and her body swung under his lead so suddenly that she caught her breath. If dancing was a duty of his time, he was a veritable sergeant, and she stumbled to keep up.

"You're little," he observed. "My apologies."

"It's quite all right," she managed, smiling tightly. Her eyes were level with his chest; she turned her throat, straining for a glimpse of Robert. Robert must see; it was the only thing to justify such a slight of fate. Yet, a faint consciousness prickled, aware of the way Wyeth's eyes settled on the bend on her shoulders. She could've slapped herself when she strained further, brushing earrings against alabaster skin. *Martha, what is wrong with you, you're shameless!*

Well, so what if she was? Wyeth was fine to look at. She glanced, watching the way his body cut through the candlelight. As frustrated as she was by her bewildering womanhood, she wouldn't deny it; despite Robert, Wyeth was very handsome. It was perfectly all right, to think such a thing. Robert wouldn't know.

"You can look me in the eye," he said, his voice low, as if amending himself.

Heat rushed to her cheeks. "I'm sorry, please forgive me. I'm distant."

"Just a moment ago you were rapt, Miss Gracey."

She rolled her shoulders, bore the discomfort, and faced him. Around his brown eyes, fine lines broke the surface of his skin. And his nose. At first meeting, she hadn't noticed what a fine shape it was. Not too prominent, yet, the structure spoke of centuries of potent pedigree.

She cleared her throat. "What brings you back to Boston, Mr. Wyeth?"

"A trade partnership, or so I hope."

"Will you stay? I've been told you've been living in New York."

"I've residence in Boston. But I have family in New York, so I prefer to divide my time."

The way he pressed his mouth made it evident that he had no interest in the conversation. It was well enough, because her attention was mangled. She caught Robert's figure, talking to Lord Tucker out of the side of his mouth. Briefly, he smiled, but she could sense from the way that he shifted that he was agitated.

She couldn't rationalize it, but seeing him like that gave rise to a new feeling. A rather mean one. His discomfort didn't bother her; in a strange way, it made her closer to him, more familiar with his mannerisms. *I shan't smile back. I shan't give him anything.*

But her countenance betrayed her in a matter of seconds.

"Really, Miss Gracey." Wyeth's voice broke her thoughts. "I certainly see where your attention lies. But to my benefit don't make it so obvious."

"I'm sorry, Mr. Wyeth." She tore her eyes from Robert. "I don't mean to be rude." Her mind raced for something to say. "You know my father?"

"I know William Gracey."

"It's peculiar, I've never heard mention of your name." She shook her head, her palms prickling with sweat. "It's just that he's very secretive with business dealings. Nothing escapes the counting room." This wasn't entirely true; Martha may as well have been an heir to Mr. Gracey's proprietorship. He kept no secrets, and though the numbers and record books were (in her opinion) boring, his attempt to include her spoke of a sweet desire to please.

"What makes you suppose I'm a business dealing?" A faint smile turned the corners of his mouth. "Perhaps we're just friends."

"Please forgive me, sir. I merely assumed since you're in trade…" She flushed, fumbling lamely. "He has many friends in trade."

All at once he threw back his head and laughed. It was such an odd sound, coming from a man so low-spirited, that she startled. And for some reason, it irritated her. The way his teeth flashed and his smile creased his eyes bothered her visceral sensibilities. She set a store by reading people, or rather, judging them from calculated perceptions, and this man was certainly not calculable.

"I am a trade connection," he said, mending his expression. "I'm sorry, Miss Gracey. Nothing more than another fellow from the wharves."

She broke from him, patting at the fine hairs on the back of her neck. "Well, you must be very busy. To be a merchant and a lawyer by trade, you must never have a moment's rest."

"Never mind, I'm a country lawyer. Petty thieves and tavern brawls. I needn't be in the courtroom for more than day." There was a dismissiveness in his tone that roused her interest, despite her irritation. *Pay mind,* she thought. He was a friend of her father, after all.

She was grateful when he fell silent again, though his eyes followed her form with stifled adjudication, as if she'd exposed enough of herself for him to determine an opinion. Or was it curiosity? It didn't matter; she was content that he'd been given the proper amount of time to observe her womanly assets.

Which he was doing, in dutiful silence. It wouldn't do to have a man ignore Martha Gracey! Even if she never spoke to him again, which she was beginning to hope that she wouldn't. Her feet ached; she was far too hot, and his body was frustrating to follow, devoid of the typical cues given by a gentleman in dance.

Her only comfort was Robert's supposed jealousy, and the fact that she looked pretty, and the man bowing low as the fiddles died was very handsome.

"I relieve you of your duties, Miss Gracey," he said, with a curt nod.

The room grew quiet, then burst with a swell of laughter and clapping of hands. Asahel Wyeth was gone. From the corner of her eye, she caught his retreating figure, fading down a corridor from the ballroom, trailed by a little man in a plain brown suit. *Papa!* She frowned, shaking her head. Yes, it was Mr. Gracey, his bald head reflecting gold. Well, it was no matter; Mr. Wyeth, after all, was "just another fellow from the wharves."

As if the dance and the games of whist had never happened, Hannah and Frances were back at her side. Robert still talked to Lord Tucker, but with his eyes averted. Perhaps he thought the danger had passed. The idea punctured the heightened irritation that had carried her through the dance. Gratefully, she took a glass of port from Frances.

"Your cousin is a funny man," she observed lightly. "A bit mean-spirited. I think he doesn't have a decent time."

Hannah laughed. "And nor do you! Unless you have had a glass, you're quite stoic."

"Don't be silly." She reprimanded herself; her tone was weak. "I'm having a great deal of fun."

"Well," said Hannah slyly, "now that you're done with that one, I've a right to the scraps." She laughed, the sound fading in the clinking of glass and the tapping of feet.

She danced with Robert until her feet hurt, and the port dissipated to a happy exhaustion, telling of a night well spent. She was sure that she'd enjoyed herself. Whether it was love, or merely admiration of his looks–she wasn't ready to decide, and who could fault a girl for that?

Yet, there was a whispering voice, from a dark corner, where the most inexcusable of her thoughts went for pardon.

He's a little silly. Isn't he?

This idea was heightened by something that had happened during the final dance. With every step they'd taken, he'd come closer, until she felt the brush of his shoe against her skirts. Then her ankle. Then his fingers, running down the length of her forearm. Every turn too close, unfamiliar to her innocence. In that moment, it became too real that he might actually be in love. Loosened by port, she'd laughed with him, making fun of someone here, gossiping there; but as the dance ended, he'd bowed, kissed her hand, then reached around the back of her neck, and taking one of the curls loosened from her exertion, he tugged it, and walked away.

She couldn't say why it bothered her so much. It didn't alleviate the infatuation. But abruptly, she'd felt any desire to be at the revel drain through the floor. The air in the room was too thick, and though she was prepared to have the horses called around, William Gracey was nowhere to be seen.

She pulled off her gloves and slipped into the parlor, where earlier the men had cast lots over her time. The candles had long since snuffed out, and the room was blue and quiet. She drew her arms around her chest and slipped outside into the courtyard.

A warmth carried on the wind, and above her the snow slid down the roof in streams, giving up against a day of uncommon sunshine. In the courtyard, the fire of the lamps cast bent rings of gold over wet brick. She lifted her head to the sky. *A nice party, though I daresay I'll leave more confused than when I came.* She sighed, watching her breath fade away.

"Rather cold to be out, don't you think."

She jumped. Asa Wyeth was leaning against the wall, half in the garden, half hidden by the shadow of the gables. One long leg bent, boot against the brick.

"I rather don't mind," he said. "But for a girl so under-dressed, I might worry." He held his pipe in one hand and flipped the lid of his tobacco box in the other.

"I'm of a sturdy constitution." She righted herself. "I enjoy the fresh air."

"As much as you enjoy dancing?"

"As much. Sir."

He regarded her until she felt the need to drop her eyes.

"A good bit of rabble." He nodded. "All right for some, though I find it grating."

She didn't reply, because she agreed, and it was too large of a thing to admit. That was why she was so grateful that parties were far and few between, and always ended at Gracey Cottage, with Judith fussing until she fell into a dreamless sleep. There was silence, and she glanced. The moonlight turned him a peculiar blue, and the embers of his pipe were just bright enough to light his nose and chin in a contradictory gold. It hung from his lips, smoke curling around his head. Her nostrils prickled with vanilla, and the scent of earth.

With a deep breath inward, he moved the pipe from his mouth and tapped it against the brick. Then, he stepped deliberately into the light, pushed his hands into his pockets, and considered her. Abruptly, he brushed past her to the door.

She couldn't think of anything to do but follow.

He reached for the latch, paused, and turned. Soft brown eyes met hers in the dimness.

"So you're aware, Miss Gracey," he said evenly. "Robert Henshaw is a proper fucking chump."

2

ROBERT COMES *to* CALL

There was no one Martha loved more in the world than William Douglas Gracey. Sometimes he embarrassed her at parties or in front of her friends, but his genuine affection was always enough to excuse him. A round little man with a musical voice, a bald head, and a sweet soppy smile, poor William had been dealt a heavy blow when he'd lost Mrs. Caroline Gracey. Martha had barely known her mother, who'd passed in childbed with a nameless baby sister, long before she could remember things; but William bore the weight of that loss in his eyes, his port glass, his rare quiet moods.

A sadness Martha couldn't understand, but she recognized the way he used his grief to propel himself forward. As a matter of distraction, everything was industry; nothing went to waste, not a conversation on the street, nor an evening in the tavern. New endeavors were a constant. At first, when he was young, he'd dabbled in agriculture. Then, he thought perhaps he should write columns, maybe even books, but all he'd managed to produce was a dictionary: beautiful, leather-bound–and mostly empty. He'd stopped somewhere in the middle of the B's.

He loved poetry. He wrote daily in his diary, but his talent lay in numbers, and *General Store, William D. Gracey, Proprietor* was one of–if not the most–profitable general store in Boston. Perhaps it was the carefully leveraged way he sold a little of everything, to satisfy the ladies who didn't want to frequent so many shops. And for the gentlemen, he passed snifters over the counter, even in the morning. The stools on the other side were rarely empty; he could talk to anyone–or talk anyone *into* anything. She'd never seen someone leave without losing at least a few schillings or signing a bill of sale. So, William Douglas, in the middle of his forties, with no wife and only a daughter, was the fastest-growing, up-and-coming proprietor in Boston, and the merchants nipped at his heels.

The mildness of his temper lent a leniency only to her benefit. He never shushed her, nor gestured her out when he met with men in the counting room; he took her on walks down Long Wharf, to the shipyards, through the Common to watch the soldiers. Because of this, she saw many things a girl of her age might not have, and she spent many an afternoon by his side, reeling with the sounds of men shouting in foreign tongues. She'd even seen a prostitute! One day, a fist brawl turned to a tar-and-feathering, and she'd strained her neck before he ushered her away.

Because of William, she could be the girl at the docks one moment, in plain cotton clothes, and the next, the wonder of the ballroom. Most importantly, Mr. Gracey allowed her to *do* whatever she pleased. He never questioned her company; he couldn't bear her distress, and she kept her side of the bargain by leaving kisses on his oily head or notes of affection on the bureau plat. In the back of her mind, she knew it was tit-for-tat, and sometimes she felt guilty; but the sincerity of her affection could balm any hurt. Besides, he had enough to do; he trusted her to manage her own affairs.

These affairs included Robert Henshaw.

Mr. Gracey didn't like Robert Henshaw. If she'd on occasion thought Robert was silly, William was convinced, and it was one of the few displeasures he struggled to conceal. He wouldn't speak; his heart was tender, and he ached to please her. So the affair was tolerated in silence. He was a long-suffering man, and she was sure that every night he prayed that his turned cheek made up for his lack of direction.

Martha certainly thought that it did.

❋

Robert had promised he would call, and every day the following week she'd risen with her heart in her throat.

She tried to forget the pestering feelings left over from the revel. That he was "silly". It was patronizing, and she didn't want to feel that way; she tried desperately to forget the brazen hand reaching around the back of her neck. A meaningless mistake, because he'd had a little too much to drink.

When he finally came, she sat in the parlor, cold fingers stabbing at a sampler, annoyingly aware that her corset pinched and pins stuck at an angle into her scalp. *Perhaps he'll walk me to town. Or at least turn around the garden?* She pressed her knuckles into her cheeks and breathed deep, hearing voices down the hall. The stamping of boots carried in, beating off thick-caked March snow.

"Let us say how-do-you-do to the lady," came Mr. Gracey's quipping voice, "then come to the office and I'll have those receipts for you." Robert entered, radiant in a crisp grey overcoat. William trailed, and behind him–Martha rose quickly–

the gloomy Mr. Wyeth from the party. Straightaway Robert strode to her, taking her hand and kissing it warmly.

Mr. Gracey averted his eyes.

"You remember my cousin, Asahel." Robert was amiable. "Don't worry, he shan't ruin our visit with his pouting."

It was in jest, but Asa didn't react save for the faint raising of a dark brow. He was far overdressed in a swallowing greatcoat, and the hat he removed was an oil-rubbed tricorn, worn and ugly.

"Good day, Miss Gracey," he said and turned on his heel. "Come, Billy, I don't have all day. I must be at the wharf by four o'clock."

His voice faded down the hall, and the billowing turn of his greatcoat stung her nostrils with lingering smoke. William kissed her hand, bouncing with a nervous energy, and followed. "Be good, my dear!" he called, chuckling. Robert might not have been in the room at all, and she wondered for a moment, frowning.

"Sorry about him." Robert grimaced. "I really thought the revel would do him good, but he's as foul as ever. I suppose that's what happens when one spends too much time in shabby society." He went to look out the window. "He seems quite friendly with Mr. Gracey, I wonder why?"

"I can't say." She was unnerved. Asa Wyeth at Gracey Cottage was off-putting; surely, such a man didn't belong in cottages. It wasn't that he was fancy. His clothes were plain, but he moved like a thundercloud.

"I suppose he's probably seeking new patrons since he's back from New York," she offered half-heartedly.

"Clever girl you are, Miss Martha." Yet, there was a hint of irritation in his tone, as if he were insulted at William going to

Wyeth and not Henshaw. She hadn't meant it to come across that way, but to her relief, Robert smiled.

"Funny fellow," he said loosely. "I'll figure him out. Henshaw-Wyeth would rule the ports if he's good for it."

Oh yes, now she remembered. *Robert is jealous of him, he won't agree to a partnership.* Thank goodness men fascinated her in other ways, or she'd become quite bored with their squabbling. Whatever gripe Asa had with his cousin had nothing to do with her, and the fact that Robert had come to the cottage just to see her! Now that he was there, the trembling in her fingers ceased; she was warm and comfortable.

"We must walk to the city again soon," he said. "I've discovered the most pleasant lane that cuts in a Southeasterly direction. If I brought my horse through it a time or two it would clear."

"That sounds very nice." The picture of herself walking through the woods, her arm through his, the sunshine slipping through the trees—it could've been a painting, as Hannah had said.

"The sun's out," he observed pleasantly. "Let's go to the garden."

She stood eagerly, and Robert helped her with her cloak. His breath brushed her cheek, and her heart jumped. He always smelled so clean and new; just to have him there put a gaiety in her step unusual to her reserve.

Outside, it was pleasant, the snow rapidly melting to lumps of brown thrown up by horse's hooves. Robert's slender bay stamped at the hitching gate, and beside it, a black horse stood lazily, ears back. It was absurdly large, gleaming haunches rolling hills of muscle, its face hidden by a mass of thick, curly mane. It must've been Asa Wyeth's horse. How odd, she observed, that a gentleman would ride such a large beast around the city—unless he wanted people to stare.

The Gracey's cottage was modest. A bit unkempt, but it made sense, nestled against fields that in the summertime burst with purple asters and dusty goldenrod. Now, the land was grey, and the cottage, (with its faded brown bricks and chipped white fence), seemed a little grey too. But anyone who'd been there knew, that despite its shabbiness from the outside, the inside could rival even the finest mansions. The mood was always correct.

Perhaps it was the lack of her mother's touch, but William had built into the cottage a style that though unusual, was fitting. One couldn't go into Henshaw House and find the faint print of muddy boots across the floor, or coats in the hall that took up half the narrow space, nor the gentle smell of herbs drifting from the kitchen. Or go into the parlor of the Tucker mansion, and find glasses stained with last night's Madeira, or bolts of cloth draped across the settee as Martha plotted her next gown. No, Gracey Cottage was a place for ease, and anyone who entered dropped their inhibitions at the door.

Perhaps that was the reason Wyeth's presence made no sense. He seemed a man of many inhibitions, and not keen to drop any of them.

Now that the leaves were gone from the bushes and the vines, the garden was like a tangled knot of brown hair. The untidiness embarrassed her, and she thought crossly, *when it's warm, I'll clean this up. I must ask Papa if we can hire a gardener!* It wasn't her duty, she insisted, (whenever these things bothered her), to run the household; if Mr. Gracey cared enough, he would've settled down with another woman.

Robert didn't seem to notice. Easy as ever, he walked with his back straight, her gloved hand resting on the bend of his arm.

"A fine day," he sighed, looking up at the sky. "I was in the city just yesterday. I talked to a regular on the Common on my way out. Funny enough, he said a farmer refused him lodging, even in the barn! Turned out in the streets at the barrel end of a musket, been sleeping on the bench of a public house for two nights since."

She glanced at him, searching for the proper response, but he spoke before it was needed.

"It's an insult. I feel for them, poor fellows shivering in the cold. I have to say I'm ashamed at the audacity of Boston, turning away our own men."

She knew no soldier lodged at Henshaw House. Yet–"I don't understand how anyone could refuse a servant of the King!"

"You're sweet. The abominations to the Crown have brought me much distress. I certainly wouldn't want to lose friends over such a thing." He said "such a thing" as if he considered it something worth losing friends over.

They walked.

"What did you make of my cousin?" he asked, after a time.

The question startled her. The sight of Asa Wyeth beneath the shadow of the gables had been peculiar enough, it must be kept it to herself, at least until it could be properly thought through.

"I can't say," she replied off-handedly. "I found him quite detached."

"I saw you speaking. I have to say I'm shocked you made it that far. Funny, he's running about to this and that, abandoning his inheritance in Boston. Hardly the proper behavior for a merchant's heir, especially one of his father's magnitude. Ah well." Robert sighed. "I think he spent too much time in New York. His sister and her husband..." His tone was apprehensive.

"Are they not reputable?"

30

"They're a bit radical, if you take my meaning? Standish is the name, a lawyer, but not the same sort. I believe he takes capital trials."

He spoke with a haughty inflection, as if his cousin were somehow "less than" for being a self-professed country lawyer. She didn't like where the conversation was going, and she noticed a particular theme, that speaking ill of Asa seemed to bolster him.

Pulling her shoulders back, she asked, "Is Mr. Wyeth a radical?"

"God, I don't know." Robert darkened. "I'm trying to get a good read on his methods before any sort of partnership. I do find it odd that he's done so well in the last few years. To turn it over two or threefold?" He scoffed. "It doesn't make sense."

"He does seem rather affected," replied Martha carefully. "You wouldn't want a partnership with a radical."

He smiled at her from the corner of his mouth and reached his free hand to touch hers. Her heart skipped.

"It would be a capital betrayal," he said softly. "I've no doubt. I would never, of course. I know what's right."

She smiled in return, dipping her head. Her stomach was hollow, and the way her heart pattered in her throat was weakening. Surely, to feel this feeble–there could be no other explanation than love! Her heart begged her to admit it, but–*not yet*.

So she listened. He talked on about the soldiers, and the Common, and the shops in the city that had cut off East India tea, the way the ragamuffins threw pebbles in the streets. After a time, it became rather exhausting. Uneasiness turned to a chill in her bones, and she was grateful when he suggested that they go back inside.

Mr. Gracey's office was at the front of the house, where he'd sit many an evening, watching the sun set. Now, as she passed, and Robert helped her take off her cloak to hang in the hall, she caught a glimpse of William through a crack in the door. Across from him, silhouetted against the yellow sun, was Wyeth; he was sitting with his boots propped up on the bureau plat, low in the chair. *Boots on the bureau plat?* She glanced again. Silver spurs cast shadow tines across the polished cherry, and the heels of his boots rocked up so they didn't touch. And he was laughing, head thrown back, white teeth flashing. The image was odd, but she didn't have time to consider it; Robert was ushering her to the parlor.

"A pleasant afternoon," he said. "I'm so very glad I stopped in."

She smiled as she pulled off her gloves. She couldn't help herself, he was so boyish, so eager–

Boyish. Robert was nine years older than she, and carried with him a wealth of experience that she had many lessons to learn before she arrived at his level. But why *did* he always smile like that? What was the reason for the buoyancy in his step? She went to the settee, irritation tumbling her thoughts, and took her sampler back up.

"Martha, I have something for you." He sat, reaching into his pocket. "Just a small thing, but I think you'll like it." He brought out a kerchief, and placed it gently in her hands, almost as if he feared she might push it away.

It was the prettiest little pocket kerchief, pure white with a lace hem, rimmed with gold thread, and on the corner, embroidered in tiny black letters, *M.G.* Her heart jumped, and the annoyance dissipated. He'd taken the time to think of such a thing! Her fingers curled around it, and she stared, unable to hold back a smile.

"It's so beautiful," she whispered. "Robert–I–thank you! You're thoughtful!"

The way he was smiling at her, she forgave her affront. At the Henshaw-Dunaway party–it didn't matter! Just a moment of imprudence, and as far as she was concerned, it'd never happened.

"I'm glad you like it." He kissed her hand, and her belly flipped. "I commissioned the brightest little seamstress in Boston. You're a talented seamstress yourself."

She was about to reply, but then, Asa Wyeth arrived in the doorway. William pushed in behind him, so little in comparison, that he slipped under Wyeth's arm bent against the frame, and walked in a swaying manner to the table.

"I'd a half-bottle of ripe Madeira in here somewhere, I'm sure I did, for I was reading a book, and fell asleep–ah yes, there it is. Not half, a quarter. Oh dear, it must've been a very good book, though I don't remember what it was about." William paused and slid his spectacles down his nose, noticing the kerchief clasped in Martha's hands. A pensive look of regret passed in his eyes. "Lovely, lovely," he muttered. "Very good, young sir."

"My apologies for interrupting," said Asa, in a voice dripping with insincerity. "I must be at the wharf by four-o'clock. Cousin, I trust you'll not miss me and Jed."

"I'll ride with you." Robert reddened at the tips of his ears; he stood, frock in hand. "Jed?" he repeated, with a scowl.

"My horse."

"You've got a horse like that, and you named it Jed?"

Asa's brown eyes under the tricorn were blank. "Yes–s'matter of fact. I have named my horse Jed." Then, he looked directly at Martha.

She balled the kerchief in her fist. Taunting William with it was one thing, but the idea of Asa being privy to her feelings was unnerving. Yet, his eyes followed her hands in one swift motion to her lap. *My God, he's uncouth!* She flushed. *I certainly hope he never comes again.* She stood as Robert pulled on his coat, and smiled warmly when he kissed her hand goodbye.

"Thank you. I simply love it." Something made her raise her voice just enough so that she was sure Asa could hear. If he cared at all, he was impervious. He stood back, pushing his hands into the pockets of his greatcoat.

"I've not got all bloody day," he repeated testily. "Ride with me or not, Henshaw, but I must be at the wharf by four o'clock."

3

an ENCOUNTER *in the* KITCHEN

A change came over Mr. Gracey in the weeks that followed. He spent more time in the office, muttering with the door shut, or he'd be gone for hours, only to return so late that Martha was already in bed. She caught him laughing as he tiptoed down the hall, and the *pop* of a bottle. He was nervous, and when she brought him his port, he turned over papers or closed day books.

His behavior was subtle enough that it wasn't necessary to be suspicious. Robert visited the cottage often as the days warmed, bringing her flowers and treats, and perhaps it could be attributed to that. William always had an excuse to keep him from conversation past the civil "how-do-you-do's" and the relieved "g'day's", so it might be a tactic he was employing to punish her for Robert. He loved her too tenderly to be straightforward, but he'd been known to jibe her with a game. She wasn't ready to count herself in quite yet.

One of the reasons for that was Wyeth. He came to the cottage often, with or without Robert, and some of William's changes in mood could be attributed to the time spent with him in the office. Hours into the evening they sat, muffled voices bothering her ears. On one occasion, Asa had nearly run into her as she made her way to the kitchen for tea. By way of apology, he'd tugged the brim of his hat, turned on his heel, and disappeared, slamming the front door behind him. The air curled with a heavy smell, sensory and sweet.

"I do find him peculiar," remarked Hannah, sitting with Martha and Frances in the Gracey parlor. Robert was at the table reading a book. "It's only too bad he has so much money."

"Hannah, you shouldn't speak so plainly," Frances reprimanded. "That's cruel. And besides," she added in a breathy whisper, "you know Mr. Wyeth is just down the hall."

"He won't hear you," interjected Robert, annoyed. "I doubt he hears much of anything over the sound of his own voice."

Martha poked at her pincushion. She was tired of hearing about Mr. Wyeth; she'd hoped that by having the girls over, they might gossip about something that actually interested her. To a degree, she understood Hannah's turmoil. Since Wyeth had presented himself back into Boston society, Hannah's constant concern was whether or not he was a prospect that carried much weight. First, she'd sworn that she found him "quite disagreeable to be around" and "no fun at all," and "he dresses as if he doesn't know his hat from his boots!" But then, Hannah, Frances, and Mrs. Henshaw-Dunaway paid a welcome visit to Wyeth Estate. That excursion seemed to have softened her.

"Frances, do you remember the hall? It's most pleasing how it's laid out. I can't say I like the floors, they're too dark. But the garden—oh my, the garden! I've never seen such a beauty!"

"Our garden is easily as many acres," Robert scoffed.

"But it's not laid out so well. Asa's has so many twists and turns, I could get lost! We must find out who planted it, and have ours freshened up."

Martha said nothing. She was unreasonably put off by the fact that Hannah had said "Asa" instead of "Mr. Wyeth." She would not have been so bold.

"What I want to know is, why he keeps coming here." Robert stood, tossing his book aside. "What can he talk about? Sign the receipts and get on, man."

"I don't know, to be honest," said Martha. "But I don't think he's hiding. Papa hates the way Judith sulks about the kitchen making noise, so he closes the door."

"What could they possibly be talking about?"

"Perhaps it's not for you to know," replied Hannah coolly. "You needn't always be poking your nose into other people's business."

"I'm sure they're just speaking politics." Frances dipped her head as if she were sorry for being a part of the conversation. "That seems to be all men talk about behind closed doors," she added hastily.

"You can't know anything of what men speak." Robert was rude. He paced in front of the window, angry at the rain that prevented a walk to the city. "Especially behind a closed door."

"Well, since *you* are a man, and you seem to know so much about what happens behind closed doors, perhaps *you* should tell us," retorted Hannah, eyes averted as she pulled a needle through her loom. "Then please do report back. For we're dying to know what Asa is talking to Mr. Gracey about in the office."

Robert sat, blue eyes hard with inner contention. Briefly, Martha wondered why, but her thoughts were interrupted by Frances's inquiry over whether or not she'd picked a color for her Midsummer's gown. This led to a discussion on the best materials, and how to pair silks with lace and lace with satins. She settled comfortably. This was the conversation she'd hoped for.

After a time, Robert rose and left, insisting he needed fresh air. Martha, for the first time, was glad to be rid of his presence; she'd never seen him in such a foul mood.

"I do wonder what's wrong with him today," said Frances. The concern in her voice was genuine.

"It's obvious what it is." Hannah was matter-of-fact. "He's jealous of Asa."

"But I wonder why he should be jealous? I would think he should be happy that Mr. Wyeth is back in Boston. Yet he's been nothing but cross."

Martha spoke up. It was easier, with Robert gone. "I agree, he might be eager to have Mr. Wyeth in Boston. My father says he's a golden opportunity in trade."

Frances flinched.

"You would think." Hannah's tone was dry. "But let's just admit it, Asa's earnings exceed ours two to one. And he tells no secrets. Rob was silly to think he would just let him in. Family ties aren't everything."

Martha was intrigued. She thought Hannah sounded smart, yet it was Robert's jealousy that roused her interest. "I do wonder how Mr. Wyeth does so well for himself," she said lightly, recalling the conversation with Robert in the garden.

"He isn't a rogue," assured Frances.

"You know nothing of trade." Hannah raised a brow. "Wyeth's creed is quantity over quality. I don't particularly mind; he's handsome enough, he could be a pirate, for all I care, if he's rich."

"Hannah!" Frances was incredulous. "A man must be of good character. And he must be loyal. I'd *never* consider anything else."

Martha winced. There was something defensive in Frances's tone, strangely suppressed, as if she knew Asa far better than either of them, and it annoyed her.

Hannah waved a hand dismissively. "Oh, never mind, Mrs. Henshaw cares too much about these things. I want a mightily rich man, who will let me have fun. I do suppose Mr. Wyeth might not be so bad after all."

Martha was silent. She didn't care to understand the business of William and his friends. At the same time, Asa's presence in the cottage planted an uneasy feeling. Mr. Gracey was passionate about his work, and perhaps he was involving himself with someone best kept at a distance. Even more, she felt increasingly anxious that Robert hadn't returned. He was far too fascinated with William and Wyeth in the office, and his irritation tripped a warning bell. Robert, she concluded quickly, must know something that she didn't. It was against her reserved will, but when the conversation had turned back to gowns and dances, she stood, an odd excitement pinching her heart.

"Goodness," she said brightly. "It's high afternoon. Let me have Judith fix tea!"

It was a relief to be on the other side of the door. Hannah's hearty laughter followed in her wake; the ice had broken now that Martha was gone. For a moment she wanted to be hurt, but it was expected; even if she was never a "country girl" to her face, the Dunaway girls were odd gems in the dilapidated mine of Gracey Cottage.

Her heart sank briefly, but she dismissed the feeling.

A variety of thoughts spun as she padded down the hall, the least of them Asa. She had Robert on her mind. He'd been strangely possessive lately, which though she didn't mind, was out of character. Of any man, he should've had no misgivings about a woman he'd set his sights on; no woman was foolish enough to stray. Not from Robert Henshaw! He was the catch of any sensible girl in Boston. Just because Asa had danced with her once, well—it was uncalled for. She was so engrossed that she barely noticed him standing in the hall opposite the office, one hand on the wall, head down, expression blank.

"Oh!" She gasped; she'd nearly run into him. She took a step back, but out of nowhere, he pressed a hand over her mouth, reaching round to pull her close at the small of her back. The gesture was so childish that her mind flickered—the tug of her hair, the way her belly had dropped. Something itched up her spine, indignation at least, irritation at the most.

"Mr. Henshaw!" She pushed him away.

He put a finger over his lips. "Please!" His voice came in a hiss, and he pulled her in by the elbow. "Be quiet."

"This isn't your concern. Really!"

"But it could be. And even if it isn't, I have a right to know of the affairs of my family. Especially when it's become about you."

"What? It isn't about me!"

"Hush, please, for the love of God, Martha. Mr. Gracey is in there. Doesn't it make you uneasy? Stay, but be quiet!"

"It isn't decent! What if—"

"What if?" He sneered. "I'm not afraid of Asahel. And you—you have even more of a right to know than I!"

He had tapped her inner contention. She couldn't argue against her curiosity; it was not like William to hide things. She stood with her head down, heart thumping, arms around her chest. At any moment, she could leave, abandoning Robert to carry on the deviance alone—but she could *not* quarrel with him. Her attachment to him was too delicate.

She watched the doorknob. *If it opens, I'll slip into the kitchen. Papa won't be angry, but Mr. Wyeth*—well, she didn't know him. He didn't seem the sort of man who would take kindly to eavesdropping. Voices rose, first William's, high-pitched and excited.

"So I can meet George Hodge at Oliver's Dock? Past South Battery. I'm not too familiar with that part of the city." While there was no apprehension in his tone, the anxiety was hard to miss.

"Hmm, no. If you're coming from King and Long Wharf, just off Long, take Kilby Street." Asa's voice was low, sending a vibration through the floorboards. There was a tapping of flint and steel, then the faint hiss of a lit pipe. "He makes berth around eight o'clock in the morning."

"Very good. I'll meet you there at eight then. Come with me to the shop, I've an order of purchase from Haddock I'd like you to look over. He claims the tea has dropped in price by a quarter percent, but I was sure that wasn't due to take place until next month." There was a clanking and a stirring, the sound of a spoon hitting a platter. "Tea for you?"

"Thank you, no." Smoke drifted beneath the door. "I'll take a glass of whatever that is. It looks bloody rancid. Stopper your spirits, Billy, or spoil them with too much air."

Billy? Goodness–it was too familiar.

"Rum!" exclaimed Mr. Gracey. "Rum, yes of course. Oh, yes. Tomorrow at eight. I have been meaning to ask if you've heard anything of Standish yet?"

"Nothing yet. Cassandra's sick with worry. I don't want her in New York by herself when none of us knows where the hell Elijah is. She's to come to Boston. Another tyke on the way, goddamn."

"Ah no, unfortunate indeed. Well, I'm sure she can make the best of it, we shall be very happy to have her. I wonder if she might get along with dear Martha. I'm so tired of her with those ninny Dunaway girls. No offense, of course."

Robert flinched.

"None taken," replied Asa easily. "I'd be happy to introduce Cass."

"I have to say I'm surprised there is no news from Beck. His own apprentice…"

"Beck is a chump. He might be good at keeping secrets, but he hardly knows what to do with them once he has them. He'll never make it as a lawyer. Bloody hell."

"I suppose you'll leave the moment you hear the news. Riding off again, for Lord knows how long, and I shall be left to manage this foul business myself."

"Don't be so presuming. I'm willing to bet I won't be gone more than a week, and if you can't manage that, you've tangled with the wrong fellow. Besides, I rather like it here in Boston, now that there's something to do. What fun Henshaw would have spreading rumors if I were to leave."

"A jolly time." Mr. Gracey laughed. His tone trilled, and Martha winced.

"Never mind," said Asa. "New York is a foul place, and it's best for me to be here. And for you, of course." A pause. "For Martha, too, if you think on it."

"Martha?"

"Yes. She's smitten with Rob. Careful, Billy."

"Now, now, I certainly know that, but I think you underestimate my girl. Martha's very clever, and I would never suppose her to be taken too far. I'll let her have her fun."

"For now." Asa's tone softened. "I don't mean to slight her. I feel a bit guilty. I didn't come to spoil all the fun. But it's better for her to stay in the dark. I don't want to ruin her in front of her friends. That can devastate a girl, aye."

"Ah, my sweet girl. You're right of course, and I do always try to break her gently." There was an interlude of silence, then– "Well, you'd better go on then, it's a quarter past three. Here is my list of the prices for the molasses, and damn both Hall and Young, for I won't go any lower."

If Martha had told herself a hundred times that she would turn into the kitchen, it would not have forced her feet to move. It was Robert who stood back as the door opened, and turning swiftly, circled in the hall under the pretense he'd been entering the front door. It happened with breathtaking swiftness; Asa was standing in front of her, eyes wide, one hand on the knob, lean fingers curled around a half-empty glass of black rum. Disbelief turned quickly to bewilderment.

Too fast–to annoyance, to anger.

In one controlled motion, he shut the door, passed the rum to his other hand, and reached forward. There was an afflicting moment, when his fingers curled around her wrist, that her eyes locked with his, and a heat struck deep in the pit of her gut. A flash, lasting only a second, but echoing in waves of confusion. Her mind hissed, and she opened her mouth to protest, but the thundering of her heart suddenly clamped her tongue.

Brown eyes narrowed and flashed to Robert, then back to Martha; then, with no hesitation at her plight, he swung past her, pulling her into the kitchen. There was a measured dominance in the way he held her wrist, loose, yet shackled; enough to contain, but not to hurt. He marched her to the back wall, where he turned her around with a patience that didn't make sense.

"What the hell do you think you're doing." It was a statement, not a question. "You don't listen at doors. You don't–whatever the fuck."

43

"Good God, Asahel, let go of her!" Robert burst through the door, exhorted. "You don't lay a hand on a woman, let go of her this instant!"

Asa ignored him. "I asked you what the bloody hell you thought you were doing." Evident anger sunk his temples, and she caught the barely perceptible twitch of a lid as if he were fighting not to narrow his eyes.

"Mr. W-wyeth," she stuttered, "I–"

"Jesus, Asahel, let go at once!" Robert was beside her, breathless. "Let go, unless you want me to bring my pistol out!" He hooked her arm and tugged; Asa's fingers tightened in resistance.

"I'm not hurting her," he said crisply, each word carefully enunciated. He was clearly as convinced of Robert's silliness as William, but it was enough. He let go with the gentlest push, enough to send her, startled as she was, swaying toward the wall. She gasped, righting herself. With her freedom regained, a weakness overtook, a tremor, spreading to her fingertips. It was instinctual for her to turn over her wrist, the feeling was so potent it was nearly physical; but her skin was unmarked. In reality, he'd barely touched her, but she burned, as if her body didn't want her to forget the way it felt.

"Be civil!" Robert's voice broke her shock. "You should leave, man! You've an audacity, to assume you can impose rules on other people's homes. Martha's right is to be here, anywhere in this house, whether you like it or not!"

"Papa Gracey might disagree." A faint smirk twisted the corners of Asa's mouth. "And you're a fool if you think I don't see what you're doing. Count yourself lucky it's not Papa Wyeth."

"You're sick, man!" Robert spluttered. "She's not yours to punish!"

She glanced fast to see Asa standing by the door, head down, as if for a moment he regretted what he'd said. But then, his eyes met Robert's. Wild, filled to the brim with spite—a hate—so raw, that a gasp caught in her throat.

"She mayn't be mine to punish," he said levelly. "But I can goddamn be sure that she isn't yours to comfort. So what'll it be, cousin? Stroke her arms, and hold her face. Or meet me in the garden with your pistol drawn." He gestured dismissively with his glass. "Trust me, I've nothing to lose." Then—"Martha, don't listen at doors. Bloody cunning, isn't it? Shame on you."

"Mr. Wyeth," she tried again. "I didn't—I think you misunderstand my intent. I didn't—"

"Martha Ann Gracey!" Out of nowhere, his voice was a gunshot. "I won't be argued with!" He took a step forward, spurs rattling, and Robert pulled her against his chest. The glass was slammed on the prepping table so fiercely, she yelped—"oh!" and swallowed a sob.

"When I say don't, I mean it, Martha! Do. *Not.*"

The boom of his voice could've splintered the bark from the rafters of the kitchen. She'd never been shouted at in her entire life; the highest form of correction William had dared to give was a suggestion, a mild variance in opinion shot down by tight-lipped silence. In that way, she barely knew that it was possible for her to misstep.

Yet in that moment, Asa Wyeth had broken her. Her thoughts were cleaved, not only by the volume of his voice but by the implication behind it. She'd made someone angry. She'd broken the pattern of her existence. And she was cowering, displaced by the unfamiliarity, in Robert's arms—a place that, for some inexplicable reason, she suddenly did not want to be.

"Really." Asa's eyes widened, head back in a show of mocking disbelief. "What would I do to you, Martha?"

45

"Leave, cousin!" Robert repeated. "You're frightening her!"

"It's really all right, Robert, please–" How her voice came out, she couldn't say, only the slightest irritation at Robert split the wide-awake fear. Only it wasn't quite fear. It was something else, something beckoning.

"How pathetic you are, Rob." Asa sneered. "I'll never lay a hand on her. But I'll think about it." He cocked his head. "Maybe bend her over my knee? Have a happy time with that picture."

"Good God, you're perverted, man!"

Asa ignored him. "Martha, look at me."

She had to. That feeling, in that moment, was rooted; he wasn't her father, subservient, and he wasn't Robert, addled by her innocence. She looked, and briefly before the humiliation broke the dam, her heart twisted again in a flash of feeling. His eyes, though dark with subdued anger, held a peculiar expression. Hunger, she decided quickly. Longing.

"Martha," he repeated, "Don't bloody listen at doors."

"Sir, I'm sorry. I wasn't trying to–"

"I mean it. Do *not.*"

Then, with a turn of his boot, he was gone, footsteps echoing down the hall.

She couldn't face Robert. She couldn't face the overwhelming knowledge of his failure, tainting the air like a bad smell. Pressing her wrist into her stomach, she brushed past him, clenching her face against tears–not of fear, but of bewilderment.

4

a CHANGE *in* BUSINESS

I t wasn't Martha's way to give in to tears. She hardly knew how it felt to be cleansed by a healthy cry, nor to think in the hollow aftermath; but even as she lay, staring at the ceiling, she wasn't granted such relief, no matter how her eyes ached, or how affronted her feelings.

Asahel Wyeth was different now. He was more than just the strange man from New York, haunting Mr. Gracey's office. No; he was viable skin and bone and lean muscle, casing a mocking melancholy she hadn't known in a person. The world hadn't held her long enough to know, and her introduction had been rattling in its embarrassment. She couldn't assume anymore that she could read people like books. Because she'd read, but she hadn't taken meaning. She witnessed but didn't understand.

Yet, one observation was clear: Robert Henshaw hated Asa Wyeth, and Asa Wyeth hated Robert Henshaw. It wasn't just family squabbles; it was more than Asa refusing a partnership, or who had more leverage at the docks. No, it was hatred, spitting fire in those awful brown eyes! *God,* she thought. *What has Robert done? What has Mr. Wyeth done?* And the words, from behind the door! Her father had lied to her before, but permissible lies. Lies of protection. But it wasn't his way to lie by omission. She could forgive the silent squabbles, but this was a wedge driven deep enough to fester.

She shook off the vision of Mr. Gracey, trailing Asa down the corridor of Henshaw House. There was no proof that man was tangling her father in illicit business, and Robert hadn't given her a solid reason to believe it was true. But why would Asa partner with humble William Gracey? What did Mr. Gracey have that other proprietors in Boston didn't? And if it was something unlawful, was he leading Mr. Gracey down a treacherous path, where he could be reproached–punished– hanged?

Her thoughts ran circles until finally, she fell into an intermittent sleep. Brown eyes haunted her dreams, filled with curious yearning. In a whirl of black rum and the spice of pipe smoke, she tangled the bedding fitfully, finally roused by Judith shaking her non-too-gently by the shoulder.

It was dark. She sat up in alarm. Her head was heavy, and she thought, blearily, *oh dear, I've slept through dinner. Now Papa will know there's something wrong!*

"You slept through dinner," Judith affirmed, bustling Martha to the dressing table.

"I might go back to sleep," she said desperately. "I've got a headache."

"I know you do. But you must see Mr. Gracey downstairs." She pulled a brush through Martha's hair, yanking at knots. "Mr. Wyeth is downstairs, too–" emphasizing *"too"* to assure Martha how much trouble she was in.

So he'd come back. And Robert–surely, if Robert wasn't there, there was no way that she could face Asa! How could

Robert see her again? Asa had shouted at her, he'd berated her like a child in front of the man she'd so long sought to impress.

She dropped her head against her chest, eyes burning.

"I don't feel well."

"I'm sorry." Judith patted her on the shoulder, clearly not sorry.

In the mirror, she was pale, eyes hollow. She stood as Judith wrapped a shawl around her shoulders, which she bound around her wrists and held in balled hands.

"Go," barked Judith, rolling her eyes. "You mustn't keep gentlemen waiting. It's rude."

※

She stood outside of the parlor with her breath held and her heart skipping paces. Everything in her wanted her to run, for Judith to tell them she was really ill; but her constitution, despite her tiny frame, was brutish. There was little that would put her out of order, and William knew it.

On the other side of the door, Asa and William sat over a muddled spread of paper, port, brandy, and tea, William with a book on his lap, spectacles low. His expression was bored, and her stomach unclenched just a little; a smile played on his lips as if he were thinking up a tasteless joke. Asa didn't seem so amused. Rather, he was impassive, and when he met her eyes, he was unreadable. He rose, nodded, then sat and poured a brandy, in silence.

"Ah! Come, come, my dear." Tossing his book aside, Mr. Gracey leaped up, took her hands, and led her to the table. "Do sit down. Tea, or whatever you like. A spot of port? Wyeth, pour her a spot of port, right now. Whatever's the matter! My poor Martha, she's not disposed to illness. She's a most sturdy woman. Strong as a horse. More like an ox, she is. Asa, pour her a spot of port."

Asa poured her a glass of port. Though she could feel his eyes, she couldn't reciprocate; her heart wouldn't subject her to the discomfort. As she took the port, the tip of one of his fingers briefly touched hers, and that flash of feeling tightened her chest. Only this time, her belly ached, hating the familiarity.

Mr. Gracey patted her knee. "Now, Martha. I've brought you up well, and Judith, a godly woman indeed, has never taught you wrong. I know sometimes we are tempted when we're curious." (He patted again). "Lord help me, I can't stand the sight of you. Have a drink of port. You'll feel better."

She obeyed. The effect was immediate; her head warmed, and some tendon that had pulled her shoulders tight unhooked. She finished and set the glass down, drawing a hand over her mouth. Asa watched, and she quickly dropped her hand to her lap. *Disgusting, rude man,* her thoughts spat. *Not like a gentleman!* But she hated that she blushed.

"There's a reason, my dear, that we keep the door of the office closed," Mr. Gracey went on. "We can't be expected to know everything about each other, but I will always tell my dear Martha what I can. I would never keep secrets from *you.* But I understand the burden that was put upon you."

Her blush deepened. It was a slight at Robert, salt in the wound. She riled, irritated by the heat in her cheeks. Her lack of incentive was *not* her fault; it was natural, when a girl was in love!

"Miss Gracey." Asa's voice came so unexpectedly after the high pitch of William's that she jumped.

"Yes, Mr. Wyeth."

"Miss Gracey." Harder. "I'd rather you look at me."

"Yes, Mr. Wyeth."

"For the love of Jesus Christ, Miss Gracey." His tone prickled with exasperation. "Look at me when I speak, aye? Billy, you've raised a contrary girl!"

"Oh dear," said William, sounding guilty. "She's tender, Wyeth, come now."

I'll look at him, she thought, *if that's what he wants.* The attitude that pushed her through such discomfort in the past rose to save her. *This is happening, and there's nothing I can do.* She raised her eyes. Asa was watching, temples tight with annoyance. His chestnut hair curled clean; there was a distinct insult in the fact of his good looks. A man so ill-tempered had no right to please her eyes that way.

"Yes, Mr. Wyeth," she muttered.

He broke, frowning, and poured himself another brandy and her, a splash of port, which she accepted, mindful of her fingers.

"I would like to make a deal with you, Martha." He cleared his throat, the frown growing darker. "Miss Gracey."

She waited.

"I consider you a gentlewoman," he said, clearly fighting to correct his tone. "But gentlewomen don't listen at doors. However, I spoke harshly with you, and I'm…sorry."

It was an apology not from the heart. Poor Mr. Gracey sat, a bewildered look on his face. He had no idea the extent of what Asa had said! *Maybe bend her over my knee?* She shivered, but aloud she said, "Thank you, Mr. Wyeth. I'll be sure to correct myself from now on."

He would've been a bigger fool than Robert if he hadn't sensed the insincerity in her tone. "Very good," he allowed, though his eyes narrowed. He put back the rest of the brandy and rose. "Billy, it's not my place to tell you what she can know. Martha, I'm comforted that you're a clever and considerate girl."

(As if daring her not to be). "I'd thank you," he added, "not to speak of this to anyone."

She nodded.

"Not anyone. Especially not Mr. Henshaw. Am I understood?"

"Yes. Mr. Wyeth."

"Not Robert," he repeated. That low voice speaking Robert's name gave her a dirty feeling, muffling the pureness of what she thought she'd had. But she pressed her lips, nodded again, and stood, placing little fingers into the palm of his outstretched hand. If ever a man offered her such homage, her vanity wouldn't permit her to resist. Something about a man stooping before her was empowering in a way that made the bottom of her belly curl with heat.

Yet, Asa loomed over her, even bowed. The lips that met her knuckles were warm, and her nostrils caught the tang of brandy. When he straightened, he held her eyes, and his fingers let go not in a dropping motion, but with a faint pull upwards, the trail of his touch cool on her palm.

"Be good," he said shortly, pushing his hat on. Then with a nod and a turn of his boot, he was gone, banging the front door.

Martha sat, hard. Heat spread to her knuckles, a curious tingling following in its wake. She frowned at her lap, for a moment so befuddled that she forgot about the boom of his voice, the wild eyes. For a man who berated her so severely, to in turn set her blushing—it didn't make sense. She couldn't have it make sense. He had no right to scold her, as if he knew how to raise a daughter!

I am not *contrary,* she thought hotly, pressing a hand to her cheek. *He simply doesn't know how to speak to solemn ladies.*

❋

52

Mr. Gracey *hem-ed* and *aha-ed*, folding and unfolding his hands, taking up a book, exclaiming at the loveliness of the day (despite it being black out, and raining). Finally, he settled and poured himself a brandy.

"Martha, Martha." He frowned, rubbing his thumbs along his glass. "My dear sweet Martha Ann. I've a little change of business I think you should be aware of."

Surely, she knew what he was going to say. She'd heard enough. She leveled with him, still uncomfortably hot. Mr. Asahel Wyeth would ruin everything that day!

"I've decided, not without thought to my friends and family, that I—" William cleared his throat. "Lord, I don't care for this brandy, he's laced it with poppy. He must stop leaving his bottles about, for what if Judith got into it after dark? Ha! That would be a funny story. Give me that port."

She passed him the bottle, and in a rush, he said: "I will stop selling Bohea in the shop."

Surely not William's notion. She narrowed her eyes. No, it reeked of Wyeth. Those lean fingers could pick through a stone wall, unaffected by whatever strife it caused—broken nails, bleeding skin. *Chipping away,* she thought. *Robert was right, he's not the sort of man Papa should be doing business with.*

"Whatever for?" she asked, fighting to keep her voice level. She knew enough to know what happened to shopkeepers who didn't sell Bohea. They were called "rebels". Families like the Henshaw-Dunaways and the Tuckers shunned those shops. On the same token, she was aware of the unrest in the city, and the resulting trouble Mr. Gracey had faced. The finger of blame was pointed at Asa, yet she couldn't discredit William's cleverness.

Mr. Gracey pushed his spectacles up his nose. "You see, I shudder as I lock my doors at night. It's a shame, that I would rather comply. My glass windows–my beautiful glass windows! If they were to be shattered, it would shatter the heart of me. I will appease the mobs, for I won't have them ruin my glass–" He closed his eyes and shook his head. "Forgive me, I don't wish to distress you. I'm a coward, some would say. Cunning, say others. I'll lose patrons, and say goodbye to Loyalist friends– Oh! Have some more port, my dear."

He filled her glass. It was a solid tactic; the only way to slacken a taut Martha was to keep the drinks flowing, though now, she felt sick in the stomach.

"Now," he prattled on. "I feel like I could fly, I'm so light. Only Asa could speak of it, and well, you know he's not the best at speaking. A short way of speaking! Strange for a lawyer, don't you think? I would think he could talk all day! Perhaps I should've been a lawyer, ha!"

The port was gone too quickly. She hung her head, the room spinning.

"Jests aside." He straightened his countenance. "You know East India merchants always stocked *my* shelves." He frowned and paused. Then–

"It some years ago I came across Wyeth at a public house. We struck up a conversation, and to my shock, I found he was attending a scallywag to court, who'd broken into my shop not a week prior, taking two silver tea caddies and two bolts of silk, sewn with real gold. And he would walk the courtroom floor as defense? I found myself friendly with a man I should've regarded as an enemy. Larceny, by the end of the night, was not but a common mistake.

"He paid me for the damages, and we settled the case without court. I showed him to the counting room, where he took an interest in my record books. I never have debts long, you know that. We spent many an evening, tipsy over numbers.

That turned into drinking at the public house every night. One day, he invited me to one of his warehouses up the coast. I'll never forget!" He sighed to the ceiling.

Martha remained still. Something was disturbing in the way his eyes lit, as if some celestial being skimmed the corners of the room. Her heart beat cold, but she kept her eyes on her lap, only moving to reach for her port.

"I'll never forget. Walking through those doors, I was hit by a mustiness. That warehouse held one thing, as far as I could see, tea, but a nasty sort of tea, from the Netherlands. Oh dear, thought I, I've made friends with a racketeer! We took a bottle of rum to the back of the warehouse and got drunk. He was brilliant then, he was; he had a lady he was going to marry, a pretty house, and endless things to do. I remember looking at him and thinking to myself, by God, to be like that! 'Billy,' he told me. 'You're an honest man. I like you. And I fancy being wealthy. It isn't boring. And you—you've a lot of potential. There's money to be had, yet you're content to divide it among those who don't lift a finger to earn it.'

"'Goddamn,' said I. 'I just want to be honest.'

"Well, I wasn't being honest. I thought about it, and he wasn't wrong. My whole world centered on being a loyal subject, paying my taxes, drinking my Bohea, playing my levied cards with my Loyalist friends." Another pause, a straightening of spectacles, then—"I started to doubt myself, and I started to see less of him. He sailed to the Netherlands, and when he came back, he went often to New York. When we did meet, he was melancholy. The fortunes never changed, but he was sick in the head over something, I think it was his lady. He never married. New York was his home, and I was—well, I was bored.

"I bothered him with letters, which he did answer, on occasion. So much time passed, too much. I gave him names. I wrote of the unrest in the city. At last, at the party at the Henshaws', he was back, carrying his despondency with his tongue in his cheek. He sought me out, and we stole a bottle of Mrs. Henshaw-Dunaway's finest sherry–ha!–and drank it in the carriage house. 'Madcaps and rebels,' I remember he said. 'Bloody golden for Wyeth-Gracey.'

"And that brings us here, my love." He smiled, reaching to take her hand. "I'm putting the proprietorship behind me, and joining my name with one of the most powerful merchants in Boston. This is indeed a golden opportunity. You can ask me anything, and I swear, I'll answer you from my heart."

She recoiled. An emptiness grew the longer she listened, and now, drunk and hollow, her words failed. This was not the sort of discussion she'd ever imagined having. Her troubles were born of the vexations of being a young lady, who'd fallen by some blessing of fate into the prime of Boston society. But this was a distinct cracking in the foundation she'd so carefully laid down. For Robert, who had been right about Wyeth all along.

"So Mr. Wyeth," she managed. "He's…running goods?"

"Well, hmm. I suppose you could say so. In a manner of speaking."

"But isn't that a punishable offense?"

William shrugged. "Many merchants are moving their accounts to the Dutch Indies. Many won't admit it. If cards are played properly, there's a fun bit of profit to be made. No American court will do much more than a slap on the wrist." He leaned forward excitedly. "Wouldn't you like to be rich, my dear?"

She smiled quickly in response, but panic welled.

If they found out–Robert, Hannah, Frances–what would happen to the way she'd grown accustomed to living? Would she ever be invited to fancy revels again? Robert could never be the same! And it wasn't just Mr. Gracey, it was Asa; if Robert understood the depths of his cousin's crimes, she couldn't imagine how he would talk! Gracey was a name as good as dead.

"Try not to worry, my dear," sighed Mr. Gracey, in opposition to her thoughts. "I'll keep my secrets if you can promise to do the same. You know, even some of the most loyal of colonists have taken Bohea off the shelves. It's not an instant expulsion from society."

Her mind flashed to the voices on the other side of the door. *"I suppose you'll leave the moment you hear of him. Riding off again, for Lord knows how long, and I shall be left to manage this foul business by myself…"* It was a desperate hope, but she latched on. Hearing of who? It didn't matter. Her immediate question was, "Is Mr. Wyeth to leave Boston? I heard, at the door. I'm sorry."

"Yes, he has a case that may take him back to New York for a time. I can't tell you when. But he'll be back."

Her heart dropped.

"His sister will be coming to Boston," added Mr. Gracey, with a nervous desperation. "I'm sure you could be good friends."

But she didn't want to be friends with Asa Wyeth's sister. The cruelty of Mr. Gracey, positioning her, threatening her livelihood–for what, soiled money? When he spoke, it was a different name he alluded to, a different life. Wyeth. Her reserve broke. To rise, and leave him, without saying another word–he deserved it!

But it was more than that, she knew, because Mr. Gracey was highly skilled. He was clever. And Asahel Wyeth–he was rich.

"You don't trust him," he said tenderly. "Remember kindly, my dear, Robert doesn't know everything. Only soften your heart, and try not to judge without measure. Asa is a brother to me."

"Yes, sir." But she flinched at the inflection. The way he said "brother" meant far more; it was nearly reverent. And it wasn't his place to discuss Robert or hold him against the brotherhood of Asa, whom he claimed to know. *God,* she thought. *I'm not even angry. It's worse, he's pushed me to the side—*

"Thank you, my dear. Whatever you wish to ask, I'll answer it to the best of my abilities."

"Aren't you…" She faltered. "Aren't you afraid of getting into trouble?"

"Ah! Not particularly, and even if I am, what of it? More than half the ships in Boston Harbor aren't trading by English rules. Redcoats must drink cheap rum too." He winked, but he must've noted her panic. "Now, please don't fret," he amended. "I'm a diligent fellow."

His eyes were bright with the excitement of discovery. But it was more than that; William Douglas Gracey was taking a risk. He'd never done such a wild thing, and perhaps that was why he hadn't brought it to her first. She would've ruined it for him. She, and Robert Henshaw.

5
the GREEN SILK

Asa still came to the cottage, but Martha only realized his presence in the sweeping greatcoat or pipe smoke prickling her nose.

Robert's marked absence had her nervous and depressed. After William's confession, she'd gone to her room, shook her hair loose, and laid with clenched fists and dry eyes. There was nothing more that she wanted than to speak to Robert. She'd reached under her pillow, where she kept the kerchief, and held it to her face in an attempt to conjure tears–but she couldn't.

She was restless.

Her infatuation with Robert was contaminated by anger, and oddly weakened. It should be that because Asa hated Robert, she must only adore him more; but his insistence on staying by the door–that cold hand clapped over her mouth–it annoyed her. If he could've left well enough alone, none of this would've come to light, and she would be as blissfully ignorant as always.

She tried to shrug it off.

It wasn't so bad, merely a change of business. And Asa wasn't *really* a criminal. At least not a bad one. Criminals didn't live in pretty houses and grumble over opium-spiked brandy.

And they certainly weren't rich. Or tall, or–handsome. They didn't kiss a girl's knuckles and make her toes curl.

Besides, there was a missing piece to the explanation Mr. Gracey had given, fitting somewhere in between Asa returning from the Netherlands and returning to Boston. Something that made him a little more human; someone with a story, not just a bad attitude. Certainly, she was still angry, but it softened her affront. Or perhaps it was more that she'd thought far too long on the fact that he'd had "a lady". That was all. A "lady". Irritatingly, it made her want to ask questions.

Furthermore, it was what Robert might do that soured her stomach, and as more time passed and he didn't visit, she could only conclude his distaste. He no longer wished to be seen at the cottage. Asa had ruined every prospect by the way his eyes dared her to betray him. That alone fueled her confusion and gnawed at her thoughts like a bellyache.

❀

She walked in the fields, Robert's kerchief clenched in her fist. It was easier to think when she wasn't trying so hard–dressing her hair just so, for his eyes. Sitting with her spine so painfully straight. In irritation, she pulled the pins from her hair and braided a rope of red. The way she'd used to wear it before she thought she could be fancy. God, it was wrong! Because Robert was a problem now. Not easy, or just cheerful–she fairly stalked into the yard, raking wildflowers from her hair with jerking fingers.

Asa was in the yard, untying Jed from the hitching post, petulant in a loose brown frock and scuffed boots. She kept her head down, but jumped when she heard: "Aye!"

She bristled. What sort of man summoned a lady that way! With a dip of his head, he removed his hat (the ridiculous oil-rubbed tricorn) and strode to hold the door. It was peculiar, and what upset her most was the innocent way his brown eyes held her own. Soft, and a little haughty, as if he'd done nothing, as if he couldn't possibly guess the reason for her humiliation. Asahel Wyeth, she concluded hotly, knew how to play games.

She passed through the door with her head down, but as she stepped into the hall, he caught her at the elbow. She startled; the warmth of his fingers spread, even beneath her sleeve.

"Miss Gracey. A word."

"Yes, Mr. Wyeth."

"I hope that you've taken my apology to heart. It was a small thing, however much it upset me." He cleared his throat. "A favor, if you don't mind. In a fortnight, my sister is coming from New York. Come by, if you want. She's nothing like me."

A faint smile moved his mouth, but the way it creased his eyes–it wasn't fair, for men to be rude, and look so well at once! Flushing, she twisted her hands, staring at the middle of his chest.

He couldn't be a friend of her father. It made no sense.

"Thank you. I'd be happy to meet her." She added, a necessary barb, "I'm sure Hannah and Frances will be, too."

His eyes tightened, but he nodded. "I'll let you know when she's settled."

There was a long pause. She held her head to her chest, heart tight. Finally, he broke and stepped aside.

"Very well, Miss Gracey."

"Good day, Mr. Wyeth."

"Martha."

"Mr. Wyeth."

"If you'd like to go riding sometime, I'll set a day. The girls expressed an interest. Rob...would go."

Rob—ugh! Why did he have to say it that way? She winced, but he was unreadable if only touched by a faint irritation. Quickly, she considered the proposition. She was a much better rider than either of the Dunaway girls. And Robert would go. At the same time, it was strange that he would extend such an invitation.

She narrowed her eyes. "Thank you, I do love a spring ride."

"Very good. Let's hope the weather will hold through next week."

"I look forward to it, sir."

"Martha." His shoulders drew up, just a little, head tilted. "Did you know," he said, blowing out a sigh, "there's a bit of aster weed in your hair?"

Heat rushed. Her fingers flew to her ear, fumbling. Stringing her hair with wildflowers was a common thing; she did it thoughtlessly when alone, sure to remove them when she returned to the cottage. It was too large a breach in her stoicism, but Asa reached, hooking a finger against her palm, and gently pressed her hand to her side.

Her thoughts dissipated.

"It's all right." His countenance mellowed. "I rather like it there."

"Sir," she muttered, "I'm not ill-mannered."

"Asters in your hair doesn't make you ill-mannered." A smile broke the corners of his mouth. "You have a strange perception of things, darling."

Darling. Her gut balled. The way he said was simple, without inflection. Robert never referred to her with such pet names, but then, perhaps it was only that Asa was older; he probably referred to all girls that way. The way Mr. Gracey did, like a father. From beneath her lashes, she watched him turn his wrist and adjust a button on his frock coat sleeve. Pressing his hat on his head, with a light tug on at the rim.

That was not like a father. Could it be, that he was flirting? It didn't matter how well he looked, men of such stature, and age, and strange melancholy–they didn't flirt with young girls. Her mind fought to conjure up an image of Robert, but her thoughts were scrambled, and her toes curled painfully in her shoes.

"Good day, Miss Gracey." His expression leveled, and he nodded. Then he turned on his heel, and she watched, half hidden against the wall, as he tightened the cinch on the horse's saddle. The toe of his boot scuffed at the ground, and in bare perception, she heard: "Bloody goddamn hell."

❋

She spent the following days in the parlor, hunched over her sewing basket, hands aching over the Midsummer's gown. There was a listlessness in her essence, persistent like a headache. Where was Robert? Was she not worth the trouble, merely because Asa was being bad? What was the point then, of sewing that gown? She threw it aside in vexation. The Midsummer's party was thrown by the Tuckers (of Beacon Hill) and everyone went to the Tuckers! This was the party where she was to be truly attended by Robert, from the door to goodbye at the end of the night. She'd lost sleep over that gown. What color would bring out her eyes? After much deliberation, she'd selected a bolt of dove grey satin, but the peacock green silk still taunted her.

Her confidence in herself had been damaged by the scolding of Asa Wyeth, however tongue-in-cheek it had been. Everything in his mannerisms, when Robert stood in the same four walls, dripped with distinct insincerity; and as humiliating as it was to be caught in the middle, she had concluded that the show had been for her eyes more than Robert's. For Robert to know how deeply it bothered her would be to discover a crack in the armor of her calculated modesty. Moreover, it was to admit, that he'd been correct, and her status in society now hung by an uncertain thread.

It was nothing less than torture.

But Robert finally did call, strangely unaffected. He wasn't angry, and the timing couldn't have been better; both Asa and her father were absent. He would walk her to the shops, he announced. They had hours in the sunshine, and it was too beautiful a day to waste indoors.

She doubled her strides to keep up. All around, the open fields were green skies, freckled with spring daisies and purple aster stars. The sun glared, but a gentle breeze countered, and it might've been perfect if it weren't for the sudden change in Robert's mood. Agitation prickled like a penned horse; his eyes fixed ahead, his mouth pulled down in a frown. It was clear he had something he wanted to tell her. She dropped her eyes, smiling. It was pleasant, (wasn't it?) to know his mannerisms so well.

As Gracey Cottage fell into the distance, he reached for her hand, running it through his arm. "I've a little news, about my cousin. I think it is imperative for you to know. He can't connect himself to your family, and keep such secrets."

Oh, how disappointing! Even with her hand on his arm, she felt foolish, and annoyance itched at her spine. Why couldn't he just forget about Asa, when she was with him–alone?

"He's going to court for his brother-in-law, Mr. Standish, from New York." Robert's eyes were bright. "But only when he's apprehended. His sister is married to a criminal! Though it doesn't surprise me. I met her a time or two, a very brash sort of woman. Not so refined as you."

She didn't respond. Inside, her heart beat out of rhythm. *Oh dear*–she wasn't sure if she was good at keeping secrets. She'd led such a simple life, there'd never been a reason to. But she'd made a promise to Asa Wyeth, and something in the authority of his eyes told her she mustn't think to break it.

She warmed. It wasn't correct to see his face, with Robert there.

"Standish, you know, is a lawyer," continued Robert. "So at first, I thought it was a legal error. But no, it's a trial of murder, in offense against the Crown! I've heard tell Standish and Asahel are very good friends–they keep correspondence often. Asahel in defense of radical murderer? I daresay he's a cad since he's come back to Boston, I'm shocked."

Martha stiffened. Rarely did the mention of licentious things disturb her; rather, they fascinated her, and her uncontested innocence gained her a distinct interest in the violence of men. Her father did little as a shield, and she was quiet enough to be ignored. Besides, it seemed fitting that Asa wasn't a "country lawyer" as he'd alluded. Principles of politics surely held no merit to a man who crafted the rules as he went.

But, for Robert's sake, she said, "I can't believe it!" She drew in a breath, loud enough for him to hear, and supposed it was good enough.

"Can't you!" Robert huffed. "I'm sure that he thinks he can acquit Standish, and if this rumor is true–well, Henshaw is damaged by his connection."

He'd clearly chosen his affront. She did not respond, fearing a slip of the tongue, and they walked in silence for a time. For a reason she couldn't explain, she ached to correct him. Wyeth was a lawyer. Isn't that what lawyers did, defend those who sought their services? He's simply performing a duty. *Oh, why should I care!* She pressed the back of her neck, annoyed.

"If it is true," Robert spoke up, "family connections mean nothing to him. Elijah Standish is a radical. I'm beginning to think Asahel has been radicalized himself! It's a shame, but I suppose it's a relief he never joined forces with Henshaw. What if he loses the case? He can never show his face in society again."

"Would there be any reason for such a rumor to spread?" she asked, in an attempt to hold her side of the conversation.

"It has substantial weight." Robert was firm. "I'm sure of it."

The sunshine, and the subject, was wearing after an hour, and she was grateful when the dirt road faded into streets and the hum of the fields was replaced by the racket of the city. She thought about what he'd said. She should've been shocked by the blight of Mr. Standish's connection; she hadn't been completely mollified by Asa, but at the same time, he had firmly clamped her tongue. So, it was with a degree of affront, that she decided she didn't like the way that Robert was speaking about his cousin.

It wasn't that she disagreed with him. Asa was insensitive, but there was something about him that interested her in a strange way. What was it…a *bodily* way. Right there, with her arm through Robert Henshaw's, her eyes on the cracked brick, she confronted the fact.

Perhaps it was the unspoken thrill. The game of avoidance at least gave her something to do; in how many ways could she evade him, or in turn, what excuses could she make to listen for his low voice? Or breathe a little deeper when he walked by, warmed by the smoke and earth way that he smelled.

She shook her head. *All he can do is make Mr. Wyeth seem ill. It's dull.* Then—*how could I think such a thing?*

"At any rate." Robert held the door to *General Store, William D. Gracey, Proprietor.* "I've got my eye on him. I'll protect the name of Henshaw at any cost from radicals. We're loyal, and we're true." He smiled and dropped the topic. They were under Mr. Gracey's roof, and surely what he'd heard at the door of the office was fresh on his mind. *He doesn't know everything,* she thought. *But he's figuring it out.* The conversation had exhausted her so much that when she smiled back, her heart didn't turn.

Richard sat behind the counter. It was a time of day William would typically be at the docks, so she browsed the shelves and crates, running her fingers over silks and satins. As Mr. Gracey had promised, the Bohea was gone, replaced by coffee tins and blank caddies, probably filled with Asa's nasty Dutch tea. She wondered with faint panic if Robert would notice, but he didn't seem to. He bought her a bag of hazelnuts and leaned against the counter as she made her rounds.

It dawned on her, eyeing the green silk, what the benefits of Asa's partnership might mean. Her father was by no means poorly situated; the simple cottage may have some convinced otherwise, but he was both skilled and pennywise, and she wanted for little. Yet, with Asa…well, if his house was as elegant as Hannah alluded, it made no sense; he dressed in a drab manner that didn't become a gentleman. *Robert is right,* she thought lamely. *He's most suspicious.* Still, a feeling of excitement tickled her spine, and the silk purred under her fingers as if waiting for her.

"What do you think?" she asked Robert, holding it out. "For Midsummer. I've started a dress in grey, but it's not too late to start again."

"I think it would look ravishing." He was light, and she felt guilty. "You should take it home."

"I wish I could," she sighed. "Papa says it's too exotic, but I do think it would look well, trimmed with black lace."

"Martha, you would be a bird of paradise." There was warm sincerity to his tone. She needed it—jealousy did so ruin his voice! "But of course," he added, "you'll look well in whatever you wear."

His smile was bright, and her heart tugged. Not affection, she observed woefully: guilt.

The door opened with a clang of the bell, and her father stepped in, trailed by Asa. Martha quickly lowered the silk, but Mr. Gracey didn't seem to notice. His energy was bouncing, and his only acknowledgment was a nod in Robert's direction, and, "Oh, hello my dear, good to see you out and about getting fresh air," as he hopped to the counting room.

Asa touched his hat. There was a wild look about him, mussed from the sea wind. A wary glance met her fingers on the silk, and a brow rose in what she could only decipher as a show of displeasure. *These are his things now. Oh dear, I hadn't thought of that!* Most everything she wanted from the shop she took, within reason. That ribbon, or a new caddy for her tea, or oils for her scented water—it was hers. If Asa started balancing the books, perhaps he wouldn't be so forgiving when he discovered the all too common "losses".

"G'day, Miss Gracey," he said stiffly.

She nodded.

"God, cousin, have you tarred your hat?" Robert leaned against the counter, haughty. "You look like a sailor."

Asa blinked. His hand rose, as if he meant to remove the aforementioned hat—but dropped. Mouth pressed, he stared at Robert. Then, "Yes, s'matter of fact. A coat of pine tar has been applied to my hat. It rolls the sea spray."

"A fellow needs a decent hat." Robert huffed, something of a scoff. "Spend some of that money, man. You've got plenty to spare. What are you doing anyway, swinging from the rigging?"

Asa countered him with a trace eye-roll, more of a flicker of movement. "Sounds like a bloody good time," he replied. He cleared his throat. "Whatever the hell, come with me to the counting room."

"Never mind," Robert said, the haughtiness giving way to irritation. "Come by Henshaw House, or put it in the mail-bag, man. I haven't the time today."

Asa's eyes tightened. He reached, removed his hat, and ran his fingers through his hair, much to the discomfort of Martha, who'd never dropped her eyes so fast. "Come with me to the counting room," he repeated. "Miss Gracey, you'll excuse Mr. Henshaw."

"Of course," she said.

He dipped his head, and Robert followed him. The door banged shut.

She paced, threading through the shelves, her brain shooting strange signals. What Asa could have to talk about with Robert, she couldn't imagine, but perhaps they'd made amends. And Asa would lie, probably. He certainly seemed like the sort of man who wouldn't mind lying, if the situation were correct. Low voices drifted, the scuffing of a chair, the pop of a decanter. She felt restless; she was supposed to be with Robert, and she was supposed to *want* to be with Robert!

After a time, Asa dipped out, closing the door quietly behind him. A heat grew around her head, and a fluttering turned her belly. Now William and Robert were alone, and on consideration, her father had never spoken face-to-face with Robert before; never a real conversation. There could be no reason for him to be in the counting room with Mr. Gracey, and without Asa, except for some sordid attempt to save face.

Asa strode behind the counter and began rummaging through papers. "Jesus, can you not be so bloody useless," he muttered at Richard, who pulled his hat over his eyes. Asa took up a quill, scribbled something at the bottom of a paper, and folding it neatly, tucked it into his waistcoat. Then he stepped out and headed for the door.

Her eyes couldn't help but follow his spurs.

"You want that silk, aye," he stated, brushing past her. "Well, I've just bought it for you."

"I–I'm sorry, Mr. Wyeth." She froze. "I don't understand your meaning."

"I've signed a bill of sale for the silk. Bills of sale are very important to me, Miss Gracey." He paused at the door, chin out. "And now that I know who'll pay this bill, I'm giving you the silk. You want it, don't you?"

"It's very pretty," she murmured. To be this uncomfortable surely ruined any kindness–yet, it wasn't kindness. It was a warning.

She flushed. Her discomfort must have been clear, and he relented, shifting, one leg slack like a docile horse. It took an inch or two off his towering height.

"You're a skilled young lady," he said. "I'm sure you'll make something smart."

"You're thoughtful, sir."

"Perhaps."

The air was tight, almost as if he wanted to say something further, but the counting room door slammed, and Robert emerged, whistling softly, heeled shoes clacking. Disappointment dropped her heart, and a hot blush tangled her unease. Oh, she couldn't be disappointed to see him! It was just that, whatever words Asa might've said hung, and dissipated too quickly. Oddly, even if it had been something useless—a comment about the weather, the docks, the sloops—she wanted to hear it.

Asa turned, clapping his hat on his head. "G'day, Miss Gracey." He tugged at the brim, nodded at Robert, and turned on his heel. The rattling of the bell smacked her ears.

Robert stiffened, eyes narrowing. He'd always been the sort of man who wore his feelings with pride, even the disagreeable ones. When she'd first met him, it had been one of the things that had drawn her to him so rapidly. He was everything that she wasn't, many of the things she wanted desperately to be. But now—*oh dear. I'm annoyed with him again.* The fact of her blush, and the sweat that rose on her palms, disrupted her balance. She wouldn't justify herself to him.

She couldn't justify herself to herself. So instead, she smiled sweetly.

"I don't like his mood," said Robert crossly, tucking his hands in his frock pockets. "Oh well! Let's keep walking." He offered his arm, and she took it, but her thoughts were too addled to care.

6

FRANCES'S MALMSEY

Despite the oddity of that day at the shop, Martha was eager to accept an invitation from Wyeth House. A spring ride would be nice, and the idea of the Estate perked her interest. Now, with the ache that had strung her weary since Asa had goaded her with the silk, the idea of seeing him in his element seemed necessary.

She'd taken that silk. It wasn't her way to turn away something she wanted, principles far to the side.

The morning of the anticipated ride, Robert arrived in the Henshaw carriage with the Dunaway girls. Jed had been stamping flies at the hitching gate since early that morning, and Martha watched from her room, curtain clutched to hide her state of undress. *I do love a ride,* she thought. Then, in an attempt to soothe her worry, *I'm so glad that Mr. Wyeth and Robert have put their differences aside*—pretending that they had, in fact, done so.

She reprimanded herself; she should be angry with Asa. Yet all she heard, over and over, was "darling". How many times that word tumbled in her head—*stop it, Martha, right now!*

"Oh, thank goodness," she exclaimed, once Hannah and Frances were in the room. "I'm at a loss completely, I don't know which to wear!"

Judith had laid out two riding habits, one brown, and one blue, and which one had been the cause of much angst and deliberation.

"Of course, you must wear the blue," said Hannah warmly. "You know blue is your color. Turn around, and I'll tighten your stays."

The blue was duly donned, corset cinched tight.

"Oh, Martha, you're so beautiful!" Frances breathed.

"Robert will be struck dumb." Hannah went to the window, pulling aside the curtain. "Let's be proper, and keep the boys waiting for a bit. Judith, get us something to drink. Madeira!" she called as Judith grumbled down the stairs. The Dunaway girls, disruptive and extravagant, were an upset to Judith. She brought a bottle and three glasses, muttering, and rumbled down the stairs.

"I'm so tired of the way they quarrel." Hannah popped the cork. "It's most pathetic."

Martha drank her port, which went too quickly to her head.

"Robert's most besotted," Hannah added. "He speaks of nothing but you, it's quite boring."

There was something in her tone that alerted Martha, to what, she wasn't quite sure. It was nearly a mindful redirection of her thoughts, and even though Hannah smiled, Frances didn't.

"However." Hannah raised a brow. "I couldn't help but notice that Asa has been sulking about the cottage quite a bit. What could that be all about?"

Martha squirmed. There were only two things that Hannah could've been alluding to, both equally terrifying—that Asa had formed some crude attachment to her, or, that Hannah knew of Mr. Gracey's treachery to the Crown.

"Yes," she replied weakly. "He and Papa are friends."

"Does he speak to *you?*"

"Of course not," she said hastily, queasy. Keeping secrets, she decided, was no fun at all.

Hannah smiled but with a different insinuation. It wasn't like Hannah, but in a flash, it passed. "Well, no matter," she said airily. "You'll be delighted by the Estate. The finest I've seen in Suffolk County."

Frances hadn't spoken, and Martha was grateful when the port was gone and they pulled on gloves, tied on hats, and descended the stairs. She hung behind the girls. Hannah's brief haughtiness was unsettling, hinting at a jealousy that questioned the fluttering in the pit of her belly. The dark ache in her heart resurfaced. The fact that Hannah considered Asa that way was *not* right. What did Hannah Dunaway know about Asa Wyeth? She didn't know the small things that made up his comforts—black coffee all morning with Mr. Gracey, brandy with laudanum in the evening. Nor his manners. The way he always scuffed the earth before he swung into the saddle. The way he tugged at the rim of his hat.

"Martha, you're a vision." Robert held out his arm. "I only wish it would rain, and I could sit in all day and admire you!"

Martha's reply was a faint blush, but her heart wasn't there. Robert helped the girls into the carriage, and despite herself, she watched as Asa swung into the saddle. He was black against the sky.

The trip was pleasant. She sat with a gloved hand pressed against the window, rapt; even Hannah was quiet (*thank goodness*). For the first time since the affair in the kitchen, she felt like herself–satisfied to be entertained, excited at the prospect of something new. The fields soared by, star-studded with wildflowers and the occasional group of men running drills.

"Poor dullards," commented Robert as they rolled by a gaggle of farm boys. "Foolish notions. They've nothing on our militia."

No one replied.

With interest, she watched as they rolled up the drive. For some reason, she'd pictured a wildness, blending into the fields, but it was meticulously landscaped. Blooming dogwoods lined the front lane in perfect succession. The house, deep red brick trimmed in white, had a Roman appeal, fronted by a broad portico with four stone pillars. It was wide, with a domed roof, broken by yawning windows, capped on each side with steps to a stone terrace. The garden must've been around back; in front was an open lawn, neatly trimmed.

A pebbled walkway turned around the house, leading up a small hill to a towering white-washed barn, fences perfectly square. To the other side of the house, just visible through the western terrace, was a pond. Oh–no, not a pond, as the carriage rolled closer; it was square, and lined with stone. A bathing pool! Heat crept into her face. Goodness, what if Asa bathed there? She glanced as he dropped from Jed with a bounce of his boot. If he *did* bathe there, she considered darkly, someone could see, out the terrace window.

The carriage rolled to a stop outside the portico, where a circle of gravel crunched under the horse's hooves. A wiry, ruddy-faced man, hair bunched in a queue, loped from the walkway and began unhitching.

"No slouching, Sam," said Asa, swatting at the man's back with his hat. Asa tossed Jed's reigns into his waiting hands, and turned, striding to the carriage.

Robert had already climbed out, offering a hand to Frances, then Hannah. Hannah was chattering, pointing to the stone pillars, Robert cross and out of sorts. She watched him, swallowing the now familiar guilt.

"Miss Gracey."

Asa was standing at the door, holding out a hand. She stared, her head fogging with heat. A firm palm, dipped in the middle, long fingers trim. *Goodness, what a pleasing hand.* Oh, dear heavens, no—Robert. Robert, *Robert.*

Robert had nice hands, too.

She looked up, caught by unreadable brown eyes. "Mr. Wyeth, I—"

He nodded curtly. Hastily, she placed her hand in his and stepped out. Somewhere, in the split moment from the carriage to the earth, his free hand pressed the small of her back. Robert had touched her there, a time or two, tentatively ushering her through a room or a door. But Asa's hand was firm, planted. Despite herself, she thrilled, and the most irritating disappointment flooded her chest when he let go.

He was flirting. He *had* to be. She knew enough about men; it was a tactic, and a solid one, because Robert was pale, arms loose at his sides. This was something about a quarrel they were having, some backhanded penalty Asa was making poor Robert pay. And it certainly wasn't fair that she was caught in the middle—but what a place to be! As Asa was relieved of her weight, warm breath stirred her hair, carrying sweet tobacco. She shuddered. *This doesn't make sense.* Frances was eyeing her with the familiar pinched expression, and she ducked her head when Martha caught her glance.

"Horses tacked?" asked Asa, brushing by Sam, who grunted.

"Yes, *sir.*"

"Very good."

Martha slid her arm through Robert's and followed to the steps of the portico, the crunching of the gravel annoyingly loud.

The doorway was arched, paneled black wood, trimmed by two windows of the same height. Inside, a yawning hall stretched, the ceiling lost in white sunlight, glaring through polished glass. The image of the messy Gracey cottage pinched at her brain, and she squirmed.

The walls were white, capped with scribed molding. Straight ahead there was a paneled glass door, leading to a parlor room, and above it, a short balcony, draped with a large animal pelt. Other than the pelt, which was evidently meant as a sort of decoration, there was little extravagance. A couple of biblical paintings in etched gold frames. Two wooden chairs against the wall. A table by one of the windows, where a daybook, a quill, and an inkwell were arranged as if they weren't meant to be touched. The entire essence was that of something not meant to be touched, a picture in a book, too perfectly arranged for real life, and the air smelled fiercely clean, of balsam and lemon.

She circled once. It wasn't fancy, yet, there were two pillars on either side of the door, each topped with the bust of a man lost in time. An iron and gilt chandelier hung overhead, simple, two-tiered. Gold trimmed the arches on the windows. It was tasteful for a rich man's house, nearly too empty. Henshaw House blared with extravagance–too many lavish things forced into too small a space.

"Good Lord, man." Robert tucked her hand protectively in the crook of his arm. "Is that a giant beaver pelt?"

"Hmm, no. It's buffalo hide." Asa paused to glance at the affronting pelt, then continued through the hall, boots beating an echo.

"Buffalo," muttered Robert. "What are you, a frontiersman?"

"Traded for it," replied Asa, his tone indecipherable. "Thought it looked pretty. A tribesman at the docks wanted my applejack, and I wanted a buffalo hide. Seems fair."

"Trading with tribesmen seems common." If Robert was searching for offense, it fell notably flat. Asa blew through the doors of the parlor without comment, and Martha jumped, tightening her grip on Robert's arm.

The sharp smell of curated cleanliness followed into the parlor, which was smaller than the Henshaw-Dunaway's, but so neatly arranged, it gave the impression of immensity. Vast eight-paneled iron-cut windows, a matching door to the western lawn. The floor was meticulously polished, dark wood set in geometric patterns. Simple cream-colored swag curtains hung, just hiding tucked Venetian blinds. A cream silk settee here, an armed parlor chair there. Everything gleamed, not a speck of dust or clutter. There was a fireplace on one wall, trimmed with marble, guarded by brass candle sconces, but little decoration—only a handful of paintings. One, she marveled, of a lady without clothes! Hair spilling over her bare breasts, hands folded against her throat. A couple more biblical pictures, hung as if the exactness of their placement were more important than the contents of their frames. Then, there were four portraits, hanging above the fireplace. A family portrait wall, she noted, taking it in.

The first painting was a younger Asa, chestnut hair tousled, leaning with one hand on a stack of books, the other slack on his knee. Beneath the painting was a brass plaque which read, *Asahel Emory Wyeth*. The next was a man, large and regal, nearly fat, as if the artist had seen a very fat man and tried to trim him up with a brush. His eyes were Asa's, large, russet, the same nose, the same complexion. He sported a long periwig and a metallic-stitched coat, trimmed with nearly ridiculous pleating.

Asahel Moses Wyeth, his plaque read. Curiously, a pistol hung between the painting and the plaque, and Martha thought it a little too deliberate.

Beside the fat man was a bright-looking woman, hands on her lap, gold hair billowing around her shoulders. She didn't look like Asa, but Martha supposed it was his mother—yes, her plaque read *Florence Rhoda Beall-Wyeth.* The last was a woman dressed in a lurid gold gown, head cocked back, her arm wrapped around the shoulder of a little boy pouting at her knee. She was beautiful, with sun-kissed skin, and the biggest brown eyes. Chestnut hair rose around her head like a cloud; her expression was decorous, yet touched with teasing. *Cassandra Winifred Wyeth-Standish | Elijah Ashley Standish.*

Goodness, she thought. The Wyeth pedigree was forceful.

"Have a seat, ladies." Asa strode to one of the windows and tugged down the Venetian blind. Martha sat beside Frances, plucking off her gloves. Robert stood behind her, a hand on the back of the cream silk settee as if he thought she needed protection. She batted away her irritation.

Asa sat, long legs crossed. "Bennet!" he fairly hollered in the direction of the door. A stiff-backed, slick-haired young man appeared, hands behind his back. "Bring Malmsey for the ladies. Brandy for two, and fetch me a Dover's, please."

"Still getting those cruel headaches?" asked Robert coldly.

"No, I've got a pain in my knee." Asa's response was jibing. "I'm getting rather gouty in my old age."

Martha blinked, glancing at him. Surely, he was joking; he was the trimmest man she'd ever seen, and there was trace self-deprecation in his tone.

The drinks were brought on a serving cart. Martha thought she'd rather not eaten enough to be drinking so much, but she couldn't refuse, because Asa poured a glass of the Malmsey and passed it to her. It was crisp, (it had clearly sat on ice, how fancy!) and bit at the back of her tongue like a sweet apple. Robert watched the gesture, and turned to the window, a chagrined expression tightening his temples. Nevertheless, he accepted a brandy, which he drank too fast. From the corner of her eye, she caught the slick-haired man dropping a white tablet in the palm of Asa's hand. He slipped it into his mouth, turning his head. She shook her head, realizing she was staring.

How odd. In all of her time with him, Robert had made her forget about everyone else in the room. Yet, it'd been too long since she'd thought of him—too many interesting things were happening. Her heart pinched, but she was not sorry about the way that she felt. Perhaps, it would pass in time. For now, the beauty of the house, and the taste of crisp port, and her racing heart—it was new. It was…better.

She settled, letting the taste sit on her tongue, and studied the portrait wall. But her mind bustled, Hannah's chattering a hum behind her thoughts.

For her to not care about his jealousy was strange. All she could feel was *that* hand, pressing into the small of her back. *Goodness*, she thought, stealing a glance at Asa. *He looks quite well today.* It wasn't fancy, but he wore a pleasant pine-green frock, fit to his waist in a way that sent a curl of heat through her belly. His boots were primed with dubbin, a proper two-toned leather nearly to the knee, clipped with a set of silver spurs.

Surely, he's not as handsome as Robert. But he does *look nice.* He caught her glance and smiled, his eyes creasing—*oh dear.* She pressed her fingers to her mouth, hastily looking away. He was *more* handsome than Robert. She admitted it, hot in the cheeks, frowning into her Malmsey Madeira. It didn't matter, it didn't mean anything, but it was true.

"I shall be so happy to see Cassandra again," Frances was saying breathily. It was easy to forget that Frances knew Asa better than Hannah or herself; it was easy to forget Frances, altogether.

"Will Standish be coming to Boston, too?" Robert fixed another brandy, delivering a jab.

Asa cleared his throat. "No, he'll stay behind. Cassandra will stay with me until the riots die down."

"Hardly a place to avoid the riots," replied Robert, clearly cross at the deflection. "Elijah really should move her to the country."

"I'm in the country. The riots I've seen in New York are bloody worse. They fancy setting fire to things. I'll take a few rotten vegetables or a piss on a wall, thank you."

The tautness of Robert's temples loosed, and a smirk played at his mouth. He flashed a glance at Martha as if she were expected to join in, but all she could manage was a tight smile. It must've been good enough.

"Will young Elijah be blessing us with his presence, then?" Robert asked casually.

"Sorry to say," replied Asa.

"Still as much of a brat as ever. If you asked me, a switch would be the best cure."

"Young Elijah has seen my venerable temper," said Asa coolly. "Discipline isn't Standish's strength."

"Falling behind on his fatherly duties, eh?"

"The law is his duty. Should've known better, lawyers aren't a marrying stock. A very bothersome trade, full of bothersome fellows." Asa's tone was light, but when he leaned forward to pour a brandy, she noted a barely perceptible twitching of his fingers.

"Someone must marry them." Robert's eyes settled on Martha–her heart flipped. Oh dear, he must've noticed the way she'd been watching Asa! She drank the rest of her port, her belly knotting with anxiety. He couldn't know when she didn't understand the feelings herself. Only, she was aware she didn't care about his opinions with the same weight.

"Well, I'm sure many ladies in Suffolk County will be grieved," Hannah interjected with a tinkling laugh. She was smiling at Asa, but she wasn't blushing. Irritation fairly crawled up the back of Martha's neck.

"Nonsense. Wyeth would be a curse on any woman," said Robert rudely. "It does answer some questions." He smirked. "Now I know why you're so old, cousin, and haven't married."

"Robert, please." Frances moved forward in her seat, eyeing Asa nervously.

It was evident why. Asa had gone stiff. Brown eyes locked with his cousin's derisive blue, and he didn't break even for Robert's leer; though he didn't rise, the tension in his jaw betrayed the effort. Finally, he leaned on his hand, and after far too long–Martha began to feel rather queasy–he shook his head and frowned.

"Fuck you, Henshaw," he said, crossing his boot over his knee. Then, as if he hadn't meant to say it– "Check yourself, Henshaw."

Robert smiled coolly and went to sit beside Hannah.

"Mr. Wyeth, you've some beautiful paintings in this room." Frances stood. "Do you mind if we take a turn? Martha, will you join me? I know how much you love to look at paintings."

Though confused, Martha was more than happy for the diversion. Her anxiety had peaked, and the level of spite burning in Asa's eyes made her forget, for a moment, about the other things he was making her feel. Frances hooked her arm through hers, and they walked, sipping Malmsey. Hannah's voice was indistinct in the echoes of the room. Martha drew a breath. This was much better. What she'd wanted, coming to the Estate. She would have plenty to think about that night–like his hand on her waist–she shivered. *I will* admit it. *I enjoyed that feeling.* Warmth pooled in the bottom of her belly, a feeling, though misunderstood, that was shamefully familiar, the more time spent with Asa. And she'd figured out how to satisfy it. Indecent, but he prodded at an inborn vein in her sensibilities, past the fluttering in her heart. Robert had never made her want to sweat through her bedding. And was it really Asa, or was she just in a rare mood?

Frances paused, her brow furrowed. She was fretful, which, though not uncommon, was out of place in the brilliance of the room.

"Oh, what a gruesome painting." She blinked up at a lady with a man's head on a platter.

"I think it's from the bible," whispered Martha, admiring the blue shading.

"Oh yes, of course." Frances turned. "Martha, may I be plain with you?"

Martha dropped her arm. Frances didn't normally speak truths; they were too bold, hidden beneath averted glances and the gentle rasp of niceties.

"I hope you don't think me crude," whispered Frances.

Martha frowned, and they both watched the painting. "Go on," she said lightly. "I'm listening."

"It's about Robert. And Mr. Wyeth. It's my understanding– I don't wish to ruin this! It's most unfair. But I feel it's only right."

Martha waited. Her body was warm, loose from the port, but her heart began to pound. Surely, bland little Frances could have nothing to say.

"It's just this." Frances's voice was a murmur. "Robert–he has an intention to–to ask you to–"

Martha turned, irritation skittering her spine. *To ask you to...what, Frances?* Her gut turned over the port. "What? Say it, I won't be mad."

"To marry him," Frances blurted, then dipped her head, as if hiding a rush of emotion.

At first, the admission fell on plugged ears. Her body reacted, hooking her arm back through Frances's. She didn't feel chilled, or alarmed, and the wild pattering of her heart slowed to a thumping pulse.

He has an intention to ask you to marry him.

"God," was all she could say.

"Don't think me rude," Frances pled. "The only reason I chose to speak is because I want you to know something before you make your decision. I can tell you, or leave it alone!"

"Well, heavens," muttered Martha. Then, it didn't matter that Robert was going to ask her to marry him–what mattered was what Frances hadn't told her yet. "Tell me, please. I wouldn't make a decision to marry if it's *so* scandalous."

"It's–it's about Mr. Wyeth. I don't wish to speak ill of him." Frances nearly gulped her port. "A few days ago," she said in a rush, "he was at Henshaw House, and Robert and some fellows from the public house were playing brag. It was late, Mrs. Henshaw and Hannah had gone to bed, and–well, I was just finishing a few stitches, I didn't mean to listen."

Martha could see it in her mind's eye–the brown wisp of Frances, barely noticed in the corner. The recollection stirred something. The door, the men, the drinks, the unwelcome knowledge. Her wrist pinched.

"What did they say?"

"Mr. Wyeth and Robert were quarrelling. I hadn't paid much mind, only it became heated. I'm sure Mr. Wyeth wished to anger Robert, so he said something–about–about you. A vulgar thing."

A vulgar thing. Immediately, her interest flared; she curled her fingers tight around Frances's arm. "What did he say? You can repeat it. I'm not offended." It was true. Her curiosity burned hotter, as always, than faux delicacy.

"I won't repeat it," Frances insisted. "I can't!"

"Well, God, you can write it on a piece of paper. Write it on a piece of paper, and give it to me!" The beating of her heart was so furious that her own voice rang dull in her head. Damn Frances and her sensibilities! Ladies spent far too much time being insulted by these things, and she must know what Asa had said about her. Especially if it was vulgar.

"Please, Martha, don't push me." Frances's chin trembled. "I won't repeat it to you, but I-I think Mr. Wyeth is…I think, what I mean is–he fancies you." Her tone was thick, as if she hated she'd had to say such a thing. "You must know, any feelings you have for Robert, can only be hurt by Mr. Wyeth. Robert–he–he made a mistake."

Mr. Wyeth fancies you.

She closed her eyes, forcing each breath. Frances was being silly. She was presumptuous, and some human folly led her to this ridiculous conclusion. Asa was merely doing what any man would, kissing her hand, helping her from the carriage, or simply admiring the fact that she was a pretty girl. Yet all at once, that feeling rushed back. The bolt of light, that burning twist, searing where his fingers had touched her skin.

Darling.

No, damn, it was nothing! She shook her head, opening her eyes. Frances hadn't finished. What had Robert done to Mr. Wyeth? What ills could he have inflicted so egregious to sway her decision to marry Robert Henshaw?

"I don't know what you mean," she pressed. "What has Robert done to Mr. Wyeth?"

"Come, we should walk." Frances pulled her along. "I've known Mr. Wyeth; I knew him before Mrs. Henshaw married Mr. Dunaway. I love Robert like a brother, you must understand, but he–he made a grave error–"

"An error? Whatever do you mean, is this a business transaction? Frances, you know I have no interest in trade."

"It's not that." Frances's eyes reddened, threatening tears. "Mr. Wyeth, he had an attachment to a friend of mine. He intended to marry her. But she was young, you know, and Robert–well he's charming. You know. He's…handsome."

"Frances. What are you saying?"

"I can only tell you what I know." Frances's tone was desperate. "And that is that he–he acted. On his feelings. Martha, forgive me!"

"Please speak. What do you mean, he acted?"

Frances breathed deep, shuddering. Then she leaned in, and whispered, stirring a wisp of hair on Martha's neck: "Robert laid with Wyeth's woman." She drew back with a gasp. "You–you know what I mean by that?"

She knew, enough. *Robert laid with Wyeth's woman.* Yes. She knew what that meant. She looked over her shoulder, and watched Robert sitting in his pretty blue coat. The pit of her belly went sour, and she rounded back to Frances.

"Are you sure?"

Frances nodded. "Yes. I knew her well–she was dear to me."

Martha frowned at the floor, desperately fighting through her feelings. After all, why should she care? Lots of men "laid with" lots of ladies. But it didn't matter; she was repulsed so immediately, it was nearly like relief. An open door. God, to feel that way about Robert Henshaw, so long the reason for her sleepless nights!

Robert laid with Wyeth's woman.

He was no less perfect. No, he *was* perfect, that body, that pure ruddy face. Smiling, even though he was clearly irritated. Childishly fraught. But for a man to break his civility, and take another man's woman—it was nothing less than malicious. A woman another man intended to marry!

Her mind flashed to her father's confession. *I think it was his lady.*

Robert laid with Wyeth's woman.

Robert is going to ask me to marry him. If Frances had told her this but two weeks ago, her heart would've grown wings. What about all the times she'd thought she was in love, all those nights she'd dreamed of his face, how she'd made herself sick with worry when he didn't call? And why was it Frances's duty to tell?

And Asa had said vulgar things about her in the company of other men.

But Robert laid with Wyeth's woman.

She needed to think. Robert couldn't propose to her, today or tomorrow, or even in a week. What would she say? *I should tell them I'm ill and I need to go home.* But no, she couldn't sacrifice this at his altar; not the new feelings stirring in her heart, the sweet haze of port and Spring dogwood flowers and—Asa! Because he met her eyes across the room, and he was smiling, a lock of chestnut brushing his forehead. The heat that pestered her groin flared in contention with her distress.

"Frances, what do you mean, Mr. Wyeth has feelings for me?" They'd almost turned around the whole room, and she'd too soon be forced to put her hat and gloves back on.

"Because I see it," said Frances in a despondent whisper. "Not only what he said. But I've seen the way he looks at you. It's no slight to Robert, but it's truth. I hope you don't find me insufferable, but to marry is forever."

"Frances. No, of course not! I thank you, very much."

"I've thought about you too. Are you sure you don't feel something?" Frances's eyes were desperate. "I'm not so clever, but I do notice things. You blush when he looks your way."

"Oh, I do *not*." Martha frowned, but she was warm, and she didn't like the look in Frances's eyes, as if she craved denial. Still, it was worse to tell the truth. "His attitude is poor," she said dismissively. "He's a friend of Mr. Gracey, that's all."

They were back at the settee. God, what else did Frances know? How many times had the vulgarity of men dropped her eyes? Even if Martha had been inclined to ask, she wouldn't have been able to. Robert stood and pulled his overcoat on, saying, "It's too beautiful a day to waste. Let's ride."

Fingers trembling, Martha tied her hat and tugged on her gloves. She didn't want to put her arm through Robert's, but she had to. Everything didn't simply go away, despite the unwelcome disgust, but it wasn't just for him; it was a counter-feeling to the one that ate too greedily at her heart.

The break of white teeth, chestnut hair, the green frock coat trimming his middle so perfectly. And the way that word refused to stop turning in her head–*darling*.

7

a SPRING RIDE

Asa led them through the back portico, where the
garden sprawled before wide stone steps. She
narrowed her eyes, putting the problem of Robert aside. It was
very pretty, but like the house, not as she'd expected. A terraced
garden, the retaining wall a half-moon around an expanse of
beds, trees, shrubs, and a maze of pebbled walkways, the bathing
pool, and a fish pond. A brindle mastiff lay in the sun by the
pond, dragging itself to attention when Asa strode by. Martha,
who liked dogs, patted it on the head, but Hannah squealed,
bustling into Robert.

"Leave off your dog, man," grumbled Robert, swatting at the
mastiff with his hat. Asa didn't respond, but snapped his fingers;
the dog loped away, and Martha felt briefly disappointed.

A dog or two had wandered the cottage yard when she was
little. All this space, with so many bends and forks—what would
it be like, to lose oneself in such a place? To run without shoes
on, like she had when she was a girl. Before she'd started to
realize that wasn't what ladies were supposed to do. She
would've chased that mastiff, and thrown sticks for him to fetch.

She frowned, watching her boots flick in and out of the gleaming blue of her habit.

She'd changed herself so much for Robert. This truth, coupled with what Frances had told her, toppled her confidence.

Asa turned sharply and led them up the gravel path and up the small hill to the barnyard. Sam, the wiry right-hand of Asa Wyeth, had tacked three horses, and rubbed down Robert's bay until it gleamed like oil. While Sam dutifully helped Hannah and Frances into their saddles, Martha twisted her hands, fretful. She was expected to ride in a sidesaddle. Certainly, she was a much better rider than either of the girls, but she'd ridden astride since she was tall enough to flip a bucket and hoist herself up by the mane. Bareback, most of the time, unless she was going to the city.

Heavens, she thought. *I'm not a lady at all!*

"Don't worry. She's gentle." It was Asa. He tossed the bridle over the horse's head, a small painted creature with a sloping nose.

"Sir, I know how to ride." Why had she said that—*just get in the saddle!*

He looked away, and she glanced, hot. A faint smile creased his eyes. "I know." He was occupied with the cinch, or pretending to be. "You don't have to ride the sidesaddle," he said quietly. "S'matter of fact, I'd rather you not."

It was such a forward thing to say, coming from a man, that her toes curled in her riding boots. Her body stiffened, and she stared at the ground.

"I would help you up, but I don't think you need that." He met her eyes directly, then slipped two fingers under the cinch, checking the tension. Then he clapped his hat on his head and strode off to Jed.

Mr. Wyeth fancies you.

It was uncommon attention, if nothing else. God, it made her want to stamp her foot, follow him, make him explain. What kind of man could slide two fingers under a cinch and make her feel like that! The air tickled with the now annoyingly familiar smell, and it went straight to her head. She curled her fingers around the pommel and swung up, tucking her legs to the side. Robert frowned, but she held her countenance. She couldn't ride astride, but at least she could mount her own horse!

Furthermore, she didn't want to talk to Robert. Not one word. If she asked him questions about what Frances had said, he would scoff–she knew it. His honor was at stake, and there were too many witnesses to contend with for him to straighten his story. No, it must fester in silence, until he asked her to marry him, and then what!

She rode, back poker-straight. On the other side of the barn, the hill dipped into an expanse of fields, fenced as far as she could see. Asa, walking with Jed lumbering beside him, unlatched the gate, kicked it open with a grimace, and let the horses pass. It was uncomfortably warm out, and sweat darkened the roots of his hair; she dropped her eyes, her heart quickening. Robert didn't sweat. He was cool and comfortable.

He must've caught on that she was angry, because he rode in silence, narrowed eyes on Asa's back. Asa held a clipped conversation with Hannah, but Frances was quiet, her expression pinched. *Oh dear, nobody's in a good mood.* Frances Dunaway, whispering with a glass of chilled Malmsey in one hand, had ruined everything.

There was a cut path at the bottom of the field, leading to the trees. Thank Christ, because it was too hot, and the back of her riding habit stuck with sweat. She hoped Asa didn't mean to take the tour too far; the cool, high-ceiling parlor was a dream, especially with her heart racing that way. The path was trimmed back, broken by a stone wall here or a bridge over a brook there. In a small clearing, there was a pavilion, and Asa stopped, dismounted, and began rummaging in his saddlebag.

Hannah dismounted too, and Martha scowled.

"How many acres do you have, Mr. Wyeth?" Hannah asked brightly.

"Don't know, exactly." (Something told Martha that he did). "Two hundred, maybe. Two-hundred-fifty."

"What a waste," interjected Robert. "You could tenant, at least."

"I've got a lot of horses." Asa stopped rummaging, coming up with a pocket flask. "Anyway, fifty is going to a fellow on down. He'll pay me to let his bloody sheep eat my grass."

"Really."

"Yes, really." Asa unstopped the flask and passed it to Robert, who reached for it tentatively, giving it a suspicious sniff.

"Do you want me to poison myself first?" said Asa testily. "I will."

"Knowing you, it's probably mixed with some rancid tincture." Nevertheless, Robert tipped the flask, grimaced, and handed it back. "What is that, rum?"

"Hmm, yes. Blackstrap rum."

Blackstrap rum. Martha nearly spoke, a memory rising–the case of molasses towering on the counting room floor. She bit her tongue.

"Rum is rather common, don't you think?" said Robert haughtily. "I'd be better off with a beer at the tavern."

Asa drank, stoppered the flask, and tucked it back into the saddlebag. "Yes, very common. Cheap, too."

There was a stone bench in the center of the pavilion, and Hannah sat down and pulled off her gloves. "Are you dealing wet goods these days, Mr. Wyeth?" she asked airily.

Martha fought a surge of irritation. It wasn't fair that Hannah could be so pert about the business of men. Mr. Gracey met with all sorts of merchants, week in and out–and she knew, at least, that the House of Henshaw dealt mostly in textiles and notions. Pretty things from Britain; things that didn't require much effort on Robert's part.

She followed Hannah's suit, pulling off her gloves, which resisted with sweat.

"I should hope he's not," said Robert with a snort. "That isn't the legacy of Wyeth Enterprises."

Asa blinked, then shook his head. "Nothing wrong with selling a case of blackstrap." It was odd, almost as if he were telling on himself to prove a point. "Nothing wrong with selling anything, really."

Martha sat, patting at the dampness on the back of her neck. Asa dipped back into the saddlebag, and came up with a bottle. He uncorked it with his teeth–a flash of white–and handed it to her.

"Cider," he explained.

She took it gratefully and drank–too much, but her sensibilities were upset. She wanted to glare at Robert, to scowl at him. And less and less did she care that her eyes wandered to Asa, following the lines of his body. She passed the cider to Hannah, and watched him from the corner of her eye.

"Too many wet tradesmen are profiteers these days," muttered Robert. "You'd best mind yourself, or they'll raid your ships."

Asa rolled his shoulders and slipped off the green frock; there was a small cherry-plated pistol clipped to one hip. Oh, goodness! For a gentleman to strip to his waistcoat, in the middle of the day, with ladies around–she flushed. His back was to her, but he *was* flirting. He had to be.

He tossed the frock over Jed's saddle. "Who would raid a Wyeth sloop, in seriousness? Goddamn."

"You're flippant." It was nearly a hiss. Robert strode through the pavilion and sat down beside Martha, despite the fact that there was hardly enough space. "You forget about the *Liberty* affair, cousin. You'd be best to go back to your history books."

"Aye." Asa nodded thoughtfully. He ran a hand over his hair, frowning at the stone floor. "Hell, I did forget about that. Suppose I was too busy, finding answers at the bottom of blackstrap bottles. I can set aside a case for Henshaw, if you're questioning your tactics."

He strode to help Frances off her horse.

Frances blushed, and Martha squirmed. She'd have to sit Frances down, and make her talk. Or maybe not; that blush had been far too deep, and the way Frances smiled up at Asa churned a new feeling in her heart. *Oh, stop!* It wasn't as if Asa were *her* man. He wasn't anyone's man! And Robert was so close, she could smell his annoyance. All of a sudden, it was too much; she flew to her feet, and fumbling with the ribbon under her chin, ripped off her hat.

"Martha! Goodness, something's gotten into you," observed Hannah, lifting a brow. "You're quite foul today."

"Oh, I'm not. I'm hot–it's too hot, I'm sorry, Mr. Wyeth!"

Asa turned, a flicker of concern passing in his eyes. His lips parted as if he meant to speak, but–

"Martha, put your hat back on." Robert's voice broke the fever in her brain. "You'll burn in the sun, as fair as you are." His concern was genuine, but there was aggravation in his tone. He'd seen it for what it was: Asa's frock was off. Martha's hat had been stripped.

And it wasn't right.

"She doesn't have to wear a hat." Asa toyed with a button on his sleeve. "Take off your jacket, if you want, Miss Gracey."

"Wyeth." Robert rose. His defensiveness was so palpable, Martha barely had time to blush over what Asa had said. "You're talking to a lady, don't forget. We're not in the back of a public house."

"No." Asa turned, facing Robert fully. "I'm talking to a woman. And if she's too hot, she may take off her jacket." There was a frosted edge to his voice, so tangible it could've stilled the sweat on the small of her back. "Martha, get back on your horse. We'll go to the house if you're uncomfortable."

But the problem wasn't that she was too hot. The problem was, Frances had ruined Robert, past the point of questioning. And she was guilty, because she'd spent so many nights hoping for him, praying for him, wanting him so badly, she'd skipped meals and stared herself ugly in the mirror. Now, her heart was too swiftly making him a monster.

"I'm all right, Mr. Wyeth," she muttered. "I'm being silly. We don't need to go back. I enjoy the outdoors." She wrapped her arms around her middle, and Frances caught her arm, leading her to the edge of the pavilion.

Hannah's tinkling laugh was swallowed by throbbing air.

"I'm sorry," whispered Frances. "You're distressed. I shouldn't have told you. I should have waited until we got back—you seem quite ill."

But she wasn't ill. She felt bolstered by anger and justified disappointment. Worse than anything, she felt…aroused. Not just in her head, but in her body. One look at Asa, and her thighs clenched. She could admit it, now, that she was disgusted at Robert, and she could admit also, it was because of Asa, that her disgust had settled with such welcome.

She'd been looking for an excuse. She had. Ever since she'd placed her little hand in Asa's palm at the Henshaw-Dunaway solstice revel.

She shook her head. "It's all right, Frances, really. You were right, to tell me."

"What are you going to do?"

"I–I don't know." She'd never thought about Robert proposing. Proposing meant marriage and estates and affairs and…babies. It wasn't even that she'd ever cared about the fancy things, the houses, the pedigrees, the enterprises. No, it was much more primal than that, when it came to men.

It was attention. Robert was a peacock among men, the strongest, the most beautiful; heads turned when he walked by. It only made sense that he'd made her sensibilities purr, and his attention said something about her as a certain specimen of woman–a lady. Only she realized it now. She didn't want to be a lady, a shell of satin and whalebone stays.

I'm talking to a woman.

God. This was not good! She wanted to slap Frances across the face. In turn, hug her. Thank her, again, at the very least–she opened her mouth, then–

Boom. The floor of the pavilion shook, and she yelped, gripping Frances by the arm. Again–*boom, boom, boom.* She pressed her palms to her ears. Hannah gasped, covering her mouth, and Robert shot to his feet, clapping his hat on his head.

"It's just musket, aye." Asa raised a brow.

"Who on earth is shooting musket in your fields?" Robert strode to the edge of the pavilion, peering through the trees. "Are those farm boys? Good God, are you letting continentals drill on Wyeth property?"

Asa shrugged, and Martha took note. It was almost as if he'd brought them there to hear it, on purpose.

"Don't fret," he said lightly. "They won't shoot at the trees."

"Are they really continentals?" gasped Hannah. Composing herself, she took out her fan. "Goodness, that's rather audacious of you. You're a Tory to the root of your family tree!"

"Fellows have to practice," said Asa, by way of an answer. "You'll never be a good marksman if you don't practice."

Robert was clearly shaken. Past subtle jibes and irritable tones, he fell silent. The musket fire ricocheted through the trees, rebounding from hill to hill outside the refuge of the pavilion. Frances, sweat coiling her mousy hair, was pale; Hannah, too interested, was asking too many arrogantly prodding questions—as if that were the sort of thing Asa looked for in a woman.

Confidence, assurance. Faux interest. *He doesn't seem to care*, thought Martha crossly. Now that she'd recognized the source of the commotion, she didn't feel the need to cover her ears. A noise like that was the source of something that needed investigation. It was the same way at the docks. If shouting voices rose above a crowd, it only meant there might be a good brawl. If a woman on the street laughed too loud, maybe she was a prostitute.

And if Asa Wyeth let continentals drill on his property, well, he wasn't just a profiteer. He was a full-on rebel to the Crown.

Robert tugged on her elbow. "Come, Miss Gracey. Wyeth, let's take the ladies back to the house. It's too hot." He seemed in genuine contention with himself, and Martha wondered where his conceit had gone. Could it be that easily rattled by a little black powder and lead? It wasn't as if he didn't know Asa had radical connections; he'd claimed it himself. Even as she'd remained tight-lipped, Robert would've been a fool not to have put two-and-two together. And less and less did she believe that Asa actually cared about the secret.

Asa didn't counter. He only nodded, touching the brim of his hat, and helped Hannah into the saddle. Martha stared at his back. He hadn't put the frock back on. Jed back-stepped, snorting, turned–her thighs clenched. The musket fire had ceased, and there was a rustling in the tall grass, followed by buoyant laughter.

She rode removed; Robert rode silent. He must've quickly come to terms with the fact that she wasn't the lady he'd thought she was. She hadn't put her hat back on, but she wasn't sorry–no. He'd goaded Asa all day. Coupled with Frances's breathy voice, she was angrier at Robert than she'd ever been at anyone.

She watched Asa from the corner of her eye. He rode as if he'd been born in a saddle, spine a little slouched, the same aura of being required to put one's boots on a bureau plat, or tell a lady she could take off her jacket. It roared at the heat in her groin. A break of shadow, slipping in and out of the trees–the rocking gate of the horse, sweat, soaking the back of her habit. The way her ears rang–*boom, boom, boom.*

Her senses were smoking, signaling to her. Not just to her heart, sore with anger, but deep in the pit of her gut. Now, there were questions, none of which she had the answer to. Robert was a thorn in her side, a problem that she had equal hand in the creation of. And if what Frances said was true–then, when?

When, when, when. And what. What would she say?

Asa led them through the west corner terrace, which opened to an airy tea-room, smaller than the parlor. A table by the wall was set with a silver service. The walls were white, relatively blank. A Jacobean cabinet, rich, painfully polished oak... Martha winced. Too much Malmsey, too much cider pushed at her bladder, and the spotlessness of the room made no sense, when she was a sweaty, uncomfortable cottage girl. *I'm not made for this—Robert tricked me.*

Frances stopped by the door. "Mr. Wyeth, is this a visitors' book?" She brushed her fingers over an open diary, displayed on a cherry drop-leaf table. Asa only nodded, and Frances took up a quill. *Signing her name in a visitors' book.* How silly. As if he'd go and pine over it later—*stop, it Martha, you're being mean.* And she regretted it, almost immediately. As Frances caught up, she brushed close to Martha, hand to hand, trembling fingers—Martha grasped a passed slip of paper.

Write it on a piece of paper. Thank you, Frances, thank you! She crumpled it in her fist.

Asa led them down a short corridor. "Have a moment, ladies," he said, opening a door, which showed a large bedroom. Robert trailed, and Martha caught him dipping down the passage to the entrance hall. So many doors, so many blank spaces…and he was questioning himself. Wrestling with himself, just as she was. She'd sensed it, since the first *boom.*

Frances and Hannah bustled into the room, Hannah deftly untying her hat. All at once, it was too much; too much anxiety, too many tangled thoughts—she couldn't stand it. She pressed against the wall, looking Asahel Wyeth straight in the eye.

"Mr. Wyeth," she blurted, "where is the necessary house?"

She flushed, her head spinning. *Why—why, you could've asked Hannah or Frances—they've been here before—*

But Asa didn't flinch. He nodded, excused her from the girls, and led her down the passage to a little room, not more than a closet, with a washstand, a pitcher and bowl, a crisply folded stack of towels, and against the back wall, a close stool chair. She slipped in, glancing at Asa as the door closed.

No scandal, no wincing. Women used close stool chairs and necessary houses, and it was all right, it didn't warrant excuses.

She dropped the lock, fumbling. Asa's boots echoed down the corridor. Then she hitched her skirts and sank back, head in her hands.

She took a moment to regain herself. It wasn't that she felt sick. She *had* drunk too much on an empty belly, but it was less queasiness, and more a wild, out-of-body feeling. Her heart beat far too fast, and her fingers, smoothing out the piece of paper from Frances, shook like a leaf. She squinted to read in the light beneath the door.

I'd work that sweet little cunt with my tongue, until she was stiff with pleasure. Have a seat and picture that—Martha Ann Gracey, cracking my skull with her thighs. She'd be hoarse from screaming my name down the halls of Wyeth House. Trust me, that girl would never forget me.

(As close as I can remember. Please destroy this as soon as you've read it—forgive me).

She read it again, and again. And a fourth time.

She wasn't an entirely innocent girl. But her freedom sheltered her with questions Mr. Gracey never answered, and her understanding of sex was barnyard at best. To lay with someone was to somehow love, with nakedness. But *stiff with pleasure*...she'd figured that out, in too many dark hours trying to understand herself. The rest was a riddle, and it didn't sound crude, or obscene.

It was impassioned, vindictive, like a secret whispered in the dark.

She rose from the close stool chair and tucked the paper under her garter ribbon. She would destroy it, but she needed to memorize it first. She was light—floating, unpleasantly so; she went to the washbasin and splashed water on her face, erasing the heat, the *boom, boom, boom*—the ringing in her ears—she scrubbed her skin raw with a towel. No more powder, no more pinched cheeks.

She was wild, infused with something inexplicable. An odd tincture. A little white tablet, in the palm of his hand. Sweat, at the roots of thick chestnut curls.

Her nostrils were rimmed with vanilla smoke.

Fingers skimming the wall, she flipped the latch and slipped back into the corridor. Thank God, it was shielded from the glaring windows; she felt safer in the shadows. She couldn't go back to that bedroom. How would she look Frances in the eye? The woman had built so much shame around a written statement, that Martha was too innocent to even bat an eye over. Honestly, even when she'd figured it out, (which she would) she still wouldn't bat an eye.

Women were so silly sometimes. Life would be so much easier if they were crude, like men. If she could simply ask Asa, "Mr. Wyeth, what does that mean, you're going to work my cunt with your tongue?" Something told her that he'd explain, without so much as lifting a brow.

The corridor emptied into the entrance hall, where the buffalo hide was taunting. Robert was nowhere to be seen, and the Dunaway girls were a distant tittering. Drawing a breath, she ducked into the passage on the opposite wall. Past a set of stairs, at the end of the corridor, there was a wall of glass windows, overlooking an empty piazza, and to her left, an arched open doorway. She passed through.

A library. There were stacks of book-boxes, from the ceiling to the floor, meticulously organized. She made out titles…in Latin, but most all of them were law books. Goodness, how many law books did a man have to read to be a lawyer? *How boring*. There was not a speck of dust, not an item out of place. A grandfather clock. A firmly latched secretary cabinet. An octagonal table, with a stack of paper, a quill, an inkwell. She turned to head back to the passage, when her eye caught something—a glint of light on liquid.

On the other side of the archway was a door, ajar. It led to a small room, centered with a burr walnut bureau plat and a beaded red leather chair. There was a decanter of brandy on the bureau plat, which had caught the light, and an empty glass, though the bottom was wet. The walls were two-toned, half a pleasant sea-green, to a neat white and gold scribe molding. Against one wall was a secretary, walnut to match. Against another, a small bookcase, a map, stuck with pins. And another—a four-winged folding screen, one panel tucked open.

She jolted. Through the open panel stood Asa Wyeth, his back to her, unbuttoning his shirtsleeves, in front of a sprawling four-poster bed.

Oh God—no! This wasn't a library for anyone, she'd walked straight into Asa's private suite! She pressed a knuckle to her mouth, backing away. *Please, please—please*—he didn't turn. Around the arched doorway, she bolted, just as a break of water-tanned skin flashed in the sunlight.

Back through the passage…back through the entrance hall, to the opposite corridor, past the room where the Dunaway girls were surely still powdering their faces. God, she hadn't just seen that—a man, stripping off a sweat-soaked set of shirtsleeves! Not meant for her eyes, yet the image fed her ravenous brain, teasing at the wild ache in the pit of her pelvis. She ducked through the doorway of the tea room—and ran straight into Robert.

"Oh!"

"Martha, whatever are you doing? I thought you were freshening up." He pushed her off by the shoulders. "Lord, you're flushed."

"Mr. Henshaw! I'm sorry. I thought I might go out onto the terrace, for some fresh air." She dipped past, but he caught her by the elbow.

"No, it's too hot. Stay inside." He led her to a settee, pressing her to sit. "Anyway, I need to talk to you." There was a dumbwaiter in the corner, and he poured her a glass of port. She took it, holding it in her lap, her heart slamming. He wanted to talk to her about something–what?

He wouldn't ask her to marry him, not at Wyeth House! Panic rose; her tongue went dry.

"Martha?"

"Robert, please." *What will I say, what will I do?*

"It's about Asahel."

She breathed, closing her eyes. *Thank God, yes. Talk ill of Asahel Wyeth as much as you want, just don't ask anything else!*

"I don't like the amount of time he spends at the cottage," he said firmly. "I know what you're going to say–business with your father. And I don't like that either." He drank back a port, too fast. "But I'm starting to think that isn't the only reason."

"I haven't considered it," she replied lamely. It was true. Or it *had* been true, until today.

"I have. He's a changed man, since he came back from New York, and he's got bad connections. Honestly, Martha, I don't want him near you."

He refilled her glass. She wouldn't argue; she didn't know Asa any better than he, perhaps less so. Yet–*she'd be hoarse from screaming my name down the halls of Wyeth House.*

The paper scratched beneath her garter ribbon. "Dangerous? That doesn't seem very fair."

He scoffed, shaking his head. "You're innocent. He's not a gentleman, Martha, stay away from him, when he comes to the cottage."

"Mr. Henshaw, I beg your pardon–" It was audacious, and as always, when someone told her *what to do,* irritation prickled her spine.

"He's taken a fancy to you," Robert claimed, nearly triumphant, as if he were the first one to observe such a grotesque thing. "I'm surprised you haven't seen it. I know him well enough, he won't stand in wait. Forgive me if I'm too bold, but I thought you were feeling something, too."

What a wretched thing to say! For a moment, she was almost regretful. His eyes turned desperate, searching for something he was clearly petrified to find. God, maybe it wasn't what she'd thought. The question she'd asked so many times when it came to Robert bolted to the front of her brain.

Why Martha Ann Gracey?

She wasn't rich. She wasn't affluent. And he'd never said "love". He'd done everything right. He'd brought her flowers, and walked with her in gardens, and paid for her treats and nice things at the shops. She'd returned the gestures by betraying herself, turning her eyes from the flowers in the fields, forcing them to stare at gemstones and rich textiles.

Her fingers pinched the stem of her glass, which he filled for a third time.

"I don't–I don't have feelings for Mr. Wyeth," she managed to say, nearly ready to cry, the ball of frustration and confusion was so tight.

His throat flexed with a swallow. He offered her a smile, not relieved, but softer. "Forgive me for asking."

"It's quite all right."

How fortunate that she was so drunk on Asa's port. More than that, she was drunk on the sight of a bronzed back in the sunlight, and Robert had no idea! Abruptly she stood, her eyesight prickling, and brushed past him to the terrace door. Every step was a fight, but she would not betray herself.

"I'm quite refreshed," she said, forcing lightness to her tone. "Let's walk in the garden, when Hannah and Frances are rested. I'm sure Mr. Wyeth won't mind."

But he followed her, circling her forearm. It was possessive; his touch was soft, but the motion was demanding. She turned sharply to find him too close.

The smell of port stung her nose.

"Martha, stay."

"Robert, please—"

He lifted her hand and kissed it. His lips were soft, wet with port, and she would've been in denial to say it wasn't pleasant. Firm, and when he let go, it lingered on her skin.

"Martha." He took up her other hand, kissing it too. His eyes were too fond, far too fervent. "God, you're so beautiful. No wonder he wants you!"

Dear God, does he mean it?

"Martha Ann Gracey, I love you," he said, under his breath. "I can't lose you. Not to him."

"Robert, please. This is fast—"

"This surely can't come as a surprise!"

"This isn't a proper place for this sort of talk," she managed. "I-I'm not of a good mind—I've had too much port!"

"Please don't evade me, love. Come here."

She was pulled in at the elbows, and he pressed her close, bending her throat, and kissed her on the mouth.

She'd never been kissed on the mouth before, and for a moment, she forgot why it was happening, and simply felt. Something she'd dreamed of so many times. It was nice at first, and faintly stirred the heat festering between her legs. But then, his lips broke her lips apart, and she tasted port. Not hers, but his. Fresh on a probing tongue–oh, what was he doing, putting his tongue in her mouth! She jerked back, planting her hands on his chest.

"Robert, what are you doing!"

"I'm kissing you." He pulled away, cradling her face. "I'm kissing you because I love you."

"Well, I–I don't want to be kissed right now, I'm sorry." She ran a hand over her mouth, trembling. Violently–the room circled.

"You're sweet. Forgive me if I disturbed you. But my feelings won't change. I loved you since the moment I met you." His hands were misted with sweat, and then–a finger traced the belly of her forearm, and she was once again pulled close. Her guard flared; she darted backwards.

"Mr. Henshaw, I beg your pardon! I-I told you I didn't want to be kissed!"

"Then sit down, and rest, love."

"I really need fresh air. We can talk–at the cottage–"

"Martha. You're *not* drunk." His tone was warning, though he still smiled. "Come now. You're a sturdy drinker. Let me talk to you, it's all I want." He caught her hand again.

He wasn't wrong. Martha, conditioned from too young an age to take port with William, handled drink stoutly. But Wyeth's port was potent, and it was more than that; it was too much to feel, too much to learn. She felt sick. He was kissing her hand, turning it over, lips skimming the bend of her wrist–

She clenched her teeth. *Stop, please–fellows aren't supposed to do that*–but the words wouldn't come out.

"Martha," he breathed. "Be my wife."

He must've taken her silence as shock, and her gaping mouth was an opening. He leaned in and kissed her again. Gently, slow burning kisses over her mouth, down the line of her jaw. Down her throat. Her shoulders locked, and she gasped, pushing him away once more.

"Martha." His voice rasped. "You don't answer. Whatever's the matter?"

"I'm unwell! I'm sorry, that you should ask me this now–"

"Should comfort make you answer with more favor? If so, we can pretend I've never spoken. Answer me yes, and I'll leave."

God, it was a nightmare. She could do nothing, she couldn't move, the earth was whirling mad. She was not lying to him; the heat had been too much, and she *was* drunk–not out of her realm, but out of touch with her sensibilities.

"Would it make a difference?" His eyes eagerly searched her face. "God, you're taking too long!"

She looked past him wildly, taking in the room. Searching for anything to ballast her equilibrium. Everything–the sunlight through the window, the smarting smell of balsam, the exasperating cleanliness–it screamed, over and over, Asa. *Asa.* Asa.

Robert laid with Wyeth's woman.

Have a seat and picture that–Martha Ann Gracey, cracking my skull with her thighs. Why did that make more sense than Robert kissing her? Because she'd struggled with Robert's way of life for too long. She'd worn hats and gloves when it was too hot. She'd sat in parlors, when she belonged in the fields. And the worst of it was, he'd believed her.

"Robert, I'm sorry, but I don't want to talk about this right now." She backed away, arms around her middle, and made for the terrace door once again. Her lips stung with kisses, virgin, swollen, and her feet begged her to run.

He followed, a wide hand locking her arm, and twisted her around.

"It's him," he said bluntly. "Isn't it?"

"What–what on earth–what do you mean? I'm not feeling well!"

"You're lying. You've never given me anything but encouragement, so I know you're lying!"

"I don't accept or decline callers at the door of my father's house." Oh yes, she *was* lying. "Sir, you'd do well to take your hand off me!"

"You're in love with him. Aren't you?"

"What–good heavens, Mr. Henshaw–"

"He's done all the right things, hasn't he? He makes you comfortable."

"Let go, this instant! You're not in your right mind!"

But he smirked, looming closer. "You gave me every reason to believe in a yes. Until now. It's on your sleeve, Martha, you're in love with Asahel. And he's a racketeering villain–he's dragging Mr. Gracey down with him!"

She gasped, yanking at her arm. It smarted to the bone. Indignation rose, hot as musket fire. *Boom, boom, boom–*

"Mr. Henshaw, I beg your pardon, but how *dare* you! You've kept me company, but you haven't given me attention. I could be a fly on the wall, and I would be enough, if only I should listen!"

"Nonsense, I've given you every attention. I've paid you every homage. Don't insult me, I've nothing else to prove!"

"You've nothing else to prove?" She stared at him. Hurt, distended, damaged by the assault on her innocence. "If you've nothing else to prove, then why do you choose to ask me such a thing, at your cousin's house? I can't think of a reason, Mr. Henshaw, I have to say–I'm embarrassed!"

"Embarrassed? You can't really think I'm intimidated by him. That's the most foolish thing I've ever heard you say!"

"You know it's true!"

"I know no such thing. This is foolishness. You're right, you're delirious with heat. I've done everything I can to assure myself the answer I expected! Please. I'm *not* asking you this out of spite. I'm asking because I love you!"

"Robert." All of a sudden, tears broke–it was too much. "I'm sorry. I'm sorry that you've wasted your time, and I'm grieved I misled you." She drew a breath, shuddering. *Just say it, Martha, rip it out.*

"I can't marry you."

There was a frantic moment, when his eyes met hers. Searching. Disbelief…her heart flipped. But any regret or misgiving was lost when he lurched forward, kissing her again. Not gentle, nothing to tease the heat. He was brutish. Before she could protest, bullish hands pinioned her arms to her sides, and she was driven backwards, hidden from the doorway by the Jacobean cabinet. From the peripheral of her vision, she caught one hand reaching for the Venetian blind, tugging it down.

The sunlight plunged.

She knotted. Her knees locked, her gut sucked in, neck bent back–his tongue was deep against the roof of her mouth. And his fingers, on her neck, her arms, her back. Fumbling at blue satin skirts, balling at her middle, hot on her thighs. Places only she had ever touched. The sound of ripping thread hissed through her skull. Her jacket–white skin met cold air.

"Robert, please stop–please–"

"Beg all you want." He drew back enough to meet her eyes. "You've made an idiot of me. When I've only ever honored you–" A lunging kiss, teeth taking her lower lip. "You'll marry me. Oh, you'll marry me!"

"Robert, this is a misunderstanding!"

Blood rose from her lip. She was against the wall, held by a fist clutching the habit at her throat. Fingers pressed ditches in her skin, down her thighs, fumbling at her garters, catching on the piece of paper. He read it fast, then tossed it to the floor.

"Frances will pay for this," he snarled.

"No!"

"Stop yelling. She's not your friend—you don't know her!"

Fumbling big hands—she couldn't move, locked against the wall by a muscled forearm. His breeches—he was tugging at the buttons, losing her skirts, a grunt of frustration, bunching them again—pressing into her—his proximity, his smell, port gone bad—

"Robert, *stop!*"

Cold air washed over her breasts, fingernails bruising virgin skin. Her tears bled into his mouth. She twisted, trying to cry out, but his kisses had her dumb.

Was this it? Bodily love, what drove men to battlefields, what moved the pens of poets? Eros, the answer to her sighing daydreams, her aching visions, was it really this—pain? Panic? Kisses in places where kisses didn't go.

Her belly roiled, and she loosened, surrendering into her misunderstanding. It was better that way. No one would explain, and she would forget.

And then, he wasn't touching her anymore. He was ripped from her with such ferocity, that even in her confusion, she knew it wasn't a change of heart. A flash of brown, and the curled, white-knuckled fist of Asa Wyeth, dragging Robert off by the back of his frock.

She caught his eyes over Robert's shoulder, stricken with something, unnamable—harrowed, chestnut curls wild, skin broken with sweat. Robert floundered, his boots clattering on the floor; he was swung, big body lagging, and pinned by the cravat against the wall. It was the most startling thing she'd ever seen. Robert was broad, muscled like an ox, and the idea that he had a match in physical strength made no sense. Something in her gut moved her to protest; her innocence, perhaps, rearing its ugly head–but abruptly, he was dropped.

Robert stumbled, and Asa seized him by the scruff, and quietly–almost carefully–reeled him backwards, and thrashed his head into the wall.

Glass rattled in the Jacobean cabinet. The tea service shuddered.

Asa rolled his shoulders and wrung out his hand. He was blank. Only a trace flaring of the nostrils betrayed any exertion.

"Get out of my house, Rob."

Robert fumbled, regaining himself. With a fist balled, he made a lunge at Asa, who stepped back almost gingerly, reached around his frock, and unclipped the pistol at his hip. He didn't point it at Robert, but instead leveled it at the ceiling, and though it was cocked, his finger lay on the lock plate rather than the trigger.

"I told you to get out of my house," he said stiffly.

"Careful, Asahel." Robert smirked. A purple bruise blossomed where his temple had hit the wall. "I'll put a bounty on your head! You're making it too easy."

"As I said, get out." Asa's finger twitched on the lock plate. "Go on, door's that way." He nodded in the direction of the beaming glass. Robert's boots shrieked on the polished floor; he stormed to the door, wrenching it open with such force that a bone cracked in his elbow.

"Cousin." Asa tucked the pistol away. "Unfortunate witness, aye. Were you hoping for Hannah? Surely not Frances, I think you know well where her loyalties lie." He crooked his elbow, arranging the pleats of his frock over the cherry-plated handle. "And as I think you already know, I didn't see a bloody thing."

Robert stared, eyes wide, temples throbbing. Then he turned and bolted, slamming the door behind him, boots beating on the terrace stones.

Asahel Wyeth grimaced, and Martha reeled, stumbled, and vomited sour port onto the spotless floor.

8

the RUINATION *of* MARTHA GRACEY

Her body collapsed into heaving sobs. He hadn't just broken her; he'd ripped her in half. She was torn skin, bleeding from the heart, her innocence picked raw. Robert's hands were crow on a carcass.

Standing by the window, squinting into the sun, Asa was silent. Once, he slipped out the door, closing it noiselessly, and she caught his figure leaning over the stone railing, staring into nothing. When he returned, he shrugged off his frock, and, stepping carefully over the vomit, dropped it over her bare shoulders. Then, he poured himself a brandy and stood, a pronounced distance away from her shivering figure.

Hannah's laugh drifted, musical. Shadows, dancing in high light, flickered and swayed, and birds outside shrilled. She was still drunk, but gradually, choking back sobs, she began to feel again. Her arms were sore, mottled with pink. The muscles of her legs knotted. Her breasts—she scrambled, gasping. One was exposed over the bent angle of her stays, white skin streaked. She pressed the edges of the frock together, rushing with shame.

Yet, Asa still wasn't looking at her. If he'd seen her breast, he did not react. After a few moments, when her weeping faded to low sniffles, he broke, plucked a kerchief from his waistcoat, and moved warily to pass it to her. She took it, pressing it into her eyes, wiping her mouth, as if it might somehow erase the taste.

"Adeline!" Asa called. A girl in a fluttering mobcap scampered in, hands clasped at her waist.

"Get a bucket and a rag, and clean this up." He gestured at the vomit. "Be quick."

Her embarrassment ate away some of the shock. Once the floor was cleaned, Asa approached her, crouching to her level with his arms on his thighs. She hunched, but a hasty glimpse punched her heart. Robert had ruined every sweet beauty that day had given her. Everything–secret corridors, to private suites. The smiles. The touch on the small of her back. Sun-kissed skin.

Ruined.

She gulped, dipping her face.

"Darling." He cleared his throat. "You can stay for a bit, I'll have a room set up."

Don't call me darling right now, please! "Thank you, sir, that's very kind."

"I'll send the girls off. Do you need anything?"

She glanced again. The concern in his eyes was unexplainable. Protective, hard. He was speaking like a father, and it made no sense coming from a man who thrashed heads against walls.

"I-I don't need anything." She sniffed, balling the kerchief. "Oh, I'm sorry, this is my fault. I drank too much port, and I didn't eat this morning!"

"Well, why don't we get you something to eat. Adeline!" (The serving girl appeared again). "Fix a plate, nothing pretty. Cheese–some salted cod, a glass of water. Hurry now."

He turned back to Martha. Even crouched, he was taller than her sitting figure, and she shivered, dropping her eyes. God, how ugly she must've looked! She blurted, "Please don't look at me, Mr. Wyeth!"

"Martha, I'm not that sort of fellow," he said, a forward tenderness matching the pitch of his voice. "You've nothing to be ashamed of. I'll talk to Mr. Gracey."

"Please!" A surge of panic pitched her forward. "You don't need to. He shouldn't know, I don't know how to explain!"

"He should know, darling."

Darling. Again. The connotation was so different, when she was wounded, and she hated it. "Please," she repeated weakly. "I-I'll be all right."

"Martha, I have a duty to speak. He's my partner." Clearly uncomfortable, he dropped his eyes. "You don't have to say anything. I won't take this out of the room, other than Billy."

At first, she didn't understand what he meant, she was so humiliated, but then–oh no, she must correct him! He couldn't leave this room if he thought for one moment the notion held any truth.

"Mr. Wyeth. I-I don't intend to marry Mr. Henshaw." She said it fast, forcing the humiliation aside.

Again, he dropped his eyes. He was frowning at his hands, a muscle working in his jaw, heartbeat in his temples. He ran a hand over his hair and cleared his throat. Then he rose and went to the dumbwaiter to fix another brandy.

"I can assure you." It was more for her aching heart than anything else. "You don't need to speak to my father. I wasn't– I didn't know the sort of fellow Mr. Henshaw was."

He stood by the window, shoulders stooped, fingers tapping lightly on his glass. Then, his shoulders rose and fell in a sigh, and he turned.

"You're a sturdy woman, Miss Gracey, to make your own choice," he said, with a tight smile. "Some wouldn't dare."

It was the highest compliment she'd ever received. Past Robert telling her she was ravishing, or Hannah, exclaiming how lovely she looked. She warmed, feeling immediately better. And even more so, when Adeline the serving girl brought in a plate on a cart. She grabbed at a piece of cheese. Thank God, an anchor to the drunken spiral! Salted cod had never tasted so good.

From the corner of her eye, she saw Asa smile and dip his head. Yet in contention, he pressed the back of his head and winced. "Bennet!" he hollered, and the stiff-backed man fairly shot into the room, hands tucked.

"Have Sam ready a chaise for Henshaw House," Asa instructed. "Two ladies. Put a Malmsey and glasses in the pocket, it must be fun—and Christ, bring me another Dover's."

The boy scampered. Martha swallowed cod, averting her eyes. She didn't understand what Robert had done, only that it hurt; but Asa was breaking it down, step by step. This must be done, and *that* must be done, after. Like a businessman. She'd vomited, so it must be cleaned up. Her jacket was torn, so she must be covered with a frock; she was too drunk, so she must have cheese, water, and cod, specifically. The Dunaway girls must be sent away in a Malmsey-packed chaise carriage, which *must* seem fun.

She blinked, chewing. The port was almost flushed out, and with it fading, what Robert had done didn't seem so horrifying. Another man had the reins, one whose short assurance was mending her shame. She thought back, reliving the feelings.

Probing mouth, tongue against her teeth–she shuddered. Something told her (watching Asa) that Robert hadn't touched her properly. That if… someone *else* kissed her, it would feel different. The rose-plated pistol glinted in the sun, clipped close to a trim hip. Bennet flew back in, dropped a white tablet into Asa's palm, and shot out.

Asa put back the pill with brandy. "I'm going to send a boy for Billy," he said firmly. "Ahem–Mr. Gracey."

She straightened. "Sir. Are you going to tell him what you saw?"

"Don't fret. Your honor is no less. Your father is a considerate man."

"I know, it's just that." She hung her head. "I-I don't want to hurt him."

All of a sudden, the truth sank her heart. Poor William, his tenderness, the sincerity of his devotion, put him in a place where he required a degree of protection. He was neither vindictive nor violent; she doubted he'd ever brawled in his life. So, if given the truth–that she'd been assaulted by Robert Henshaw–what on earth would he do?

The only thing close to hatred he'd ever felt had been channeled to Robert and Robert alone. He'd drink himself silly, most likely. Die of a sore heart.

Asa frowned into his brandy. "Fuck," he muttered. He bent his head, one side to the other. "Stay for a bit. Settle down. Adeline will fix a room for you."

He wouldn't promise not to speak. It was a stark reminder that he was not her friend, no matter how considerate; he was a brother to William Gracey first. The foolishness rushed back, and she felt wretched, shrouded in his pine-green frock, in a room now haunted by the ghost of her slaughtered innocence.

"Sir," she muttered tearfully, "may I have a port?"

117

He strode to the dumbwaiter, took up the bottle of port, and firmly corked it. "No." His tone was clipped. "You drink too much for a pint-sized girl, I've noted." She flushed, half-rising from her seat, but he circled and stoppered the brandy decanter as well, tucking it under his arm. "I'll send Adeline for coffee. I won't argue," he said, in a manner that riled an image in her brain—black rum, a booming voice, Robert's flustered indignation. Her wrist pinched. It was unbelievable to her now, that she'd forgiven Robert for circling in the hall.

He headed for the door again, and she saw it, at the same moment he did. The piece of paper. It had fluttered and landed, just beneath the Jacobean cabinet. *No...no, no!* She bolted, forgetting her weakness, and snatched it up.

"I'm sorry." (*Oh, thank Christ!*) "I've written something private on that. I was playing a game. Ahem—with Frances."

He cocked his head. "With Frances, aye?"

"Yes." She swallowed a bite of cheese, tightening her grip on his frock. "I'm sorry. Ladies play such silly games."

He must not know. Something told her, that if he knew that she knew, she would never find out what it meant.

She was shown to one of the bedrooms in the corridor, opposite the passage to Asa's suite. Asa wouldn't, in fact, be argued with, about Mr. Gracey nor her consumption of port; and it barely mattered, because she was so tired, that as soon as the riding habit was shed she collapsed onto the bed and slept—hard. Her brain had been battered with thoughts all day, and shut off so abruptly when Robert had made his move, the exhaustion caught up the moment her head hit the pillow.

She slept, for hours. When she finally opened her eyes, a grey light throbbed against the glass, and exuberant birdsong told her that it wasn't high afternoon, but the following morning. She pulled the covers to her chest, examining the room. The first visit to Wyeth House, and she'd spent the night! It was a pretty room, clearly arranged with a woman in mind. There was a neat cherry dressing table with a mirror, set with a brush and a powder tin; a matching wardrobe, a washstand with a basin and towels, a chair in the corner. It was simple and airy. The windows were hung with white patterned brocade, pulled open.

Adeline the serving girl was poking in the wardrobe.

"Best get you dressed, Miss Gracey," she squeaked, a hint of resentment in her tone. Martha put her feet on the floor, realizing that all the girls in Asa's service probably sighed when he walked by.

Adeline brought out a simple cotton petticoat and gown, too large. "Breakfast is serving. Mr. Gracey is here, he's going to take you home."

"Oh–I'm not hungry." She wasn't; she'd eaten the entire plate of cod and cheese. She ached, but it wasn't as bad as she'd feared. A line of bruises circled her upper arms; her collarbone and shoulders were tender, but otherwise–she glanced in the mirror. Her lower lip was a little swollen, but to someone who didn't know, it wouldn't have raised questions. Strangely, she didn't remember the pain. It was the embarrassment that ate her.

"You must go to breakfast," insisted Adeline. "Mr. Wyeth won't have anything else."

She fairly stuffed Martha into the petticoat.

Her head didn't want her to dwell on Robert. Perhaps it was forethought, making her stay the night, to wake in a new house with so many other things to think about. Things that both annoyed her (Adeline) and upset her (the fact that Asa had a room so readily set up for a woman). And things that excited her. The whispers, scampering feet, the ducking heads, cogwheels turning in a flawlessly ordered household. No wonder it was so spotless. She lost count, trailing Adeline, of all the bodies, dusting, scrubbing, polishing.

The dining room was adjoined to the tea-room by a set of double-pocket doors, which, thank goodness, were shut. The room was bright and white, like most of the house, curtains open, centered with an extended mahogany drop-leaf table. Asa sat at the head, an untouched plate of thick rye cakes and a cup of black coffee in front of him. He was frowning over a record book, wire-framed spectacles low on his nose. Mr. Gracey sat to his left, and Sam to his right.

Her throat closed when she saw William. Everything swelled; the bruises were wine-red. The bite was a chunk of flesh, torn from her lip. And her shame spelled a bad word, etched into the skin of her forehead.

Asa barely looked up. "G'morning, Miss Gracey. Bloody hell, there's a missing number here somewhere, or I've got a bandit on my hands." He muttered, running a finger down an impeccably penned list. "Sam, send that new chamber boy to my office. What's his name…Edward…Edmund…something."

"Yes, sir." Sam leaped up, shoulders straight, and loped away.

"My dear." Mr. Gracey bounced to his feet. "I heard you weren't feeling well, poor thing. Too much heat is the worst thing. I can't imagine anything worse. You're in the best care at Wyeth House, however, and I hope you rested well." He caught her hands, kissing them repeatedly, and led her to sit across from him at the table. Very close to Asa, who smelled scrubbed clean. He glanced, frowned, and bent back over the book, scribbling.

"Sleep all right, Miss Gracey?"

"Oh. Yes, thank you, sir." She bunched her hands on her lap.

"Let's get you something to eat, my dear." Mr. Gracey pushed away his plate, which was scraped clean. "We'll go directly home when you've eaten. Wyeth and I are headed to Wentworth's Wharf this afternoon, I thought to ask you to come—"

"She's not coming to the wharf," interrupted Asa flatly.

"Well, well," said Mr. Gracey, turning red. "Never mind, you're too delicate, you must rest all day—"

"I thought she was sturdy as an ox." Asa removed his spectacles and met Martha's eyes, directly. For a moment, she was affronted. But then, she glanced at Mr. Gracey. His blue eyes were eager, strangely happy. Relieved.

So Asa hadn't told him everything. It was the worst secret to keep, but Mr. Gracey didn't need to know, not when Robert's presence had already caused so much pain. *Thank you—thank you, Mr. Wyeth!* She tried to convey her gratitude. There was a flicker, an understanding, as raw as it was. Asa dropped his eyes, cleared his throat, and stood.

"Right," he said. "I'm going to go rap some heads. See you at Wentworth's, Billy. G'day, Miss Gracey."

He put back the last of his coffee, turned on a booted heel, and was gone, the air curling with tobacco and castile soap.

Mr. Gracey sighed and reached across the table to pat her hand. "Martha, my dear sweet Martha Ann. How could I lose you?"

It was too formidable a question to lead with. She pulled away, pressed her palms into her eyes, and burst into tears.

Poor Mr. Gracey! He'd never seen his daughter cry, she'd never had a reason to cry. The bumps and the bruises of childhood, the sore knees, the bee stings, the rare disappointments… She'd always taken them like a boy. Because it meant she could do the things boys did. How terrible it was that this first misfortune was a direct insult to her clumsy womanhood.

"There, there, my love." He sat beside her. How odd he was in Asa's chair, too small, too sweet. The purest man, not a shadow on his being. Thank God Asa had spared him. Cunning, good with figures, good with people, was William Douglas Gracey–but he was just as innocent as she was.

"I-I refused him," she gasped through tears. "Papa, what will I do, we still have Midsummer's!"

"Oh, dear child. Don't you worry about Midsummer's. I'll have Wyeth come, you won't have a thing to worry about. He can be properly foul."

She sniffed, running a hand under her nose. "What about–about Hannah and Frances? They were my only friends!"

"Don't fret, we'll find you new friends." The relief in his tone was palpable, as if he'd been holding his lungs for all those months, and he could finally breathe.

"I don't know what came over me. I should've said yes!"

"Oh no, child. Your heart knew why. Time tells us our hearts are always correct, no matter the pain. I know my Martha. She is wiser than the most educated of men, for she knows herself more thoroughly. Oh, please don't cry, you're breaking my heart!"

He took her hands, but she stood fast, pulling them away. His kindness was too much, or rather it wasn't enough. Oh, that he'd teased her! That he'd laughed at her poor decisions; it wouldn't have cut so deep!

"Robert–" she started.

"Don't worry about that brute." He went to a dumbwaiter by the fireplace, snatching up a port. It was a celebratory gesture, and her heart stung.

"A spot, my darling?"

It was the only thing he knew how to do; it was the only thing she'd allowed. She nodded tearfully, and he took Asa's empty coffee cup, wiped it out with a napkin, and filled it to the brim. She took it, and went to the window. In the garden, the roses hung low from a morning rain, and water clung in orbs to the glass, taunting her with her reflection, over and over.

"Martha, my love." William's voice drifted. "You are among good friends at Wyeth House, I promise you that. We can come here, whenever you want. Asa will not mind."

Asa. God, she couldn't look at Mr. Gracey.

She'd had time to rest, to return to her feelings, and her heart still beat far too fast when Asa was near. She could admit it, on the other side of Robert. She was deeply attracted to Asahel Wyeth. Those long legs, the lean lines; the deep voice, clipping words with a blunt New York tongue. And in the same room as her father, she was reminded that the reason she'd said "no" to Robert Henshaw was ridiculous. Frances's affronting tale threw fuel to the fire, but it was the ridiculous reason that roared.

Mr. Gracey's partner. A man she didn't know, even if she'd memorized his mannerisms. If he didn't flirt with her anymore, she would have to wait for the feelings to go away, and it was nothing short of torture when she was undeniably on fire. She'd witnessed a new side to him, and despite everything–his clumsy way of dress, his raw manner of speech, the scowls–he was incredibly…decent. And she ached for that decency like she'd ached for nothing else.

Because chivalry wasn't kissing hands and holding doors. It was thrashing a head against a wall. Kindness was taking away the port, when she'd had too much. Consideration was seeing that she was scared, understanding that he was too tall, and crouching in front of her on the floor.

Her face crumpled. Mr. Gracey was patting her shoulder, but she wanted nothing more than to swat his hand away. Asa had seen far too much, and now, she sensed it; he was retreating. Because it was the right thing to do. But madly, now that she was free, there was nothing she wanted more than to do the *wrong* thing.

She sobbed, and drained the coffee cup of port, praying that her lips touched the same places as his.

9

HIS FAVORITE SUMMER FROCK

Without Robert, she had too much time to think. Everything had happened so swiftly, from the moment Frances ended her story, that she hadn't had time to realize that certain, uncomfortable things could be true. The fact that, if Robert had taken a woman away from Asa, perhaps all Asa wanted to do was serve him right, and the flirting was for Robert's eyes. Worst of all, she didn't care. Whatever his motives were, her attraction festered, held at bay by a very half-hearted dam.

She tried to forget what Robert had done, and for the most part, it was suppressed. Misunderstanding was a benefit; her only worry was, what if he'd ruined her, forever? What did it take, to ruin the honor of a cottage girl? In whispers behind hands, she'd heard of girls who kissed fellows too much. Or fell prey to lascivious men, tumbling into marriage traps. And Robert had done far more than kiss her. He'd done things she hadn't realized men enjoyed. Things between what she knew to be true—romance, and rutting, like dogs in a barnyard. She hated it, but she wondered, long into the night, tossing, turning.

She couldn't ask Mr. Gracey. He would turn red, and shuffle his feet, making excuses. For the first time, the absence of Mrs. Caroline Gracey–the woman with no voice, and no love–was a marked hole.

The only thing she'd gotten was a piece of paper, and even that, despite the connotation, was too much. She stared at it far too long, then ripped Frances's apology from the bottom with a grimace. The rest, burning with Asa's words, she tucked into her bedside table.

❀

The following day, sweating in a June fog, she tied on an apron, pulled on a pair of gloves, and took to the garden, ripping at the brambles and weeds with a ferocity she prayed would rile some sort of feeling.

The disarray of the cottage was maddening, after sleeping in that airy room. After watching tight-lipped servants polish things that didn't need polishing. Asa was there; Jed shifted at the hitching gate, but she didn't care. He'd seen worse. Some men would've acted differently. Some would have made a show and insisted she marry Robert. But he hadn't, and she ached with gratitude.

It was the worst thing. She was just starting to figure him out, and now, she must punch down feelings. As she ripped and pulled, sweat curling her hair, a sullen voice formed in the back of her head. *Fuck you, Robert Henshaw.* Oh dear (but yes) *fuck you.* She'd heard Asa say that. Again and again, in her head; then silently on her lips, then a whisper. Then, she flung down an armful of brambles and yanked off her gloves.

"Fuck!" she shrieked, stamping her foot. "Fuck, oh *fuck* you, Robert Henshaw!"

"Careful, darling. Thin edge of the wedge from there."

She whirled, turning to see Asa standing in the path, hands behind his back, a suppressed smile creasing the corners of his eyes. She blushed, but the sudden interruption flared feeling to her fingertips.

"I'm sorry," she mumbled. "Please don't think less of me."

"It's all right, to have a time of it. We all do, here and there."

She should thank him, but it wasn't right. She knew he'd saved her from something terrifying enough that "thank you" seemed pathetic, but how could she say it when he looked like that? One glance, and her heart seized. Robert had cast a shadow, only because he commanded more space; he'd been brighter, louder, happier. Yet, there stood Asa Wyeth, hands tucked, chestnut hair curling on his forehead, boots to the bottom of his knees. Shirtsleeves loose. No waistcoat, no frock.

She blushed, harder. All the feelings rushed, too fast, when she knew she shouldn't feel them.

"Cassandra will be settled by Friday," he said. "If you'd like to come by, I've talked to Billy."

"Yes, I'd like that very much." She hadn't wanted to be friends with his sister, but Robert's insult was dead.

He nodded. There was a pause, and she watched the toe of his boot scuffing the path.

"Martha."

"Yes, Mr. Wyeth."

"She's not like me. Cassie's friendly. She'll be easy." He dropped his eyes. "I rather don't want the Estate to be foul to you. She'll make you comfortable."

Was he checking himself? "You don't make me uncomfortable, sir."

He nodded. "Happy to hear it."

"I'm excited to meet your sister. I enjoy making new friends."

"Well." He cocked a brow. "Her favorite pastime is breaking my balls, so take it with a grain of salt."

"Oh–yes, of course." She burned, still new to the way he spoke–with every inflection of a gentleman, but with none of the right words.

He turned, taking a step towards Jed, then–

"Martha. I was… admiring some of your samplers in the parlor. You're very talented with your needle."

She stared. What was this…what the hell was this? Not flirting. It was more in vein with an apology. "Thank you, sir. I sew my dresses as well."

"Cassie likes to sew, too."

"I can bring my basket, when Papa and I come to visit."

"Hmm, yes." A nod. "I was rather wondering if I could ask a favor of you."

A favor. She breathed, fighting the urge to narrow her eyes. "I'm afraid–I'm afraid I must know what it is, first." *Oh, God. Why did I say that?* Was she reverting back, that quickly, from Robert?

"Of course," he said, smiling. "I was at the docks, you see, yesterday afternoon, and tore my favorite summer frock climbing the sloop. Adeline could sew it, but I rather don't like her stitches. They're too big."

"Too...big?"

"Aye. Too big. Is there a way you can mend it so the stitching doesn't show?" He sauntered to Jed, flipped open a saddle bag, and produced the offending frock. She took it, fingers trembling. It was a dark blue, well-worn coat, fraying at the wrists, and ripped halfway up one forearm along the seam. She inspected it, fingering the tattered thread. Then she swallowed, looking up at him.

"Yes, it can be fixed. I can remove the lining, and sew it from the inside, so you won't see the stitches."

"Very good. Do you mind? Have Billy bring it to the shop, I'll come pick it up tomorrow."

She clutched the coat, watching him swing into the saddle. "I'll have it finished by morning, sir."

"Very good." He nodded. "Thank you."

A faint breeze caught the linen of his shirtsleeves. Skin flashed at his collarbone, and she jolted, staring at the ground. Skin, bones–strength. Thrashing Robert's head into the wall. She hoped there was a mark there forever; if there was, the Estate would never be foul.

He touched his hat, smiling softly. She couldn't smile back. Sweat prickled her back, and she watched as he turned Jed in a burst of dust and stone, and was gone.

Hand on her back. Smiles across the room. Passing her Malmsey Madeira–such a small gesture, but so calculated. And somehow it made maddening sense, coming from the same man who cracked heads. Cracking Robert's head was done with the same deliberation with which he touched the brim of his hat. Simple and necessary; a means to an end.

Suddenly she knew. It wasn't done, because she wouldn't let it be done. She turned, the coat pressed to her breasts, and bolted into the cottage.

The first thing she did, on the other side of her locked door, was lay the coat over her bed and stare at it. Such a big coat, crafted for a very tall man. Worn thousands of times. He had a lot of "favorite" things. Jed was his favorite horse, the only she'd ever seen him ride. He always wore his favorite hat, the ugly one, rubbed down with oil. His favorite boots, leather worn and supple from so much dubbin. Black coffee was his favorite thing to drink in the morning. God, she knew so much about him—no, she would *not* let this go!

She turned out the pockets. Nothing, in one. She dug deep into the other, and came up with a folding knife. She squinted, rubbing at it. It was engraved, with his name and birthdate, *Asahel Emory Wyeth | 1735*. She must've read it twenty times before she broke, placing it reverently on the dressing table. Then she slipped into her house dress, settled into bed, and went to work. Her stitches wouldn't be seen; Adeline was a stupid girl, to sew such big stitches in a fellow's clothes. Carefully, she broke the seam on the lining of the sleeve, pulled it back, and mended the tear, mad that it only took a few minutes.

The fabric smelled like him, potently. She looked around the room, and though she felt foolish, she brought it to her nose and breathed deeply.

It shot to her groin. God—he had *not* given her this coat just to mend. No, he was too deliberate! She poured a glass of port and put half of it back. Thank goodness, Robert hadn't ruined the taste of a good port! She drew the coat to her nose again, closing her eyes.

That hand on her back. What if…what if it had gone a little lower, like Robert's had? But not the same. What if it were gentle, caressing? Yes, caressing made sense. She'd said *no* to Robert repeatedly. But what if she said yes…to Asa? Did he kiss with his tongue? He worked cunts with his tongue, whatever that meant. Did he bite? Did he put his hands on a girl's breasts? Her heart pounded, but in her head, it was right. Those thoughts, next to his name. Slow, not hostile, but exploring, intent, and reverent.

She closed her eyes, and slipped a hand between her legs.

130

A rapping sounded. She scrambled, just as the door flung open and Mr. Gracey burst in, bald head shining in the candlelight.

"Just saying g'night, my love." He'd been frustratingly attentive since she'd returned from Wyeth House. "Are you all right? More port?"

"No, thank you, Papa." Her face burned; his eyes landed on the coat in her lap almost instantly. "I'm quite comfortable," she added hastily.

"I say, is that Wyeth's frock? He's about worn holes in the elbows."

"I—um, yes, he asked me to mend it for him on the way out. He said he wanted very small stitches. And—and that you must take it with you to the shop, in the morning, so he can pick it up."

"I see," he said dubiously, smiling, though his brow knotted. "Very well, don't let me forget. G'night, sleep well." Then he was gone, shutting the door with barely a *click*.

She breathed deeply. There was much, much more to hide than there ever had been with Robert. Flushed, she gulped the rest of her port, and squinting at her needle, sewed the lining back into place.

When she awoke the next morning, she was tangled in Asa Wyeth's favorite summer frock.

❀

Friday arrived, and Mr. Gracey readied the wagon for a visit to Wyeth House. Martha was in a very good mood; Asa hadn't been to the cottage, but the coat had been scrubbed clean, dried in the sunshine, and delivered by William. She'd left the folding knife behind; she would bring that herself, because it promised something. A conversation, a smile.

Listening to Asa speak about his sister, (that she enjoyed "breaking his balls") she'd gathered that formality wasn't a concern. Judith did her hair prettily—low on her neck, woven with purple asters. *Asters in your hair doesn't make you ill-mannered.* Well then. She admired herself in the mirror, pinching her cheeks out of habit. A simple cream linen would do, and a cotton apron with pockets, where she dropped the folding knife.

The thought of returning to Wyeth House—the scene of carnage—had bothered her, but passing back through the airy hall and into the bright parlor, the discomfort faded. A tall, lean-boned woman sat on the settee sewing, and a boy of nine or ten stood glowering by the window, hands deep in the pockets of his britches. Asa lounged low in a chair, a book in his lap; he rose, marking his place, and dipped his head by way of courtesy. Robert, she marveled, would've bowed and kissed her hand.

He was wearing the mended frock coat, which her frazzled mind understood as flirting. She almost stared, blushing hard, and opened her mouth to speak, when the woman rose, marched forward, and pushed Asa aside, taking Martha's hands.

"Martha Gracey!" she exclaimed. "What a pleasure to meet you. William, so good to see you again!"

"Ah, my dear Cassandra," sighed Mr. Gracey, kissing her hand twice. Martha was faintly affronted. He'd kept secrets, and it wasn't fair—but she smiled, her nose filled with Asa's scent.

"Miss Gracey." Asa nodded stiffly. "Cassandra. My nephew, Elijah." The sulking boy bowed, hands behind his back, and Martha nearly jumped. He was Asa, in a child's face. Big brown eyes, chestnut curls, set mouth. His lip rose in a sneer, and he returned to the window.

"Hell," muttered Asa, frowning. "I'll have him shoveling shit in the barn, in a minute. Elijah! Straight like a soldier—Billy, my office." He brushed by the women, Mr. Gracey bouncing behind him. Young Elijah grumbled but followed, dragging his feet.

"Cass, don't leave your sewing things on my settee." Asa's voice faded down the hall. "I nearly stuck my ass with a pin this morning…"

Cassandra led Martha to sit.

Her heart was beating far too fast, but Cassandra Wyeth-Standish was easy. She was beautiful, in the same striking way as her brother, tall, straight, potent. Her eyes were Asa's, soft brown, stunning in a feminine face. Her hair was darker without quite the same chestnut gleam, tossed over one shoulder in a loose braid. Certainly, formalities were nothing! When she smiled, her eyes creased, and Martha warmed; Asa had left her alone with Cassandra, on purpose. She wasn't Caroline Gracey, but she was a woman.

"How nice it is for Emory to have good friends in Boston." Cassandra picked up a set of shirtsleeves and began mending. "I feared after so much time in New York, he'd be lonesome. But he seems to be getting on. Your father is brilliant to him."

Martha pushed back her shoulders, glancing at the portrait of Asa by the fireplace.

"Oh yes," she murmured. "They're very good friends."

"Of course. New York is unlivable these days, I'm so glad to be in Boston." Cassandra's voice carried the same New York accent, but softer, as if she had a definite hold on it. She smiled warmly, hand on her belly. Martha noted the faint rounding evident in the clear absence of stays. No stays, and *oh dear*—Cassandra's ankles were crossed, and her feet bare. Just like that, bare feet, out in the open, soaking in the sunlight.

133

Thank goodness she hadn't worn a fancy dress.

"I heard you were having a baby, Mrs. Standish," she said, losing her remaining reserve.

Cassandra patted her middle. "This little one, I've been waiting for him. I've not had the best of luck, but fingers crossed. I've always longed for an army of boys. Here." She rummaged in a basket and came up with frock sized for a child. "Help me mend. Emory tells me you're skilled with your needle."

Martha blushed. She took the frock, identified a tear in the pocket, and began to sew.

"I'm sure you know why I'm here." Cassandra kept sewing, a small smile on her face. "Boston Tories can't keep the gossip at bay when it comes to Emory. He lived for so many years in New York, mingling with low-life lawyers and radicals…"

Martha opened her mouth, then shut it quickly, realizing Cassandra was only teasing.

"Now with my husband under a bounty." Cassandra sighed, gazing out the window. "They'll never run out of things to talk about."

Robert's indignation came to mind. *Asahel in defense of radical murder?* "I'm very sorry," she muttered, "it must be so stressful."

"It's all right. As much of an ass as Emory can be, he's a decent enough lawyer. I trust him." She nudged Martha's shoulder gently. "And he seems to have taken quite a fancy to you, aye?"

"Oh! I-I'm sure I don't know what you mean."

"Don't be silly. One letter, he's making mention of a red-headed Boston girl, the next, he's written a novel. I've seen this. Don't let him fool you with his moods, he's soft as butter on the inside." Cassandra was pert, sewing. "He falls in love and turns himself inside out trying to hide it. It's amusing to watch, really."

134

The discomfort was a secondary feeling because she didn't want Cassandra to stop talking. Her casual attitude shot confidence straight to the heart. "I'm always in the way at the cottage," she mumbled, watching her fingers pass the needle.

"Oh no, it's not like that." All of a sudden, Cassandra sobered. "Just be mindful, Miss Martha. The last girl sent him out of Boston for seven years."

The last girl. Mr. Gracey had been right. Martha met the brown eyes in the portrait. Younger, much younger. Not much older than she was. Seven years was forever, to mourn the loss of a romance, when there were so many pretty girls in Boston to fall in love with.

Frances had been friends with that girl. Well, she'd have to explain; Martha would make her explain!

"Do you—do you know Frances Dunaway?" she asked lightly.

"Hmm, yes. Here and there." Cassandra's tone was cautious. "Emory's acquaintances aren't so much mine. I've been in New York since I married Elijah. Papa Wyeth…well, he didn't fancy radical lawyers."

"Cassandra. Why do you call Mr. Wyeth, Emory? That's not his name."

Cassandra smiled. "I like you—you're forward. He was always Emory when we were growing up. His name has a bit of a connotation to it. He got on quite poorly with Papa, and I think it softened the blow."

"But he goes by that name now."

"Well, he's on a warpath to the ports. Everybody knows who Asahel Wyeth is. His name is at the bottom of quite a few bills of sale." Cassandra admired her stitching. "I want to see him settle down. Set up a firm in the city, maybe. But he keeps bloody doing things. Law, trade, depository…." She shook her head. "Good luck, I say."

"Oh, is Wyeth Enterprises merchant banking?" Martha was proud of herself; she hadn't ignored everything Mr. Gracey rambled on about.

"Some." Cassandra grimaced. "Very careful investments. He had a bad debtor, once. I think it scared him for life–kindness taken too far. I hear the Tucker's are having a Midsummer's party," she added, changing the subject. "Are you going?"

Martha's head spun. She knew Asa was rich. The extravagance of those families, the Tuckers, the Henshaw-Dunaways…it'd always seemed so far away. Only Robert had brought her within an arm's length. Yet Asa wanted her at Wyeth House, where the coffers burst, but Cassandra Standish mended her own clothes in the parlor, no shoes on her feet. She kept a light conversation, but her mind was on fire. Why Mr. Gracey? It still made no sense. Even less so, when he sprang into the room, an hour or two gone. Her belly was full of apple betties and dusty Dutch tea, and her head rang with Cassandra's loud New York voice.

Asa sauntered to the dumbwaiter and fixed a brandy. She followed his form, heart in her throat.

"Where's my boy?" Cassandra rose, hand on her belly. "You've not sent him to his room? You're cruel!"

"I have not," replied Asa shortly, corking the decanter. "He's outside, thrashing at my flowers with a sword."

"Not a real one, I hope!"

Asa's response was a grunt. Martha rose; Mr. Gracey was pulling on his coat.

"All right, Wyeth, I'll catch you in the counting room. I've sold the last of the glass…"

136

Oh–the folding knife! She fumbled in the pocket of her apron. "Mr. Wyeth, I–when I was mending your coat, I thought to wash it." She held out the knife. "I'm so sorry, I forgot to return it with Papa."

She dropped it in his outstretched hand, her fingertips brushing his skin. Not on purpose, but God, that no one else had been in that room! He smiled, that smile, the one that had started to haunt her, striking a light behind his eyes. Her heart stopped, and her ears rushed.

"Ah." He considered it, glancing at Mr. Gracey, (who was halfway to the door), then he pressed the knife back into her palm. "Why don't you keep it? For now." He closed her fingers, a temperate pressure, and dropped her hand. Then, he stepped forward, and his voice met her ear:

"Keep my name in your room, sweetheart."

He turned and followed Mr. Gracey through the hall. Her heart thundered; her mouth went dry. *Sweetheart.* It was a slip of the tongue, it had to be. Cassandra, pretending to busy herself with her sewing basket, ducked her head.

Keep my name in your room. Again and again, all the way back to Gracey Cottage, until, by the time she was in bed that night, it was different.

Speak my name in your room.

10

HOLDING HANDS

Cassandra was her excuse, but also, steadfastly, her friend. As Midsummer drew near, and Mr. Gracey recognized the solace Martha found in Cassandra, trips to Wyeth House were frequent. Loud laughter meant open doors, sunshine, bare feet. Cassandra, though a Wyeth in breeding, was evidently used to a simpler life; she worked alongside Adeline in the kitchen, and Martha followed, learning the names of the girls in Asa's service. No pale satins and silks; only homespun and aprons, in a household so abundant, it could've paid for a sloop of the best textiles in the world. Cassandra uprooted one of the rose beds and planted it with herbs. If she wasn't found sweeping, dusting, or sewing, she was in the kitchen, brewing tinctures and powders.

"You'll be staked and burned," snapped Asa, blowing in from the public house, worse for wear. "You're acting like a witch, aye, how dare you dig up my plants. You've ruined the garden! Hallo, Martha."

"Ruined it?" Cassandra scoffed, working a mortar.

"Well, it doesn't match anymore. And this—" gesturing at the prepping table. "Crumbs everywhere. God, you're such a pig! Where the hell is Billy?"

He stormed off, snatching a bottle of blackstrap as he went. Martha sank, blushing.

Cassandra gave her the courage to sit in the sun-scrubbed parlor, drinking coffee. Laughing. To walk the garden in the afternoon, or dine through an evening soft with Madeira. In the candlelight, she caught Asa watching, eyes alight. He looked away, at first. But one evening, when she'd mustered the nerve to hold up her head, he didn't look away anymore.

It was worse because Cassandra encouraged it. She knew Asa's loose schedule: meetings or court in the morning, wharves in the afternoon, office hours after dinner. It wasn't by accident that there was a book Cassandra must show her in the library, at exactly the time he'd retire. Or that the busts in the hall needed dusting, just as he blew in from the docks in a gust of ocean air. Visiting Wyeth House was a throbbing daydream, and the thrill of seeing Asa in his element bellowed on the fire. She flushed scarlet when he ambled in, dripping from a swim, and stripped off his shirtsleeves before he'd even turned the corridor. She swooned when he'd nearly tossed Sam out by the scruff, for the crime of saddling Jed with a bur under the blanket. It spun her head like a rich drink when she floated down the corridor, breathing in thick Virginia tobacco.

The folding knife was home beneath her pillow. She sewed so often with Cassandra that she moved her basket to the parlor, including the mass of green silk for her party gown. By now, she knew the road like the back of her hand, and only rarely did the picture of Robert Henshaw, clawing at her virgin skin, rise. It *had* hurt, but it was over now, and new things bloomed. She was free. Scrubbed clean, like the floors of Wyeth House. When she rode in the fields, she spun flowers through her hair and didn't take them out. She skipped meals. But when she looked in the mirror, she couldn't find one ugly thing about herself; she was beautiful, colored high with something beyond infatuation. Beyond longing.

Lust.

It made her want to hitch her skirts, and run, all the way to Wyeth House. Bare ankles whipping in the grass, up the portico, burst into his office…and then, what? It was then, that Robert returned, when she thought about those things.

❋

One afternoon, bored, too hot in the muffled parlor, she rode to Wyeth House without Mr. Gracey. He'd be there once his work in the counting room was satisfactory, and Gracey Cottage didn't match up to the way she felt.

Entering through the kitchens, she found Cassandra, rifling through a tray of tinctures. She was sweating, one hand on her back.

"Oh, Cassie, are you all right?"

"G'day, Martha. Yes, I'm all right, this scoundrel's got my belly twisted." A kettle whistled on the stove. "Tea for you? I'll make Emory drink it. Tired of him moaning about his bloody head."

"Oh, no thank you." Martha watched as Cassandra prepared a cup of pekoe, tipping in a few drops from a bottle. "What's that?"

"Valerian root. It helps the muscles relax." More rifling, another bottle, a cork popped, and *tap, tap,* a few drops of amber liquid into the tea. Martha watched, something itching at the back of her brain. The bottle was fixed with a label; she couldn't

140

make out the words, but there was a drawing, ink blurred, of a skull and crossbones.

"That looks dangerous," she said lightly.

Cassandra smiled wanly and picked up the tray. "It's opium elixir. Don't worry, I'm not poisoning my brother, as much as I want to. Here, come with me. Maybe talking to you will put him in a sunny mood."

Martha followed her through the corridor, bewildered. Asa was home, and she'd expected he'd still be in the city! It wasn't yet high afternoon. White sunlight warmed the dining room, which was empty, the table neatly folded against the wall. She trailed Cassandra through the double-pocket doors into the tea room, where Asa sat low in a chair, spectacles perched, a day book in his lap. He'd been writing, and he snapped the book shut. At his boots, the brindle mastiff lounged; it rose dutifully, and Martha patted it on the head.

"There's your witch's brew," snapped Cassandra, dropping the tray on a table beside him. "And Bennett will *not* be getting you anymore Dover's. You're capped for the day. Go to bed, if you've still got complaints."

Asa ignored her. "What are you doing here, Miss Gracey? You shouldn't be riding alone. All sorts of rascals about in the weeds."

His tone was faintly scolding, and she warmed. She hadn't thought about riding alone. Mr. Gracey had never stopped her.

She twisted her fingers. "Papa was held at the shop—a fellow was upset about his bill. He said he would be by this evening."

He removed his spectacles and regarded her, brow cocked. "You're deflecting," he observed.

"Oh, don't scold her," interrupted Cassandra. "You can't know how annoying it is for a woman, idling about for a man to

141

take her on a ride. *You* get up and go whenever you want. Nice, isn't it?"

"Hmm, yes." Asa tossed the day book on the table. "Quite nice. Martha, go to the parlor, don't sit in the bloody tea room. I'll be in in a minute."

"Why can't she sit in the tea room?" Cassandra planted her hands on her hips. "She can sit in the tea-room if she wants to."

"I don't want her sitting in the tea room."

"Sir, I don't mind sitting in the tea-room," Martha spoke up, then shrank. She knew what he was alluding to, and it bothered her doubly that he seemed to mind more than she did.

"If she's comfortable here, let her sit," Cassandra retorted. "Oh, you two squabble it out, I'm going to go and lay down before I lose my stomach." She brushed by Martha, muttering, "Good luck, you're going to need it."

Martha thanked Cassandra silently. The woman was too astute for such an encounter to be an accident. Asa uncrossed his legs as if to rise, but Martha sat down quickly. He was hard to trap, and Robert–what did he even look like, when she was in a room with Asa?

"I really don't mind," she said quickly. "I-I think it's good for me." She placed her hands in her lap, one over the other. "I'm sorry you have a headache. It seems you get them often."

He eyed her warily. "Do you want tea? Or coffee."

"No, thank you."

"Hmm. Very well." He frowned and crossed his boot over his knee once more. "Couldn't bloody stand it on the sloop, too hot. What a chump am I. It's all right, I wanted to talk to you about something."

She straightened.

"It's better coming from me than Billy, but it's about the shop." He took up the tea, regarding her over the rim. Steam curled, but his eyes cut, and her heart lurched.

"The–the shop?"

"Yes. Wyeth is wholesale, you see." He grimaced, pushing away the cup of tea. "I have warehouses, I'm afraid, not proprietorships. Once the stock is cleared, Billy has made the decision to close the doors."

Close the shop. For a moment, she forgot that she was alone with him, and her heart sank. The shop was an integrated part of her life, since the day of her birth; as much her home as the cottage, if not more.

She swallowed, looking at her hands. "Oh. I see."

"We're keeping the building, though." He cleared his throat. "For something. Not sure what."

"I understand, sir."

"Your father is a very talented businessman. I want you to know, this is not just an opportunity. Billy is a friend."

"I haven't thought any less," she replied, and it was true.

"Good." He frowned. "Bloody hell, don't look so glum. A fellow can't stand it, from a pretty girl like you. I'm not trying to wreck your life, darling."

"You haven't, sir." *A pretty girl like you.* She may as well forget the shop altogether! She brightened. "I'll miss it, of course, but I'd love to see the warehouses sometime."

"I think not. Musty boxes and trunks, nothing to see." He rose stiffly, hand on the back of his neck, and went to the dumbwaiter to fix a brandy. It was marked that he didn't offer her a drink, and she supposed she should be grateful, but–would Robert be a ghost forever? He opened a blind and stood staring out into the terrace.

"Martha."

143

He turned. Her heart picked up pace; he was cut by the sunlight. Frowning, as always, but through his shirtsleeves she caught quickened breath. A chestnut curl fell, and he ran his fingers through his hair with a grunt of frustration.

"It's only this, I don't think you'll like the sort of man I am." He gestured at her with the glass. "Look at you. You're goddamn stunning. I mean that. Glad it's off my tongue." He rolled his shoulders. "It's a pleasant feeling."

"That's very nice of you. Thank you." How the words came out, she was baffled; it seemed impossible.

"But I'm a right foul old bastard, I am," he went on. "What's worse, I've come to Boston feeling rather mean. I don't laugh at things that aren't funny, and I certainly don't like parties. I'd rather spend my time at the ports, carving my name under the planks. You see? Foul."

"You're not foul." She didn't know what else to say, and it didn't matter; she could barely breathe. If this was a move, it was nothing she'd ever seen from a man—certainly not Robert.

"I am, though," he insisted. "I never forgive debts. And I don't mind pilfering accounts from other merchants. It only means I've done a better job, aye." He tapped his glass, thoughtful. "The cleverest way to a full coffer is selling things that everybody wants, but never last. Rum, tea. It all goes away. My point being—I *am* a racketeer." Chin out, he smiled. "What do you think?"

"Sir—I-I don't—I just don't think about it. Papa said it's nothing to worry about. It's not against the law to sell wet goods."

"This isn't just about wet goods. It's about the fact that I raise my right hand, and I lie. And nobody says anything. It's bloody unbelievable. Once—once." He corrected himself. "I was taken to court. It was over in an hour, and I didn't pay a shilling."

"I'm not sure where this is coming from," she said. There was a foreign tone in his voice–not desperation, but something more akin to discomfort, and she ached to soothe it. "Papa has always worked with all sorts of merchants," she explained lightly. "I don't think you're a criminal."

"His Majesty's port officers would say differently." He regarded her seriously. "The ones I pay off, to keep it under their hats."

"Are you trying to make me think poorly of you? I-I can't– Papa would never do business with someone untrustworthy."

"No." His brow furrowed, and he shook his head. "No, that's not it. What bothers me is that you don't ask questions. I came in from New York like a six-pound cannon, and you don't even blink. A girl should be suspicious, aye, of a fellow who comes in like six-pounder."

She knew, then, what he was trying to say. The ghost was still there, and he was fighting it, even when she'd almost let go. *Robert laid with Wyeth's woman. The last girl.* Well, she wasn't like the last girl. She knew it.

"When I–when I was with Robert." She cleared her throat. Even blushing, her fingertips went cold. "I-I wasn't honest with myself. I did a lot of things, but I'm just a cottage girl. I don't really get offended."

He met her eyes. *Don't look away–don't you dare look away!* His expression softened; he'd been heightened, by something. Opium perhaps. She didn't care. If it was opium talking, or the brandy, let it speak–because it still came from his mouth. *His* mouth. Against her will, her eyes wandered. A perfect mouth; not too full, lines in the skin, maps through his story. There'd been a time when he'd laughed, far more than he did now.

"You're just a cottage girl, aye," he said softly.

145

She lifted her chin and nodded. The mastiff shook out its ears and settled its huge head on its paws with a sigh.

"Martha. Come here, please."

How–her knees weren't there–but somehow, she went. The sunshine seared through the windows, and his shadow fell long, over the floor to the door. And he smelled so good–God, he smelled good! Smoke and ocean, salt, summer.

She couldn't look up, she couldn't breathe.

A finger caught her under the chin, raising her face. "Martha." A hint of brandy. "What are you doing here? That's what I want to know."

"Sir. I'm sorry I rode alone, I–"

"I don't mean that, though don't do that again." He met her eyes. Soft, but–under a veil, burning holes–a spark, a flicker of something…wild. His hand dropped, and he tipped his head back. "You walk around my house with your hair down. Every time I turn a corner, I see you, whether you're there or not."

"I don't mean to be in the way."

"You do, though. And it's working incredibly. You walk in the room, and I lose twenty years. Goddamn, I could run with you. And when it's all said and done, well–I'll be honest." He smiled softly. "I want to kiss you. I said what I said, but you know it's not right."

Her ears roared with a low sound, broken by the thumping of her heart, yet she couldn't look away. "Why isn't it right?" she asked in a whisper. *Don't let him stop. Don't!*

"Well, because we're here. You rode to Wyeth House alone. And I've downed enough Dover's I'll be coughing up chalk, trying to get rid of this headache. So no." He nodded, agreeing with himself. "No kissing for you."

She dropped her head, but he lifted her chin once more. Her thighs clenched, her toes curled. A thumb ran over her chin, her bottom lip. Tipping her head, further. *Breathe, Martha, remember to breathe.*

"I'd like you to do something for me, darling. Do you mind?"

"Y-yes, sir. I-I mean, no, I don't mind."

"Take the pin out of your hair." He nodded. "Go on, it's all right."

Her fingers were numb, but she obeyed. Her hair fell, swinging down her back.

"Jesus." He wasn't smiling; his eyes were on fire. "I'll be honest, darling, I've thought of myself, tangled in that hair."

Tangled in that hair. I'd work that sweet little cunt–words she didn't understand, but that still made sense. And he wasn't looking at her face anymore. His eyes lingered on her throat, and she felt it like a touch. On her collarbone. Over the rise of her breasts, pert and new.

"Darling." He reached forward, around the back of her neck, fingers skimming her spine, and drew her hair over her shoulder. Then, he leaned down and kissed her on the forehead. She closed her eyes, sucking in a breath, trapping it in her lungs. She stared at the floor, at his boots, but felt only one thing. His lips on her forehead. His lips anywhere on her skin–white heat, just like it had that day outside the office. Robert was truly gone. It didn't matter that she was in the tea room. It only mattered that she was with Asa, and he was holding out his hand. Not his arm, like Robert.

His hand.

"Here, let's go to the parlor."

"I-I don't know about holding hands–"

He tilted his head. "What don't you know about it?"

"It's only, I've never held hands with anyone before."

"It's easy." He reached out, raised her hand under the palm, and placed it in his. His skin was cool and dry; God, if her heart beat any faster, her ribs would break! He turned his wrist, and his fingers slipped through hers, loose, yet bound.

"You can let go. But it feels nice, doesn't it?" And he started to walk, pausing to tuck the daybook under his arm.

She followed. It was unquestionable.

She lay wide awake, too late. Clutching the folding knife, while the candles faded from gold to blue. After Asa had walked with her to the parlor, Sam had interrupted with news of a squabble in the ice house. But it didn't matter; Asa had clearly said all he wanted to say. It didn't matter, because he'd held her hand, for the longest, yet briefest moments. Only when he'd sat, had he let it go, and now she burned; the spaces between her fingers were wide, stupid, without his to fill them.

She'd never felt this way about Robert. Even when her heart thundered, and her mind drew blanks, she'd been excited. Light. Robert had been easy. Tea in the afternoon, hidden smiles, common fancies. But now, she was aching like a wound, swollen, infected. Not just longing for Asa, but wildly angry that he wasn't there.

She was in love. That was all there was to it.

From the top of her head to the bottom of her feet, she was in love. Her body, her heart, her soul, every part of her wanted that man. She wanted to mend his coats. To fix him pekoe tea, or brandy, or whatever he wanted. She would leave her hair down, forever; she would run in the garden, and ride astride her horse. Never again would she lie to herself—because he'd set her free.

She put the folding knife on the table and slipped out of bed. At the dressing table, she poured a port and pulled open a drawer, where the kerchief Robert had given her lay. She fingered it; her name, created under his direction. His affection, because he might've really been in love with her. Robert, Frances, Hannah…silk, satin, ballrooms, and dances—God, she'd wasted so much time! Her skin itched, and with a squeal of disgust, she tossed the kerchief into the dead grate, lit a match from a candle, and burned it.

The moonlight shone crisp blue. She was heightened, her senses teased, sounding limb to limb. It was starting to make sense now, that Asa had broken. *I want to kiss you.* His eyes, on her neck, her breasts, the lobes of her ears, as if she were a cornucopia of good things, and he was starving—God! She flung herself onto the bed.

The folding knife flashed. She picked it up again and held it in a fist, so hard it sank into her skin. *No, Martha—don't. Don't you dare.* But his face, filling her mind's eye—he wasn't saying no. He wasn't saying anything.

He was watching.

She placed the knife on the bed beside her. *Remember the way he smelled? God, yes, like the ocean*—her hand slipped between her legs. The door was locked. Her thoughts, and Asa's eyes, and that feeling. Lust. Pleasure. It rushed like it never had. *Don't stop— never stop!*

Her fingers, at first, were enough. Slow, circling. *Listen to his voice.*

"I could run with you."

Mr. Wyeth, say that again. Please—

She flipped on her belly, and ground into the palm of her hand. Her hips needed to move against something. Eyes on his name, twisting, kneading—sore. Sweating—and she was done, panting, legs shaking, limp on the bed. The house was silent. The moonlight was silent. His name, carved in bone, was silent. But his eyes were on fire, and he nodded, touching the brim of his hat.

"Asahel Emory Wyeth," she breathed. To speak his name in her room was to strip her apprehensions bare, to bind him to her lust. As soon as she put the words into the silence, it was right.

11

RUNNING *in the* RAIN

The following morning, Jed stamped lazily at the hitching gate. *It could've been a dream*—but no, her fingers burned between each, held by the ghost of his touch. She stared at the bed, blankets twisted, pillows flung. *God, Martha, you're an animal.* How could she face him, knowing she'd touched herself to the image of his face?

Trembling, she stepped into her shift and fumbled through the wardrobe. What did Asa want to see in a woman? She'd taken cues, but things were different now that he'd made a move. Everything spoke of Robert. Bright colors, lace, too much lace! Finally, the girl in the mirror calmed her throbbing heart. Hair low, homespun dress. An apron. She sucked in a breath and went downstairs on the tips of her toes.

She went to the kitchen to fix tea. It was so untidy! *God, what good is Judith, Papa should tell her off!* A chicken scratched at the hearth, and she snatched it up, its wings flapping wildly, and tossed it out the door. Wyeth House would never have chickens in the kitchen, unless they were roasting with herbs and potatoes! One of the scrabbling claws nicked her finger, and she sucked it, frowning. This was going to have to change. She stamped her foot—goodness, being in love made her angry!

"Judith!"

"I've sent her down to Marshall's, we're out of sugar, my dear!" William's voice rang.

Her heart sank. Those things that Asa had said to her weren't right, when Mr. Gracey sat in the office; and the reality of him, so completely different, pinched. Perhaps the things Asa had said he hadn't meant the way she'd taken them. Or they were influenced. Or she'd dreamed them.

She stared at her teacup, fingertips pink against the heat, and closed her eyes, remembering. Touching, teasing, her mind drawing blanks when it wasn't filled with his face. Stroking, kneading—his touch, not hers—his eyes, flaring at her pleasure. *Oh, stop it, Martha!* To hold his hand like that, his fingers laced through hers. It was sensual, blithe; it wasn't like a gentleman.

She opened her eyes, startled by a drop of blood that had risen and broken over the side of the teacup. She shook her head, pushing the wound into her mouth once more. The henhouse was riddled with holes, and only sheer luck found Judith gathering eggs in the morning. Now, she resented it. It wasn't that Wyeth House was fancy, but it was wide open and clean—

"Martha."

She jumped. Asa was standing in the doorway, a record book tucked under his arm, hat in hand. He was scrubbed clean, shirtsleeves tucked under his favorite (mended) blue summer frock.

"Finger out of your mouth, darling," he said blankly.

She flushed, twisting her hands behind her back. "I'm sorry, Mr. Wyeth. I was sewing, and my hand slipped on a pin—"

152

"What were you sewing, bloody feathers in your hats?" In a stride he was close, plucking something from her hair: a feather from her scuffle with the chicken. She burned, eyes on his hands. Robert was a brawny man, his hands muscled and thick. But there was something about Asa's, lean, strong–

"Christ, Martha, how do you get anything done, with that voice in your head?"

"Oh, I'm sorry!" she gasped. "I-I'm not sure."

He studied her, for too long. She squirmed, and he broke.

"Right."

In all her discomfort, he was flawlessly passive. Perhaps she *should* flirt; it had always worked with Robert. The wound on her finger had ceased to bleed, but still, in a swell of nerve, she pushed it under her tongue, throwing him a glance.

"That really doesn't do much for me." His brow rose. "I know what a woman's mouth is capable of."

"Mr. Wyeth!"

He smiled, his countenance softening. "I'm sorry, I'm a bastard, as I'm sure you can attest. Here." He reached for her hand, kissing the top of her fingertips. "All better, aye."

Heat rushed. Her fingers were wet from her tongue, and she was sure he'd felt it; his breath deepened, and his eyes went soft.

"Wyeth?"

Mr. Gracey bounced through the doorway. Asa jolted, but hastily righted himself, brow settling into a frown. Yet it told on him. As uncomfortable as she was, he was not impervious! If Mr. Gracey could make him shift like that, he knew he'd been doing something bad, and her heart glowed.

William paused, glanced at Asa, then Martha, then back again, and shuffled his feet. "Hello, what's going on? I'm off to knock Richard on the head, will you come with me, Wyeth?"

153

"Bloody no thanks," replied Asa testily. A faint blush rose at the tips of his ears, and she smiled, dropping her eyes. "Go on, I'm off the wharves," he muttered. "Got a fellow at Hunt's."

"Good idea," mused Mr. Gracey. "See you later, fine sir. Martha, be a good girl. When Judith comes back with the sugar, send her out again for some millet. It's a game I've been playing to annoy her." He chuckled. "She needs the exercise!"

Asa stepped aside as he strolled out the door, humming to himself.

"Are you really off to the wharves, sir?" she asked, once the front door had slammed.

"S'matter of fact." He watched the window, narrow-eyed, as Mr. Gracey plodded down the drive on one of the old mares. The realization that she was alone with him, as she'd been in the tea room, warmed the pit of her belly. He could do anything, say anything! *Be a good girl.* But looking at Asa, long legs, straight spine–the way his hair was tousled from the ride over–well, she didn't feel like being good at all.

His shoulders settled, and he set the record book down. "Martha, I wanted to talk to you. I was a little out of sorts yesterday." He went to the basin, searching the pile of unwashed dishes with a grimace, and gingerly selected a teacup. "Do you mind?"

"Oh! Of course." Quickly, she fixed him a cup; the caddy was on the butcher block, loose leaves littering, and he flipped the lid.

"Billy had better not be hoarding Hyson. It smells like it."

"It's Dutch. He used to keep Hyson there." She pressed the front of her dress, heart hammering. "Do you take anything in your tea, Mr. Wyeth?" What if he took sugar, and Judith had let it run out?

"Nothing past my usual poison." He accepted the cup and leaned on the prepping table, legs crossed at the boots. *Please, don't take anything back,* her mind begged, yet–

"I wanted to apologize for yesterday. Too much of the poppy can turn a fellow on his head. Forgive me if I upset you. You're a clever girl, and I appreciate your trust." A curl had fallen loose over his forehead, and he ran his fingers through his hair, not breaking.

"It's really all right," she managed.

"Yes, well. Pathetic, to ask for justification when it's uncalled for." It was faintly arrogant, and she fought the urge to smile. "I would never put Gracey in a compromising place," he assured her. "And you'll be happy to know, I'm putting him at twenty percent next month."

"Oh, that's quite generous!"

"Hmm, yes. And *you* can have anything a girl wants. Provided, of course, there's a bill of sale. Bills of sale are very important." He coughed into his elbow. "Bloody ipecac."

"Is your headache quite gone?" For a moment she forgot the teasing ache, and a faint pass of unease split her thoughts. He looked well, fresh even. Plenty of sun-kissed color in his face. Yet, she recognized the laudanum and tablets as something of a requirement in his day-to-day. She shrugged it off. Plenty of fellows dropped laudanum to relax.

"Quite gone," he replied. "I'm a new man. Now, if you're not affronted I acted like an eager ass, I should wonder what's going on in your head. You don't have much to say."

She pressed her palms into the tops of her thighs. He couldn't possibly see, but they were clammy, and it was off her tongue before her brain could tell her "no".

"I'm thinking that I'm very attracted to you, Mr. Wyeth."

She heard the words, but she didn't feel them leave her throat. *Too much, Martha, too much!* He wouldn't force her to be a lady, but she'd forget she was even a woman, and she was simply Martha! Her heart beat so fast, too high under her collarbone, that she almost couldn't breathe.

He considered her, his mouth set. "Goddamn, darling. You've proved me wrong."

"Why do you say that?" She bunched her skirts in her fingers. *Oh, stop being Martha, for a minute! Stop it, now–*

"Say what?"

"Darling. You call me darling all the time. Is that what you call every lady?"

"It certainly isn't." He scowled. "It suits you. Jesus, you're pint-sized, but you're vicious. I don't care how sweet you are." A flash passed through his eyes, lighting a peculiar gold. "I'd better watch myself. You're bloody beautiful, but I bet you'd stick a man's eyes out if you felt like it."

She twisted her fingers. "It's how I feel. I-I want to hold your hand again."

He watched her, for too long. When he broke, there was a curious sadness in his expression, and her heart sank.

"Martha, I'm not going to sigh over poetry, all right. I don't stop for flowers along the way. I'm just not that sort of fellow."

"You don't like parties either."

"I do not."

"Then what do you do with a lady, sir?"

The question was genuine. She was locked, while he looked her over. Then, he set his tea down, pushed off the prepping table, and closed the distance. His eyes were measured; he gathered up the record book and hat. Her heart sank, but–pipe-smoke, so close, prickling her nose. She fought the urge to close her eyes; he moved a step closer, reached out, and with deft fingers, tugged the busk from between her breasts and placed it on the butcher block with a quiet *click*.

She stopped breathing.

"Don't wear a busk anymore, darling. Your breasts are quite beautiful as they are."

"Mr. Wyeth, that isn't–"

"It's the sort of thing I do with a lady." He smiled and touched the end of her nose. There was an authority to the gesture, and she blushed, staring at the busk. It seemed so naked, so foolish. What else was foolish? Her corset, her pins? It'd been a demand, that she take the pin out of her hair, even if he'd asked politely. All of those things, that she'd fretted over with Robert, meant nothing to Asa. And now, though he'd moved a step away, his eyes were lingering on her mouth.

Her heart thundered.

"I said I was sorry for being an ass." He reached, tipping her chin. "I suppose I've got to keep saying it."

"I-I'm not offended by anything you said."

"It makes you uncomfortable," he said evenly. "I hate that."

"No, sir. It doesn't make me uncomfortable."

A gentle touch moved over her chin. "I see how it is." To her bottom lip. *Please, please!*

The front door slammed. She jumped, rushing with heat. Judith! It took everything–a bit lip and balled fists–not to scream the woman's name. Asa dipped his head and pushed his hat on, eyes flickering with what she could only construe as exasperated mirth. She'd never been so disappointed in her life. It could've been her first kiss; Robert's didn't matter!

"Someone's getting sent for millet," Asa sighed. "Don't fret, darling. You know I'm a haunt around here. Let me think about this." He kissed the edge of her jaw, by her ear, while Judith's lumbering steps rattled the floorboards. God, it felt good, to have him so close, to be right about the way he felt! She brightened, and her anxiety eased. Confidence–it was all a girl needed, when in love.

"Yes, sir," she managed.

He nodded, touched the brim of his hat, and–in a sudden move, enough that she jumped–he snatched up the busk and tossed it into the empty hearth. She watched him saunter around the kitchen door, her head purged of thought. Her groin was tight, and her breasts ached.

If that was the sort of thing he did with ladies, well–he was wrong, and she was very much a lady, after all.

※

And so, it was him. All day, all night, eating her thoughts to nothing but the image of his eyes, lit with lust. Robert was less than a ghost. He'd never been, to begin with. She'd never been touched, and her body ached for the moment Asa felt she was ready.

His patience infuriated her when he came to the cottage so often. Yet, he didn't come to court; it was only business. It was a problem, but one that he seemed to be solving carefully in his head. The fact of Mr. Gracey seemed to make him uncomfortable, though not enough to keep him from flirting when poor William's back was turned.

It was nothing less than torture. Asa's particular brand of flirting was not subtle. If something was intended for her eyes, it was visceral. Reaching past her, leaning too close. Pouring her a glass of port, holding her eyes too long. Running his fingers through his hair. He did it with his entire body, and she pierced her palms with her fingernails to put up with it. He had work to do, and it was evident he was plotting; yet, she ached so badly

158

for confirmation that her doubts brought her to tears when she was alone. She'd be a secret lover for him, she didn't care! But no, if he was to court her, Mr. Gracey would know–eventually. Everything must be sorted. And he must contend with Robert, even if he would never admit it.

She did everything she could. At her shaky behest, he took dinner at the Gracey's (Asa's variety of dinner, which meant indulging in a brandy and pipe while his food went cold). All afternoon, she'd fretted, ripping stitches in a green fitted-back gown, until the neckline was lowered a distinct inch. It fit like a dream, and the absence of a busk was a compliment to her figure. He was right, and paired with a set of emerald drop earrings, she was exquisite. Judith growled in displeasure, but Martha silenced her with pure ice. Judith was appalled by anything, and it was clear she'd caught on, a fact that seemed to amuse Asa endlessly–flirting was almost as much for Judith as it was for Martha.

She sat, taking a deep breath. No assets would go to waste, and the effect was as desired. Asa cleared his throat, eyes snapping to the toe of his boot. Mr. Gracey, absentminded and pleasant as ever, hummed and poured a port.

It was contrived, but there was something freeing about the absence of her busk. She could bend now. And it was pleasant, not to waste so much time fussing over her hair. As Judith cleared the plates, and William strolled to the office (a bottle of Madeira had him convinced Asa must admire his dictionary), Asa reached across the table and touched her nose.

She closed her eyes, her heart wild.

"You're a good girl, aye." His tone was tender. "But don't try too hard. Just be Martha. That's what I'm here for, darling."

"Actually." She fought to keep her voice level. "I rather am glad you made the suggestion. It was quite uncomfortable if I'm being honest."

"Well, that won't do." He tapped his glass thoughtfully. "You must be comfortable."

"Yes, I'm beginning to see that."

He rose and circled the table. She looked up, and deftly–unquestionably–he reached, his wrist brushing her throat, and slipped the emerald drops from her ears, regarding Judith coolly over her head. She didn't know whether to laugh or sigh with relief. Judith's nostrils flared, and she stormed off, plates rattling in her arms.

Asa placed the earrings mindfully on the table.

"There now." He crouched, leveling with her eyes. "Try that next. Let me know what you think."

Even past the frantic fluttering of her heart, she knew what he wanted her to say. "I will, if it suites me. Thank you for the suggestion, Mr. Wyeth."

He laughed, and she flushed scarlet. But he was telling the truth–he didn't want her a certain way, and it felt so good, to be comfortable in her skin again!

The door to the study banged shut. She closed her eyes, fighting her disappointment. *Just a few moments–three, two, one. Mr. Wyeth, please*–she shuddered deliciously. Warm breath brushed her neck, and a kiss, light as a feather, pressed into the bare lobe of her ear. *Oh–my God.* One more, more–kisses fell in a gentle line down her neck, to the top of her collarbone. Her thighs clenched. It felt so good, she almost didn't care if she was found out. She sighed, rolling her head, catching each one. How could a girl have her neck kissed, and feel that way between her legs– it made no sense!

"Sir," she gasped, "is that a place you're supposed to be kissing?"

He rose, a smile playing at the corners of his mouth. "I don't know," he mused. "You seemed to enjoy it."

"Kisses are for hands." She frowned at the table. "For lips."

"Well, you have a beautiful mouth. But whatever you think, darling." He ambled to his chair and sat, crossing his legs and resting his hands on one knee. Mr. Gracey rounded the door, cherry-red with happiness, but none the wiser.

So she left her earrings on, but he made no comment. Aching days passed, and she took them off, flinging them in exasperation. She wanted it, so badly, but he was too patient! He'd been coming to the cottage more than Mr. Gracey had been to Wyeth House, and she missed Cassandra. She needed someone else to talk to, to calm the tempest of her thoughts. Being in love was *not* easy.

But she couldn't be angry at Asa. It was impossible, especially when, in rare moments, she caught him, chewing at the end of his pipe, staring out the window. Eyes closed in the parlor chair, fingers pressed into the back of his neck. It was evident there was a demon that checked him, even if it passed swiftly and he was back to teasing her. She could only guess because he wouldn't speak. A headache, maybe. Worse—maybe that girl, the one Robert had taken from him.

❀

On a gray afternoon, she decided to go to the Estate, aching for Cassandra's company. She knew the path well, so she hitched the wagon, tied her hat under her chin, and started out. Asa's prior warning fell on deaf ears; barely remembered, and disregarded out of habit. Thunderclouds roiled overhead, but she shrugged. She'd ridden in the rain before. The paths were dry, and she could be there and back before any damage was done. She kept the mare at a quick pace, clutching the reins, her brain whirling with anxiety.

In contention, she hoped Asa wasn't back from the docks. She couldn't stand his conundrums when she was in such a mood; she needed Cassandra, brash, honest Cassandra, who kept no secrets. *She* would understand. It couldn't go on forever. Asa would have to break, and tell Mr. Gracey.

She rested the reins on her lap and reached round her neck to pull the pin out of her hair, shaking it loose. He wanted that. How in the hell did he know that she wandered the fields, spinning her hair with wildflowers? As if he knew who she was, from her toes to the top of her head, and no amount of finery could shield it.

Frances's secret voice, her warning whispers, ate her alive. *Asa's woman.*

What had Asa done with that woman? Because he hadn't married her. He hadn't married any lady. His argumentative nature, the inelegant way he dressed, his fixation with competition, told of a man well integrated in the ways of bachelorhood. So why was that woman so important? Some fellows went through many ladies—she could be nothing at all, if he'd had that many ladies! She wanted to cry.

Rain fell, speckling black, and the thunder tumbled, rolling through slate clouds.

What had that woman's name been? Had he held her hand, the way he'd held hers—loose-laced fingers, tender warmth? Had he kissed her on the mouth? Had he kissed her with his tongue, the way Robert had? She shuddered; she hated the way Robert had done that. But it drove her mad that when Asa's lips had met her neck, he'd lit a fire between her legs, and he'd done that to a different girl, too. That he'd done more, when all she wanted was more!

The thunder clapped, splitting the sky. Summer rain came in sheets, soaking her through in a matter of seconds. The mare jolted, but regained herself, plodding on. The earth drank greedily, and a flicker of panic broke her thoughts. She picked up the reins and slapped them across the mare's back.

In a surge of spite, she felt gratitude to Robert. If he hadn't fallen to his impulses, she might not have known Asahel Wyeth. She would never have been at the end of the drive, soaked to the skin, wild with uncertainty. The usual serenity of the dogwood trees bent subservient to veils of rain, and she could just make out Wyeth House, a beacon in the distance.

There was a dip at the end of the drive, a churning mess of water, stones, and white petals, deep enough that she worried the wagon might lodge. The earth rose to the right of the path, so she slapped the reins and rounded the trees. But she hadn't gone a few feet when the wagon pitched, rocking so far to the side that she lost her seat, rolling against the wall. Her ribs smarted, and she yelped, more annoyance than pain. God, she was making a fool of herself! Asa's warning should've meant something, if only to save her the embarrassment.

She clambered out of the wagon. Her shoes sank, and she growled in frustration. The wheel was lodged firmly between two stones, washed from the grass by the torrents, and no amount of kicking or yelping would shake it loose. *God, please. Don't let Mr. Wyeth be home from the docks!* She could walk the rest of the way, and Cassandra wouldn't betray her–

"Martha Gracey!"

She'd never hated to see him, but her shame brought the feeling close. Striding down the hill, boots kicking up rain, black

163

frock whipping in the gales. His tricorn spilled water in a manner that was nearly ridiculous, and when he reached her, he ripped it off, flinging it into the wagon.

"What in the hell is this!" he shouted.

"I was coming to see Cassie!"

She stood shivering as he unfastened the halter. She could see the anger, tight in his temples, and she was useless to it. Leather halter straps were freed, and the tug fell to the ground with a thud and splash; he slapped the mare across the rear with such force that Martha winced. The horse started, and with an aggravated snort plodded up the hill.

"I really don't give a fuck what you're here for." He rounded. His eyes were nearly black, and his hair, curls wet, had lost the chestnut gleam.

"I told you not to go out on your own. Didn't I?" His voice rose over the noise. "I've got troops drilling who the hell knows where. These are not gentlemen!"

"I didn't think–I'm sorry!"

"No, you know what, darling, you're not sorry. What, did you suppose I told you not to come for the fun of it?"

Tears burned. If she cried, he wouldn't see it; she was soaked to the bone. Yet, there was something in the urgency of his tone that gave rise to indignation. He couldn't tell her what to do, it didn't matter how deeply in love she was!

"I needed to talk to Cassie," she insisted. "You're not being fair!"

"Not fair? You don't know my grounds. This isn't your home. You'll end up in a ditch!"

"You don't talk to me at the cottage. It is not fair, and you know it!"

He stared at her, incredulous. "Well then, if you want my sister to speak for me, by all means, you're welcome. But don't you dare ever ride alone again. Christ, you're drowned!"

"I beg your pardon, but I *can* ride!"

"This isn't a question of your skills!"

The way the rain ran off his skin, pulling his hair limp, fought the wild ache. Eyes wide, furious. His frock was open; shirtsleeves clinging to bone—she dropped her eyes. It didn't matter that it was a summer rain; she started to shiver.

"You told me to just be Martha." Her voice was a faint whisper, empty in the noise. "This is what I used to do."

She hated herself then, from her toes to the ends of her wringing hair. She didn't need to say Robert's name. He must know what she meant. There was a moment, too long, too uncomfortable, that he simply stood and stared. Then, he broke, seized the tricorn from the wagon, shook it out, and pressed it on her head.

Then he held out his hand.

She took it—again, it was unquestionable. She knew she made a ridiculous picture, in her drenched dress, hem muddied, his hat a guttered roof over her head, but when he stepped ahead, she followed, clutching his fingers, head down, eyes fixed on silver spurs.

He paused, and turned; his eyes were on fire.

"Please don't be angry with me, Mr. Wyeth," she gasped.

"I'll be angry at you if I want to be. Now pace up, let's run."

Run.

She surged, fighting to keep up, whipping through the grass, skirts balled at her knees. If she'd been sitting, warm and dry, in the Gracey parlor, the idea would've been absurd. That men like him—royalty at the ports—ran anywhere, much less through the rain, was curious at the least. She tripped, but he pressed on;

165

briefly, he turned to look back, and a smile broke the anger. Deep laughter blended with the roaring torrents, and suddenly, it broke her heart–yet, it wasn't a wound; it was a split along a perforated seam, bursting with light, lifting her under the heels with a wild rush of freedom. He stopped, slowed to a walk, and turned to face her. One hand slipped around her waist, pressing the small of her back; he tugged off the tricorn, drew her in, and kissed her on the mouth.

The rain didn't feel cold anymore. Heat shot from her belly, through her limbs; she curled her fingers, clutching the sleeves of his frock.

She didn't know how to kiss, but she didn't need to. The way his lips stroked all the right parts of her mouth, in gentle assurance, told her he didn't expect it. Over and over, temperate yet urgent; he gathered her hair, pulling it over her shoulder in a rope. He had a taste–and God, it was good! Sweet, like the first bite of an apple, like the sugar at the bottom of her tea. And for Asahel Wyeth to kiss her under a broken sky, snuffed the fires beneath her burning doubts–gone, in the pressure of a tender, searching mouth.

She was limp when he drew away and took her hand again.

"Come." He smiled. "Let's get you dry."

12

WE CAN'T SAY LOVE

S he followed him up the southern terrace, into the bright piazza. With the kiss over, she was furious; rather, the ache was wide awake, and the swelling in her heart hurt. It didn't matter how gentle he'd been. Her spine was snapped straight, her gut on fire, and she stood, running rain onto naked stones.

"I would offer you my coat," Asa muttered, "but I don't think it would do you any good." He held open the door, and she ducked her head and slipped under his arm into the library.

"Goddamn, you had to catch me without my tarpaulin, didn't you?" He took her hand again, leading her through the library to the office, and ushered her in. It was marked, that he didn't shut the door all the way. An opening, an easy escape. It almost made her angry.

"I'll get you something to wear. I'm sure Cassie's got something, though you're so damn little, you'll drown in it." He frowned. "You're staring at me."

Of course, she was staring at him. How could she not? She squared her chin. "Is this what you do, Mr. Wyeth?"

"Is what, what I do?" He peeled off his frock, muttering. Wet white linen, skin seeping sun-gold…Because his back was turned, she indulged her eyes. It was the closest she'd been to seeing his body, in proximity, and it suddenly made sense why the masters removed the clothes from a man before they painted his picture.

"Is what, what I do?" he repeated, tousling his hair.

She swallowed, then blurted: "Is this what you do, go about kissing girls, and then don't say anything about it?"

"Hmm. Not something I regularly do. I was under the impression you wanted to be kissed."

"I did!"

"Then I can't see a problem." His brow rose. "I don't know, darling. You're very young. You need a lot of kissing."

"I'm really not so young, I'm twenty." But her heart sank. Something about the kiss he hadn't enjoyed, and it hurt, because it'd given her wings.

"Most ladies would be satisfied with a kiss," he said, by way of explanation, "and wouldn't ask so many questions. This proves the opinion I formed the day I met you. You're not a lady, you're feral."

"I beg your pardon, but that is rude!"

"I think not, I rather like feral women." And he rounded, two strides to her shivering figure, caught her at the back of the neck, and kissed her again.

She sank. His fingers passed through her hair; her spine was pliant, and she pushed off the balls of her feet to reach. For a split moment, she felt his teeth, smiling against her mouth, and then he was back to kissing until it was impossible not to respond. Her lips parted. *What am I doing?* Without understanding, she'd offered him something, and he took it, softly, in a trace of sweet fire. His tongue. Not probing like

Robert, but a mere break in the rhythm of a kiss, a stroke of heat and flesh.

Mouth to mouth, tongue to tongue. What else could touch, and feel so good? Her thighs clenched, and she swallowed when he drew away. His taste was real, so potent, it *could* be swallowed. Like a sip of Malmsey Madeira.

"Goodness." She flushed. "Kissing is nice, Mr. Wyeth."

His mouth set, holding back a laugh. "Very good. I'm fond of it myself. Now sit here." He pulled out a chair in front of the bureau plat. "I'll be back."

She sat willingly; her knees were weak. Once the sound of his boots faded down the passage, she rolled her shoulders, face to the ceiling, and nearly squealed. *Yes, yes!* Nothing could make this day any better, only maybe a glass of port.

She turned her eyes around the room. It was spotlessly clean, the four-paneled folding screen closed. Only his wire reading spectacles, a daybook, and a wet brandy glass proved his presence. Curious, she leaned until she could make out an entry in the daybook. His penmanship was deliberate; he clearly never crossed things out.

June 12, 1773. Stapleton & Co refusing to move on quadrant three, North Warehouse, from April. On inquiry, reasoning is unsteady. A matter of comfort with Bleeker, and has nothing to do with the quality. Figuring J.S. to be a proper waste of time, and off the shit end of the docks. Meeting at ten tomorrow, with John Neale from Neale & Sons distillery in West Sussex County.

Weather ill-tempered. Could impact docking at Hunt's in the morning.

His boots were easily heard in the echoing corridor, so she rose and circled the bureau plat. To see his things, his element, was to know him just a little better. A sterling inkwell with a glass stopper. The brandy decanter, the distinct absence of a speck of dust. Then—*oh*. That skull and crossbones, glaring at her from a paper label. She lifted the bottle, frowning. The letters were worn as if it had been picked up many times.

Laudanum: sedative hypnotic. Dosage 10-25 drops. Poison in excessive quantities.

She dropped it fast, her spine crawling, and turned to the bookcase. She skimmed the spines, curious; some of the titles were almost untouched. Volumes of Shakespeare, Milton and Dryden, works expected in a gentlemen's collection. Then, her eyes drifted to a worn spine, brown leather cracked. *Love in Excess, or the Fatal Inquiry: A Novel*. A novel! How interesting; Asa didn't seem the sort of man who read novels.

Curious, she plucked it out. It was well-read—nearly tattered. Below the inside title, in loose script, was written:

My Asa. This one made me laugh. Meet me in the pavilion on Tuesday. Bring this book, and I'll read you a chapter if you can hear me from under my petticoat. Affection—because we can't say love, can we? Damn, I just said it. I'm free. I love you, I love you, I love you! Forever, G.

She stared, the wild elation escaping through the bottom of her feet. G. And what did that mean, *if you can hear me under my petticoat*? It mixed up, drawing lines to a different set of words. *I'd work that sweet little cunt with my tongue, until she was stiff with pleasure.* That taste...of his tongue...could it be? *No, you're disgusting, Martha Ann!* She grimaced, pushing the book back in its place. His boots sounded in the corridor, and she swung around the bureau plat and narrowed her eyes at the cork-board map.

Asa sauntered in, a bottle of port tucked in his elbow, two glasses in hand. Once again, the door was left open. A brown calico dress and petticoat were draped over his free arm, and he set the bottle and glasses down and tossed her the clothes.

"Glass of port, sweetheart?"

Oh, thank God, he'd moved past something! "Yes, that sounds nice." She held the dress at arm's length. It was simple, trimmed with cream lace. Cassandra was tall and lean-boned; this dress wouldn't have fit her. And that lace at the sleeves wasn't cream at all. She fingered it, her heart turning. It was age.

She cleared her throat. "Where—where is Cassandra?"

"Resting. Go on, I'll give you some time."

"Sir, I don't have a dry shift."

"Are you going to make me ask my sister for one of her shifts?" His tone was incredulous, but the amusement behind his eyes taunted her doubts. She flushed. Of course, it was Cassandra's dress! She watched as he dipped through the folding screen, tucking it shut behind him.

She scrambled out of her wet things and pulled on the petticoat and dress. It was far too large and laced up the back. She could lace it herself—yet, it wasn't by accident; she pulled it tight enough so it wouldn't drop, and turned back to the corkboard map.

Asa was back. He fastened the buttons on a fresh set of sleeves, tucked under a green waistcoat. A knitted pair of cotton breeches, held at the knee with a silver clasp. It was the first time she'd ever seen him without boots, and she had to stare at his face not to follow the lines of white hose to brass-buckled shoes.

God, she thought. *What right has a fellow to have legs like that?* The sight of him could almost put the book out of her mind, past a gnawing in a subconscious corner.

"Oh, thank you." She accepted a port and squinted at the map, feigning interest. "Have you been to all these places?"

"Hmm, no." He poured himself a glass. "The Indies, for a stint when I was—Jesus, probably your age." It was self-deprecating, but he smiled. "Bloody hotter than hell."

"For business?"

"I suppose you could say that."

She sipped her port, slowly, because he was watching. *You drink too much for a pint-sized girl.*

"Where else?" she asked. "There are a lot of pins."

"It's a merchant's map. Money, not memories." He drew her hair over her shoulder, following the length. "The Netherlands. I did go to London, every law fellow does that."

"Oh?" She shivered. "What for?"

"To drink a lot of clear spirits. Fuck off at the Inns of Court. Pretend to be a lawyer. Christ, you have beautiful hair."

She closed her eyes. He was behind her now, pulling the laces of the calico taut. His breath stirred the fine hairs on the back of her neck, and everything—his proximity, his scent, the faint haze of port settling her doubts—made her want to whimper. His fingertips brushed her skin, working upwards…and his mouth touched the top of her spine in the barest of kisses. One, two, three—she lost count as his lips moved until his nose was in her hair. She'd taken off her shoes (they were soaked) and her toes curled into the cold floor.

He turned her at the waist, and she sank into another kiss. She was weak, but it was surprising how easy it was to reciprocate. Her mouth searched, tasting; little hands went by instinct to his chest. The waistcoat couldn't hide his warmth. His breath deepened and swept, a sweet sigh over her cheek. Not by direction from her head, her fingers slipped to his waistline.

Martha Ann Gracey!

"You taste incredible. That's the problem, darling." Gently, he pressed her hands to her side. "Bloody cunning, you are."

172

That kiss had done something fierce. The ache was so swollen now, that she studied her fingers, considering if she should touch it herself. Maybe he would like that; he didn't seem to be embarrassed by anything sexual. The thought, rather than confusing her, twitched a smile on her lips. *Goodness, I really wish he'd shut the door.*

A fellow couldn't be properly bad unless he shut the door.

"What exactly is so amusing?" he asked warily.

"Oh. Nothing." All at once, in a surge of assurance, she pushed back a chestnut curl that had fallen over his forehead. The familiarity of the gesture was thrilling. "I was just thinking how silly I must've looked in the rain. I'm sorry you had to get wet."

"You aren't sorry at all." He regarded her over his port, chin tipped. "But you won't do it again."

She didn't reply, only dipped her head and dropped her lashes.

"Well, you came all this way to talk to Cassie. What's so important?"

"Oh, just ladies' things." She shifted, a flush creeping in her neck. *Cassandra will explain G,* she thought. It was dark to consider while Asa sat (on the bureau plat) observing her with bright eyes.

"Hmm. I see. You drove in the rain to talk about ladies' things." His long legs still touched buckled shoes to the floor, and she followed, up white hose, breeches snug, up–more. *Stop it, Martha. No, don't you dare–*

Her fingers slipped down her glass. "Ahem. To be fair, it wasn't raining when I started out."

"Most girls wouldn't do that."

"I've been riding since I was little." Her defense was necessary. "I've taken the wagon to Boston many times."

"Well, you shouldn't. In fact, I'm going to talk to Billy. Redcoats in the alleys, they aren't so friendly in the dark. All manner of scoundrels in the trees."

She frowned into her port. The subject must be changed when there was still more kissing to do. Even then, something in the way he'd said "Billy" indicated, with limp inflection, that he knew William Gracey wouldn't do a damn thing. That truth was mutually recognized in silence.

He studied her thoughtfully. "You know, I saw you mucking in the cottage yard once. Probably ten years ago. Old bastard, I am. You were squatting in the garden, turning over stones."

She blushed. "I would've been a child."

"Gathering worms was more fascinating than fellows. I rather think that's what struck me, seeing you at that bloody revel. All grown up. I'll be honest, I didn't know you by sight."

"I didn't know you either, Mr. Wyeth. I had no idea Papa was so close to you."

"Well. It's all right at a revel, aye. But goddamn, you look beautiful in the rain. To be honest, I don't mind mucking around." His tone was gently searching, though he hid it by clearing his throat. She smiled and rolled her shoulders.

"Sir, I don't mind either. I like the rain, it feels nice."

"Christ." His eyes sharpened, taking on a luster that pulled at the ache. "Come here."

She went. He slipped a hand around her waist, pulling her in for another kiss. Her innocence was strong, but any shame she'd felt about being kissed, after Robert, was gone. She wanted Asa to kiss her, and her desire made each touch a sweet gift. Besides, he was very tender. In a surge of confidence, she brought her hands to his waist once more. Hip bones, evident. Skin, warm, muscle hard—oh! His hand skimmed the small of her back, down—firm, over her backside.

So that *was* a place that men touched.

Light pressed at her eyes. The storm had broken, and the sun pushed heat through iron-cut windows. *I'm dreaming.*

Only she was sure she wasn't, because of that ache. It was roaring. Asa drew back, hand moving up her waist. He kissed her nose and chin and turned to pour another glass of port. The crack of the door bothered her even further. He was too considerate, it should've been slammed shut and bolted!

"Sir," she breathed.

"Yes, sweetheart."

"I'm very attracted to you."

"So you've said." He leaned, opened a drawer, produced his pipe, and began packing the bowl. There was a deliberation in the way he brushed loose tobacco leaves into his palm, leaving the bureau plat spotless.

"I am," she repeated, "but you make me feel a certain way."

"Hmm, how's that?"

"Why didn't you shut the door?" She shifted and sat. "You're behaving quite badly, you wouldn't want anyone to see." *God, put the port down, put it down now! What else are you going to say?*

"Trust me." Smoke drifted, prickling her nose. "This is not me behaving badly. If I choose to be bad, I'll shut the door. I'm sorry you're feeling a certain way, but please leave the door open."

She stared at him. Sitting on the bureau plat, pipe perched on his lips, hair mussed. She wanted to punch the ache down. "I just–I don't know if kissing is going to make it go away," she said, downcast.

He frowned, tipping his head. "Does it need to go away?"

"Yes, I'm sure it does." The port was talking, but the words were hers. "It bothers me."

"If it goes away then, aye, what if it comes back?"

"I-I don't know. I suppose I'd want to keep making it go away."

He watched her, for too long, without saying anything. His breath quickened; the port glass tipped, throwing lavender rings over the wall. "I'm not sure what to say." Palms resting on the bureau plat, he leveled with her. "I might suggest one thing."

"Oh?"

"You could touch the feeling."

She couldn't speak. Staring at him, she couldn't breathe; the ache pulsed with each beat of her heart. He knew. He was looking right through her; she was a frame around that image of herself, grinding into her hand, twisted in the bedding. Eyes locked on the folding knife. *Asahel Emory Wyeth | 1735.* Over and over and over…

"Sir, I have." She gasped. It was her voice, but she hadn't felt it. No vibrations on her tongue. Her fingers flew to her mouth, and she watched him, wildly. He was unreadable, but then, there it was, that haughty smile. Heat curled, whipping from her toes to her heart.

"You're some kind of woman," he stated, clearly happy with her response.

"I'm sorry, I shouldn't have said that!"

"Why so?"

"It's just that, well—the ladies say—"

"I don't think the ladies say the same thing the fellows do. I rather think the picture of a pretty girl like you, with her hand between her legs, might have a man set for life."

"That doesn't sound decent," she muttered, flushing red.

"It isn't, I suppose, by proper standards." He sighed, a finger tracing the rim of his glass. "But women do feel that way. And you." He stood and reached down to take her hand, pulling her to her feet. "Darling, look at me."

176

She met his eyes.

"Don't feel shame. If you want to touch, touch. And enjoy yourself, no less." Gently, he touched the tip of her nose, tipped her chin. Her face was on fire, but it was all right, just like he said. To move past her inbred shame, in tandem with her blunt curiosity–it wasn't the hardest thing to do. In fact, he was making it easy.

"Sir. It–it feels so nice when you kiss my neck. Could you, please?"

He smiled, but it wasn't teasing. "There, you see. You need a lot of kissing, and there are many places to kiss." Firm fingers caught her neck, and he obeyed. He obeyed! Sweet indentations pressed her jaw, her throat. Her heart skipped and surged. It was one thing to ignore the opinion of a man, or pretend to listen to him; but for him to obey, with that much enthusiasm, was intoxicating.

She sighed to the ceiling, each kiss sending shooting signals to the fire. She caught him, from a crack in her eyelid, putting the pipe down, and then, his hand was on her backside, cupping soft flesh. God, it was molded to be gripped! Her fingers flew to his chest, his shoulders, to his head; she'd wanted for so long to feel those chestnut curls. She buried her fingers, and then–

She felt something, just above the base of his skull. A scar? No, not a scar; his hair was thick. It was more an unnatural indentation in the bone, about the size of a shilling, and about as deep. She felt again, ignoring the tightening of his muscles, and outlined a blunt diamond, deeper on one side.

Suddenly, the excitement died. An image flickered. Asa, sitting in the battered parlor chair at the cottage, pressing the back of his neck. By the tea-room window, staring at Robert's retreating figure, fingers pressed into the back of his neck.

Dover's. Valerian root and pekoe tea and opium tincture. *Laudanum: sedative hypnotic. Poison in excessive quantities.*

He flinched and pulled away. "All right, darling. I've got to pace myself, you're too damn sweet."

"Sir, what happened to your head? Is that why you have so many headaches?"

"I'm sure Cassie is up by now. Ahem." He turned, frowning at the bureau plat. "I know you've got pressing ladies' things to talk about. Besides, I've got things—bills—very good."

"I don't mean to pry." Panic ached in her chest, an awareness she'd made a mistake. "You can talk to me."

He rounded and went to sit in the red leather chair. The port was abandoned, and he popped the cork from the brandy decanter and poured a glass. The shift in temperature was marked, though he was clearly attempting to right himself.

"I'm sorry, sir," she said hastily. "I didn't mean to offend you."

He scowled. "What are you talking about, aye? I'm never offended. Say, are you still going to that Midsummer's party?"

"Mr. Wyeth, you sound angry."

"Not true, I'm not angry, are you going to Midsummer's?"

It was a pointed change in subject, and he would force her to accept it. Maybe it wasn't anything, she reasoned, a malformation from birth that embarrassed him. "Oh. Yes, I suppose," she said lamely. "I've almost finished my gown. Papa will want to go."

Papa. The air cleared for another problem. The mention of Mr. Gracey (when Asa's hand had a moment ago gripped her haunches) wasn't right, because Asa wasn't just Asa Wyeth; he was the other half of Wyeth-Gracey. The thought of William Douglas, sweet little man, rocking on his heels, sipping at his port, seeped both guilt and curious anger in her belly. She'd come to talk to Cassandra, but she was wasting away the afternoon, being bad with Asa in his office, where so many times William had sat pouring over receipts! If he found out–

He wouldn't even be angry. It was worse. He'd be hurt. Disappointed.

Asa's expression was stoic, but it was evident he was thinking something similar, or at least a thought that warranted a pass of guilt. He considered his brandy, forehead bunched with a scowl. "I can take you back to the cottage," he muttered. "Or send one of the boys for Billy."

"I don't know what to say to him!"

"You won't say anything." The guilt wasn't gone, but he cocked his head. "I'll send for Billy. We'll have dinner, Sam can shoot a duck. I've got a bottle of port your age in the cellar."

She stared at him, incredulous. "That's not very nice! You say you're not angry at me, but I don't believe you."

"I'm not angry with you." He put his shoes up on the bureau plat and sank low. "Well, I *am* angry you took the wagon out. But never mind, and don't worry, darling, your claws are sufficiently sunk. But I need to think about this. In the meantime, please don't ask questions."

"Oh. Are you not going to kiss me anymore?" She sat, forlorn.

"I'm going to kiss you plenty. But understand, you've put me in a bit of a spot." He was serious. "I don't want to take anything away from you. You've got the world at your feet, aye, when you're twenty. But well, the older you get, the smaller it becomes."

Even if he was right, and she knew it, she didn't care. It was an easy truth to ignore when he was in essence so tender. And so, *so* handsome–it was breaking her heart, to look at him, shoes up, pipe lit, the faintest sunset blush on the skin of his collarbone. From kissing, of course; she was warm there too, and it felt exquisite. But, the surging happiness of kissing in the rain was fading. It was far off when he'd shut down that easily, just because she'd asked one innocent question. The wings that had lifted her heart were rudely clipped, and she was planted on her feet, straining to see through a cracked door. Feeling real things, bodily things, embarrassing things. Things she'd pretended didn't exist with Robert.

She glanced at her fingertips, remembering the dip in bone, and realized something about Asahel Wyeth.

If there was something he didn't want her to know, he would never, ever tell.

It wasn't that he was done. Some time, a bowl of Virginia tobacco, and a glass of brandy, and he was back to kissing. She was careful to keep her hands out of his hair. Her own hair was thoroughly dry, her knees weak, and her lips smarting by the time Cassandra lumbered downstairs, barking orders, and began sweeping the dining room floor. Asa sent for Mr. Gracey, and sauntered to the cellar for the twenty-year port. But he was unreadable, as she sat, blushing, fingers twisted on her lap. William would know nothing because Asa wasn't ready for him to know.

She lay awake, long past midnight, exhausted from trying to satisfy the ache (it hadn't worked, despite Asa's encouragement). Alone, with just the walls and her doubts, she was outnumbered, and the words crept back.

He had kissed her, he'd touched her like she'd longed for. It was beautiful, but—it wasn't perfect. A dream, yes, to feel his mouth on her mouth, to feel his hands on her body, even through clothes. To taste him, to ache for him. But in the darkness, she had to admit it. It wasn't necessarily a good dream.

It wasn't a daydream for chasing, hoping, wanting. Hitting walls and going hungry. It was both, and it hurt.

It was clear now. Robert Henshaw's ghost didn't walk the halls of Wyeth House alone; he walked in a crowd.

We can't say love, can we?

"Love," she whispered into the darkness. "Damn, I just said it."

13

the SWEETEST FIRE

Since the moment of the first kiss, it was him: all day, all night. Knotting her belly, sick with doubt. Kisses stolen around William had her wild, making mistakes, punching walls. Judith, stumbling across a fierce embrace in the kitchen, was ready to wring necks; William was industrious and very innocent. Yet, no doors were shut. At night, no matter how hard she tried, her hand wasn't enough. And if too much time went by without his touch, she was melancholy, and uncomfortable things crept back in. *Forever, G.* Laudanum. Her finger, dipping over the strange indentation.

But she was veritable opium, and he was, despite any contrary muttering, addicted. That moment in his office was an innocent intrusion, and must be corrected; he had not meant to react that way, and even if he'd never admit it, he was sorry, and his sorrow was expressed by mulishly pretending it'd never happened. She tried to do the same, and for the most part, she could. Only a muffled warning bell rang when his muscles tightened under her fingertips, and she had to remember not to touch the back of his head. She could touch his curls, she just had to be careful; and the more she kissed, the more she learned.

❀

The morning before Midsummer's, she slept past dawn. It wasn't uncommon when she saw every midnight, eaten alive by the image of his face. It was almost disgusting, she admitted crossly, how infatuated she was. *You did the same thing with Robert—* yes, she'd felt the same angry obsession, yet with Asa, it lacked a marked element: the question of his integrity.

She pulled on her dressing gown, raked her fingers through her hair, and fairly stomped downstairs.

Never had she questioned his intent. Anyone who knew Asa Wyeth (which she felt that she did), knew that despite his oddities, he was a good man. Close to sweet. And considerate, past his blunt New York mannerisms. She'd never experienced such a thing from a man, and it was intoxicating. What were her feelings to Robert? If a woman was angry, it was because she was too hot, or her stays were too tight, or she was on her "courses". And Mr. Gracey, well—if her woes were too evident, it made him uncomfortable.

But while Asa could be bullish, the fundamental problems were addressed head-on, as if he had a checklist of things to do to make a girl feel easy. She needed to use the necessary house? He led the way. She was wet and cold, so here was a fresh dress; she might feel better if she had a glass of port—but just one. She'd stated that she liked it when he kissed her neck, so he'd kissed her neck. And he'd been right to leave the office door open.

She huffed, rounding into the kitchen. *If he'd let me, I would've slammed that door shut. There's got to be more than kissing!*

183

"Oh!" She jumped, manifesting him behind the prepping table, leaning on his elbows over a cup of coffee.

"Sir! Aren't you supposed to be in the city?"

"I've to meet a Dutch fellow on Merchant's Row. I'll be late." He rounded the table, caught her by the waist, and kissed her. Her taste buds nipped with black coffee. Just like that, the doubts were gone. What had they even been, when her senses raged? Her thighs tightened; it was subconscious, to plant little hands on his chest.

"Mr. Wyeth, I'm not dressed!"

"You're not."

"Where is Papa?" She pulled the dressing gown so tight, stitches hissed. Nothing held her breasts, and vexingly, they'd hardened the minute his mouth had met her mouth.

"The shop. He's gone to tell off Richard." He returned to his coffee, and she glanced. Of course. No waistcoat, no frock, wind-tousled hair. His countenance had shed a decade; the elixir of youth, evidently, sprang from her lips.

She considered for a moment. Should she get dressed…or, perhaps not. No doors were closed, Judith was absent, and Mr. Gracey was at the shop. "I don't like Richard anyway," she said warmly. "He's lazy."

"Hmm, yes. And he's been slipping off to watch the militia drill. Told Billy he wants to be a drummer."

"A drummer? Oh, that's silly." She could feel his eyes, following the sway of the gown as she set a kettle to boil. She frowned, rifling through the tea caddies.

He cleared his throat in an attempt to stifle a laugh. "Is it silly? Men love war, you know. Nothing finer than a good brawl."

"That is just silly, too. You wouldn't brawl, you're a gentleman."

"Bloody wrong, on both accounts." He leaned, chin on his thumbs. "I can pretend to be a gentleman. And I can attest there's no better feeling than getting decked on the jaw in the back of a public house. I used to brawl quite a bit," he mused.

She dropped two sugars in her tea, fingers trembling. "I don't believe it!"

"An honorable man must brawl." He nodded, agreeing with himself. "Some would duel, too, if you can think it."

"I can, but it doesn't make it any less silly. I can't think of a good enough reason–" She was cut off by a kiss. A perfect kiss, lazy and warm, a signature of his, maddening because it teased. She pressed her fingers into the back of his neck, and it changed, out of nowhere. Eating, open mouth to open mouth–she gasped, and pulled away, her lower lip smarting.

"You're a good enough reason," he stated, his voice stifling triumph.

"What–oh, for heaven's sake!"

"It's true, though. A fellow will do just about anything for a pretty girl."

"Are you saying you'd brawl for me?" All of the uncomfortable heat centered in her groin. Kissing with tongues, kissing her neck…it was tentative, a finger skimming the rim of a brimming glass. Suddenly, she knew what he was doing, and she detested it. Robert had bitten her first. And so much time had passed, yet Asa still had it caught in his head.

He may as well have sat her down and lectured her. *Fellows do* this, *you see, and it can feel very nice. But it doesn't feel so nice if you don't want it…*

Without further thought, she locked the doubts in a cupboard in her brain, and dropped her arms to her sides. The effect was immediate; his eyes darted to her breasts, which were perked with agitation.

"Hmm, yes. I'm saying." His eyes snapped to her face. "I would, s'matter of fact, brawl for you."

"Well." She drew a breath, dramatically deep. "I do thank you, that's very nice of you."

"Goddamn. You seem rather miffed this morning, have I tripped up?"

She watched him, crossing the kitchen to put his empty cup in the washing basin. Aware, abruptly, that her shoulders were heaving, and her heart rate had increased so much, that her tongue was dry.

She swallowed, digging her nails into her palms. "I *am* annoyed at you, Mr. Wyeth."

"Well, I suppose I'm to guess why that might be. I'm definitely going to be late to Merchant's Row."

"It's just that. You're being too nice, and I don't prefer it."

"That's an interesting complaint."

"Maybe nice is not the word." She cleared her throat. "But I-I'm not a fragile doll. You're too careful with me!"

"Really?" His brow rose. "Your lip is bleeding."

"Oh! You don't have to close doors," she said hotly, wiping fiercely. "I want to be alone with you."

"And what exactly do you think is going to happen, if I were to shut the door?" He was haughty, but she sensed the faintest strain of longing in his tone, stifled by amusement.

"Well, I don't know," she muttered. "But it's got to be more than kissing."

"You don't like kissing anymore? Ah, too bad."

"No–no!" *Too much, Martha, you're making an idiot of yourself.* "It's just that I don't want you to think that I'm scared. I'm not!"

"You know." He was thoughtful. "Society says you shouldn't even be kissing a fellow before you're hitched. I reckon you're on the road to hell, at the rate you're going."

"Oh, that is *not* nice! I'm sure you've done more than kissing with a girl!" She clamped a hand over her mouth. It was pathetic, skirting around the problem, the tangled knot in the middle of all the beautiful things he was making her feel.

Robert.

"What do you want me to say, darling? That I've fucked so many women, I've lost count? And you're the anomaly. Incredible, really." He shook his head, clearly irritated. "Or could it possibly be that I'm aware of something that continuously flies past your pretty head. That you're very young, and I don't give a damn what you say, you're delicate."

"Delicate." Her nostrils flared, despite her best effort. "Sir, that is *in*correct. I am not delicate."

"Yes, you are."

"No, I'm not. You said I wasn't a lady!"

"That doesn't mean you're not a woman."

"Well, maybe I don't want the things women are expected to!"

"Jesus." He pushed off of the prepping table, rounded, and was in front of her. Her heart shot to her throat–his shadow, his scent, his essence–it tightened the walls. She dropped her eyes, wrapping her arms around her breasts.

"Sir–I–I'm sorry. I'm being rude. I'm sorry."

Yet his hands went to her waist, to her backside, and he lifted her, placing her on the prepping table. Her hipbones smarted on impact, and she squealed, wrapping her arms around his neck. Like she weighed nothing, she was a feather! Still, he was taller, and he leaned to kiss her, from her lips, along the line of her jaw, to the lobe of her ear.

"I didn't mean to offend you," she gasped.

"I'm not offended. I'm a reasonable fellow." He drew her hair over her shoulder. "Jesus, you've got beautiful hair. And you." He tipped her chin. "You've got an appetite. It's salacious, really. I can smell it when you walk in a room."

"That doesn't sound right!"

"Oh, it's very right. A fellow could tie you to a bedpost with a cravat, and you'd scream, but you'd love it." He smiled, but there was a warning flicker behind his eyes. "I could strike your ass, and you'd love it, wouldn't you? Yet." His thumb ran over her chin, down her throat–tracing hills of flesh and bone, toying with the ribbon of her dressing gown.

Her head clouded with heat. *I said too much*–one simple tug and the gown was open, a parallel of silk. She closed her eyes, fighting to breathe. Slick cloth ran over blushing skin, dropping to her elbow in a heap.

"Look at me," he murmured.

She opened her eyes.

"Yet," he finished, "you have no idea what I'm talking about."

He traced the lines of her shoulder, watching her breast almost reverently, taking her in. A touch followed. Skimming, a feather over the rise of flesh, to the hardened climax of something she didn't understand. But it didn't matter, because it felt so, so good! Under the gown, his hand followed her curves, bending her neck; her throat arched, her spine supple like a sapling. Kisses, kisses, down…that ache, now a gaping wound, was screaming at him.

His mouth met her breast. Her thighs clenched, and she dipped her head, pushing her fingers into the hair at his temples, fighting the urge to pull. A break of white teeth, then his tongue, circling the dark skin, teasing the hardened end. His lips moved, tender points of pressure, to her collarbone. Down, to her other breast, nudging the silk aside, until it fell, too, and she was naked to the waist. She leaned on her palm, nearly panting. Honeyed kisses, burning the spitting ends of her nerves, working up her collarbone, to her throat–then he drew back, tipping her chin.

"Do you like that, darling?" His eyes were hazy, his voice hushed. "You don't have to say yes."

"It–it feels very nice." Her tongue went dry, sticking to the roof of her mouth. Robert's mauling–pink rivers eroding virgin flesh–was erased. Kissed clean.

"You see, kisses can go anywhere you want." Mindfully, he drew her dressing gown together and tied the ribbon. "On your lips." He traced them– "Your breasts. You have beautiful breasts, exquisite."

"Oh! Thank you." Then, a begging thought, an answer to a shuddering question, indistinguishable from a dream. "Where–where else?" she whispered.

"Wherever you want."

She wrapped her arms around her middle. "Down my belly?"

"Certainly, there."

"On…my back?"

"Aye, that's a pleasant place to kiss."

"What about." She frowned, too warm, but he was easy. "What about my legs? And my feet. You can't kiss feet."

"I can, though. If I want to." His hand slipped under her gown at the split of her legs, down her shins, to her ankles. He lifted one foot under the arch, glanced at it, then dropped it gently.

"You've got the prettiest little feet. I'd happily kiss them." And he kissed her, hungry again. She responded, her toes curling, cold in the stagnant air. His lips worked around her throat, into her hair, and she sighed, taking in the lines of his shoulders, her forehead falling against his collarbone.

For a moment, she forgot about her body.

She'd seen that part of a fellow once, on a drunk man, streaking through the streets. Ladies, behind hands and through giggles, whispered about it mockingly. Yet, it was a rise, fighting against linen, almost begging her to touch. He was distracted, his nose in her hair, so she indulged—from the floor to his waistline. Spurs. Boots. Breeches. Cock. Yes, that was the word. *Cock.* On the streaking man, it'd looked so limp, so useless. Yet, Asa had a cock, and it was…well. It certainly wasn't limp. Without thinking, she reached out and ran her fingers over the form.

Oh—goodness. He was hard as stone.

He pulled back, tucking her hands in her lap. "All right, darling. Hands to yourself."

She flushed, realizing she'd made an error. "You don't keep your hands to yourself, Mr. Wyeth."

"This is me, keeping my hands to myself." He stepped away. "You're very sweet. What I want, is for you to enjoy yourself. That takes time."

She patted at the hairs on the back of her neck, watching him cross the room to gather his hat and frock. She noted, pouting, that he buttoned it, which he rarely did. Flushing, she asked, "Have you decided if you're going to Midsummer's tomorrow?"

"Yes, s'matter of fact." He stooped to adjust his spurs. "I have an opportunity."

"You can have fun at a revel," she reminded him.

"I'm not dancing, never mind that. But I might be in the mood to have some fun."

"Oh? What do you do for fun?"

"The most fun is had at a revel," he stated, straightening, "outside of the ballroom. Try it sometime. Take off your shoes and walk in the grass. I put back a bottle of applejack at a party

190

once and stripped for a fountain swim. If I remember correctly, it was the governor's social."

"Mr. Wyeth, that's scandalous!"

"I'm sorry. I suppose the sight of my ass pulled the stick out of his, he made a story of it eventually." He pushed his hat on. "All I'm saying is, you're a beautiful girl, Martha. You'll look damn fine in that dress, but you've ruined me, I'm afraid. I'll only ever see you naked, no matter what you're doing." He crossed the room and leaned in, thumb on her chin, to kiss her again. "Has that feeling gone away yet, aye?" he murmured against her mouth.

"No, sir." There was not a damn reason in the world to lie to him about that.

"Ah, I'm sorry. Why don't you try again, before you go to sleep?"

"Mr. Wyeth, those are private things!"

He took her hand, pressing the knuckles into his lips. A nip– she jolted. Then he turned her palm up, fingers loose, kissing each one. "Put this little hand to work tonight. Think about whatever you want."

She tried and failed to be indignant, but he caught her in another kiss. She felt better, but there were still secrets. She wouldn't make him guess who she was–it was on her sleeve, out of her mouth, in every part of her body that he would put his lips to. *Every part…I should've asked. If he can kiss something as silly as feet–*

"God help me! God save me!"

Judith gaped in the doorway, a basket of washing slipping from her arms. She dropped it, stormed into the kitchen, and seized Martha, yanking her to her feet.

"Hello, Judith," said Asa pleasantly. "All right, now, there's no need for that–"

191

"You," Judith hissed, pointing a finger at his chest, mobcap fluttering. "You are the devil himself. You are Satan himself! I will starve myself, to purge this house of your spirit—"

"Christ, don't do that," Asa muttered. "There's got to be a healthier way to purge spirits."

"Don't you dare speak his name with your forked tongue!" Judith's barking followed him to the doorway, where he turned to smile at Martha. "I'll see you at the rabble tomorrow, darling," he said. "Look for me. I have a surprise for you."

"You'll have no such thing," snapped Judith, "in the name of all that is holy and good!"

❋

She didn't enjoy herself that night.

As Cassandra prepared her the following afternoon, she was heavy-eyed from lack of sleep, belly gnawing with worry. She hadn't thought about it much before, but it had occurred to her (faced with nothing but her thoughts and a blank wall) that Robert Henshaw would be at this party.

Hannah and Frances certainly would. Hannah would never say no to a Tory revel, and Frances was a follower. And the families that attended Tucker parties were affluent, well-connected—textile merchants, nearly all of them. But, she'd started to get the sense, towards the end of her time with Robert, that the House of Henshaw wasn't doing too well. Not only that, she'd struck him down. A blow to his pride, that surely a man like Robert wouldn't let go with grace.

The day was cool and dampened by a mist of rain. As usual, when she prepared for a party, she'd kept to her bed until the middle of the day, though she barely slept. She rose, took coffee, and packed her gown in a box to send to the Estate. Cassandra wouldn't go, but she'd insisted that Martha prepare herself at Wyeth House; she wouldn't miss seeing the final production with so many of her weary hours spent, threading needles and pinning lace.

But Martha was angry at that dress. She'd planned it for Robert; Midsummer's was going to be *their* party. Asa would tell her she looked beautiful, but she couldn't shake the feeling that inside, he'd be stifling a laugh. And thinking about her feet, probably.

She blinked and yawned, her head lolling as Cassandra brushed her hair. Judith, insisting she attend, was sent to fetch port. ("I won't have you acting like a harlot at Wyeth House!" she'd hissed, snatching a pouting Martha by the arm). Providentially for Judith, Asa was absent, locked in the office with Mr. Gracey. William would attend her in one of the Wyeth carriages, Asa insisted, but he would only ride on Jed.

"Everyone will stare at you, riding in on that beast," said William pleasantly.

"Stare at me?" Asa appeared genuinely confused. "Why? I just don't want a bloody introduction. I'll come in through a window if I have to."

Martha hung her head. The "introductions" had been her favorite part of revels, her arm looped through Mr. Gracey's, ears pricked to hear "Robert Henshaw." She tried to make herself feel better. Asa had a surprise for her–that might be interesting.

Now Cassandra stood behind her in the airy bedroom, steady fingers twisting and tucking, pausing here and there to admire her handiwork. "Don't be disappointed if Emory doesn't dance with you," she said drily. "He's most boring at a revel. Don't worry, he's in love with you. I'll make him do something. I don't know, bring some flowers. What a chump."

"Please." Martha blushed, grateful when the door slammed behind a hustling Judith, who brought Madeira and two glasses with little poise. She was grateful for the port. Since the days of preparing with the Dunaway girls, she'd relished doing so under a haze of drink; and now, with the gray light that cast from the windows, and the buttery-sweet smell of honeysuckle, the distant spinning was welcome. She tried to apply it to the worry.

Cassandra tucked a final curl. "You're a dream. Emory could be the envy of every man, if only he had the bollocks."

Every man. She set her port aside, annoyed that her palms were sweating. "Cassie. What—what will I do if I see Mr. Henshaw? I don't want to be rude."

Cassandra was well-versed in the tale of her woes with Robert. Asa had evidently given her a skeleton of the story, (though he would never admit it) in an attempt to heal her wounds with his sister's motherly understanding. It worked, as a tipsy Martha had spilled one day, sniffling over a port on the settee. The sincerity of Cassandra's affront was true, and her comfort, as a woman, was soothing.

Cassandra paused, regarding Martha in the mirror. "Your thoughtfulness is pleasant." She sighed, arching her brows. "I'd advise you not to hurt your pretty head over it. We're women, we must be cruel sometimes. Not every man can walk away happy. Besides," she added, placing a final pin, "he won't speak to you, with Emory there."

"Are you sure?" Martha was doubtful. "He's never been timid."

"Trust me," said Cassandra grimly, "Henshaw wouldn't dare."

Martha may have been demure, in her entrance to the ballroom of Lord and Lady Tucker (of Beacon Hill), but she was anything but silent. Everything, from the silk hose to the pearls and black beads woven in her hair, shouted in proclamation of her newfound potency. She was on fire, from the copper crown of her hair to the slippers on her feet. (Which pinched, excruciatingly).

But as William dropped her arm and left her for his initial glass of port, a sense of vulnerability sank her expectations. There was no bullish Hannah to mimic. No Frances to calm her with low whispers; and as she stood alone, the throng spinning, she felt distinctly lost. The Dunaway girls were suddenly a much harsher loss than Robert.

She took a port and worked her way to the safety of the wall. In a moment, she caught sight of Asa coming from a muted corridor, and her heart seized. He wore the most exquisite honey-colored suit, barring only some of Robert's more extravagant ensembles. A satin pleated frock skimmed his middle, over a cream waistcoat stitched with green and mauve florals. Lace, at his sleeves–she'd never seen lace, in the vicinity of Asa. White hose, gleaming buckled shoes, a neckerchief.

He turned his wrist, adjusting a button at his sleeve, then took up a conversation with a fusty gentleman in a silver wig. Mr. Gracey floated through the throng, port in hand, and joined them, face red, blue eyes earnest. Asa had that effect on him, she noted, pushing down guilt. Almost as if, the moment Asa was by his side, Mr. Gracey's simple life was complete. She felt panic rising–*Papa can't know. No one can know*–but she still had the feeling Asa was going to be bad. How could a fellow be bad, in a room full of stuffy people?

She narrowed her eyes, searching for familiar faces, then– Robert.

Cassandra's comfort dissipated. A snifter of brandy in hand, he was to all accounts the same Robert. The same beautiful face, the same impeccable dress, the same perfect body. She'd almost forgotten, in her race to sink her claws into his cousin, how handsome he was. Yet, the long shadow he cast in the candlelight was grim; his countenance was smooth, stone-hardened. Blue eyes were grey glass. The line of his mouth pressed thin, his shoulders knotted to his ears.

A strange feeling pinched her heart. Certainly not regret–no, not after what he'd done! Almost as unwelcome, she felt guilt.

She shrank further. Guilt, what a horrible thing to feel, for someone who decidedly didn't deserve it! Frantically, she searched for a distraction. Oh, there was Frances! Frances had always been kind enough, even if she was a bit annoying. Her dull brown eyes were soft as always, and she smiled timidly, moving to Martha in the throng.

"Frances!" Martha exclaimed. "It's so good to see you!"

Frances took her hand, leaning to kiss her cheek. "How I've missed you, Martha, dear. Hannah–" But she was cut off. Asa approached, and Martha stiffened when his hand brushed the small of her back. Her nose prickled with a new scent, zestier than usual. She fought the urge to swat his hand away, smiling tightly at Frances.

Two sets of eyes were watching her. Mr. Gracey, and Robert.

"Ahem. Hello, Mr. Wyeth." She moved pointedly away. "Frances–"

"Excuse Miss Gracey," said Asa firmly. He nodded, and turning on his heel, steered Martha towards the refreshments.

"That was very rude, shame on you!" she blurted, stumbling to keep up.

"Shame on me for nothing, she's not so much a friend."

Hadn't Robert said that? Her brain pinched. "What? Frances is sweet."

"You women use that word in the cattiest way." He poured a brandy. "You look fantastic, darling. Good enough to eat. I'm starving."

"Sir." She turned red. "You cannot behave like this at a revel. You're going to get yourself in trouble. Oh, you look very well, too, I've never seen you dress like a gentleman!"

He smiled. His eyes were a curious color in the candlelight, the deepest coffee brown rimmed with gold. Her own wandered, taking in the honey frock. It was the perfect color for his complexion, sun-kissed; it made his hair look darker than it really was, bringing out the grays around his ears. Her fingers tingled, and she fought the urge to push back a curl.

"Why would you say that about Frances?" She doubled down.

"Because it's true. Jesus, it's bloody hot in here. I've to talk to a fellow, Sanders is his name. He's opening a distillery in the city. If you see him…little, dresses like a preacher, you wouldn't know him to brew spirits…"

She glanced. Robert still watched, blue eyes blank. Her skin crawled, though she smiled up at Asa, not really listening. He was rambling, clipped New York accent accentuated in the low thrumming of polished voices.

Something pooled, dark, in the middle of her heart. She leaned close. "Sir, what is the surprise?"

He paused, cocking a brow. "After a bit."

"It's just that I don't–I don't *feel* very comfortable." She saw his eyes, flickering to Robert's face. His body stiffened, and in a deft movement, he turned, shielding her from Robert, took up his brandy, and guided her away from the table. Through the crowd, down the corridor.

Her heart pounded. Flesh fell from Robert's bones once more, and he resumed his position as a pest of a ghost.

Asa pushed open one of the doors at the end of the corridor. Had Mr. Gracey seen them walk away? *God!* She slipped under his arm. Brown eyes met hers, burnished oak in the candle dim, and he shut the door, and turned the latch. *If I choose to be bad, I'll shut the door.*

He kissed her, long and slow. It calmed her heart, and the low ache of sleeplessness fell away.

"I don't know about kissing at a revel," she said, feeling weak at the knees.

"You wanted to leave." He took her hand. "Besides, since you can't be patient, I've got something for you."

He led her to a settee, a red silk damask in front of a hollow fireplace; a polished harpsichord stood regal in the corner. It was a small sitting room, clearly one of many (the Tucker mansion, the pride of Beacon Hill, boasted forty rooms). She sat, curling her toes. Her dancing slippers hurt badly, and she was annoyed that she'd bothered to wear them. It wasn't as if she'd be dancing.

"That harpsichord is from London," he noted, settling beside her. "Out of tune from the ship ride over, I think. This." He reached, taking her hand, and ran her fingers over the damask. "Spain. Quite expensive. It seems a bit ridiculous. Working yourself to the bone, and you're a bloody harpsichord, that no one knows how to play."

There was something in his tone that was almost warning, but it lit a flare. A secret, just him, just her, alone. Her eyes circled the room, and she checked herself, quickly. She didn't feel trapped. Quite the opposite; he'd rescued her, again.

"That being said." He reached into his pocket, bringing out a little velvet box. "If it means something to you, it means something to me, darling."

A present! She took it, fingers trembling, and plucked off the lid. Inside, glittering on black silk, was the most beautiful pair of earrings she'd ever seen. Georgian sterling, sparkling with rose-cut diamonds–long, like sheets of rain. She stared, mouth open, heart pounding.

"Mr. Wyeth, I don't know what to say. They're beautiful!"

"Aye." His eyes went soft. "And you. Cottage girl, my ass, you look like a princess." Gently, he slipped the earrings she wore (her old emerald drops) out of her ears. "Put them on. I want to see you."

"They won't match my dress!"

"Really. I might disagree, I can be a drab fellow, but anything matches with diamonds."

She blushed, sliding the earrings through her lobes, and shook her head. The stones caught the candlelight, throwing snowflakes over the walls; they were so long that they tickled halfway down her neck. She couldn't help herself–she squealed and laughed. Robert had given her what, a pocket kerchief?

God, who was Asa Wyeth? He was watching her, eyes lit, the slightest smile curling the ends of his mouth. For a moment her heart froze. A man had never looked at her like that before, as if only she made him proud. As if only she brought him respect.

"Ahem–what do you think?" She turned her throat. "They're very heavy."

"From England," he said softly. "Though not on any of my sloops. I think you're hurting my eyes, woman." He dropped his head, frowning into his brandy. "For the ones I took off. You know, I've thought about what you said, you're right. I haven't been giving you what you want. I don't want you to make yourself a certain way because you think it's what I want. I'm here for Martha, all right? So wear your pretty earrings and ride astride your horse. Do you promise, darling?"

He was oddly vulnerable, something she didn't know he was capable of being. Where was this coming from? She knew she was in love, but she'd never called into question his feelings. Was Asa Wyeth in love? To be loved by a man who read *Love In Excess* to tatters was nearly frightening. More so, because he was looking at her with heightened reverence, as if that little sitting room was a church, with Spanish damask pews.

"I promise," she answered, her voice shaking.

"Another thing." He cleared his throat. "Look at me, darling. This isn't going to work."

"What—oh, what do you mean?"

"I can't steal around anymore." He reached, tipping her chin. "I'm going to talk to Billy. Tomorrow, after all this. I've got to shoot myself in the foot and be done with it, all right?"

Her nerves pinched. Mr. Gracey was the only man in the world who'd never raised questions to her. This was going to hurt him—badly. "It's all right," she said quickly, "if you're not comfortable."

"No, I want to court you properly. You deserve it, and I'm sorry I didn't see that. I'm just—I'm a little out of practice." He leaned, pressing his lips to hers in a quiet kiss. His fingers brushed her neck, toying with one of the earrings.

She leaned in, sinking into red silk. It didn't matter that her heart pounded, wild with nerves, at the prospect of William finding out. Asa was right, of course; it had to be done. He would handle it, like an order of business, and there was little that she did that William Douglas couldn't find a way to forgive.

What really mattered was a closed door. Rose-cut diamond earrings, brandy on his tongue.

"I've been thinking about what you said." He leveled with her, serious. "In the kitchen."

"Oh?" What *had* she said?

"I'm not particularly fond of revels. If you want to go back out, we can." His eyes flickered to the door. "Or, would you want to try something?"

That door… he'd latched it. *You said that's what you wanted.* "Try something?" she asked, annoyed at how suddenly she warmed. "What–what do you mean?"

"Just for you. You'll have to take your panniers off, though."

She stared at him, her belly curling. The noise of the assembly was a distant drumming, accentuating the crisp silence of the room.

"T-take them…off?"

"Mhmm." He nodded, as if he'd taken the panniers off a hundred different ladies before. "I can help you put them back on."

She dropped her head to her chest, eaten with heat. In any other circumstance–in the kitchen, his tongue teasing her breasts, in his office, with the door cracked open–she wouldn't have felt quite the degree of shame over her innocence. It was easy, to ask him questions. But her heart was beating very, very fast…and the door was shut.

"I–um, I-I don't know, sir. I'm not sure what you mean."

"Well." He crossed his ankle over his knee. "I get the feeling kissing isn't enough for you anymore."

"Oh, that's not what I mean. It just doesn't–well, it makes me feel angry. Like I'm not getting everything. I'm sorry, I don't mean to sound selfish!"

"Not angry. Excited. And you're allowed to be selfish when it comes to what feels nice. Every woman deserves that. Besides." He took a drink of brandy, leaning on his hand. "Nothing pleases a fellow more than pleasing a woman. I can say that definitively."

There was a moment of silence; she sipped her port over a swelling in her throat.

"Would you take your panniers off, darling?" he asked.

"Oh–I-I don't know." She fumbled. "I suppose I would need to know what you're going to do first. I-I'm a virgin." The word sounded so silly coming from her mouth, but her brain was signaling, remembering the way his cock had felt under curious fingers. So hard, too hard. It was the fundamental means to an end–the only thing she was sure she knew about sex. Barnyard animals. Catching a prostitute and a fellow getting busy in an alley.

The diamond earrings were nearly too heavy.

His brows rose, a trace. "I won't take your virginity, Martha."

"Why would I need to take my panniers off?" The heat in her face was an annoyance, and she batted at the back of her neck. "They're awfully hard to get back on."

"I can put them back on," he said simply. His tone was light, nearly flat, as if he could sense that his suggestion might frighten her. He dropped his eyes to his glass, tracing the rim. Silence, for uncomfortably long, then, he leveled with her. "When you touch yourself, it feels very nice, doesn't it? And you can finish with your fingers if it's right. Martha, you can look at me."

"I'm sorry, this just–this isn't a very proper conversation." The image flashed in her head, pathetic little Martha, sweating, grinding into her own hand. Eyes locked on his name, lips pushing it into the darkness. Yet, there was no shame in his voice.

"I can do that for you," he said.

"Oh–do what?"

"I can make you finish. If it's something you'd like to try." Not a flinch. Not an inflection out of place.

"I-I really don't know what you're saying." Yet her curiosity roared out of control, surging alongside her slamming heart.

"Well. If you think about how you use your fingers, I can do the same for you. Only with my mouth, and tongue. If I do that for long enough, you'll finish. If you can relax, and not think too much."

God, was he really talking, or was she trapped in a sordid dream? A man, calm as a stagnant day in summer, explaining the vision she couldn't show her mind's eye. "That seems like–not– not a very nice place to put your mouth," she said, attempting and failing to sound indignant.

"It's a pleasant place to put my mouth." He nodded thoughtfully. "Just thinking about it is pleasant. More than that." He leaned, touching one of the earrings, fingers skimming to her throat. From the corner of her vision, she saw it again–that animal part of him, unapologetic, straining against the front of his breeches. She met his eyes through a haze of blush. Port? No–*excitement*.

"Do you–do you get excited, too?" she asked, forgetting that she should be appalled.

"Of course I do."

"Right–right now?"

"I'm very excited right now. Because I feel like you need this, darling," he said, soft in the candlelight, his insistence the gentlest thing. "All you have to do is lay back on the settee. You don't have to touch me. That's your choice. Enjoying yourself is what matters."

"So–so you'd use your mouth, like kisses?" Her body, involuntarily, turned to him, and foolishness pinched at the back of her brain. Like a child, waiting for a story–she flushed, harder.

"Like kisses." He shifted. "I suppose you could say. For you to be wet brings the most pleasure. That's why I'll use my tongue."

She pressed her hands between her knees. The door was locked, and on the other side, somewhere in the sea of eyes and glinting teeth and clinking glasses, there was Mr. Gracey. And Robert. *Robert.* He had seen them, she was certain, blue eyes stinging the back of her neck. *Stop, this isn't about him!* She leveled, chin out. Her fingers trembled, her gut was hollow, and Frances's shaky riddle beat at her brain. *He licked my breasts. He said he'd kiss my feet.* And he was offering her the answer, simple as that, as if there were nothing he wanted to do more. *Work that sweet little cunt with my tongue.* She opened that answer like a gift, her heart unfolding like a tucked box—tingles shooting to her fingertips, fire rushing in her ears.

"Just—just my panniers?" she asked, her voice trembling.

"Well, yes." His mouth twitched, and he dropped his eyes. "I wouldn't mind taking your stockings off, too."

She stood, her feet cold, and blurted, before her pounding heart could change her mind: "All right, sir, I want to try."

Her legs were unsteady, and the rose-cut earrings shook like leaves. He set his brandy down and took her hands. "Easy." He pulled her down, framing her face for a kiss. *Like kisses…*The intent was black, rooted, and forgotten. She kissed him back, and he stood, turning her to the side.

"Gather your skirts, and hold them at the waist."

She obeyed. The silk weighed like a stone, pulling on her muscles. "Sir, this—is it something you've done before?"

His fingers flinched, tugging at a knot on the pannier. *God, why would you ask that?* He didn't reply, and for a few moments, he worked in silence. The hoop dropped, finally (he seemed to be having a bit of trouble) and he placed it in front of the grate. It looked so silly, a linen and bone birdcage.

"Other side, sweetheart. Turn around."

She bunched her skirts and petticoats over the second hoop. That one dropped in a matter of seconds, and she let go, green silk cascading in an emerald waterfall, too long without the lift of the panniers. He took her hand, stepping back, and ran his eyes over her form, from the folds on the floor to the earrings, brushing her throat. That light, again…a quiet reverence, yet holding back something more formidable. Hunger. An ache. Was it fear?

"Sir." Her voice trembled.

"S'pity I can't see your breasts," he stated, in a hasty reversion to his usual self. "Society's got you women bound and gagged."

Her shoulders loosed, a little. He pulled her close and kissed her, a searching kiss, working from her mouth, over her jawline, to her earlobe. Gentle, biting–her heart surged, and she clutched his shoulders, aware of a curious wetness accompanying the ache in her belly. She pressed her thighs together, trying not to squirm.

One hand on her backside, the other steady in the middle of her back, he lifted her and carried her to the settee, laying the crook of her neck on the bend of the arm. She watched, attempting to swallow the wild pounding. Revenge wasn't even a question. In a break of shadow and smooth movement, he reached into the pocket of his frock, turned, then–hand to mouth–and a sip of brandy.

Dover's. Her heart sank.

"If you have a headache–"

He shook his head. "Darling." Another wash of brandy. Then he shrugged off his frock, rolled it neatly, and tucked it beneath her just above her hips, where it filled the gap between the small of her back and the settee. She shifted, settling.

He sat, one shoe tucked, and studied her for a moment. Then he rose over her body, planting kisses up her throat, to her mouth. Her lower lip smarted, bit, again. Owned, again–she sighed into his mouth. The familiarity made it easy, and a little of the fear faded into the more pleasant roaring of anticipation. His lips moved from her mouth, back to her throat, nipping at tender skin, then–a clamping bite. Fast, but agreeably painful; her body seized in a natural reaction.

"Ouch! That hurt!"

"Martha, listen to me." He drew away, taking up his brandy again. "If I'm to court you properly, as I should, I'll happily empty my coffers for you. But one thing needs to be understood. By you."

She shifted, suddenly impatient. "What's that?"

"You." He touched the end of her nose. "You're a headstrong girl, you know? But you've said yes, so I'm going to make you finish, if I have to keep you locked in this room all night. Don't forget that."

The chestnut curls had resorted to the customary wildness; framed by the soft gold of low candlelight, she absorbed everything. God, he was beautiful. What was he even saying, when he had a jaw like that, a mouth like that? Her eyes wandered…a cock like that. Her fingers prickled.

"Martha." He cleared his throat. "My eyes, please."

"Oh, I'm sorry!"

"I know you're very young. But one of these days, I'm going to start coming home to you. Be a lady, or be a scholar." He softened. "But you'll be there."

Forever, G. *Oh, heavens, why would you think that?* Of course, she knew why. The fear she'd noted suddenly made a little more sense. Then, a hush of silk, a break of air, his hands on her ankles. Her breath quickened.

"I'm going to take off your stockings. Is that all right, sweetheart?"

"Not—not just panniers?"

"I'd like to feel your skin, if that's all right."

Something changed in the pitch of his breathing. Lungs lifted, a little less room for air. *He's already touched your feet.* "Y-you can take them off," she managed.

He lifted one foot by the ankle, gently tugging off the pinching dancing slipper. The pain swelled and dissipated, and she sighed with relief. Soft fingers rounded, pressing gently, kneading through the ball of her foot. He tipped his head and kissed the arch, meeting her eyes; it tickled, but not in the usual way.

"I just—I just don't know." She gasped, hating her ignorance. "You really shouldn't kiss people's feet!"

"I told you," he said quietly. "I would happily kiss them."

A tug, and her garter ribbon broke loose. Her stocking was stripped, like a layer of skin, as if he were a craftsman, and undressing ladies in secret rooms was his skilled trade. Even the small amount of struggle he'd met with the panniers looked well. More than that, it spoke directly to the ache pushing at that private place, deep in the hollow of her hips.

The other slipper and stocking joined their mates, lined on the floor in front of the settee.

"I'm going to tuck up your skirts, all right." He reached to touch her cheek, as if checking her. "Around your middle. Are you comfortable, darling?"

Comfortable? She considered, biting her lip. No, she wasn't, she was scared. But could she admit that when he was being so tender? "Yes," she said quickly. "Thank you."

She glanced at his mouth. It didn't seem right, something her dreams had conjured, aching for him in the middle of the night. She closed her eyes, a tiny sigh escaping as her skirts came to rest on her thighs. Her petticoat followed; her legs were laid bare, toes cold. She clenched her knees together. *I don't know if I can do this, it does seem awfully silly–*

"Now." A kiss, his body warm over hers. Close to panic, she clutched at the shoulders of his shirtsleeves, the muscles of her middle bunching inward.

"Now, if you don't mind," he murmured, "open your legs."

She jolted, rising on her elbows. "My–my legs?"

"I want to see you. If I'm going to taste you, I want to see you first." He took her hand, winding her fingers through his. "Trust me when I say, there's nothing you need be ashamed of. I would kiss every inch of you."

His free hand moved up her shin, over her knee, and she snapped her eyes shut. *Just do it. He's done this before, it's obvious–*

"Breathe, darling." A kiss, soft as a feather, on the top of her thigh. She sighed out her mouth, and loosened. *Breathe.* Another kiss, only this time, on her belly, at the bottom of her stomacher. "That's it, keep breathing. Don't think about me. Think about this." Another kiss. Parted lips. And his tongue, drawing a line from the middle of her thigh, over the channel of her legs.

She lurched. *Oh my God–*

"We're just trying something, sweetheart. Just for you." A kiss, a nip, a sweet slow circle on tender skin. She sank. With each new sensation, the ache between her legs clawed for him. He was too close to that place, coaxing her body, one breath at a time, to let go. A little more. *Breathe.*

She split her knees, opened her eyes, and dared to glance at him. Her heart was throbbing, her face on fire.

"Jesus." He smiled, slowly. That reverence–it was new, and it was frightening. Before she could move, or protest, or even think, he leaned, his breath a warm sigh over her cold thighs, and pressed a single, closed-mouth kiss on the peak of her pleasure, that place her angry fingers had worked so uselessly to satisfy.

The tightest flower, too new to bloom.

She inhaled harshly. His mouth, by her ear. His voice, the sweetest whisper, tapped to the marrow of her bones.

"Sweetheart, I'm the luckiest fellow in the world right now."

The tendons in her legs pulled tight. Her body jerked, involuntarily, because he'd touched her there. Between her legs. One long, gentle stroke, then deep into tender flesh, pushing–not even a fingertip–inside the heat of her body. Gliding back up, skimming over raw nerves, like she was open, skinless, everything felt times a thousand.

It was terrifying. She whimpered. *Don't you dare cry. He'll stop, he'll run–*

"Martha." His tone dripped with approval. "You sweet thing, you're already wet."

"What on earth–I don't know what's happening to me–"

"Don't think. Just breathe." He was smiling, ten years younger. Beautiful, heartbreaking, and she had nothing to say. She only nodded, and he kissed her, slow, hot, long. And then she watched, following chestnut curls over black ribbons and lace, over hills of forest silk…

She curled a hand back, pressing her palm into the arm of the settee. *God–God!* Her hips lurched. Breath, a stirring summer breeze, tickled her thighs. His mouth settled once again, only this time it wasn't a simple kiss. Warm lips parted, heat and wetness; she dug into Spanish silk. His tongue circled, settling deep, the gentlest pressure kneading like a hum over the sore endings of her nerves.

God, this can't be right. Her thoughts tangled, fast, spilling down a hill. *How is he breathing? The smell–the taste?* Too many thoughts to make sense of. The tumbleweed faded into the distance, rolling away a strip of her inhibitions in a deep turn of his tongue. Her hips lurched. And another. Hot, languid caresses caught at her apex, pushing through the ache. Working her slow, just like that, as if his lips were meant to eat her, as if his tongue existed for no other purpose.

A low noise vibrated against his mouth, shooting signals to her head. *God, he likes doing this–what on earth*–another stroke, his tongue catching beneath the shield of skin, sent her legs shaking. It was a cue, and he snatched it, fast, as if he'd been waiting for her to agree. Sweat prickled at the back of her neck, behind her knees–

"Oh!"

And he broke. She gasped, nearly a yelp of disappointment.

"I want to taste her, sweetheart. Are you all right?"

"That–that wasn't tasting?" *Good heavens, could you sound any sillier?* "I-I'm fine, sir." Abruptly, it irritated her that he'd broken the rhythm to speak, because never mind her ineptitude, her hot face, her racing heart–God, it'd felt so wildly, naturally good! Her dry fingers and aching legs were foolishness, her solitude was forever broken from her pleasure.

"I'm fine!" she repeated.

Then–*Jesus God. No!* She could feel his fingers, parting untouched flesh. A sigh. A low noise of admiration. The pressure settled, teasing, for a moment, and then, her spine went rigid. His hands, firm on her hips, settled her flush, and heat pooled inside of her body, a radiating channel. Her thoughts screamed. *You need to tell this man to stop. Right now! I don't care how in love you are–*

Her pelvis clenched. Tasting. Oh, he was tasting, everything! Deep inside her, at the mouth. Working, teasing, catching that curious wetness on his tongue as if it were the only thing that would satisfy his thirst. Pulling over sensitive tissues, skimming tender points of pressure. It hadn't occurred to her that anything could rival the satisfaction of grinding into her own hand, but this was like a vein, bursting with fullness. A surge of pleasure faded, surged again. *Judith is right, he's the devil himself!* Because he was working her hard, his tongue inside of her body, his fingers serving the ache outside of her body, and now she could feel it. Tenderness, not angry bursts; coaxing, not clenching; thorough investment, not the frantic means to an end.

A familiar pleasure ebbed and flowed, and she rocked her head back. It was only when he moved away, that she realized her fists had been clenched so tight her nails left purple crescents in her palms. She let go of her lungs, breath coming in short, shallow gasps, and in the silence of the room, she heard him swallow. The brush of his jaw on her thigh tickled, and a noise escaped her throat–something between a cry and a snarl.

Frustration. She looked down; the chestnut head was still bent over her hips, as if she'd interrupted a feast. But his eyes were locked with hers. His lips were wet, flushed.

"Do you want to know what you taste like, darling?"

"I-I took a bath last night. With lavender oil–"

"No." He shook his head. "No. You taste like I've been at the wharves." A kiss landed on the inside of her thigh. "And I'm tired and I'm hot. And I come home, and I sit at the bureau plat, and I can finally breathe." Another kiss, a nip. "And I pour myself a brandy. And it bites the tongue, like the sweetest fire."

Brandy. An elixir, a drug. Flowers, sunshine. Sugar. *Of course not.* He rose over her body and kissed her on the mouth; her lips pressed shut, trembling.

"Open, darling," he coaxed. "Open your mouth. I want you to taste yourself."

"I–I don't know–"

But even as the words came, her lips parted, and she obediently opened her mouth. Hot breath. The smell of…what? A high tension in the air. Clean skin, the faintest ash of a pipe. His tongue entered her mouth, pressing into her own. Glancing over the sides, rolling taste-buds to taste-buds. Smooth as silk, a bittersweet tang–sharp, yet honeyed.

God, I do taste like brandy.

"Do you taste that, sweetheart?"

She nodded, fast.

"It's nice, isn't it?"

"Yes–yes, sir."

"Now, one thing needs to be clear, before we go any further."

She blinked, her vision blurring like a fog. Or perhaps it was threatening tears; she managed to say, again, "Yes, sir."

"Do whatever you want with your hands. Your thoughts, I don't care. But this." His finger ran through tender skin, and entered her again–just a little. She gasped, closing her eyes. A little more. And withdrew, a dragging touch spitting fire over angry nerves.

"Once you finish, because you will. This cunt is mine."

Mine. Her heart was furious just looking at him; there was no doubt that she was in love. And he was waiting for an answer, brown eyes eager, blushing mouth–God, he belonged there! He belonged between her thighs, he belonged to her pleasure. If

212

done once, it could be done again. She wouldn't sacrifice it for anything. Not embarrassment, not anxiety, not tears–

Do what he wants.

"Sweetheart." He regarded her seriously. "I'd like you to say it."

"S-say what, Mr. Wyeth?"

"Once you come, this cunt is mine. So think about that, before you say yes. Say it to me, darling, I'll work all night, I will, until you're satisfied."

This cunt. Speaking the answer to Frances's riddle, written on his mouth, running down his tongue. Her words came with no further hesitation.

"It's–it's yours," she breathed. She'd already known what he meant. It was a horribly embarrassing thing to think about saying, yet he was weathered. And it was just her. Just him. Anything could be said, anything could be done.

"Say it's yours, Asahel," he corrected her.

"Sir, I-I said it already–"

Kisses seared her throat. Her middle, back over folds of silk–

"Say it or I'll stop."

"It's yours!"

"No. Be specific in your speech, darling. Tell me this cunt belongs to Asahel Wyeth. Say it out loud."

"It's yours!" *Just words. Just say it–* "Asa. It's yours, Asahel!"

Out of nowhere, a warning flared. Asa, not Asahel. Why had he said that? The man in the periwig, the pistol, the plaque–her hips lurched. A tremble ran through her legs, starting at the ankle, and she forgot his words. Sweet, deep caresses of his tongue, over and over–the desire to clutch something, punch something, grip the muscles of her belly. Her heart was manic. In a fevered moment, she surrendered, slipped her feet through the bends of his arms, and watched through the split of her legs.

213

Gleaming curls, moving, the rhythm, found and kept, rushing hard—*yes*—there it was, a pulse of tight pleasure, just as his tongue glanced the head of her sex. Only it wasn't clamped anymore. Swollen, it was swollen. As if it must burst and drain out her pleasure.

Another surge. And then, it happened every time, every single time—insistent strokes, the turn of tender flesh on tender flesh, hellbent on her surrender. She shook like it was winter, but she was bathed in heat. For a split moment, he looked up and met her eyes, and she gasped, horrified, but still, she couldn't look away—because he smiled. From a forbidden dream, a man, eating her body from the outside, feasting on her like a crow on carrion. *I'm going to hell. I'm going straight to hell, don't you dare look away!*

She watched, feverishly following the rise of his shoulders, hating the spasms in her legs, so far beyond the control of her head. His body shifted in response to her digging heels, and she caught, heart in her throat, his hips, pressing into the settee. The rhythm didn't change. But in a calculated move, his hand cupped her backside, tipping her flush with the rolled frock coat. He placed the other on her belly, just above the rise of private flesh; and before she could move or protest, a sharp pressure seized the tender muscles of her pelvis. She threw back her head, wide eyes to the ceiling, one hand flying to the top of his head; her body clutched him, tightening hard around a finger, working inside her, beckoning. Pleasure rang like a gong, beyond anything she'd ever felt. Tight-wound, scraping with angry claws at her mangled innocence. At the next stroke of his tongue, her body locked, and the ache burst.

Pleasure shot from limb to limb in plush, sleek surges. An exhausted cry bled from her mouth, never mind how hard she tried to stop it. Her nails shredded silk, her fingers fisted his hair, she must've bruised him with her heels. A rush surged around his fingers, dampening the settee, cold and strange outside the heat of her body, and she rose on her elbows, pushing at his forehead with a sweating palm.

"Stop–stop, please, stop!"

The pleasure was angry, spinning in and out of a strange, enjoyable pain–beyond anything she'd felt on her own. It was too much. He obeyed, drawing away with a reverent kiss on the smarting flesh, fully bloomed and raw. He drew a hand over his mouth, then kissed the side of each of her thighs; she lurched when his finger left the heat of her body.

"First time, and that's what I get," he murmured. "I'm a very lucky fellow."

All the embarrassment, all the indignant modesty, was leaving in dragging waves. Her body sank, exhausted, into the settee, and for some reason–*oh please, no*–the tears that had threatened her earlier broke free, running rivers down her temples, bleeding into rose-cut diamonds.

She hadn't realized how scared she'd been. The physical feelings had masked it, but now, it was evident; her body had been shielding her. Her innocence had hidden her fear, again. He hooked a hand around the middle of her back and mindfully drew her to a seat, pulling her into his arms, against his chest. She sucked in a breath, aching just from his warmth, her body against his body. The tears wouldn't stop. Against her ear, his heartbeat thrummed her sobbing into sniffling, into silence.

"Darling, I know it's a lot to feel," he whispered.

"I'm sorry, I don't know what's come over me!" She'd said things, in a heightened moment. Made promises. Bared her heart. Obeyed.

"Look at me." He turned her face. "That was beautiful. You did exactly what I wanted. Exactly what you were supposed to. And you taste incredible, darling."

"I–I did?" The wound muscles in her belly loosened. She lifted her head, meeting his eyes. His mouth was blushed…God! Fiercely, she wiped tears with the back of her hand. What else did she want, if it wasn't what he wanted?

"Yes, of course. You came under my mouth. That's a goddamn gift, I won't forget it." He kissed her, sweetly, no tongue, only comforting lips. "Lay back, for a minute."

"Sir, I-I can't–"

"Of course not. Just lay down, and relax."

She obeyed. He reached around his neck, tugged off his cravat, and folded it into a square. Then, splitting her legs at the knees, he gently dried her damp skin. Some sweat. Some of the wetness from inside her body. Softly pressing into her sore sex, running down her legs, teasing behind her knees. He picked up both of her feet, kissing the arches, and settled them into his lap. In the weak hush of exhaustion, she was aware of the hard rise of his cock against the side of her foot, but he didn't move. He didn't do anything, save for lightly massaging the bones of her ankles.

The earrings tugged at her lobes, tickling her neck, and she swallowed the last of the tears. How silly, to cry! It *had* been frightening, but at once, better than anything. And he was deep against the settee, eyes bright, the smallest smile on his lips. Watching her.

Gazing at her.

It was nearly impossible to believe that the heat, the rawness had come from the same man. In the lowest candlelight, he looked like an angel, who would never say such dark things.

Who would never make her say, *this cunt belongs to Asahel Wyeth.*

14

FEEL THINGS UNDER
YOUR FEET AGAIN, DARLING

"Darling. Martha. *Martha*."

She opened her eyes blearily. A dim room, an empty grate, red silk…pipe smoke prickling her nose. Asa was gently nudging her shoulder. *Oh, God!* She scrambled, hands to her breasts. Her earlobes pulled, and it all rushed back. Rose-cut sheets of pure extravagance; surges and strokes and licks and kisses, and tears–she ran a shaking hand under her nose.

"You were out cold." Asa settled in the corner of the settee. "But it's been almost two hours. Billy's probably worried."

"Oh!" She clapped a hand to her cheek. "Papa. Oh dear–" She stood, wobbling at the knees, and rounded on him. "Two hours? We're going to be in trouble, you know people saw us! Oh, what will I say?"

"To be fair," he said reasonably, lost in a cloud of smoke. "You were asleep for most of it, that's not my fault. My task was sweet, but surprisingly short–you're about as ready as a lad at his first country revel."

"Oh—I am *not,* and you could've woken me up!"

"Would've been a crime." He turned to his brandy. "You were charming, you snore a little."

"Good heavens, this is silly!" She flushed, stumbling to the grate for her panniers. She was weak, and squeezing her thighs together, aware of how sore she was. Sore in the best way. With her back turned, she clenched her fists, and nearly squealed. Asa Wyeth had spread the legs of a cottage girl on a rich man's settee, and eaten her alive! *Goodness, that noise you made. You and Mr. Wyeth are going straight to hell!*

"Bring those here." Asa set his glass aside and she obeyed, placing the panniers on the settee. "Skirts up," he said with a frown. Perhaps the slip of the knot earlier had only been her question, because the panniers were raised with bewildering aptitude. She glanced at his groin, her palms prickling, while he worked. With the veil of the unknown ripped, her diffidence faded, and she pursed her lips.

"Sir, you can't go out into a revel like that."

"Frock will cover it. All these bloody pleats and frills must be good for something." He turned her hips.

"I can go by myself," she retorted. Nearly better than a first kiss, she felt bound to him under a secret awning, like a joke only they shared. He rolled the silk over her panniers, took her hands, and pulled her down for a kiss.

"I'll walk you out, we'll find Billy, and I want you to stay with him. All right. Then I'm going to need a little time to myself."

"Sir." She stared at him. "You are bad!"

"I think not. I can't talk to Preacher Sanders with my pecker stiff as a mast. Christ. I wore this lady's neckerchief just for him. Does it look pretty?" He tugged at his cravat, which he'd tied incorrectly.

219

Her toes curled. *He wiped me dry with that. He's going to wear it into the assembly like nothing happened?* "Maybe you shouldn't wear it," she suggested lamely, flushing. "You look well without a cravat."

"I'm at the Tuckers', I must wear my neckerchief." He stood, catching the back of her neck and kissing her deeply. She sighed, savoring every tang of flavor on his tongue. Sweet brandy was fresh, and the musky Virginia tobacco stung. "Besides," he murmured against her ear. "I want to wear it. To have Martha Gracey's pleasure wrapped around my neck—I can't think of a higher honor."

"Oh, stop!" She pushed him off, hands on his chest. "For heaven's sake." She tugged loose his cravat, unwound the cloth, and adjusted it properly under his chin, arranging the folds of lace. "There. You look well."

"Damn." He brushed a finger over the side of her throat. "I've left a mark on your neck. I'm sorry, sweetheart."

Her fingers flew to the place he'd bit, flinching at the memory. Fast, animal—she shivered. Branded. Fumbling, she unpinned a curl over the mark. The idea passed, like a shadow, that it would serve Robert right to witness such a thing; but not poor William, when he held Asa in such veneration. The thought made her belly turn, but she shook it off, standing on her tiptoes for another kiss.

She brushed by and gathered up her stockings and slippers. A barrier was clearly broken. For weeks, it had loomed, impatient, for something to topple it, but now, there was familiarity. She didn't need to shake so hard when he walked by, or swoon with balled fists. She was an open book, and he could skip to whatever chapter he wanted! She was the girl astride her horse, wearing the most expensive earrings in the city of Boston, if not the colonies. She halted by the door.

"Sir," she asked tentatively, "can you see my feet under my hem?"

"What, now? No, I cannot. Those skirts are ridiculous."

"It's just—well, my slippers are too small. They pinch my feet. Do you suppose I could go barefoot?"

"I won't tell." He smiled. "By all means, feel things under your feet again, darling. No one will ever know."

She trailed a few paces behind him, the floor cold beneath her bare feet. It was a delicious feeling. He had to be the tallest, most handsome man in the room, and it wasn't just because she was in love; he *was*. His shadow was the darkest, on the golden walls, his strides the longest, his scent the strongest. As if successfully pleasuring a woman made him ten times more of a man, and she was that woman!

He held to the walls. She kept her eyes on the honey-colored suit, amber in the low light. Mr. Gracey, of course, was by the refreshments, pouring what was most likely his dozenth glass of port. Asa rounded, coming at the table from the opposite side, and Martha met William from behind, threading her arm through his. Her face burned and she stumbled a little, but she smiled as innocently as she could. Asa frowned and fixed himself a brandy.

"Ah, Martha, my love!" William patted her hand. "I was wondering where you were off to. Hallo, Wyeth." He reddened, and his eyes lit up. "Where the hell have you been, man? I was having the most amusing conversation with Lord Tucker, about the Committee. I say, good sir, you were missed at dinner."

Asa scowled, plucking a pear from a sterling basket. He inspected it, then dropped it with a grimace. "Not hungry, Billy," he said, by way of explanation.

"You never eat, Wyeth, you're thin as a reed."

"Right." Asa took up his brandy. "Got papers for Sanders to sign, left them in my saddle bag. Martha." He paused, eyes landing just below her chin. "Are you all right?"

Mr. Gracey turned, curious eyes on Martha. "I'm *fine*," she managed through gritted teeth. Asa nodded, and head down, circled the table. There was a faint reddening at the tips of his ears, and she might have found it endearing if she were able to breathe.

"The gentlemen are retiring in a few minutes!" Mr. Gracey called eagerly after Asa's retreating figure. "Port in the courtyard on a summer night, nothing more splendid!"

She watched Asa fading down the corridor and tucking back inside the door to the little sitting room. She flushed again, turning Mr. Gracey back to the table before his eager eyes could witness the crime.

"Papa—" She was faintly miffed that *she* hadn't been missed at dinner. Where would she have typically sat? Next to Hannah and Frances...

"My dear," William sighed. "I've got to get a handle on that man, he's going to kill himself one of these days. Ah! There's Sanders. Pardon me, I must rush and have a word before Wyeth scares him off..." And he was gone, dropping Martha's arm and zig-zagging through the throng.

For a moment she considered following, but her obedience to Asa (who was still, after all, a man who had told her what to do) was far easier to give under the threat of his tongue, which was currently lifted. Things were different in the light, with her embarrassment, and all of these people, to contend with. She squeezed her thighs together, bothered by a sudden heightened irritation. Mr. Gracey hadn't even noticed her earrings. She wasn't sure if she should be insulted or grateful.

"Martha!"

Frances Dunaway. *Oh, Lord have mercy on me.* "Frances, hello," she muttered. "I was just fetching a port." She fumbled for a glass, shaking as she poured. Why *had* Asa said that about Frances? He'd invited her to Wyeth House, after all, so she couldn't be all that bad.

Frances smiled, the same wisp of a smile that had always irritated Martha, as irrational as she'd argued that it was; yet, there was a strained quality in her eyes. She touched Martha's arm.

"Mr. Wyeth is very attentive to you, my dear. Let's step outside, and walk for a little."

"Frances." Indignation rose, chilling the heat in her face. "Don't spread rumors, please."

Frances flinched, working her bottom lip. "I'm sorry, my dear. A slip of the tongue."

Jesus Christ. Her hand around the glass slid, but she righted herself and put back the port in a gulp. Inwardly, she shrugged. Fresh air was a dream, and besides, Asa had no reason for alluding anything about Frances, when the woman had always been sweet, if a little stupid. She accepted Frances's arm. There was something comforting about the gesture, hailing to the simpler days of Robert Henshaw. Only when they passed by *that* door in the corridor did her heart begin to pick up pace again. She thought she caught a whiff of pipe-smoke, and heard the faint sound of a cork popping. She smiled, dark and vindicated despite her wild heart. Frances had, no matter how "sweet" she was, made eyes at Asa more than once.

And Asa was Martha's man now.

Goodness. She shivered, the diamond sheets brushing her neck. *I wonder what fellows do when they're excited like that?* He'd have to touch it, of course–touch his cock. Pleasure himself. A brief image conjured of Asa, head back on the settee, cravat loose, stroking himself in the candlelight, and all of the heat returned, balling in her groin.

She nearly pulled poor Frances through the remainder of the corridor.

The dim light of the passage broke into a torchlit terrace paved with red stones, which stepped down to a courtyard, busy with carriages, footmen, and other loitering figures. The stones beneath her bare feet were wet from a light summer rain, since passed; the air carried grass and summer rose, and the splendor of the mansion cast long shadows, broken by rings of fire. For a moment she stood silent, arm through Frances's. The feeling of being rather ridiculous–a cottage girl lost in the middle of the gentry–crept for a moment, but a dark rebuttal shot it down. They didn't know, none of them knew.

Well, maybe Robert had figured it out. Still, the realization struck her–of course, she wasn't high society. She never would be, but she *was* rich; she was the daughter of Gracey, of Wyeth-Gracey Enterprises, and she was draped in Asa's jewels.

A dark part of her wished they all knew. That someone had opened the door, and a crowd had gathered to watch Asa Wyeth feast on the throbbing between her legs. *God, Martha, stop it, right now. You really* are *disgusting!*

"Here." Frances paused at the bottom of the stairs to pluck two glasses off a serving tray. "I really was going to stay put tonight," she murmured, slipping her arm back through Martha's. "I've seen too many parties. But dear Hannah wanted so badly to go…"

Martha took the port. It wasn't so bad to walk, warm feet against cold stones, through the courtyard, down a paved path through the rose garden. The Tuckers' roses put Asa's to shame, she noted. If Hannah wanted a lovely garden so very much, she should've married James or Hiram; to be married to the son of an English Lord–well, she couldn't imagine anything more elegant. Asa was a lot of things…handsome, with a body that made her want to sink her claws, but he was decidedly not elegant.

"You've seen Robert," said Frances in a whisper. "Poor thing! He's taken the blow rather hard."

"Frances, how is that fair?" Martha stopped, turning to face her. "You were the one who told me what he'd done. What was I supposed to do?"

"Oh, I didn't mean it like that." Frances kept walking, and Martha skipped to keep up. "It only hurts to see him so despondent. He is family, after all, and I do love him."

"I'm sorry I've caused him any pain." She wasn't, yet a twinge of unwarranted guilt passed again. She frowned at the stones. It was her fault, a little (right?) even if it didn't matter. It certainly didn't make Robert a good man; it was only that she regretted wasting so many weary hours entrapping him before she'd figured out who he was.

"*Is* Mr. Wyeth courting you now?" Frances broke her thoughts.

Martha stopped again, irritation flaring. "Frances, why would you ask that? I told you, he's a friend of my father."

"I'm sorry." Frances dipped her head. Her tone held back the same sense of want, searching for denial, as it had that day of the ride. The confession that had blown holes in the fabric of Martha's well-laid plans (even if they'd already been tattered at the edges). "I just assumed," she added in amendment. "I do know him a little."

Martha scowled, the delight of her lost innocence fading behind an angry curiosity. It was perfect. Even if Asa didn't want her to talk to Frances, he would never talk himself. She must get what she could, where she could.

"How well do you know him?" she asked, fighting to sound amiable.

Frances looked guilty, glanced, and moved briskly, head down. "I told you, I was friends with a lady of his."

"Ahem. Who—I mean, do I know her? What's her name?"

"Martha, you said he wasn't courting you. It doesn't matter."

Martha's heart rose to her throat. A question teased, ripping fissures in the beauty of her affair with Asa. It was, after all, a secret affair. But once William knew, what exactly did Asa plan to do with her? *Don't think it, Martha, don't—*

She thought it.

Marry her. Of course, he would have to marry her, he couldn't maintain a household, a trade enterprise, and a law practice while wasting time courting. It was a grave enough realization that she gave up her fragile loyalty, and stopped once again on the garden path.

"Frances, I must confess. Mr. Wyeth is courting me. In—in secret."

Frances nodded quickly. "I suspected." She seemed nearly ready to cry. "Of course, it's only right. Robert was in his way, all the time. I-I am happy for you, I really am."

"Frances." She shook her head, fighting to control a flaring in her nostrils. It was far too easy to be angry at Frances's timidity. "That girl, the one you were friends with. He seems a bit fixated on her. I mean, he doesn't talk about her but—he still has some of her things. Could you tell me her name, so I don't have to wonder?" It sounded exactly as desperate and hurt as she wanted, even while her true feelings were different.

"You wouldn't know her." Frances shook her head. "We were childhood friends before Mrs. Henshaw married my father. Meriton was the name."

"Frances." She gritted her teeth. "Please."

Frances's shoulders dropped, and she sighed. "You mustn't torture yourself with things that don't matter. Her name was Grace. But it doesn't matter."

Grace. *G. Forever, G.* She fought a sickness, roiling at the bottom of her belly. What had the pleasure felt like? *Remember, his tongue, his fingers—God!* She shook her head, her toes pressing into stone. "Thank you," she said stiffly.

"You won't find her, Martha. She wasn't part of this society."

"What, is she low-bred?"

"No." Frances shook her head. "She was perfectly bred. Mr. Meriton was a stationer on King Street. Not anymore. He moved out of the city."

"Frances. Why do you keep saying that?"

"Saying what? You wanted to know. I'm sorry if it hurts you!"

"No." The pleasure was a whisper, barely heard. "Why do you keep saying that—*was*. Did something happen to her?"

Head down, skirts bunched, Frances kept walking. They'd circled the garden and were almost to the courtyard before she stopped. In the shadow of the rosebushes, broken by torchlit gold, she was a frightened deer, trapped by predatory questions; yet, there was something in her tone that lit a warning flare. Her willingness to talk, how she only fought the inquiries, just enough. Almost as if she wanted to tell on herself—to tell on other people. It occurred to Martha that in all the time she'd known her, she'd been nothing but a body.

She didn't know Frances Dunaway at all.

Silks and satins, like blooming flowers, spilled from the ballroom into the courtyard. A reprieve after a dance, that for perhaps the first time, Martha was happy not to be a part of. She slipped her hand around Frances's elbow and tugged her back into the shadows.

"Tell me," she insisted. "Please."

"Oh–Martha, you mustn't talk to Hannah. She's very angry with you–"

"What on earth, I don't care about Hannah. I haven't said a word to her!"

"She wanted Mr. Wyeth. You took him away from her!"

"Oh, God, who cares!" Martha nearly stamped her foot. "Hannah wants every man. Now tell me!"

Frances turned, her eyes no longer soft. The sadness, the tears, dissipated into a foreign chill.

"She was dear to me," she said, her chin square. "She was my friend. Mr. Wyeth loved her, and I'm sorry if that's not what you want to hear. He barely speaks to me anymore. But I can assure you, she is not an obstacle to you." She straightened, her eyes flashing. "Grace Meriton is dead, she's bones in a churchyard in Salem. And don't ask me any more questions, because it hurts me, too. She was a sister to me, she was an angel–who–who made one very grave mistake."

"Frances–"

But it wasn't Frances. It wasn't any girl she knew. "The House of Henshaw lives because of Grace Meriton," Frances went on, her chin shaking. "And now–now he's unhappy. He's angry, and–and he's out for blood!"

"Robert? Frances, these are riddles, I don't understand!"

"No, not Robert." Frances's face crumpled, and she dropped her head. "Not Robert. Asahel Wyeth!"

Martha's heart tightened. Cold sweat prickled her palms, and she pressed them into her skirts. "Frances, why are you telling me these things? Why are you talking to me? You sought me out, you know it."

"I've made mistakes too, if you can believe it." Frances drew a shuddering breath. "Mistakes I lose sleep over. You will too, when you get a bit older, and you'll try to right the wrongs. Before it's too late."

Then she turned and floated back into the courtyard, exuding all the grace of a woman nearly comfortable in her spinsterhood.

Goddamn Frances Dunaway! Once more she'd rattled the foundation of Martha's ideas, her convictions. She stood clenched, breathing fast, bare feet cold. Uncertainty seeped over everything beautiful Asa had given her, locked in that room. Disgust, not at him, but at herself. She'd taken too many of his kisses, without knowing who he was—she was making the same errors!

But no. Asa, he was sweet. Always tender, and considerate. It wasn't his fault that she was so angry, nearly sick to her stomach, that he still thought about a dead girl. That he'd kissed a girl now ash in the ground under Salem. That he had made that woman finish with his mouth, too; that maybe—he'd really loved her. More. To read *Love In Excess* that many times, to shred the pages, was strange. Obsessive. It wasn't right.

But G–Grace–was dead. The first thing she'd felt when Frances had said it, was relief. She didn't have to battle skin and bones; this Grace was just another ghost, drifting down the corridors of Wyeth House. Yet, the truth of her left a sour taste in Martha's mouth. All of her kisses, her ridiculous cry of pure pleasure–those things had been his, and only his. But who had he been thinking of, with his hands pinning her hips? With his tongue deep inside her body? When she was sitting on his lap, when his fingers were tangled in her hair?

Was he reliving something? *God. I could be just that, a memory!*

She glanced over the courtyard. In a group of ladies, Frances had settled into her familiar place, silent with her arm through Hannah's. Lord Tucker's daughter was there. A few others, she wasn't fancy enough to know. *Oh dear,* she thought, nearly ready to cry. Everything was crumbling, and the night was still very young. She would have to talk to people, without Hannah. And she couldn't hang off of Asa's arm for the rest of the night–there was Mr. Gracey to consider!

There *was* Mr. Gracey, ambling down the steps, port in hand. Asa trailed him, long legs flashing stark shadows on the stones. A sour blend of guilt and anger churned her gut. They shouldn't be talking, laughing like that, not when that chestnut head had moved so languidly between her thighs, not when he'd branded her with those perfect teeth. She watched Asa pluck a glass off a passing tray, easy as ever, and they both settled into a group of men. Lord Tucker, the little man who must be Mr. Sanders (dressed like a preacher, as alluded). A few others she didn't know by name.

And Robert, standing a little outside, brandy snifter in hand, blue eyes ice.

Maybe it hadn't happened, maybe it was a dream. Slowly, she lifted trembling fingers and touched the place on her neck. It was very tender. It did happen, it did! And how awful was it, that even after what Frances had told her, just looking at Asa already had the ache smarting again. *Martha Ann Gracey, you are pathetic.* Pathetically, hopelessly in love, in lust.

Swallowing down her heartbeat, she clutched her skirts and skimmed through the courtyard to the blur of wild colors. Frances averted her eyes, staring at the back of her fan, and Hannah raised a condemnatory golden brow. Martha, despite her painful apprehension, smiled sweetly. The girls were in the midst of an in-depth conversation about men, and Tucker's daughter, Abigail, was motioning at Asa with a glass of sherry.

"What say you ladies to that one? I hear he makes dirty money, but he's very handsome."

"I don't care about dirty money." Hannah threw Martha a deliberate glance. "I could clean it up well enough if I wanted to. He's rude, but I find it endearing." She flipped her fan open, and Martha watched the golden coils of her hair drift. She bit her tongue, hard. *You hush your mouth, Hannah Dunaway!* Asa *was* rude, and it *was* endearing. *Keep your eyes off my man, or I'll stick them out— oh, goodness!*

"He's not so rude." Frances was sweet. "He's a handsome carriage, and a pleasing smile when he *does* smile."

"I find him grim." Abigail shrugged her shoulders. "Now Robert. I hear rumors that he's re-entered the prospects. Whatever happened? I felt for sure there'd be wedding bells by this time of year."

Martha had known that she would have to contend with the question of Robert, and there had been many a night she'd lain awake, strung with anxiety, wondering how she would justify her behavior. How quickly Asa had killed that beast! Yet, not one of those girls had cried out because of him. None of them had been kissed in the rain, nor sat on the lap of a man clearly aroused.

She lifted her shoulders. "We were not meant to be," she replied, as easily as she could.

"An upstanding, loyal man! What were you thinking?"

"Oh, never mind," said Hannah, irritated. "Robert's a chump, he'll find some other girl. They can both be chumps together." It was a deliberate barb, but her indifference deflected it. The conversation was boring, and Martha must not be the center of attention.

Through tight eyes, she watched Asa. He was looking over a piece of paper with Lord Tucker, spectacles perched on the bridge of his nose. He caught her eye briefly, and frowned; of course, she'd disobeyed, leaving Mr. Gracey's side. At least he hadn't seen her talking to Frances. He turned back to the paper, the glare sufficient punishment. He was composed. Not like a man who'd insisted she say silly things while he licked her raw. Not like a man who put his tongue inside of a lady. She flushed, balling her fists at her sides.

Certainly not like a man who was "out for blood."

Frances is so stupid. She ran her eyes down his slim middle to his groin. Calm, besides only the gentle rise that was always there.

Good heavens. She was so engrossed that she hardly remembered Robert was there, too. He was hazy, blonde hair yellow from the lanterns, eyes pricks of light beneath a furrowed brow. One hand tucked in his frock, the other around a glass of brandy. The bite burned on her neck. In a wild moment, her heart hammering, she brushed the curl out of the way, tucking it behind her ear. She looked away, but she could feel his eyes piercing her skin; she held her breath, watching in the periphery of her vision as he turned in disgust. When she glanced again, his back was turned, and he kept an excited conversation with a gentleman in a white wig.

She grimaced, shaking off a chill. The rabble of men's voices sent vibrations to her bare feet, and the ladies' giggling was an annoying trill. Politics, men, textiles. She sighed, gazing at Asa. Would that she could just go home! Curl up in her bed, and just think. About what Frances had told her. About the bewildering fact that she'd felt relief at the truth of someone's death. And what would Mr. Gracey say, when Asa came to talk to him in the morning?

For that matter, what would Asa say? If his intent was in fact to marry her, what would *she* say? Well, yes, of course. Her heart knew it in an instant; none of the painful things mattered when it came to that question. She would figure those out as she went. One, at least, had been laid to rest in Salem. *Grace.* Ugh, she

232

hated the woman, without knowing her face, and she hated herself because it wasn't fair. Yet, Frances had taken the trappings off yet more wounds, even as that one healed. *The House of Henshaw lives because of Grace Meriton.* Certainly, Robert had slept with Grace and deeply affronted Asa. But whatever that stupid, dead girl had to do with the House of Henshaw made no sense.

Frances spewed riddles, and she did it on purpose. She really wasn't such a friend.

She was so lost in her head that she hardly noticed that the men's conversation had become rather heated, Lord Tucker's booming voice cutting through a chorus of arguing chatter. Robert had moved inside the circle, and Asa stood, lounging against one of the pillars of the portico, nursing his port. Mr. Gracey was at his side, smiling radiantly. Apparently, she gathered, the port officers had raided one of a Mr. Chestney's sloops–*oh dear*–raiding sloops was decidedly not a good topic, with a true racketeer in the midst! She glimpsed Asa's way, and he smiled and nodded. Mr. Chestney, a stringy man with thin hair tied in a failing queue, was gesturing frantically.

"I paid my dues before the first cask hit the docks," he spluttered. "The simple fact of a fellow wanting a day's break is enough to make him a criminal. And the port officer, loitering about with his hands in his pockets, waiting for a bribe–"

"The port of Boston isn't so respectable as it once was," observed Lord Tucker. He was a large, brawny man; his sons took after him starkly, and he was nearly ridiculous in the trappings of an English Lord. A meticulous snow-white wig rested on his head, not a faux hair out of place. Glancing from Tucker to Asa, Asa did appear rather reedy. *Goodness,* she thought, forgetting about Grace for a moment. *Once we get married, I'll have to fatten him up a bit.*

"A fatal error you've made, Chestney," Asa said, extracting his pipe from his pocket. "Say your vows to His Majesty, lay down your virgin body, and unload within one hour, no less, or you'll come out looking like a rat."

"Over a hundred casks of Madeira, in an hour? It can't be done, with my crew!"

"Pay off." Asa shrugged. "I used the *Brilliant's* crew to unload glass. A bloody broil at the docks, you do what you must." Smoke curled around his head, and Martha thought he sounded too blithe.

"Certainly, an expert at paying off, Asahel." It was Robert. Her belly chilled, and her eyes flickered to where he stood, snifter tipped. "It's the only reason you're so goddamn fortunate. Gentlemen–" He held out his arm. "I'm afraid you've been duped. If your pocketbooks have been feeling rather sad, let me introduce the reason. My cousin, Asahel Wyeth. The Dutch Whore."

"Now, now," said William, with a nervous glance at Asa. There was a collective shuffling of shoes and incredulous coughs. Lord Tucker chuckled, clearly thinking it was a joke. Asa was unreadable, brown eyes bright through veils of pipe-smoke.

Robert shrugged and took a drink of brandy. "Laugh all you want, but those accounts you lost, you know whose name is signed at the bottom of them. Coffers light? The whore was feeling a bit frisky, I suppose."

Still, Asa said nothing. There was something calculated in the way he leaned against the pillar, legs crossed at the ankles. Almost as if he didn't care if they knew, and this had all been a set-up.

"It's a simple thing, to make bountiful profit at the ports," Robert went on. "If you don't pay your levies."

Asa broke. "I pay my fucking levies, Rob," he muttered, half-hidden in a cough against his elbow.

"Oh, my apologies. He does pay some levies." Robert laughed, shoulders drawing to his ears. "Every time he straddles the Netherlands, he gives them a profit cut."

"Come now, good sir," William interjected, "leave the man alone, don't be a dandy. This is a revel, let's not worry our heads with levies! Everyone should get another drink."

Martha was shocked at his forwardness, unusual when it came to Robert. Perhaps it was because he was no longer the looming threat, goading him with his own daughter. Her heart swelled with fondness, but no one was listening to Mr. Gracey. He was dispensable. Every eye had turned in incredulity to Asa, who regarded the stares with an eyebrow cocked. The moment of initial shocked silence broke, and exclamations of protest rang out. Asa frowned, biting at the stem of his pipe.

"Good Lord, Wyeth, tell us Henshaw is joking!" exclaimed Lord Tucker. "You owe everything to the East Indies. We can't lose you on the docks! We've lost too many honest tradesmen already."

"I assure you," said Asa coolly, "I'm not lost."

"Was it you who countered my Ashton account?" Mr. Chestney pointed with a trembling finger. "He was perfectly satisfied for years!"

"This isn't stagnant, Chestney. I'm allowed to have a better price for molasses."

"He certainly gets a better price." Robert's voice cut again, agitated. "Because he sells cheap. Not one thing in his warehouses has passed the standards of the British East India Trading Company!"

Asa, finally ruffled, turned to Robert. He was wild in the golden light, hair mussed, eyes bright. "What's the goddamn point, Henshaw?" he snapped. "Is this some kind of crusade for you, licking the docks clean for the king?"

"You're a profiteer traitor to the Crown! At least if you had principles, I might have a shred of respect," Robert sneered. "Never mind, I only advise the rest of you upstanding fellows to watch your accounts. If something smells a bit too sweet, the whore has come for some trifling!"

Asa shook his head in exasperation, turning back to his pipe. "Jesus, Rob, you know nothing about trade," he muttered. "Pretty cloth and thimbles, ladies' things. It's a wonder you made it this far. Have you ever rolled a bloody barrel?"

"Always the trouble with you, Wyeth," interjected Lord Tucker. "You don't roll barrels, you're a merchant. I should've sensed there was something off about you!"

"Merchants roll barrels all the bloody time." Asa was clearly exasperated. "Christ, you've never been to the Indies, have you?"

"One more thing, fellows," continued Robert, ignoring Asa's retort. "Have a care to keep your woman close. If he's feeling randy, he might just pull her into the nearest closet and get busy!" He laughed and threw back the rest of his brandy.

Martha's heart stuck in the back of her mouth. Asa's eyes were closed, forehead against his fingers, and William was studying him, hands behind his back, an expression of sorrowful curiosity in his eyes. But the damage was done. Suspicion, trepidation, even anger; she could feel it like a hand had fisted around the courtyard. Robert stepped back, sneering, and tossed his glass into a rosebush. Muttering voices rose to a dull roar; Asa was impervious, shaking his head, grumbling in response to fervent questions. She wanted nothing more than to run to him, take his hand, pull him away–but she could only watch, in bewilderment, as they henpecked him, and she felt like crying.

She met Mr. Gracey's eyes. His expression was resigned, and he smiled just a little as if to say, *it'll be all right, my dear.* And that faint dubiousness, processing what Robert had said. Oh God, Asahel Wyeth had explaining to do! He hadn't come back from New York to apologize, he hadn't come back to play by the rules.

May we go home, please, Papa? We don't need to be here anymore. We can all go back to the cottage and have a drink.

You and me, and Mr. Wyeth.

"Wyeth, if it's true you are profiteering at the docks, I'm afraid I don't let pirates under my roof." Lord Tucker was mocking, though the inflection was serious. "I shall have you thrown out on your ass, and don't expect an invitation at harvest!"

"Oh, God," replied Asa testily. "However will I bear the shame?"

"So it's true then. You've relinquished your contracts with the Indies?"

"Christ, Tucker. A proper tradesman never reveals his secrets. Besides," Asa added, smirking, "if any of you chumps were any good at it, you would know this already. Yesterday's news, aye. Goddamn, I'm going for a brandy."

"No, you're not." Tucker stepped forward, hands on his hips. "You are leaving my house, and if I ever see you on the docks again, I'm turning you over to Hutchinson!"

"Turning me over to Hutchinson." Asa laughed, head back, white teeth flashing in the dimness. "God, you've spent too much time in bloody England. Anyway, I make Hutchinson more profit than all of you fucks combined. Move off, Tucker."

His testiness muffled anger–true anger, and there was silence.

Then a sudden movement broke, rippling through the crowd. A clattering of heeled shoes, a collective gasp. *What on earth?* She frowned, peering past Hannah's ample gown.

"Henshaw, Henshaw." It was Asa, hoarse, level. "All right, man, put the gun down. Put the gun down—"

She followed his eyes to Robert, standing halfway in the garden, white in the shadows. His face was dripping sweat, and at the end of an outstretched arm, he gripped a silver flintlock pistol. It happened in a matter of a split second; a clapping rattled the stones, the crowd broke, and a throbbing silence dropped like lead from the clouds.

Asa lurched, his voice ringing in a shout.

"Billy! Jesus, Billy!"

Her nostrils stung with smoke, and her ears shrieked. The glass of Asa's reading spectacles sprayed with blood, and William Douglas Gracey dropped his port, folded with a sigh, and landed on his back with a soft thud.

There was a sickening calm.

And then flaring bursts, shooting from every atom of her senses. Screaming, the beat of heeled shoes, the flash of shadow cutting torchlight. She was frozen. Asa crouched, hands on Mr. Gracey's head, crying out again and again—"Billy, Billy!" Blood leached between his fingers, staining the portico steps. Then he was gone, sprinting, ripping off his frock as he disappeared into the darkness.

Robert was nowhere. The flintlock pistol smoked in the grass just off the garden path. He was shards and pulsations, splinters of light, fragments of sound. Frances shrieking, her hand over her mouth. Hannah swooning, crumpling to the ground in a heap of satin.

Martha's vision pounded. A sound streamed from her mouth, like vomit, on and on, retching up screams, curdling her insides. Her lips wouldn't close, even as she felt her teeth, striking again and again. Blood seeped down the steps of the portico, a midnight waterfall, slow under the dim suns of torches, towards her bare feet, trickling through seams of red stone. Stone by stone, step by step, to the well from which it ran.

William Douglas Gracey, the simplest, smartest, sweetest man, was dead on Beacon Hill.

He was peaceful in the uproar, impervious that his silence was the cause. Heart to the sky, blood mingling with a new summer rain, eyes open. His face wasn't bright anymore; the cherry red had drained to a quiet misted white. Above his temple was a scarlet hole, pulsing thick blood into his ear.

And he was smiling. Just a little, as if he were about to tell a joke.

She dropped to her knees, hands slipping in blood. Stumbling, crazy to reach him, but someone held her back, her bare feet skidding.

Blue eyes ice. Hand deep in his frock. Hurt. In the shadow of roses, a beautiful face turned to stone with pain and vindication. And disgust. A smoking pistol, burning through the earth. Now gone, eaten by blackness—her vision spiraled. She saw Asa, a nightmare, blood sprayed over the side of his face, blood powdering his shirtsleeves, blood from his hands to the bends of his arms.

"Go!" he shouted. "Go, goddamn it, get her out of here!"

She was dragged, thrashing against frantic arms and whispers holding her in. Her bare feet slipped in the oil pools of blood, past William's body bathing in the mist, into the garish light and laughter of the assembly. Behind her, red tracks trailed all the way through the corridor.

Feel things under your feet again, darling.

No one will ever know.

15

PASSING THROUGH *a* DOOR

Suspended above the noise, she was a shaking, screaming little redheaded girl, led in an army of skirts, pushed to sit on a damask settee. An empty bottle of port. Whispers in a spinning room. Blood on her feet, blood on green silk, blood on her hands—*did I touch him?* The settee was wet against her cheek, and her fingers passed through pearl blood.

Blood was white, it was pure. Death was little things. Everyone, trying so hard to be quiet, they hissed like snakes. A faceless body fed her bitter syrup on a silver spoon. Hands passed her around like a wooden doll. Ringing ears. A silent harpsichord, in the corner, keys oiled with blood—not blood, Madeira. Madeira, everywhere, soaking the strings, warping the wood, shards of glass winking in the candlelight. Or was it blood? It could be. Sweet Mr. Gracey, he'd loved his port. Perhaps it had given him life; perhaps it had run through his veins and fed his heart.

It was sometime later, lolling in a carriage, going somewhere, that she stopped crying. The tears simply went away, and her eyes locked, dry. She didn't remember anything, other than rocking, bumping, trying to control her streaming nose with the back of her hand, but it dripped on and on, sticky on her lips, stiffening her sleeves.

No one else was in the carriage. No one was driving the carriage.

No footmen, no horses. Simply moving, skimming over hills, jump-skipping over brooks, as if the carriage had grown legs. She was swallowed by plump satin in a far-away corner.

She closed her eyes. Open. Where? Wyeth House–the party was over? Cassandra, Judith, whispering. Her head, on a pillow, her body, soaking in a brass tub of pink water. Petals drifted…roses. She reached and picked one up, cradling it in the palm of her hand. But it wasn't a petal–it was a strip of flesh. Tongues. Tongues floating in the water, not pink anymore; it was white and thick. Pearl blood on the settee. She stared at her fingernails, and they started to bleed.

How beautiful, it looks like a flower…

She opened her eyes to blackness, her ears haunted with whispers and the low thrum of Asa's voice. Footsteps paced in the corridor, echoing in the hall. After waking so many times, she was grounded; her head throbbed, her feet were ice, and her belly begged her to vomit. She dragged herself to her feet and retched into the wash basin.

The picture of Mr. Gracey, sweet face to the sky, was fading. The boom of the pistol no longer pummeled her skull. Only fragments remained, and clutching her pillow, staring at the light under the door, she started to forget the dreams. The visions. They were amber liquid, on a spoon. The effects on a girl so small and unconditioned were potent, and as the laudanum faded, the worst feelings must be felt. The worst words must be listened to.

241

Long past midnight, she heard doors shutting, feet scurrying. Whispers, Cassandra, Judith, bringing her tea. Hollow, she rose, almost too weak to walk, wrapped a shawl around her shoulders, and followed the voices into the hall.

Cassandra paced. Asa gestured, frock over his arm, his face still speckled with blood. Two uniformed men nodded, muttered, shook their heads. Deputies. Why on earth would Asa have sheriff's deputies in the house? He was too blithe, he was going to get himself in trouble!

"Mr. Wyeth." Barely a whisper. "Mr. Wyeth, what are you doing? What happened at—at the party?"

He met her eyes in a flicker. God, he must've brawled, he had so much blood on his face, on his hands!

"Martha, go back to bed, sweetheart."

"Did Papa go back to the cottage? I think—I think I drank too much at the Tuckers. Can I go home?"

"Martha." He brushed by the deputies and turned her gently by the shoulders, back to the passage. "Go back to sleep. Get some rest, we'll talk in the morning."

Panic hardened like ice. She shook him off, turning to stare at his face. He was old. Haggard. A hundred years old, his eyes shattered with an unnamable thing. Close to grief, but too hollow. Disbelief. Shock.

Why would Asa Wyeth be shocked? Was there anything under the sun that ruffled his feathers?

"I don't want to go back to sleep," she insisted, her voice breaking. "I want to talk!"

"Martha—"

"I-I had a dream! Where is Papa, please!"

"Martha, go! Cass." His eyes were pleading. "Go and lay down, Cassie, get her some more laudanum."

242

"No. No!" A wild fury unfurled sharp wings. He had no right to look like that, he had no reason to have blood like war paint on his face! He must've brawled, he must've dueled, and he was in trouble with the deputies–

"I don't want more laudanum, I want you to tell me right now why I'm here!"

Cassandra stepped forward, lacing her arm through Martha's. "Go," she muttered, brushing past Asa, and directing Martha back down the corridor. "Come, my dear," she said levelly. "I think it's best you lay down. I'll send Judith for valerian, all right? No laudanum. It's not the answer to everyone's ills," she added, glaring over her shoulder.

Back in the airy room, she sat Martha down on the bed. Her figure was black, darting around the room, closing curtains, and arranging things that didn't need arranging. Finally, she stooped in front of Martha and took her hands. Her eyes were Asa's. Martha searched them, wildly, for the truth that her heart already knew, but refused to tell her head.

"Martha. Mr. Gracey passed away last night."

Passed away. It sounded so simple–walking through a door to another room.

"I'll tell you the truth." Cassandra looked at the floor, then back. "Asa will torture you with deflection, because he loves you, Martha. But–but Mr. Gracey died last night. A coroner took his body to the city, but we'll have him back at Wyeth House by the end of the day. We must prepare for a funeral."

She stared at Cassandra. "A coroner."

"Yes. Mr. Gracey was shot. Emory is motioning for a coroner's inquest and a jury examination. So he can take it to court."

Martha stared at her hands, cupped in Cassandra's rough palms. Her fingernails weren't bleeding. The room wasn't spinning, there were no tongues, no pearl blood. "If–if he was shot–"

"Robert Henshaw." Cassandra didn't blink. "Robert Henshaw drew a flintlock in the courtyard and shot him."

The swelling burst, and she fell against the pillow, soaking it with tears. She cried (it must have been an hour) until her throat was raw, and her head split, pausing only to heave up the nothingness in her belly. Cassandra sat patiently, smoothing soaked hair from her face, tracing circles on her back. When the sobbing dissipated to sniffling, she rose, pressing her hands into her apron.

"Do you want more laudanum?" Cassandra asked. "It'll help you sleep."

"Oh–no, I don't like it at all!"

Cassandra nodded. "I will help you, Martha." The pain in her eyes was different; controlled and familiar. "The best thing is to busy your hands. Sleep, and we'll ready for the funeral. It's a woman's duty to prepare the dead. I'll have Adeline take your measurements to the city, for something black. You won't have time for sewing."

❋

William Douglas Gracey, aged forty-five when he died with a smile on his face, was laid to rest beside Mrs. Caroline Gracey in Boston's Granary Burial Ground.

His Christian guilt, never appeased during his lifetime, ("Oh dear–I've missed service again? Martha, you *must* remind me") would not be catered to in death. His bones would rest among fellow men and women, untouched by the angels of a churchyard. The service, held at Old North Church, would've been laughable if she'd had any remaining feelings. William was purely loved in Boston, and the pews were packed shoulder to shoulder. So many men, who'd put back snifters at the counter; so many merchants, whose bills he'd once paid. So many sniffling ladies, who had thanked him, over and over, for having Indian silk *and* dried apricots under the same roof.

Martha sat, clasping Cassandra's hand, her palms prickling with sweat. Flies buzzed; one settled on Mr. Gracey's nose. She cried because her body told her to, but she didn't feel it. A few times, she glanced at Asa; he'd insisted on sitting on the other side of the aisle. A veritable heathen, it was clear he was immensely uncomfortable, and close to ridiculous in a pocket-less black frock, a cambric cravat, black breeches, and overly-polished shoes. His expression was nothing short of pure, wretched shock.

The sight of Mr. Gracey's body had ceased to disturb her. He had returned from the coroners on his second day of being dead, a smile still on his face, but not the same man. Drained, tucked in a coffin, and smelling far too strongly of lavender, it was easy to pretend it was someone else. She knew he was dead; she accepted that he was dead. But he didn't have a body to bury. He'd simply dissipated, bouncing down a hall, turning around a door into a bright light–never to be seen again.

It was a better thing to picture than a stiff corpse, not flinching when the coffin clapped shut.

Everyone was "so sorry" and everyone squeezed her hands, patted her shoulders. Cassandra loomed behind her, a wary crow in her mourning dress. Judith bawled so loudly people started to stare. Elijah Ashley Standish refused to stop sneering, and Martha caught his uncle rapping him on the back of the head.

Asa was clearly balancing on a final nerve; when the last bit of earth was patted down, and the crowd trickled into the streets, she caught him pulling the stopper from a pocket flask and pacing away through the markers. A heron, wading in reedy headstones, miserable, impervious to tears and well-wishes. It was awful to look at him. He was an open daybook, with one entry, one word, written all over his beautiful body.

Guilt.

Guilt on his forehead, on his lips; guilt on his tongue–especially his tongue. Guilt on every atom of every strand of chestnut hair, dampened with sweat. It was disturbingly hot, and far too bright a day to be burying the dead.

When she caught his eye, he looked away. It made her want to vomit sour port onto the Granary grounds.

A stop at the cottage was made. She gathered a few of William's things, necessary items to soothe her grief. His favorite port glass–it had a chip on the rim, which he claimed brought him good luck. Little things; a snuff tin, his pipe, his favorite books, mostly poetry. She circled his room, eyes throbbing with tears. The bed was still made up, but under the pillow, she found his diary. She started, once again, to sob.

Her eyes could read his words, and his voice could speak to her until she fell asleep.

❀

Back at Wyeth House, the mourning gown peeled from her sweating skin, she curled in bed, lit a candle, and opened the diary. William had been a meticulous keeper of records; every entry was prefaced with the date, the day of the week, the weather, and a sentence or two detailing his mood. Most of the time, it was the same–*hopeful. Feeling quite chipper this morning… giddy as a schoolboy…* and one word, one name–over and over and over.

Wyeth.

She settled on an entry from April.

April 8th, 1773 – Thursday

Weather: Skies are gray and the breeze is cool, but the air smells of Spring. A lightest mist of rain caught me on my way back from the docks; had I been any closer, I would've mistaken it for sea spray. Otherwise, a splendid day.

Temperament: I have to say I'm feeling a little melancholy.

I was all right until I rode into the city with Wyeth. He was in a rare mood—fire in his veins, and on the way back from Hancock's he suggested we stop at the Sign of the Red Stag on Fifth Street. I said all right, I wouldn't mind an ale. He was rather raging at that point, as if he'd lost ten years at the wharf. The tavern went under the city, and I must say I felt rather uncomfortable when my eyes adjusted to the dim. I will pen it here, but never say it aloud; it was clearly a "disorderly house", and I, a man of tender ways, have never set foot in such an establishment in my life. Wyeth had an itch, so I took one ale and left him to his devices. The last I saw he'd slung a lovely young lady with black hair over his shoulder, and was ambling down a hallway. I rode home alone, feeling rather sorry for myself.

Which I still am, if I am honest. Why ever, I can't say. A man is entitled to his strumpets, and perhaps it is simply my nature to turn the other way. Caroline owned my whole heart, and she will forever—but I must confess to these long-suffering pages that I was not thinking of my beloved wife when I left Wyeth at the Sign of the Red Stag. But, I am thinking of her now, and I'm heavy with guilt. My happiness has forever been owned by sweet Caroline; but I rather detest to admit, that my heart has sprouted a feather of a wing, and blackened just a little with jealousy when I think of him.

She flipped pages, her eyes eating words, her heart frozen.

April 23rd 1773 – Friday

Weather: A day from a dream. The sun is out, the air is warm, and all around the cottage, flowers dance like stars in the night sky.

Temperament: simply elated. I couldn't be happier. Guilt will do nothing to stop the skip in my step; it's a feeling so familiar to me, I will gladly hold its hand if I can continue this sweet suffering.

And my guilt is nearly forgiven. Wyeth must know what a proper choice he made—we have been twofold since March. I know my numbers, and I know my speeches by heart; I do love this foul trade. I knew I would be good at it, and Wyeth doesn't seem to begrudge my insistence. I wonder what it was that I said that brought him so swiftly back from New York. I don't remember the letters I wrote. I rambled on, because I couldn't get him out of my head, and it was like talking to him across the bench of a public house. I'm sure he supposed I was quite drunk, most of the time—I wasn't—though I do admit, I am now.

This is why I have the courage to put down, for my eyes and my heart alone, that I will happily endure any suffering, if I may stand by his side for the rest of my life.

I will stand by his side for the rest of my life.

By a shake of the hand, and our names inscribed on papers of legality, this is possible. My heart, and the pains it must withstand until the end of my time, are mine to bear. He will never know. But it doesn't matter; this suffering is as it should be.

I will happily hold it. The faith of my fathers will damn me to hell a thousand times, but every moment bursts with worth. For on earth, I was cursed with the sin of his smile, and the agony of watching him walk away—time, after time, after time.

He will never know. He will never, ever, ever know.

Caroline, sweet Caroline, I am very drunk. I'm crying on the pages. But I am so, so happy, and I would kiss your feet with gratitude if you were here. You alone could have the grace to step aside, after haunting me so beautifully all these years, through tears, and regrets—and watch me fly.

"Miss Gracey!"

She'd been staring at the wall. Crying, though she didn't feel the tears, a trembling finger marking her place in the diary. Someone was knocking on the door. She scrambled for her house dress and dabbed her face dry with a sleeve.

"Oh—come in!"

Adeline poked a rose-gold head around the door. "Miss Gracey, Mr. Wyeth requests you come to his office, if you're feeling up to it."

"Of course—thank you, Adeline, I'll be right there."

"I'm very sorry for your loss, Miss Gracey," muttered Adeline, shrinking into the shadows. For a moment, Martha considered getting dressed, lacing her stays, putting up her hair—but it made no sense. There was no reason for it when he'd seen the worst of her. The Martha who vomited on floors, the Martha who'd been assaulted, the Martha who laid back on settees and let a man lick her senseless. The Martha who'd cried until her nose was swollen, and her eyes were split spiderwebs.

She put her head down, pulled her house dress over her shoulders, and padded down the corridor, feet bare. The idea haunted her that if she looked back, she would see her footprints, following in blood. God—Mr. Gracey had loved so hard, and so purely, that he'd locked himself in the walls of Wyeth House, doomed to wander the passages and halls with his ghostly peers.

Asa was sitting at the bureau plat, shoes up, smoking his pipe. The pocket-less mourning frock was shed, his shirtsleeves were untucked, and his hair, tousled, gleamed like polished brass. He stood, poured a glass of brandy, and slid it across the burr walnut.

"Drink."

She drank, wincing at the fire.

"Have a seat," he said, sitting himself, pulling open a drawer. He brought out an assortment of papers, perched his spectacles (cleaned of blood) on the bridge of his nose, and began sorting, a frown darkening his eyes.

She sat, folding her hands in her lap.

"Some legalities to consider. The will." He shuffled papers, and she watched his throat move as he swallowed. "And this." He drew up a crisp parchment and passed it to her tentatively. "You'll hate me, I'm afraid, but it's what he wanted."

She reached for the paper, squinting to read it in the pathetic yellow candlelight.

"In the event of untimely death, be it accidental or natural, the guardianship of my daughter, Martha Ann Gracey, is to be transferred to the undersigned effective immediately, to be absolved in the instance of her marriage, or on the day of her twenty-first birthday, whichever occurs first…"

Her vision blurred; she shook her head. "I-I can't read this, sir. What does it mean?"

He cleared his throat, dropping his eyes to his brandy. "It means you're a ward of the Estate." He gestured, pointing at the bottom, where his name curled in meticulous script. "I signed it back in May. Billy was insistent his affairs be in order, in consideration with the partnership."

She watched him. Business, legalities, crisp talk… yet, there was a sense of wild insecurity behind his eyes. Perhaps he thought she would be angry about such a thing. He was wrong, painfully wrong. Even after all that had happened, her heart didn't feel any differently; it was ten times more powerful a feeling, knowing the reverence William had held him in. *That* hurt–brutally.

She drew her shoulders up. "Does that mean you own me?"

"Own you?" He shook his head, grimacing. "Goddamn. No. But you are under my guardianship for a few more months. You're twenty-one, coming up, is that right?"

"Yes, Mr. Wyeth."

"Right. So until then, Wyeth House is your home. By law, I mean." He slid the paper aside and picked up another. "Billy left all of his effects to you, including the cottage. What was it–" He pushed his spectacles up. "Forty-three and two-thirds in acreage. The mares are yours, I had Sam pasture them here. Everything else, his library, his valuables, it's all yours. Judith is to stay here, I'll take her on." He dropped the paper and leaned back in his chair. "He left me two things. That bloody dictionary, God knows why. And the shop."

Of course, he'd given the dictionary to Asa. She swallowed back tears. Each page was a labor of love, even the unfinished ones. "I-I understand, sir."

"I'll have the cottage closed up, for now. You can think about what you want to do. Darling–please."

She'd started to cry. She couldn't help it. It was too hard, to look at his beautiful face, and feel the same things William had felt. God, if her heart could make it through this, she was invincible! Should she be angry, should she resent him; should she kill him with guilt? Jesus–no! Things that would have upset her before–the fact that he'd slept with a prostitute, not a few months ago–were nothing. Insignificant, forgivable.

He was only a man, and her jealousy was only a feeling.

Grace Meriton was dead. William Douglas Gracey was dead. And Asa was hiding behind frowns and papers and brisk instructions. But she could see it, a spilling wound, blown through the center of his chest, no matter how many useless things he applied to ebb the bleeding.

Her shoulders shook, and she surrendered. Asa was around the bureau plat in a moment, crouched in front of her, clutching her hands. Holding them to his mouth, pulling her head down, pressing her forehead to his. "Darling, I'm so sorry—I'm so fucking sorry—"

"Sir! It's not your fault—it's not—"

"Please." He held her face, locking her eyes. "Please. Martha! Martha, listen to me." Brown eyes, completely shattered. He wasn't crying, but she wished he was; it would've made more sense than anguish. Heartbreak. As if it had always been there, hidden behind a veil of time and happening, and the reaper had sheared it too short.

"Martha." He kissed her twice, fast, her tears seeping into the split of his mouth. "I-I'm sorry—I'm sorry. Understand one thing, all right? That I'm fucking sorry. I will always, always take care of you. No matter what. Anything you need, anything you feel, darling, I'm here."

She could only nod. It was wrong to have him so close, to feel his warmth, to breathe in the way he smelled around dying sobs. Nevertheless, she clutched his shoulders and wept, until she was ragged.

She lost track of time. She lost grip on her thoughts. Her throat burned with brandy, her belly gnawed with hunger, and her heart broke again and again with shame and regret and the purest sadness. He was making her smile, and her feet were growing roots. He was holding her by the window, stroking her hair, catching her tears.

She was gasping, drunk, laughing over words and memories.

"Mr. Wyeth." She paused by the door. So much time had passed, the house was settling, sighing cracks and groans. The decanter was empty, and her face hurt.

"Darling." He smiled, distant, tipsy. He looked like an angel, sitting with his shoes up.

"I just–I really think–I believe it, sir. Papa was happy. He was happy–I'm sure of it."

"I'm glad you think that, darling."

"I know it. I know because he was standing beside you. It's all he wanted."

He watched her, a muscle working in his jaw. Then, his head dropped, and he nodded slowly. The candles were snuffed, the moonlight was blue. But it didn't feel like midnight; it felt like morning. A new day, a different life. Dewdrops were tears; Madeira was blood. Tea was a disease, and coffee was the cure. Laughter only meant something if it echoed in the halls of a haunted house.

And William Gracey had spent the rest of his life by Asa Wyeth's side, and had passed just in time. Because if he'd known the truth, perhaps he wouldn't have died with a smile on his face.

"Thank you, sweetheart." Asa's eyes were soft. "Go to bed. It's late."

16

DON'T MAKE ME SLEEP ALONE

Wanted under the ordinance of Sheriff Greenleaf, having fled following the murder of William Douglas Gracey: Robert Frederick Henshaw, of the House of Henshaw, aged thirty, the likeness of which is referenced above.

He was last seen in the courtyard of Nehemiah Tucker's residence on Beacon Hill, sporting a gray frock, a white lace cravat, gray breeches fastened with sterling knee buckles, white hose, and black shoes. He stands about six feet, one or two inches, is of a broad build, and a healthy countenance. His hair is a bright blonde, worn in a queue, and his eyes are blue.

Upon this notice he is a convict on the sentence of murder of an innocent. Whoever shall apprehend and secure the said Robert Frederick Henshaw and report him to the Boston Gaol, or deliver him to a deputy of the sheriff, shall thereby be rewarded in the sum of two hundred-and-fifty pounds.

"Two-hundred-and-fifty pounds," muttered Cassandra, over a copy of the *Boston Gazette*. "Hardly seems worth it. He'll trip over his own feet and break his neck, before anyone finds him alive."

"I'm footing the bounty, it's not any skin off Greenleaf's nose." Asa snatched the paper from her hands. "Give me that. Martha, are you all right?"

Martha had memorized the drawing of Robert. She'd stared at it, until it almost didn't look like Robert anymore–or, she couldn't remember his face. Asa had done everything right. Robert's name was put in the papers; his picture was the source of a tumultuous wave of scandal. Bounty hunters, bloodhounds, warrants, and searches. But it was evident, as days turned into weeks following the funeral, that Robert had fled the city, and he'd done so under the cover of darkness, the same night he'd robbed the earth of William Gracey. His tracks were lost, erased by panic and disbelief.

The primary problem was time. Time passed, and when that happened, people started to forget. They would go back to revels and assemblies, and no one would miss Robert Henshaw, just another fellow in a proper coat. She smiled weakly at Asa, who was offering her a port, not knowing in the deadness of her room, she'd already put back several glasses.

It was her lifeblood, the only thing that kept her heart pumping.

❋

Summer was high. Horrible, really. She was too hot, all the time, and she itched in corsets and petticoats, hating that Asa walked around the house in loose shirtsleeves, and Cassandra never wore shoes. She'd been in the middle of changing when Mr. Gracey died, and his death had stunted her transformation. Was she Robert's girl, in satin, or Asa's, in an apron, barefoot in the kitchen?

Neither. She was held, crumpled, somewhere in between.

Asa's particular brand of "caring" didn't help. He was sweet, but he pointedly neglected the things her heart needed to heal. To be held and kissed, to be loved like she had during those blissful days before Midsummer's. His position as warden had reached into his ear, perhaps, and tapped an idea in his head, and that was it. What hurt the most was that he thought he'd made an error. She could see it, and it was almost worse than her sorrow.

She forgave herself any guilt she might've felt. The sort of man Robert Henshaw was, was not her fault. There was no room for guilt, not with so much grief. It would change nothing. William couldn't be cried back to life. Asa wouldn't find the rights to his wrongs at the bottom of a bottle of laudanum. The earth continued to spin past her pain, over and over, spitting with injustices. And that morning, sticky with August heat, her bare feet in grass wet with dew, she smiled.

She hated herself for it.

She'd been wandering the rose garden. The brindle mastiff (whom she'd learned, thanks to Asa's remarkable talent for naming things, was Ham) loped at her heels, and her foot caught on a fallen stick. She picked it up with a grunt of frustration and tossed it. The dog took off like a musket shot, his ridiculous tongue lolling from the side of his mouth.

For that moment, she forgot. She forgot about the blood she couldn't seem to scrub from between her toes. She forgot about Asa; she forgot about everything, watching the dog, rippling haunches tipped, tiger-striped tail whipping in anticipation. At that moment, she was a little girl again. Mr. Gracey was in his office, watching her from the window, and she was picking bugs out of underneath stones. She'd never been kissed. She'd never even thought about boys in that way. She hadn't noticed them.

Until they were men, and she was still a little girl, in the middle of her heart.

She smiled.

She could've punched herself. She left Ham in the garden, sad brown eyes following her—soft, hurt, the same way Asa's looked when he dared to glance her way. She wrapped her arms around her middle and hurried through the western terrace, through the tea room, where Robert had nearly raped her; through the passage, to the room that had now become hers. Hand under her nose, eyes burning.

"Oh, Miss Martha!" Adeline was standing at the foot of the bed, a large wooden box in her arms. The rose-haired serving girl had taken over most of Judith's duties; poor Judith, who had devoted her existence to Mr. Gracey, was useless in her grief.

"Sorry, Miss Martha," she chirped. "I thought you were in the garden. A delivery for you, from the city."

"Thank you," muttered Martha, dipping her head so Adeline couldn't see the tears. It wouldn't do to have her see. She didn't know how to comfort; no one did, except for Cassandra. When she was alone, Martha wiped her nose on her sleeve and pried the lid off the box.

Inside, folded neatly, was a cloak. She pulled it out, and it rippled to the floor. Sweeping folds of lush black velvet, with a rabbit fur lining. On the bottom of the box, folded in half, was a piece of paper. She snatched it up. In impeccable script: *It'll be cold before you know it. Asa.*

Time. Time, time—always time.

It was a beautiful cloak, and probably cost him a pretty penny, with all that fur. She hung it in the wardrobe and poured herself a glass of port. Then she sat on the edge of her bed, and stared at the velvet and rabbit fur, sullen like a mourning dress. Time passed. She cried, thinking about the way she'd smiled at

Ham. For the first time, she didn't come out when Adeline called for dinner, insisting she had a belly ache. Finally, as the sunset light hushed to sullen blue, she heard the familiar *bang* of the front door and boots in the entrance hall.

She waited, counting the beats in her head. One, two, three–frock off. Four, five, six–deep in the red leather chair. Seven, eight, nine–*pop*–a glass of brandy, boots up. Head back, a sigh. She slipped out, padding through the hall and the library. The office door was cracked, and she knocked.

"Whatever the fuck, Sam. I just got in."

"Sir, it's me." She pushed at the door. It was always open to her; he'd made that clear, in a curt lecture a few days after the funeral. He was sitting at the bureau plat, a book on his knees, boots tucked against the side of the burr walnut. A book–*God.* He may as well have crossed the room, opened her chest, and squeezed the blood out of her heart.

Love In Excess.

He straightened, pulled open a drawer, tossed the book down, and closed it with a hollow thud.

"Martha."

"Sir."

"What do you need?"

"I-I wanted to say thank you." She swallowed. "For the cloak."

"Of course. Whatever you need, Miss Martha."

"Sir." She twisted her hands. "I was wondering if I could talk to you."

"Whenever you need. Have a seat."

She sat hastily, tucking her skirts with trembling fingers. She hadn't been close to him in weeks. He hadn't touched her; he hadn't kissed her since those hard kisses on the mouth, the night after the funeral. His scent caught her like a slap to her senses, already raw from tears, from too much port, tender with grief. Rushing her back to the days of flirting. Sweet kisses, in secret; kisses in the rain. Holding his hand, rough from sea-air.

"Sir, can I have a brandy?"

He eyed her with a brow up, but poured her a glass without protest. "What now, darling." He was haggard. Sleepless, pale. The bridge of his nose blushed with a faint sunburn, which, if she wasn't so purely miserable, she might have found endearing.

She sipped the brandy. "Was it very hot on the sloop today?"

"Wasn't on any sloop today. Court this morning, then I waited in the Common to watch the fellow hang."

She stared at him. The brandy bit at the back of her throat, and she swallowed fast, putting back the sting. "Are you–are you joking, Mr. Wyeth?"

"Why would I joke about such a thing? If I send a fellow to the gallows, you'd better believe I'm going to listen to the sound of his neck snapping."

"Doesn't that bother you?" She frowned into her glass. "That you send people to die."

"Not in the least. I say some pretty words, and a jury decides if they like what I say. It isn't on my conscience. It's American law."

He was testy, but something lit behind his eyes. A flash of the old Asa, betraying the fact that something made him happy.

"Are you a good lawyer?" she asked. "Do you win all your cases?"

"I do now." He put his boots up. "I didn't, at first. The first two years in practice, I was so fucked in the head, I lost most of them."

"You were…fucked in the head?"

"Hmm, yes. Very." He leaned his head over the back of the chair, eyes on the ceiling. "What did you want to talk about?"

259

She studied his profile. His words had stirred a memory, something she hadn't considered since Mr. Gracey's passing. *Fucked in the head.* The indentation on his skull was a haunt, pressing a finger into the tenderest part of his thoughts.

"I was just thinking," she said tentatively. "Reading the note you put in the box. About—about time."

"Time."

"Yes. That it would be cold before I knew it."

"It will."

"Sir." Her fingers clung to her glass. "It's been two months. Did the bounty hunters find anything?"

He cocked his head, his eyes settling on hers. Other than that, he didn't move. He didn't tense. He simply studied her, then sighed, and turned back to the ceiling. "They took it as far as the Neck back in July. He must have been lifted by someone after that. Dogs lost the scent."

"So that's it, then?"

"Martha, please. Trust me when I say to you, I've got this handled." He closed his eyes, pinching the bridge of his nose. "You have to trust me. The legalities aren't simple."

A lump swelled in her throat. Of course. Orders of business, calculated plans. "I was out in the garden this morning with Ham. I smiled, sir."

"You should smile, I want you to smile."

"*You* don't smile."

"I'm a lot older than you, Martha." He shook his head. "I've seen a lot more."

"I've seen horrible things too." Tears broke. "I have and I—just—I'm afraid that too much time is passing, too quickly. I-I'm not ready to smile. But I couldn't help it. I-I hate myself for it!"

Boots hit the floor. Glass hit hard on the bureau plat. Elbows on the surface, eyes level, suddenly bright.

260

"Martha, listen to me. Look at me."

"I-I can't, I'm sorry–I'm crying!"

He stood. With a turn of his heel, he was in front of her, pulling her to stand. He tipped her chin, wiped her tears away with his thumbs. "Time isn't passing too fast, I can promise you that. Billy is here–all the time. And I swear to you, he would've wanted to see you smile weeks ago." He smoothed her hair away from her face. In a moment of weakness, driven by a wrenching sob, she dug her little fingers into his forearms and pressed her head into his chest. His arms circled her shaking body.

"Martha, please. Trust me."

"I-I do trust you!"

She wasn't lying. But as always, when he didn't want her to know, nothing would pry his lips apart. So she was awake, long past midnight, her forehead smarting from the gentlest kiss. Pacing the floor, over and over, burning prints into the floorboards. The windows were dark, and a summer thunder rolled. Rain was worse than silence, scratching at her ears, roaring against her raw senses.

She flung her dressing gown around her shoulders and once again followed the corridor.

It'll be cold before you know it.

It wasn't hard to stand in front of his office again. She'd done it so many times, defeated by her sorrow, knowing he wouldn't hold her the way she needed. But now, she pushed it open. Through the screen, she could see his figure, the darkest shadow in a room lit with splitting currents, breaking the sky, shaking the floors. He was sitting on the edge of the four-poster bed, taking off his spurs.

"Martha, what do you need? You should be sleeping."

"Mr. Wyeth. I-I can't sleep alone." Her nights were broken by the darkest dreams, no matter how hard she slept. No matter how full her belly, or how fast her head spun with port. Her eyes always opened to the same image.

Not William Gracey. Not even Asa, his spectacles sprayed with blood. No; always Robert. Leaning against the counter in *William D. Gracey, Proprietor*. Smiling, as she held up the green silk, and telling her she would look so, so beautiful.

"I can't," she sobbed. "I just can't. Please, don't make me sleep alone!"

She opened her eyes, drowsy. Vanilla smoke. Sea air. The room was dim, gray with a predawn glow, and from the open panel she caught Asa, bouncing on his shoe to reach a book.

She'd slept there all night. Hard. No dreams, no nightmares. He'd slept with his clothes on, arms around her belly, his nose in her hair, almost warily, as if he weren't allowed to sleep properly. The bedding all around her was rumpled, threaded with his scent. The pillow, cool against her cheek, smelled like castile soap.

She propped her head on her palm and watched him. He flipped through the book, reading a line or two, then tucked it back in its place and reached for another. He was already dressed, more dapper than usual in knee-buckled black breeches and black frock, polished low shoes catching the candlelight. He must have felt her eyes; he glanced over his shoulder, marking the page with a finger.

"G'morning, love. Sorry if I woke you, getting ready for court. Coffee?"

She sat up, pulling her dressing gown tight around her shoulders. "Oh, yes. I'll take coffee." Her feet hit the floorboards, pleasantly cool. Fresh air... she knew the smell like the back of her hand. A ride in the field, a misted summer morning. Around the panel, the window behind the bureau plat was wide open, the curtains swaying in hushed gusts.

She sat, hands between her knees, as he poured her coffee. "Do you always wake up before dawn?" she asked.

"My head's the best in the morning." He sat, producing his pipe. "I've got to be sharp before court. Brush up on some law tricks."

She stared into her coffee. Black. It was an acquired taste, one that, since she'd been deprived of the privilege of Hyson and Bohea, had been heartily masked with milk and too much sugar. She sipped, and it snapped at her tongue.

"What are you going for this morning?"

He considered her–then, "Rape," he said, eyes on his shoes.

"Rape." Perhaps he thought she would balk at the word. "I didn't know such a thing went to court."

"Rich people take it to court. It's the worst kind of case. Never ceases to amaze me, how many *ahems* can be said in a minute." He raised a brow. "You know me, darling. I don't blush. Nevertheless," he sighed, leaning back in the chair, "the bugger will be howling at the post by this afternoon, of that you can be sure."

She glanced at him. There'd been decidedly nothing sexual about sleeping with him last night; it was comfort, and comfort only. A strong pair of arms, to right her pitching equilibrium. *Yet.* He was deflecting, as always; the guilt hung around his neck like a noose. Tied with his tongue, at the gallows.

She cleared her throat. "Good luck, sir. I hope you win."

"Hmm, thank you. Now. I've something I wanted to show you. Thought you might get a smile out of it." He opened a drawer and brought out a thick, leather-bound book. She knew it in an instant; her heart sank to the floor. The dictionary. The labor of love…thoughts, feelings, something that he'd given Asa

263

that had nothing to do with work. Just his hands and his heart. He opened it and pulled out a loose leaf of paper, passing it to her.

"Billy had quite the way with words. A veritable poet."

She took it, her fingers shaking. She wouldn't know, she'd never bothered to read anything he'd written, before the diary. It had seemed silly. A waste of time, when she could be outdoors. His shaky penmanship sprawled on the page, slanted words, ink spills, and cross-outs. At the top, poorly drawn with flowers and birds, was a large, illustrated letter M.

Martha. A definition, in my own words and experiences. Affection or familiarity does not blemish; anyone who lays eyes on her would swear in a court of law, I speak the truth. Oftentimes, this exquisite creature is the daughter of William Douglas Gracey, though one might wonder how *and* why *when considering her beauty and poise. A wildflower, an American rose. The Middle of the Mist. Watch the turn of her wrist—see that? Flawless. Her pout has killed him so many times, William is rather weary from rising from the grave. But he'll bury himself again if she'll kiss his grizzled head—which she does, every night before bed. And in the morning, her fingers, slim and quick, fix him tea and cakes. Then she's gone; she is a wood nymph, in her soul. Sunset hair, dancing feet. Yet she could make a man bow too low in a ballroom, and make a fool of himself.*

I loved her before any man, I held her before any hands. She confuses the heads of men. For who can make sense of innocence, beauty, and wit, all in the same little girl? I am well certain the only one who will win her hand is he who drops to his knees. I know as I've already done it, begging her silently to stop leaving her pins on the settee.

She smoothed the paper on the bureau plat. She couldn't hold it; her fingers were shaking too hard. Asa was watching her, something desperate dulling the spark behind his eyes. *Oh dear, he thinks he made a mistake.* She smiled quickly, holding back tears.

"It's beautiful," she managed. "Thank you."

He smiled, just a little. And then—her heart stopped, and the paper was nothing. A jumble of twisted black vines, blurred in the corner of her vision. A touch brushed her cheek, tracing the line of her jaw. Down her throat. And gone.

She hated herself in that moment, like she hated herself when she smiled. Because with just that touch, it wasn't like sleeping with his arms around her. She'd read Mr. Gracey's words. And Asa had touched her, in a motion he surely perceived as comfort, yet he'd awakened a monster. A two-headed beast, that she'd fought wearily for weeks after Midsummer's. One head, dull, bleary eye cracked. Guilt. The other, writhing, snapping, nipping—lust. It was the memory, in nightmares, of Asa's tongue. Of his hands, pinning her hips. Of rustling silk and sweat, and long, deep strokes.

Every time she thought about it, the other head grunted. Shifted. Reminding her that it would never be a separate thing.

He stood, leaned, and kissed her on the forehead, then rounded the bureau plat and slipped behind the panel.

She snatched up the dictionary.

A. A, r…A–A, s.

Asa. Ares, the unloved God of War.

The American God of War. His sword is a quill, plucked from the back of the sagest pheasant in the trees. Running for centuries, ever evading the flintlock fowler. Old enough. Made up of mistakes, running wisdom through his sighs. His words hang from a noose, dripping with honey—justice for some, the end of the world for others. His smile breaks apart the heavens, his eyes bind a woman's hands behind her back with a glance.

Yet I am a man, and he has cracked my kneecaps with too much prayer.

She stood, fast. Cold sweat rose to the surface of her skin, and her heartbeat surged. Grotesque. Beautiful. Her heart and William's fit together too perfectly. *Bind a woman's hands behind her back. Tie her to a bed with a cravat.* Strike her ass.

Eat her as if she were his last meal.

Asa rounded the panel, brown eyes innocent, holding a black cockaded tricorn. Jerky, her head blank, she stepped forward, snatched the hat away, and tossed it on the bureau plat.

"Sir—no!"

"Martha, I have to go to court."

She balled her fists. She wanted to cry, to scream, to slap his face. Rattle his bones, the way Grace Meriton still did, the way he'd rattled Mr. Gracey's. Her tongue went dry. "When is court?"

"Well, I need an hour to ride to the city." He brushed by her, taking up the hat with a grimace. "I usually sit in the gallery, for an hour or two. Makes some notes, right my head—"

She made a snatch at his wrist, fingers balling black cotton.

"Mr. Wyeth."

"Martha—"

"How long does it take to fuck?"

17

DANCING *in a* ROOM
WITH GHOSTS *and* DEMONS

There were simpler ways to manage grief. Cry, would've probably been the easiest. Walk in the garden, or talk to friends. Or, if things were particularly ugly, a drink or two, or three. Remedies could be a white pill or amber syrup on a spoon. And Martha was a shaking fool, punched in the gut, numb in the mouth, appalled at herself for saying something so utterly foolish.

But then, he broke, and she forgot.

His hat dropped to the floor. She met him halfway, wrapping her arms around his waist, sinking her nails into the small of his back. His mouth met hers in a hungry kiss, desperate, as if he were afraid she might bolt. She scrambled, trembling, tugging at buttons; his shoulders tightened, twisting off the black frock.

"Martha, you don't want this. You don't!"

But she wrapped her hands around his neck, searching for his mouth. He relented, opening to her lips. Her breath came fast, cold. She buried her fingers in his hair, curling around the back of his head, grazing the ghost of that wound. She touched it, eating his taste; dense like a thicket, taunting her with the unknown—now, she must know. To feel, to be fucked, to be given something beyond the ugliness of grief, was all that she needed.

She circled the wound again, then pressed it, hard.

"Slow your tongue." He jolted, his voice husky, disbelieving. "I'll bite it down!"

"Then bite it!" She lunged again, raking her fingers through his hair. God, if she could've bathed in that smell, she would've! Sweet Virginia tobacco, a sensory storm of the cleanest things, and his hands eating the length of her body, cupping her backside, lifting her above all the things that nipped at her heels. Sour memories fled, as if terrified of her kisses, as if threatened by the way he loved her.

"You don't want this," he insisted. "You don't!"

"Don't say that! Please, show me!"

"It'll hurt, Martha!"

"I don't care!"

"I'm a bastard of a man, I am!" he hissed. Yet she spun, driven against the wall, biting down a shriek, shot through with wild excitement. God, she was nothing, a sack of grain, dragged down the planks of the docks! Sweating, but she couldn't feel it; she could see it, gleaming on her skin, slipping flesh to flesh. In a rush of wild confidence, she raked her fingers down his middle, balling his shirtsleeves and jerking them from his breeches. He was clearly on the precipice of losing himself, so blindly, she pulled her palm over his fall-front, once—then lingered, searching with shaking fingers.

That part of him, she'd so long ached to touch—why, but she had, sore with conflicting unhappiness, forcing her eyes to the floor when he stood after dinner. When he teased her, after a swim, carved through like a sculpture, veined with clinging fabric. Lust was winning, clear in the flush at his throat, the rapidity of his breath, and she snatched his weakness. His hands were lost in her hair, his mouth lost on her mouth with wild kisses, and she pried her fingers under the buttons and plunged her hand. Her fingertips tickled with coarse hair, skimming plush flesh; through misted heat, lambent candlelight, and heaving breath, she pressed her forehead to his collarbone and took him in.

She'd never seen something so foreign, yet something she desired so much. It wasn't enough to touch him. He demanded more–to be stroked, teased; a womb to reach, a body to ransack. A frightening desire took over to drop to her knees, to put him in her mouth. That was to taste him, truly, to choke on him while he watched, to use him in every way to hurt herself, to validate him–

Trembling, she ran her fingers up his length, then down, curling her fingers. A thrill started in her chest, shooting to her fingertips; the motion was hardening him, and she increased the rhythm. Within seconds he was stone. Yes, just like she'd imagined that night at the Tuckers! Beautiful head on red damask, lips parted, eyes closed, stroking, sighing–

He pushed her off with a noise close to a growl.

"Who taught you to fuck with your hands like that?"

"Sir, I don't know–it just feels right!"

"You want to be fucked, aye?"

"I want to be close to you!"

"Martha, you're not in your right mind." His tone was warning, laced with desperation. "You're sad, this is foolish!"

"Foolish? I beg your pardon, but how dare you!" She gritted her teeth, jerking his hips to her hips, pressing him into the softness of her middle.

"You don't know what you're saying. You're a virgin!"

"And I'm giving you my virginity!" She lost grip on her tongue. "It's my choice to make! I'm sick of your open doors, but I want them now. I want you to kiss me in front of everyone after dinner, and in the morning, before you leave. I want you to show me how to fuck, and then I want you to fuck me wherever I want, with the doors and the windows open for everyone to hear—how much—how much I love you, Mr. Wyeth!"

She was gathered again by eager arms. Pushed again into the wall. Something fell, thumping, breaking. A gust surged through the open window. A candle died; her nose stung with smoke, and his fingers sunk into her flesh, lifting her thighs around his hips. Bones hit the floor—on his knees over her, her body sinking into the heavy shadows of the bureau plat. His lips, eating her lips. In a distant dream, she was aware of the speed of her heart, and the cold, clean feeling of cloth slipping over porcelain flesh.

She closed her eyes.

The house dress splayed open. His mouth was on her neck. His teeth nipped salt from her skin. Her back bunched, arching like a cat, responding to slick warmth on the peak of her breasts. There was no moment of clarity, no room for hesitation; no tender assurances, nor explanation. She had asked to be fucked. Her knees were pushed apart, his body shifted over hers in an animal lunge, and he obeyed.

Pain tore through her pelvis. The back of her skull drove against the floorboards. She clung, her nails pinning linen to flesh, her eyes clamped shut.

Her body jolted, ragdoll. One thrust, two, three—she counted, her teeth sinking into her lip, clenching in blank, screaming pain. No room for regret. Her womb balled, and she clawed at the back of his head, pulling his teeth from her neck, fighting the primal urge to cut off the pain, to throw him. Only, a deeper instinct fought in opposition, insisting she hold on. She clung, fighting to breathe, and with the passing of a few moments, the pain dulled, giving way to a thick, velvet sensation of fullness and heat.

She rolled her head to the side, cracking her eyelids. His palm anchored him to the floor. That same whispering comfort instructed her to move, and she met the sharp bones of his hips in a primal movement, wound with kisses and sighs. Little by little, feelings rose, separate from the pain. A bursting ache. Her fingers, spun up in soft hair. Her feet, arches stiff, knees bent around the small of his back. Her body opened to him like a brimming cup, begging to be spilled.

No one had told her about fucking. The conjugal act. Yet, her body was performing it as if she'd known it the moment she'd laid eyes on him. Touching him, digging into sweat-damp cloth; watching him, distantly amazed. Through the open window, birdsong trilled in a chorus, and his breath was a tempo, matching the melody of a summer morning. A war beat, threading strings through her limbs; arranging her bones, shifting her flesh. To feel the best things. A low throb, building at the front of her womb, that secret door once coaxed open by his fingers, now teased by a new part of his body.

She arched her neck, pressing her heels. He was whispering, sweet things, breathless in her ear. "Fuck, you're beautiful, darling–" Sweet nothings. "Jesus, you feel like heaven–" It was a fever dream, where smoke ate her nostrils, where her fingers twisted in ivy curls, gripping at his scalp. Without thought, she brushed the indentation again, tracing the diamond. His pace increased, pushing her into the floor, her backside numb. Then the oddity of it struck her, and she pulled her hand from the back of his head, but he snatched her wrist.

"You want to touch it. Touch it," he whispered, pushing her fingers back into his hair.

"Does it hurt? I don't want to hurt you!"

"Why don't you touch it, and find out? Fuck it with your fingers, darling, yes. Jesus, like that, fuck it harder–"

For a moment, her heart fell to her spine. He'd moaned, a primal noise, that coming from Asa (as diffident as he typically was) was just shy of startling. But she brushed the feeling aside, burying her fingers obediently. His hand trailed her free arm, pinning her wrist. Her pulse strained, and her hand grew hot; she clenched her fist, raised her hips, and dug her middle and index finger into the center of the wound.

It wasn't that she was close to the height of sexual excitement. She wasn't; the hurt was too much, the feelings were too new. And she was too busy touching and kissing, wild with disbelief, that she cried out when suddenly, he stopped. She leaned on her palms, dragging herself up. On his knees, one hand on the floor, the other cupping the small of her back, he pulled back with a cry; a hollow feeling took her breath away. Against the soft skin of her belly, her curiosity was appeased. He finished, his eyes locked on her eyes; thick heat met trembling flesh, rolling pearls down her sides.

She gasped, shifting backward on her hands. "Asa!"

"Darling! Jesus, I'm sorry–"

He pulled himself up on his knees. For a moment her mind locked on the stark image of him, lording over her, slick from the secretions of her body. Yet the guilt in the air was palpable, and if she'd taken the gesture that way, he clearly hadn't meant her to. He turned, fumbling in the shadows, and when he dropped beside her, his breeches were closed.

She frowned, falling back on her elbows. Curious, she toyed her fingers through the mess, a hazy memory stealing in. Red damask, pearl blood, dripping in a spinning room...

"Martha." His voice broke her thoughts. "I'm a bastard, all right. A girl shouldn't be shaken up like that her first time."

"I want–" She stared at her fingers. "I want to be close to you."

"I know, but not like that. I want to kiss you, Martha." He smiled tightly. "Properly. From your toes to the top of your head. It's just–I don't make love in beds very well."

Her heart sank, but she reprimanded herself. "Is a bed where you're supposed to make love, necessarily?"

"Hmm. Not necessarily." He slipped his arm under the crook of her neck, his breath tickling her hair. "I think you rather belong in a field somewhere. Bloody tangled up in wildflowers. With the moonlight turning your body blue."

There was silence, broken only by distant birdsong. Then–
"Martha."

She turned, studying his profile in the low light.

"Remember the night I met you?" Gently, with the barest brush, he touched her cheek. "You were wearing blue satin."

"Yes. Papa wouldn't let me take the green silk," she whispered. "It was a compromise."

"You looked like a bluebird. With your red hair, pinned and pretty." He pushed away stray hairs, stuck with exertion, and leaned to kiss the end of her nose. "I took one look at you, and I was done for."

"Really?" Her heart pinched; her fingers, drawing circles in the wetness, paused.

"I was. You made a fool of me that night. You had me dancing, and I don't dance for anyone."

His words resonated with something—deep, uncomfortable, yet pure. Not poetry from Asa's lips—he was hardly a man of romantic caprices. A chill froze the foreign deposit on her skin; a ghost passing over her body, rapid feet in heeled shoes, a fast chuckle dissipating into stillness. Guilt sprang and shrank in the middle of her heart.

She'd have a man bow too low in a ballroom, and make a fool of himself.

"You don't," she agreed quickly. "You don't dance."

"Except for you. You let me know, darling. I'll fold up the tables. I'll spin you dizzy."

"You would do that for me? I-I miss dancing."

"I told you, I would brawl for you. You think I can't handle a dance?" He smiled, tracing her jawline. "Look at you. I wish you could see yourself right now. I'm sorry but just fucked, God, you're a sight."

She flushed, but her heart went cold again. For a second time, her path was crossed by an unwelcome ghost; her feet slipped into different shoes. In that moment, she knew what it felt like to be loved by Asa Wyeth. A blameless wilderness, meant for sweet things. Running in the rain, kissing while the clouds broke. Laughing with a brandy in her hand, while he sat with his boots up. Fucking hard and making love slow, not like this—he'd made a mistake, and she recognized it with an unwelcome twinge of guilt.

She fought a grimace. Everything was making up for it. Quiet strokes on her skin, the bursting silence, roaring the words "I'm sorry" so loudly, irritation prickled in her sternum. Abruptly, tears rose hot behind her eyes. Was everything haunted, was nothing just hers? Grace had kissed him first. Grace had taken his cock before her, and now here she was, lying in a spreading pool of shame, without the changes her raging heart had so longed for.

274

Because Robert wasn't gone. Fucking hadn't answered the question of justice. Mr. Gracey's ghost had already passed, oblivious as ever, through the room and out of a door he'd open again, and again. And again.

She willed away the tears. "Mr. Wyeth."

"Sweetheart."

"Why would you say that? About your head."

"My head?"

"Yes. You have a wound on your head, and I know it's a wound because it gives you headaches." As she knew he would, he rose to a seat, but she persisted. "Why would you want me to touch it like that?"

"I didn't ask you to touch anything. You fairly latched onto my skull, woman." Abruptly, he pitched forward onto his feet, crouching. "Nothing of particular interest, if you ask me."

"That's not fair. You can talk to me, I want you to!"

"Not everything must be talked about." It came as nearly a snap, so odd considering what had just occurred that even he startled, and turned with a frown. "Sweetheart, I–" He paused, biting at his lower lip. "Jesus, you're bleeding quite a bit."

Bleeding? She strained her eyes. Fuchsia pink streaked her thighs, matting the curls between her legs. Her heartbeat doubled, racing to her throat. Bleeding, after so much love? It was one more blow, and she fought not to cry. Only her innocence, because he was being sweet; a man who'd taken the virginity of other girls, and knew what to do in the aftermath. She closed her eyes, sighing to the ceiling as warm, strong arms lifted her from the floor. He carried her through the panel and laid her mindfully on the bed, rolling the covers to the foot. She watched as he soaked a cloth in the washing basin, closing her eyes as his weight dipped the bed. Gentle hands eased her legs apart. He worked from her knees to her thighs until she drifted, bones dragging.

"Sir." She reached, stopping his hand, rolling his palm, skin worn by ropes and sea. Without thinking, she pressed his knuckles to her mouth, then let go.

He studied her in silence. Shirtsleeves untucked, hair mussed, nowhere near the man who needed to stand in court in an hour. And he looked like an angel, in a room that lingered with sex. Rich coffee. Summer morning, laced with distant rain.

"Martha, I—"

"You can talk to me," she whispered.

"I meant that, what I said. That first night I saw you. I went home that night about half-sick. All I heard was Martha Ann." He laughed softly. "I didn't hear Gracey. I guess my head didn't want me to."

"I'm sorry if I complicated things for you."

"You did, though. I was going to win that dance if I had to swing sherry-sodden Mrs. Henshaw around the room first. I remember, when I walked you out, you looked so disappointed." He took her hand, playing with her fingertips. "But you started to dance, and I saw you, with your hair just—whipping all around your face. You had wildflowers behind your ears. In a plain cotton dress, on your bare toes. And I watched you, just spinning, laughing at me, because I was being such a prig." He shrugged. "That was it. I fell in love."

"You fell in love?" The sleepiness dissipated, and her heart pinched. "That night?"

"Aye." He nodded, thoughtful. "That night."

One look. One touch. The end, right at the beginning. "Sir," she faltered. "I didn't fall in love with you that night."

She hadn't. It had been a slow-seeping feeling, a beckoning light, that she'd glimpsed through the broad shadow of Robert

Henshaw. Bursting, the sun breaking the clouds, the moment he'd stepped aside.

"That's all right, darling. I wouldn't have expected it."

"I thought you were very handsome."

"I was an ass. I still am, of course. And darling, don't doubt yourself." He leaned forward on the edge of the bed. "You're perfect to me, all right. I don't want to ruin that with things that don't matter."

Tears threatened. She followed the darkness of his form, hating the quiet sadness, and out of nowhere, the image filled her head–Asa in the rain, black coat whipping in the gales, reaching for her, laughing. *Goddamn, I could run with you.* Tripping blindly through the grass–she didn't need to see when she had his hand to hold.

She reached, brushing the small of his back. "I wasn't at first," she said quietly. "But I am now."

"What's that, darling?"

"I am," she whispered. "I'm in love with you."

"Aye." He smiled softly, leaning for a kiss. "Darling, I have to go to court. I'll lose this case, but it'll be worth every minute. Martha–"

"Mr. Wyeth."

Her belly turned. She'd only seen it once, in his eyes. Fear. And now that the fucking was over, the passion had passed, the familiar beast, the ugliest haunt.

Guilt.

"Martha, will you wait for me?"

His guilt made him broody. Tea was ordered, and extra pillows, "willow bark powder, Cassie's nonsense" for the pain, if she needed it. How many times had he returned to the bed, to brush hair from her face, to kiss her temple, she lost count.

Through split moments of wakefulness, she caught him, long legs cutting her vision. Pushing his hat down over mussed curls. Tucking books into a saddlebag. Pausing, for a brief moment to grimace at himself in the mirror, as if he hated the way he looked. Leaning in for a kiss on her slack mouth, brushing her cheek with his thumb.

"I love you, darling. I'll see you this evening."

I love you.

She sat up with a jolt, bleary. It had to be past midday.

Everything rushed. Warm flesh, long kisses. Heavy breath, wild pain; the thin skin of her virginity, torn in two. She scrambled off the bed, hands over her breasts—they were sore. And Asa's cleaning hadn't done much of anything, because her thighs were streaked with new blood, and the bedding was spotted with it.

She jumped, clambering for her dressing gown; Asa had mindfully draped it over the foot of the bed. The passion seemed far away, mangled by the more sinister things, glaring at her in summer sunlight. *Touch it, you want to touch it.* She spread her legs, peering. Her sex was swollen, the soft skin of her belly tight, the ghost of white pearls tickling her sides.

Her throat caught, and tears welled. *Oh, Jesus, stop it, Martha! You wanted it!* Her eyes searched the room. Asa's room. Spotless, of course, the wood floor polished to glare. The walls were a pretty sky blue, trimmed with white scribing. A burr walnut dressing table and mirror, a matching wardrobe, all doors and drawers firmly shut, nothing out of place.

She grimaced, circling her eyes again, trying to feel comfortable. But it was simply too airy. The ceilings were too high, the sunlight too bright. He'd even pulled up his side of the covers and plumped the pillow before he left. The bed was framed on either side by a set of single-drawer side-tables, matching the other furnishings, and in a surge of morbid curiosity, she tugged open the drawer. Nothing. Her fingers prickled. She padded to the other side of the bed, and pulled open the other.

A flicker of metal. She reached, fingers trembling, and came up with a hairpin. A little silver hairpin, set with a piece of yellow glass. She stared, her belly cold.

That is not my hairpin.

She flung it and clapped the drawer shut. Had that woman– Grace–had she slept in that bed? Had he fucked that woman, in the same bed? God, his secrets were not forgivable yet! Panic welled. *I need to leave, I need to leave–I've made a mistake*–she bolted for the panel, out of the office, into the corridor.

There she paced. She'd wanted it so badly, and it had been beautiful; not in the way she'd expected, but in a way that certainly made her want to try it again. But, if he kept other ladies' hairpins, if he were eaten by a secret so dark that he must chase it away with opium, day after day–no! Her thighs clenched around seeping wetness, running down her legs. Blood. Pink and streaked with crimson red. She balled the dressing gown, turning to bolt through the hall.

"Martha?" Cassandra halted in the opposite corridor, a basket of sewing things tipping in her arms. "Whatever is the matter? You missed breakfast. And you look as though you've seen a ghost. Are you ill?"

"Oh, no! I'm fine, I was just tired." She bit her knuckle, but the ploy failed. The dam broke, and she burst into tears.

"Cassie, I-I did something–with–with Mr. Wyeth. I'm bleeding, I don't know what to do!"

❋

In Cassandra's room (windows heavily curtained, crooked paintings all over the walls) a bath was drawn. She shivered in a copper tub, standing as Cassandra worked at the dried blood with a cloth. The water around her ankles was pink, and her brain pinched with another dark memory.

"Less of a ghost, more of my brother's pecker." Cassandra grimaced, scrubbing. "Enough to scare the wits out of any woman. Not to worry, I'll butcher his balls when he gets in."

Martha wrapped her arms around her chest. Cassandra was, as always, unperturbed; virgins were broken, and they bled. Or perhaps this wasn't the first time she'd mended a shivering girl on the other side of Asa's passion.

"Don't fret, most women bleed," Cassandra replied curtly. "Though you're so little." She paused, rinsing the wash rag, then sighed pointedly. "Careful, dear. You don't want to end up like me."

Martha blushed, glimpsing at Cassandra's protruding middle. Any fear of losing the child had passed, now halfway through her pregnancy. She was twice as beautiful as she'd been the day Martha met her, amplified by the fact that she padded around the house, belly swaying, like a bred wood nymph waiting for spring.

Martha glanced at her hands, then at the top of Cassandra's head, bobbing as she cleaned. "Cassandra."

"Hmm, yes?"

"*Should* I be worried?"

Cassandra rocked back on her heels. "You should always be worried when a man is involved. But I know what you mean," she sighed. "Did he finish while inside you?"

"What—oh." She blushed. "I-I don't think so. There was something—it came out, on my belly."

Cassandra cocked a brow. "I see. At least he's being mindful. But watch yourself, men suppose themselves the dog's bollocks for having the control. Goes straight to their thick heads." She stood, wiping a hand over her brow. "In the meantime, wrap it up pretty with a bow." She swayed to the bed, took up a freshly folded towel, and shook it out. "Sheepskin condoms worked well for Elijah and me. He courted me for two months, but that didn't stop him from dropping his britches before we were hitched."

Martha rolled her shoulders. It was comforting, listening to Cassandra's prattle, easing away some of the panic. A simple fact; people just fucked. The towel around her shoulders was warm, smelling softly of sunshine; she was sore, but the bleeding had stopped, washed away in soapy water.

Perhaps the hairpin was a mistake. Maybe it wasn't even Grace's; maybe he'd slept with a prostitute again. Or one of the maids, maybe. It certainly looked like a cheap hairpin, with that ugly yellow glass instead of a real stone.

If love wasn't a factor, she reasoned, neither was jealousy.

"What is a condom?" She pulled her hair over her shoulder, raking her fingers through. "Can I get it at the shops?"

"Wraps up the cock, so he doesn't leave anything behind. I'm sure he has one," Cassandra muttered, lumbering to the dressing table and pouring two glasses of sherry. She rolled her eyes. "The man's been a bachelor his entire life. He's been to England enough times. If there's not a sheepskin in the top drawer of his toilette table, I'll be damned." She passed a glass.

Martha watched her, eyes narrowed, as she sidled around the room, wringing towels, shuffling curtains. She considered, hearing Asa's voice low voice–*I love you, darling.* Cassandra was a definite ally against Asa's strange moods, and she was transparent as glass.

She drew a breath. "Cassie, I noticed–*ahem*. I noticed that Mr. Wyeth has a wound of some sort. On–on the back of his head. Did he have an accident?"

Cassandra halted. Her back was turned, and her head dipped against her collarbone. Her elbows jerked, fingers fumbling. The silence swelled. After too long, she turned. Her eyes were dull, and her mouth had settled in a flat line.

"I'm sorry, Cassandra," Martha amended, startled by the change in demeanor. "I didn't mean to pry."

"An accident," said Cassandra, by way of answer. "I suppose if you want to call a pistol-whipping an accident."

"Pistol-whipping, what do you mean?"

"He was clipped with the butt end of flintlock." Cassandra broke, hurrying to the washbasin. "Fractured his thick skull. Fool should've got it trepanned."

A cloud passed, even though the day, outside the iron-cut windows, was garish. Martha's heart slowed, sluggish, to a dull drum in her ears. *You want to touch it, touch it, darling. Fuck it with your fingers.*

Her mouth went dry. "Who would do such a thing?"

Cassandra paused. Then abruptly, she turned, plopping down on the unmade bed with a sigh. She passed her hands over her face, then rested her elbows on her knees, staring at the floor. "I suppose if he's going to fuck you," she amended, "it's only fair you know what you're dealing with. But." She eyed Martha, sideways. "Go easy on him. You're a good girl, and he really loves you."

"Of course." She nodded, fast. "It's only, it seems to cause him a lot of pain. I wondered what I could do to help."

"That's sweet." Cassandra smiled, though there was a trace of apprehension in her tone. She tipped her sherry, draining the glass, then wiped her mouth with the back of her hand. "It was

Papa Wyeth," she said in a breath. "He pistol-whipped him, the day Emory got back from the Inns."

Martha stared at the floor, her eyes cold. She felt her mouth open, and words, addled by the sherry, slipped into the contradictory brightness. "Oh, my God." The connotation, in the open, was brutally foolish.

Cassandra rolled her eyes. "He's alive and well to tell the tale. At the time, knowing Papa, it made sense. Emory was such a fussy old codger, even then. All he did was read his bloody law books in his room, he was so boring. If he wasn't reading, he was lost somewhere, in the woods, or whipping his horse through the fields. Always away, though." She was distant. "Always away from Wyeth House."

"Cassandra." She forgot about the fucking. The fear, the blood. "How could such a thing happen?"

"They never got on." Cassandra shrugged. "Took it to fists on more than one occasion. Emory was supposed to be–*it*. You know? The heir to the enterprise. Papa went through two women and three dead daughters before he got the son he wanted. But, I don't know. Emory was wild when he was young."

"Wild? What do you mean?"

"Just–I don't know, different. It's not like he was going through whores, it wasn't like that. But he wouldn't behave. He'd pack up his law books, and leave, sometimes for days. He slept on tavern benches, in barns, out in the middle of the woods just to get away from Papa. All he wanted was to be an attorney. It was annoying, how much he wanted it. God." She rolled her eyes again. "He was going to do this, and that, he was going to open a practice in the city. On and on. By the time he was twenty-five, he'd spent ten years apprenticing under three different lawyers. But his feet were dragging when it came to

Wyeth Enterprises. He did enough to keep his name at the bottom of pieces of paper, and that was it. It drove Papa mad."

"But a pistol-whipping…" Some of the feeling in Martha's tongue returned, and she corrected her shock, frowning into her sherry. "It doesn't warrant a pistol-whipping."

"Papa Wyeth was a man with a controlled temper." Cassandra frowned, a finger tapping. "He never touched me, and he never beat his wives. Instead, he took everything out on Emory. I understand his frustration to a point, Emory was very disrespectful. The enterprise was in textiles back then, and Papa was fighting to keep it afloat. But Emory's nose couldn't be pulled from the law books. He wasn't behaving like an heir."

The floor creaked. Distant voices grumbled, servants squabbling in the kitchen, laced with shrill birdsong. But it was separate. A different day. A different hour.

Cassandra shifted, wincing. "One morning I woke up to a note slipped under my door–*to the Inns. See you in four.* And he was gone, four years in London, just like that. He wrote to me, but he never wrote to Papa. Naturally, Papa was furious, but he made good of the time. He was close to the Henshaws, taking particular notice of Robert. I guess I can't blame him."

"Robert…why–why Robert?"

"Robert was considerable. Young, but he was enthusiastic, bright-eyed. Easily trained." Cassandra scoffed. "He was an heir, through and through. And a doubly convenient one, as a relation by blood, and already invested in textiles. A formidable threat."

"You're saying." Martha paused, fighting to ask the question past the wildness of her heart. In less than a moment, so many things too quickly made sense.

"He leveraged Robert Henshaw," she whispered.

Cassandra nodded. "Robert came close, and he knew it. When Emory came back, you can imagine how it went. He and

284

Papa brawled. It was bloody ugly, it went all over the house. Papa earned himself a black eye. Funny thing, he was an enormous man, as tall as Emory, but as round as a barrel." She laughed softly. "They looked ridiculous when they fought. He landed Emory a good split on the chin, and I suppose that was enough because Em took off running for the terrace. Papa followed, pulling his pistol from his frock. He always carried that pistol. Emory was halfway across the lawn when Papa caught up–he swung it, butt-end."

She was staring at the floor. One hand around the empty glass, the other, palm to the ceiling. "I was in the tea room," she said under her breath. "I saw it happen. I watched Papa making off to the barn. Emory was down in the grass, convulsing like he was trapped in his body. I was sure he was going to die. The whites of his eyes turned red while I watched. So." She cleared her throat. "I ran for help, he was put up in bed. The skin around his eyes went–went black. For two weeks, he lay like that, shaking, all the time. He tried to walk, but he couldn't stay on his feet. A surgeon said that the skull was fractured, but the depression wasn't deep enough to trepan." She shook her head. "I still wonder how he would've been if they'd trepanned. He did recover. But the headaches started, and his mood changed. He was melancholy, all the time. And he started dipping into the poppy, every night."

Staring at Cassandra, Martha felt sick. There'd been a passing time or two she'd rolled her eyes to herself, watching Asa tip the laudanum into his brandy, thinking to herself that it was a bit dramatic. "I didn't realize it was something so horrible," she said hoarsely.

"It's not so bad. When he was on his feet, I sat him straight back down. I motherfucked him properly, I did. Wyeth Enterprises would *never* be Henshaw's, over his dead body. I was shocked, but he listened…he buckled his shoes, put on a fancy coat. Papa had the sugar sickness bad, so if Emory could prove himself, Wyeth was his. And he did, almost to the point of being fake. In the last year of Papa's life, they got on quite well. They always had their heads together over the accounts. I even caught them laughing over brandy. And then one morning, well–Papa was dead. Stiff as a board, with a plate of almond-crumb pie in his lap." Cassandra laughed drily. "He was happy when he died. He had an heir. Emory's name was at the bottom of every inheritance Papa had to offer. Little did he know," she finished with a sigh, "his son was drafting queries to the Netherlands that very night."

Martha couldn't speak. Her head felt dull, jumbled with memories. Pictures of things, that now made so much more sense. The portrait in the parlor, the pistol, her pressing fingers. It was sickening. She clenched her lips, fighting a hiccup.

"You know," said Cassandra, her tone lightening. "Wyeth House wasn't always like this." Her eyes circled the room. "These walls, they were filled with beautiful paintings. Furniture and trinkets shipped from France and England and Spain. We used to have howling good revels. We were better at reveling than the Tuckers, if you can believe it." She chuckled. "Papa Wyeth would skimp for nothing. It's silly, but I miss it sometimes."

"I'm very sorry you lost your father on those terms, Cassandra. I didn't know."

Cassandra huffed, batting at the air. "Good Lord, don't be. I hated him. The night he died, Emory and I, we raided his liqueur stores for the best ratafia, stirred it with blackstrap, and got roaring drunk. It was like a snap of the fingers. I saw Emory again. Not Asahel, just Emory."

Abruptly, Martha weakened at the knees; her insides hollowed, as if he'd emptied her by penetrating her. She backed, plopping into the dressing table chair, her groin smarting on impact.

"Martha." Cassandra eyed her. "My brother isn't a bachelor because he loves his women half-way. Don't think that, dear."

"I didn't think that," she said quickly, flashing a tight smile.

"He wanted to marry. He wanted Wyeth babies everywhere, whooping in the yard. He wanted a wife in the kitchen. But, he always lost himself to the sort of women Papa hated." Cassandra crossed her arms with a huff. "Women that brought out the threat of Henshaw. A barmaid, print-maker's daughter, a fisherman's daughter. You see. The daughters of laborers, when his pedigree ran through the gentry."

"Like Grace." She brought a hand to her mouth. *Why. Why did I say that?* Hastily, she corrected herself, "Like me."

"Grace wasn't like you," said Cassandra drily, misunderstanding. She rose, untying her apron and shaking it out. "A word of advice, my dear. Don't let the ghosts follow you. They're busy enough, trailing Emory all over the place. And if a man is tended to, in the proper way–" She scowled. "Well, men are fools. As you've discovered, they think with their cocks more than their heads. And I've observed if they ignore a problem long enough…"

She reached, brushing Martha's cheek with the barest touch. "It simply goes away."

❀

Will you wait for me?

She waited, in the tea room, where Robert had ruined her. It was late when she finally caught his figure, black in the summer

287

dusk, coming in from the barn. Ham trotted down the path to greet him, and he crouched, dropping his saddlebag to scratch behind the dog's ears. She watched, fingers on the glass. New truths made him younger, as if he were in the middle of a second chance, nearly free. He tossed a stick into the bathing pool, and the dog flung into the water, spraying the stones wet.

Perhaps he thought she wasn't going to wait. She watched him sit, tug off his shoes, shrug off his frock and waistcoat, and sink under the water.

She snatched a bottle and two glasses and padded out onto the terrace. "Mr. Wyeth!" Her voice cracked from too many silent hours. "Are you celebrating?"

He broke the surface, shaking his head, running his hands over his face. For a moment he just stared, as if he couldn't believe she was there. She hitched her skirts and skipped down the stairs to crouch by the edge of the pool.

"Did you win?" She poured him a port and held it out. He bobbed, then plunged; the shadow of his body made a dart of darkness through the water. He came up by the edge, shaking his head like a dog; droplets scattered, and the water lapped the rim of the pool, soaking her hem.

"Sir!" She laughed, jumping backward. "Did the fellow get his lashes on the Common?"

"As he properly should. I'm surprised you couldn't hear him hollering from the house."

"Did you stay and watch?"

"'Course I did. What's the fun of watching the gavel go down on a rapist if you don't watch him take his lashes?"

"You are bad!"

"Martha." He put back the port and set the glass down. "Come here."

"I cannot! My dress will be a hundred pounds if I get it wet!"

"Then take it off." He held out his hand. "You can swim in your shift."

"I don't know–" But she was already untying laces. Stripped to her shift, she sat on the edge, dangling her feet in the water, her palms on cool stones. Like a little girl, like she should be catching fireflies in the moonlight, or splashing through a brook with bare feet. It was strange; he made her feel that way. He always had. Wild, in the gentlest way. As if she were that smell, before the rains came, or the newness of watered earth and washed leaves, right after.

"Come in the water," he insisted, tugging at the backs of her knees.

"I don't know how to swim!"

"That's all right, it's not deep. Hold your breath and pinch your nose, I'll catch you."

And he had her doing things she hadn't thought of doing. Nose pinched, eyes screwed shut, hurling into nothing. Breaking the surface of the water, sinking like a stone, only to be caught in strong arms, spluttering and shrieking. Laughing, even though she wanted to cry, her arms binding his neck. Her hair twisted on the surface of the water, and he ran his fingers through, breaking channels through copper rivers.

The bottle was empty and the moonlight blue when he carried her inside. It didn't matter that his room was haunted, and the ceilings were too high. He made love to her again and again, in between breaks and sighs of sleep. Laughing. Chasing her down. Reading, only to say it took too much time, and making love again. At a pivotal point, rigid and sweat-soaked in the oldest hour of the night, the aching fullness broke apart, and she finished, her muscles clutching him like a trapper's snare. The condom, found (as Cassandra had dryly alluded) in the top drawer of his dressing table, was abandoned at Martha's shy behest. The velvet skin, the heat, the pure power of feeling him inside of her body, of binding herself to him, was too addicting. The only thing in the world that made her forget her grief, and remember that it was all right to smile.

She danced in a room full of ghosts and demons all night, skirting the teeth gnashing at her hem. Was it Grace? Frances? Robert? Papa Wyeth? Even as the tongues lashed, she smiled, and she did not hate herself.

Would Asa smile—would he smile—was he a fool, like Cassandra said? His affliction, the cross that weighed him down the lowest, was guilt. It never went away, as the days turned over.

No matter how many times he fucked her.

18

a COLUMN *in a* PAPER

The muggy days of New England summer seeped into a fiery Autumn, one hour bleeding into the next without a sense of time. During the day, she sewed in the parlor with Cassandra, or watched her in the kitchen, grinding herbs and boiling tinctures, the air smarting with sharp thyme and rusty pepper. Several letters came, unmarked, assuring her that Elijah Standish was alive and well—but still on the run.

But the question hung in the air, palpably tense.

"He should turn himself in, and be done with it," snapped Asa. "How'm I supposed to come up with proper statements for a fellow who's God knows where?"

Cassandra paced. "My Elijah will never turn himself in," she gasped, incredulous. "He's innocent! God, you're the worst Whig, I really hate you sometimes." She flung the letter into his lap. "Put this in your pretty evidence file. It'll be cracked and yellow by the time you come up with a shred of patriotism!"

"Bloody hell," muttered Asa, folding the paper and tucking it in his waistcoat. "Oh, Christ, Cass, don't cry. I'm sorry, all right, come here–"

Martha, who hadn't put much consideration into the situation, watched in silence while Cassandra bawled, wrapped in her brother's arms. It was easy to forget outside suffering when she'd been so consumed by her grief. Yet, gradually, as the day-to-day molded into habit, the problem of Elijah Standish became a sore subject. There was a distinct parallel that bothered Martha, raising the fine hairs on the back of her neck. They were hastily patted down for Cassandra's sake, but the truth itched at the back of her brain.

Elijah Standish was a convict. Robert Henshaw, though a ghost in Wyeth House, was a convict too. And they were both on the run from the same accusation. The only difference was the question of innocence, which, in Elijah's case, was boiled down to a mere legal "trifle". She found Asa, cheek in palm, scribbling on the other side of a stack of books. He paced, reading. He built towers of paper, black with notes and courtroom speeches.

She made him pekoe tea and measured out the laudanum herself, so he didn't take too much. She sat on the other side of the bureau plat, feet up so he could see her ankles, and tried to ignore the glaring fact that more of his effort was poured into Elijah than Robert. Still, she kept every newspaper clipping. She clung to every conversation, every small action; a time or two Asa had a deputy in the office, but it ended in nothing that he would recount.

Though impatience roiled beneath the surface, she found a place for herself at Wyeth House. It was a little easier to see past her own grief, with heightened tension in every room. It wasn't that it went away; little things still made her cry, but they were silent tears, alone in her room, concealed and corrected.

There was hardly a night Asa was willing to forgo making love. Well, sometimes it was "making love"; most of the time, it was riotous fucking, which Martha, ever impatient, grew to enjoy more than sweet slowness. He'd once accused her of having a "salacious appetite", and it seemed his mission to tamp it down. She learned to look into his eyes without turning away in embarrassment, so she was flipped on her belly, knuckles in her mouth, and rutted like a dog. His hands, pinning her wrists, turned into her palms, leaving sweat-prints on the wall. Her backside stung with handprints, and Asa left the house in the morning with her teeth tattooed proudly on his neck.

She lived for every minute of it.

Yet, quiet discomforts were amplified, with so much time to think. Things that hadn't bothered her before gave her pause. Once or twice she'd dared to chide Asa about his consumption of poppy, which was a daily occurrence; even when he wasn't complaining of a headache, she caught him tipping the bottle or washing a Dover's down with brandy.

"If your head doesn't hurt, why are you taking it?" she challenged.

He scowled, half-hidden by *The Third Part of the Institutes of the Lawes of England* by Sir Edward Coke. By now, even though he'd never admit it, he'd clearly caught on that Cassandra had spread his story, and it made him wary.

"I know when you have a headache," she pressed. "You don't have a headache. You're taking it because you like it."

"Isn't that why anyone does anything? Get out, I'm trying to read. I love you, but get out. Christ."

She went to the door, but it was easier to chide him when he had full access to her body whenever he felt the itch. "I read the label, it says twenty-five drops. You take five times that in a day. How many drops is that?"

"Do the math, you're clever. And stop watching me, find something useful to do." He grunted, slammed the book shut, and poured himself a brandy. But she knew that she was right, and it settled, like so many things, in the hollow place in her heart. It was easy to make love to him; the easiest thing in the world. But loving him…her brain hurt, just trying to pick apart the knots enough to catch a glimpse of who it was she'd given her heart to.

❀

The air was crisp, the house smelled like apple-nut cake and soda biscuits, (Judith's grief was mended, fixing Mr. Gracey's favorites) and the tension in the air was so potent she could've scratched it open with a fingernail. She was stirred from a hard sleep by a drowsy wave of pleasure—a bleary glance found the chestnut head working languidly between her legs. It was later in the morning than he typically would've left the house…*thank God*, she thought, pushing a palm into the wall. *If I could wake up like this every day!* She rode the swells and pitches, finishing with a shudder and a sigh.

He dropped her thighs, rolled her hips to the side, and smartly rapped her on the ass.

"Asa! What was that for?"

"You fell asleep with your legs spread. What's a man to do?"

She narrowed her eyes, pulling the blankets to her chest. He was well-dressed, suspiciously so, in an indigo wool suit and crisply starched cravat, which he'd tied too low. Boots, polished black, hit just below his knee.

She sat, crossing her legs. "Are you going somewhere? Not to the docks, dressed like that. You look dandy."

"I certainly do not. I've a meeting at the *Dragon*." He frowned in the mirror, running his hand over his chin. "Goddamn, I'm going to lock my jaw trying to keep you satisfied."

"A meeting with who?"

"A fellow."

"A fellow, for what?"

He circled the bed and leaned to kiss her. "Please stop asking questions. It's bloody annoying, you know."

She untied his cravat, adjusting it to its proper place under his chin. "There, you always place it too low. It's meant to cover your throat."

"Thank you. I'm going to stay at the public house tonight, all right? I've to be in court early in the morning. Larceny case, won't take long. I should be home by midday if I don't stop at the wharf. You be good."

Her eyes followed his sauntering figure to the door. Yet, her mind raced. His office, the daybooks, the secrets hidden in the bureau plat. She blinked, clearing her countenance.

"Oh." He paused at the door. "Good news from New York. I've word from Kit Beck. He should be here by month's end, and I can start a deposition."

"Kit…who?"

"Beck, Kit Beck. Elijah's apprentice. Can't stand him, insufferable hand-wringer. I'm going to be in a bloody foul mood, the entire time, mind you. G'bye, darling."

He was gone, with a heady bang of the door.

She scrambled to her feet, tiptoed to his side of the bed, and tugged open the drawer of his bedside table.

The hairpin was gone, and her heart dropped; it was like snapping a book shut in her face. She peered out the window, making out his figure striding to the barn, then moved on to the dressing table. An odd assortment of things—a bottle of scented water, fresh candles, a silver tobacco caddy, a little bag of brittle molasses (Cassandra insisted he keep close by, in case of what she called the "blood drops"). The sheepskin was there, long abandoned for the preferred method of *coitus interruptus,* which he practiced with maddening precision. It was useless; she searched every nook and cranny, but the hairpin was nowhere to be found.

Of course. Now that every night had her tangled in long legs, he'd purged the room of anything suspicious. Pouting, she stood in front of the mirror, pulling her fingers through knotted hair. Well, why not? He was gone, until tomorrow. And it wasn't fair, the way he kept secrets.

Most everything to be said about Asa was in the office. She slipped through the folding panel and stood, arms crossed. It was frustrating, how fussy he was. Not a spot of dust, everything in order—brandy glass washed, decanter stoppered, his current daybook, shut and alighted square. If she touched anything, he'd probably see her fingerprints. It was nearly laughable, but she pulled her sleeve over her hand before she began opening drawers. Nothing, past what she already knew. Neatly stacked papers, stoppered ink, trimmed quills. Laudanum, and a bottle of Dover's.

She flipped the daybook open to the day.

November 2ⁿᵈ, 1773. Sons of Liberty, Dragon at eleven o'clock 'til three in the afternoon. Hancock. Cooper on King at four. Deposition two, three and six.

She flipped backward, finding the words scattered here and there over the summer. *Sons of Liberty.* The *Dragon* was the most common public house in the city; she hurried by it herself many times in her days of freedom, wondering how the doors held back so many bustling bodies. *Oh, maybe it's a secret code for the freemasons. How fascinating!* Mr. Gracey had attempted freemasonry, attended two meetings, and left with the assessment, "a bit too dramatic for my taste."

Or perhaps. She pursed her lips. It was sometimes easy to forget that by action, Asa was a Whig. Everything was done with his tongue so firmly lodged in his cheek, it was easy not to take him too seriously.

She shrugged and moved on to the secretary. It showed some degree of life, only because he filed bills of sale there, crumpled by less meticulous hands. A maze of drawers, dividers, and shelves, he'd labeled everything with cut pieces of paper, stuck with a coat of fish glue. *Billed. Past Due. Paid.* Names, in alphabetical order. Closed accounts, current accounts, leads...names floated. Hodge...Patterson...Randall...Sanders (*oh, he'd gotten Sanders after all!*). She was about to close the doors when she caught sight of an unmarked drawer, to the bottom right.

Inside was a lettercase, clipped shut with a steel buckle. She plucked it out; it was stuffed to the point of creasing the leather. She pulled it open, straining to see. A printed piece of paper was at the front. She removed it and tipped it towards the window to read.

"Mr. Isiah Cooper
Cooper & Sons Practices of Law
King St., Boston
Province of Massachusetts Bay, Wyeth Enterprises
v.
The House of Henshaw, Robert Frederick Henshaw

In response to your request for written testimony, I promise the truth of the following, under the seal of the honorable Mr. Jonathan Holmes, notary public.

On the evening of June the twenty-first, 1773, I witnessed the murder of Mr. William Gracey, by the hand of Robert Henshaw, in the courtyard of Nehemiah Tucker's residence, on Beacon Hill, Boston, Massachusetts. I will not be of much use to you in understanding the events that led to the occurrence, as I was detained in another room for the better part of the evening.

In the exit from the ballroom, there is a corridor that leads to the courtyard through a set of eight-paneled double-doors. For purposes of confirming my account, I was in the room behind the third door on the left, when entering the corridor from the ballroom. It was a small sitting room with a red silk settee and a harpsichord in the corner. You would find the harpsichord wet with port; I spilled a bottle before I left, as Nehemiah can attest.

I was behind that door with William Gracey's daughter, the named Martha Ann Gracey, as stated, previously attached to Mr. Henshaw. I had formed an affection for Miss Gracey some time prior, and I had seen fit to remove her from the assembly when she expressed discomfort with Mr. Henshaw's presence. I witnessed (before closing the door), that Mr. Henshaw saw my hand on Miss Gracey's back; I was not careful in hiding my affection, as I intended to expose our affair to Mr. Gracey the following morning.

Please note case B, the argument for a crime of passion.

Miss Gracey and I departed the sitting room after about two hours, and re-entered the ballroom. I left her with Mr. Gracey, and returned to the sitting room for a reprieve. I found her later in the courtyard, just outside a circle of ladies: Abigail Tucker, Nehemiah's daughter, as well as Hannah Dunaway and Frances Dunaway, the defendant's stepsisters.

Some of the men gathered in the courtyard, breaking for drinks and a smoke, including Mr. Henshaw, Lord Tucker, Mr. Sanders, Mr. Moody,

Mr. Chestney, Mr. Dole, and the late Mr. Gracey. (These gentlemen, excluding Mr. Gracey of course, are on the list of witnesses I gave to you on the twenty-ninth of June). I was standing on the steps of the portico, leaning against one of the columns, Mr. Gracey at my side. The conversation was, for the most part, civil. Sanders mentioned the Committee of Correspondence, and the mood livened a little. This led to banter about the port officers, stemming from some trouble Mr. Chestney had faced unloading Madeira casks at Wentworth's. Nehemiah Tucker was affronted, but it was nothing that I thought warranted argument; I'd had a few drinks, and was feeling pretty mellow.

Mr. Henshaw, however, seemed intent on ruffling feathers and began presenting statements about me, (supposing to be derogatory) regarding my partnership with the Dutch Indies. His accusations properly upset the Tory company, and with the damage done, he stepped aside, tossing an empty snifter into a rosebush.

(To note: it did come to my attention, on first witnessing Mr. Henshaw in the courtyard, that he seemed fairly intoxicated. He was pale, on edge, and confrontational).

Mr. Henshaw wandered to the lip of the courtyard, and I was so caught up in defending myself, that I did not see the moment he extracted a flintlock from beneath his frock. When I saw the weapon, it was my reflex reaction to speak, in an attempt to talk him down; in retrospect, it was foolishness; my words were idiotic—I said something to the effect of, let's talk, put the gun down—I don't exactly remember, but it only goaded him further. Within seconds of me speaking, he fired.

When he did so, Mr. Gracey and I were about a foot apart, Mr. Gracey angled towards the house. Mr. Henshaw stood at approximately a forty-five-degree angle from the rosebush to myself and Mr. Gracey, and about thirty-five to forty feet in distance. The pistol was fired with a fully outstretched arm. I can attest that Mr. Henshaw is a poor marksman; all that given to conclude, it is impossible for me to say if the bullet was intended for William Gracey, or myself.

Mr. Gracey fell to the portico steps, dead upon impact; the bullet had entered through his skull, just above the right temple. In the ensuing panic, I witnessed Mr. Henshaw attempting to put the pistol back under his frock, but as he moved to run, he abandoned the weapon. Though the attention was on Mr. Gracey and the aforementioned Miss Martha Ann, I witnessed Mr. Henshaw sprinting down a cobbled path that wound through the roses. I pursued him, but only to the end of the drive; it was fruitless in the darkness. I then returned to the scene of the murder.

That is my account. The pistol was recovered, as well as Mr. Henshaw's brandy glass, which I found in the rosebushes. A deputy took these items from me the following morning.

I swear the truth of this statement, again, under the seal of Mr. Jonathan Holmes, notary public.

Signed,
Asahel E. Wyeth
July 7, 1773

On unfolding the last of the paper, a small, handwritten note fluttered to the floor. She snatched it.

Whatever the truth, I fully expect a plea for manslaughter on the part of the defendant. If taken to court, his appeal will be firm: the bullet was meant for me, and William Gracey's death was an unfortunate accident. I would prefer to arrange a meeting in person, to explain the complexities of Mr. Henshaw's grievances against myself and Miss Gracey. These details may provide a clearer path for charges of murder of the first degree.

Copy B, July 7, 1773

She slipped it back into the letter case, heart hammering. How sickening to see it written out like that, like a column in the *Gazette.* And flipping through the papers, some printed, some Asa's slanted script, told a dead-end story; transcripts of conversations with sheriff's deputies. Letters, to names she didn't know, responses–copies made in his hand–to the warrant reward. *I saw a blond fellow on the ferry to Charlestown…a man in a drab knit cap, skirting behind the Sign of the Thistle & Crown on Wing's Lane.* Printed maps, drawn with zig-zagged lines, circles, notes.

She tucked the lettercase back into the drawer and slammed the doors to the secretary.

The notion that Robert hadn't meant to end William's life at all–that it had been Asa–was jarring. He could've been dead if Robert were a better shot. She pressed her fingers into her eyes, turning to sit at the bureau plat. She poured a glass of Asa's brandy–so what, if he found her fingerprints? His guilt made sense, too much sickening sense. Mr. Gracey had died for nothing better than a lover's predicament.

A petty one at that. Bite marks. Tossing curls. Closing doors.

She put back the brandy and stared at the wall. She chewed her lip until she tasted blood, she burned her mind with too many thoughts. Robert Henshaw…Elijah Standish. If Elijah's case could be won, every victory was a loss for Robert Henshaw. *Justice for some, the end of the world for others.* But did Asa see it that way? She sat in silence, unsure where her tears ended and the brandy began.

Because he should have told her. Showed her, and comforted her…but he had kept his tongue still.

19

ELIJAH STANDISH
is an INNOCENT MAN

Richard's apprenticeship was clipped short, and he was free to pursue his dream of drumming for the continentals, which Martha still thought was quite silly. She was careful not to voice her opinion out loud; however much it pained her that the stock was cleared and the shop was shut with a bang, Asa's meetings with the *Sons of Liberty* were not insignificant. No matter how irreverent his attitude, he still rose early several times a week, "dressed like a fop", and was off to the *Dragon*. A few times, much to her unwarranted irritation, she found Cassandra, hands folded over her belly, chuckling with Asa at the bureau plat.

They understood things she didn't. Things she'd ignored, because they were "boring." She started to read the papers, not simply for Robert's name. The *Sons of Liberty* was not just a man's club, no matter the mockery she'd made of the title; it was a Whig society. Some of the most powerful men in Boston–Hancock, Adams, Warren–haunted the news. Names connected to crimes of high treason; racketeer merchants of the same variety, who, when put down on a piece of paper, spelled "Asahel Wyeth" a little too crisply.

❀

Kit Beck arrived from New York, and Martha quickly understood what Asa had meant by "insufferable handwringer". He was a ratty man, barely taller than Martha, with a nervous energy—not bouncing, like Mr. Gracey, but glitching and odd, as if he'd been slapped about too many times as a boy. Stick-thin and small-boned, a shock of fluffy brown hair stood like a tumbleweed on his head, wiry and motionless.

He came in from the road with a strung countenance, as if haunts had chased him all the way from New York to Boston. Cassandra showed him to the parlor, bustling with her hand on his back as if he were a child. Martha perched on the settee, ears pricked, mending a set of Asa's shirtsleeves.

"Now," said Cassandra, in a low hiss, "tell me where he is, and I promise you, I'll spare you Wyeth's tongue-lashing."

Kit blinked, his mouth opening, then clapping shut. He pushed a pair of laughably large spectacles up his nose. "Mrs. Standish, as a c-courier you m-must understand—"

"Courier, my ass! You cannot deviate from Mr. Standish's account. No—you listen to me—" grabbing at Kit's arm so hard, he lurched in his seat—"Wyeth is going to grill your bones to dust, Christopher Beck! I don't care what you saw or what you did or who you told what, but Emory better have his head wrapped around self-defense, or I swear to Christ—"

Martha noted Kit's trembling lip. "Get him some tea, Judith," she muttered out of the side of her mouth. Judith, by then accustomed to Cassandra's brazenness, nodded. No sooner had she gone, boot steps stormed through the corridor and Asa blew in, hair on end, face pale, temples tight. *Oh dear,* thought Martha, sighing to herself. *A headache.*

"On your feet!" he roared, crossing the room and hauling Kit by the scruff. "Pockets out, Beck. Straight like a soldier, pockets out!"

Kit, shaking like a leaf, turned his pockets out. Several folding knives fell to the floor with a clatter. A dirk knife was extracted from his boot, two penny knives plucked from the waistband of his britches, and two razor blades removed from the lining of his hat. Nearly in tears, he handed over a flintlock from his belt, and another, tucked into a strap on the inside back of his frock.

"Is that all?" Asa pressed. "Jesus, you're a walking armory!"

Kit scrambled, producing from the hem of his waistcoat a bone bodkin needle and a sewing awl and placing them in Asa's waiting hand.

"Hell," muttered Asa, eyeing him with a cocked brow. "Martha, make use of these, darling." He tossed them on the settee. Martha, hardly daring to look up, tucked them in her mending basket.

"What were you doing on the road?" snapped Asa in Kit's direction. "Sewing pretty petticoats?"

"Of course," mumbled Kit.

Judith returned with the tea, but it was abandoned to chill on an end table; Kit would need a stiff brandy, Asa alluded, by the time he was done with him. In fact, poor Kit's testimony must have been grating. The office door was closed for hours, long into the evening. Martha sat faithfully with Cassandra, who was drawn, pale, and silent; Elijah the Younger lurked by the window, sneering.

"Papa's a murderer, isn't he," he chided, lip curled. "Uncle Asa's going to turn him in. What an angel."

Martha glanced at him, then back at her needle. It was a fine line to tread, when Cassandra, (for some unexplainable reason) adored her son, almost to the point of fawning. Yet now she sat, head hung, mouth tight.

"Elijah, that isn't very helpful," Martha corrected him mindfully. "Can you go to the kitchen, and have Adeline bring some Madeira?"

Cassandra didn't move or speak, and Elijah, brow cocked, (uncomfortably like his uncle) sauntered out of the room.

She had no idea what time it was when the office door burst open, and Asa's boots echoed in the hallway once more. She flinched; he only walked like that, in eating strides, when he was good and angry. Kit trailed, expression pinched as if he'd been properly shouted at.

"Cassandra *Winifred* Wyeth Standish!" Asa's voice boomed to the ceiling.

Cassandra rounded fast. "Don't you dare shout at me, Emory, I will rap you on the shins!"

"Self-defense, aye? Fine scrabble with a tyke in an alley?" Asa threw up his hands, wild in the candlelight. "A British ensign at Whitehall. I've been wasting my time!"

"Don't you dare say such things!"

"I'll dare what I want, this is as good as dead!" Asa stormed to the dumbwaiter, poured a snifter, then turned on her, eyes flashing. "You need to get a handle on that man!"

"He was running letters, so what? Everybody does it!"

"What! No, they do not! Elijah's an attorney, not a rebel courier! He belongs behind the bureau plat and you bloody know it. Jesus Christ, we've got manslaughter at best."

Manslaughter. Martha put her mending to the side, giving up pretense. Where had she heard that word? *Manslaughter.* It was so familiar, written on the back of her brain, tucked away as something to remember.

"Elijah shot in self-defense!" Cassandra shouted, "and you will argue that or I'll rip your tongue out!"

"Bloody poor argument I've to make, for a man who starts alley brawls! Benefit of Clergy. That's what you get. Let's hope it saves his ass from the gallows!"

"No!" Cassandra's voice rose to a shriek, and she leaped to her feet, tossing her mending to the side. "You will not bring my Elijah home branded like a market pig! I thought you were a good lawyer!"

"Oh, I'm an excellent lawyer, Cassandra Wyeth, and I will argue self-defense if I have to go to court every day for a week. But mark my words, if Elijah comes back to Boston, he'll be squealing like a pig with a fire spit up its ass!"

"I could slap you right now!" Cassandra's lip quivered, her eyes brimming with tears.

"He's going to lose the practice. I'll hand him a broom, and he'll be sweeping the floors of my warehouses for the rest of his life!"

"Oh, Jesus–fuck you, Emory!" Cassandra flung her hands, gathered up her skirts, and brushed past Asa, sobbing. Her wails bounced around the walls of the hall, more little ghosts added to the grief.

Martha sat with her hands on her lap. Perhaps it was guilt– she should've put her arms around Cassandra, or at least patted her on the back–but she leveled with Asa, lips pursed. Close proximity had stripped away most of her apprehension.

"Sir, I beg your pardon, but that wasn't very nice," she reproached. "You know she's not feeling well."

"Goddamn." He reeled, running his hands over his face. Another glass of brandy was poured, and he circled the settee and sank, elbows on his knees.

"You're right darling," he muttered. "I'm sorry. I'll talk to her."

"She's just anxious. With the baby."

"I know." A hand cupped the back of his neck, two fingers pressing into the back of his skull—just for a moment, as if he'd done it by mistake. "I've got a bitch of a headache. Bad bottle of Madeira, I suppose."

She watched him for a moment, then tentatively slid her fingers into his hair. His skin was hot, unusually so, and a throbbing pushed at her fingertips. She kneaded, working her way up; when he didn't flinch, she circled the wound, careful not to touch, and worked his scalp.

"Should I leave?" piped Kit Beck. Martha had forgotten he was standing in the corner, looking like a trapped rabbit.

"Yes, and go fuck yourself while you're at it," snapped Asa. Kit scampered, shoes clapping.

"Sir, what is Benefit of Clergy?" she asked.

"A guilty man's way out of the gallows. Last resort. Not that he's guilty, but Elijah's going to come back branded or he's not coming back at all. If he's not branded he's not free. I know it's not what Cassie wants, but he won't be pardoned otherwise." He sighed. "He's on house arrest in New York. He needed to be turned in, I had to turn him in."

"Oh." She frowned at the floor.

"It's not as ratty as it sounds. Elijah agreed to it. I have to make it look the absolute best for the courtroom. I paid off a limp Tory fellow to bring him to the deputies. He's lucky he gets to stay at the house. If he can just bloody behave himself, I've got a chance."

"Did–did he really murder a British Ensign?" she asked, even though she was confident in his silence. It was predictably bestowed, and she worked her fingers, scowling. It was all right; it gave her a moment to think, and a match flared in her head. Asa's written testimony. *I would fully expect a plea for manslaughter...if taken to court...the bullet was meant for me...Mr. Gracey's death was an unfortunate accident.*

She cleared her throat. "*Hem*–I didn't realize a man could be pardoned for killing someone."

"Oh, trust me, it's far too easily done." He rolled his shoulders. "Far too easily. Darling, I'm sorry, but can you stop touching my head?"

A pinched feeling, of being unexpectedly hurt, flared in the middle of her chest. She dropped her hand to her lap, staring at her fingertips. "I'm sorry–I was just trying to help."

"Isn't that always the bloody case." He stood, jauntily, and snifter swinging, he began to pace. She watched his legs breaking the firelight, back and forth, back and forth in front of the portrait wall, fighting the lump swelling in her throat. Papa Wyeth's eyes were black in the dim, soft, and obscure. "Isn't that always the bloody case? I'm not angry at you, Martha, please, don't cry. That isn't going to help!"

She hung her head, tears slipping hot down her nose. Hurriedly, she brushed them away when his back was turned, his boots beating loud enough that she fought the urge to clap her hands over her ears. Heel to toe, over and over–manslaughter. Manslaughter.

Manslaughter.

"You like what you saw in my letter case, darling? Aye?"

She froze. Even her heart stopped beating, lodged at the base of her tongue.

"Don't worry. Because I'm not angry with you. How could I be angry with you, you sweet thing?" He halted in front of her and curled a finger under her trembling chin. "I won't even lock you out of my office. There's not one thing in this house I won't answer for, or keep my silence if I see fit."

His hand dropped. The pacing started again.

"So go ahead. Go through my things. Empty my coffers. Try my locks. You'll hardly find anything that isn't written on my *goddamn* face!"

A smattering hit her ears. Glass powder blew, sweeping over the floor like a gust of snow. She lurched, her belly twisting in a knot. The snifter had found impact squarely in the middle of Papa Wyeth's face, splintering the glass shield in stealing spider-claws, reaching to the gilded frame.

"Fuck—fuck!" He reeled. "I'm sorry, darling, I'm sorry, I'm sorry—Christ, don't cry!"

But she couldn't help it. She sobbed, fingers over her mouth, and in a moment his arms were around her, and she collapsed into his collarbone. He held her, rocking, his nose in her hair, but it was half-hearted. She could feel his muscles, pitching and trembling. His eyes were shot through with blood, his heartbeat, wildly paced, hollow under his ribs. After some time, his arms slackened and she pulled away, finding him slumped against the back of the settee, eyes staring into nothing.

"Elijah." It was barely a whisper. "*Ahem.* Elijah is an innocent man, Martha." He winced. "Let me get Bennet to clean this up. I'll have Sam bring in a pane from the city—Christ." He unraveled to his feet, holding out his hand. She took it and followed him through the hall. Her tears were dry. Her heart and her thoughts were hollow, save for that new and bitter word.

Manslaughter.

She stood at the side of the bed, chewing on her thumb. A shot of pure laudanum, and he'd gotten as far as his frock and waistcoat and fell, face to the ceiling, one leg slung over the side of the bed, one arm limp over his head. She'd put out the candles, knowing that the harsh light made his headaches worse. The room was cold, the fire too low in the yawning grate. A draft whispered.

Flexing warmth back into fingers, she pressed her knuckles briefly against his forehead. His skin was hot, and his breathing was markedly shallow. She sat, elbows on her knees, and stared at the floor. Then, in a moment of nerve, she gripped the heel of one of his boots and tugged it off. Then the other. He shifted, rolling his head, but his eyes remained closed. Gently, she moved him to the side at the hips and pulled the bedding over his legs. He was drifting, somewhere else. Somewhere where the letter case was empty. Somewhere where the glass hadn't broken, and he'd kept his cool.

She tugged his shirtsleeves gently from his waistband.

She froze, her heart pounding. A sigh slipped from his mouth, pushing brandy; his back curved at the small, then collapsed. He was aroused. God—she ran a hand under her nose, her cheeks smarting with old tears. How could he be aroused, lying there, punched in the head with laudanum and brandy? With all those things to think about. Manslaughter. A murder trial, tight like a cat ready to pounce, toeing the line of impermeable shadows.

"Asa." Her voice was tiny in the hollow room. "Asa, what are you doing?"

She knew he didn't hear her. She slipped her hand underneath the blanket and pushed his legs apart at the knees. Fingers trembling, she unfastened buttons, and worked him over the waistband of his breeches. His eyes flickered, briefly, but his head was slack on the pillow. She circled two fingers and her thumb and traced the velvet skin, once, twice. His hips tightened, his head pushing into the pillow, the tiniest sigh dissipating into blue air.

She moved on the bed, a knee on either side of his thighs, stroking him with slow fingers. From somewhere in a cold, clean corner of the room, in the dead space overhead, she watched herself, bent over his long body, her eyes aching for movements affirming his enjoyment. His fingers, sinking into the mattress. His chin, tipped, lips parted, breath dropping. *Oh, my God*—she bent her ankles, her arches aching, taking him in. He flared, growing harder and angrier under her power.

Then she leaned, pressing a palm into the firm barrier of his belly, and pushed him into her mouth.

How many times, seeking to escape the pain of loss, had she ground out her pleasure on his face? Too many times to count, as the lush leaves of summer roared with fire and crumbled to ash, one by one. She slid down on her knees, taking more. Tasting, relishing salt, like the Boston harbor lived in his body. The glands in her mouth rushed, and she swallowed, her eyes smarting. A tremble ran through his hips. She trailed her mouth, closing her lips, letting his taste roll on her tongue.

She hardly realized she was crying, while she moved her mouth like his fist. Again, and again, watching as his muscles gathered. One of his legs bent in, then the other, caging her; lean fingers met the sides of her head, twisting her hair, piercing her scalp. Tears scalded, pulling in her nose in sharp breaths, stinging her throat.

"Angel." His hand clamped the back of her skull, pushing him deeper into her mouth. "Angel, don't stop—"

She took it, choking, pulling back, dipping down. He was in the throes, and watching him in the darkness lit a wild, aching

311

fire in the pit of her heart. Her neck burned. She couldn't breathe, and she couldn't stop crying.

She knew she was not the angel he was talking about. But it didn't matter.

She cried, and sucked and licked, until her nose ran, and his hand on the back of her head locked, pulling her hair at the roots. He couldn't be harder–he was stone in her mouth, filling her from wall to wall, swelling, throbbing, hot as fire.

"Don't stop, angel–don't stop–"

His spine pulled, neck arching. He was bathed in sweat, sick, trembling–his eyes flew open, his grip working her mouth down his length in a final aching push, bursting in the back of her throat. He cried out. She heaved, closing her eyes, swallowing against rushing bile. One swallow, one more. *Taste the pearl blood, soaking the tongue, stinging the throat with port salt. One more. One more, one more*–and he was done, limp, wrist over his eyes, breath shallow.

She sank back, running a hand over her aching mouth. Her lips tingled, swollen. Carefully, she moved his legs to the side and covered him with the blanket. Her knees were gone, but she made it to the dressing table and poured a brandy, burning a path down her throat.

She turned and watched him, palms on the edge of the table. He was serene, eyes closed, mouth quiet, just sleeping. Hard, like she'd never seen him sleep. Like he'd never written the word *manslaughter* on a piece of paper. As if he wouldn't wake in the morning, and send one man to the gallows, and set another free, for the same crime.

Her mouth smarted with the taste of semen, and it was suddenly humiliating. A strange, silent mockery.

A guilty man's way out of the gallows.

To question the American God was not so hard to do, when she was privy to his witches and ghouls. She had never doubted him before. But to have him beg burned one question, etched deep in the pulsing muscle of her heart. Perhaps he did not have the power he thought he did. And if that were the case—

Asa, what if you fail?

20

TEA SHIPS *at* GRIFFIN'S WHARF

A man, the morning after having his cock sucked by a pretty girl, supposed himself capable of conquering the world.

A truth that Martha stored away, innocently, watching Asa over breakfast. He'd lost ten years overnight. He cleared his breakfast plate, something she'd never seen him do. Fingers flew over the house records; he declared everything to be in perfect order, and called for more coffee.

He'd risen early that morning (Martha watching him dress from a bleary crack of her eye) to right his wrongs with Cassandra, which seemed to have been successfully done. She was chipper, convinced that there was no better situation than for Elijah to be comfortably on house arrest. Much better, of course, than being on the run. The trial was set for the end of the month. Asa was to leave for New York in three weeks, giving room for travel, margin for error, and time to solidify the case. Whatever Kit had alleged, whatever had him clatter into Boston with an armory strapped to his bones, had been duly considered, and smoothed out to the same innocent conclusion: Elijah

Standish had been accosted by an ensign while running letters, his life had been threatened, and he'd shot in self-defense.

Martha, (yawning), sensed there was more to the story, but it was useless to pursue. In the world of law and order, tangible truths were not so important as convinced truths, and a good lawyer could convince anyone of about anything.

"Could he hold the right to practice?" chirped Cassandra, sipping her tea. "I was thinking, I'd like to give up the house in New York and come to Boston. Emory, you and Elijah must open a practice in the city!"

Asa grunted, not looking up from the *Boston Gazette*. "Where the hell is Sam. Useless son of a bitch, this is yesterday's news. Speak of the devil," he muttered, as Sam burst in, nose bit red with cold. He removed his hat, bowed low in the direction of the ladies, and then tossed a folded newsprint in front of Asa's plate.

"East India ship at Griffin's," he announced breathlessly.

Asa took up the paper, unfolding it with a grimace. "That's a bit of a broad statement, don't you think?"

"Sir, a tea ship at Griffin's. The fellows at the wharf are making a row, you're to head to the *Dragon* at once."

"What ship? Give me a name, man, for God's sake."

"She's a British East India ship, sir. She's moored, last night– the *Dartmouth.*"

Asa was on his feet fast, chair scraping. Martha jumped. "*Dartmouth*," he muttered. "*Dartmouth*…" He began to pace, knuckles to chin. "Yes, yes, I know whose ship that is. That's a bloody big ship, that is. A whaler of a ship. Nantucket Island. What's the fellow's name, Sam? Jesus, I can't recall for the life of me…"

"Rotch," said Sam eagerly, "Joseph Rotch."

"Rotch. Right, of course. A Quaker fellow. Been to London, aye. So she's dropped off his oils and come back with some tea, all right. I've got to think about this." He ran a hand over his hair, shrugged his frock over his shoulders, and rounded the table. "G'bye, darling. Off to the *Dragon*." He leaned to kiss her, squarely and audibly, on the mouth. She flushed, glancing at Kit, whose eyes snapped to his plate. He sat gnawing Johnnycakes and gulping ale, still clearly unrecovered from the ills that had plagued him in New York.

"Emory, you can't keep secrets!" Cassandra called as Asa disappeared, Sam at his heels like a trained dog. "This is exciting! What're you going to do?"

For several days, no one knew what Asa was going to do. The tensions at Wyeth House rose to a grating pitch. Even his headaches must've known he didn't have the time; he was blown through with a near childish vigor, roaring in and out of the house at all hours. The days were strung thin between the business at Griffin's and polishing Elijah Standish's case to shine, and Martha trailed Cassandra, maintaining her silence. He didn't lock the office or the secretary or the drawers to the bureau plat, and when he sighed and dropped into bed beside her, her mouth watered with the urge to ask about Robert.

She had to believe he hadn't forgotten.

Barely four days after the offending *Dartmouth* was tethered to the port, Sam brought news of another ship. This one, the *Eleanor,* was the cause of not just curiosity, but firm outrage.

"Rowe's ship. Rowe's!" Asa blew in from the cold, face chapped. "A Boston fellow. God, I've tied my sloops at his wharf I don't know how many times." He threw a pile of paper down on an end table, uncapped an ink well, and strode across the parlor, tossing a quill at Cassandra.

"The note on top," he snapped. "Copy it twenty-five times."

"What?" Cassandra brushed the pen aside. "You can't tell me to do things, Emory!"

"Why is it," he said, in evident irritation, "that I'm to run around Boston, freezing my ass off, while a gaggle of women sits pretty on my settee sewing dresses? Copy the note, and mind, because I'll check your spelling. Not *you*, Martha. Your handwriting appalls me."

"Oh," said Martha, feeling small. She sat, fingers cramped, sewing clothes for the baby. There was little else to do when she couldn't wander through the roses with Ham, tickling her feet in the grass. The kitchens bored her. Cassandra was broody, most of the time. Kit Beck, wide-eyed and skittish, was no companion, and the days of sitting on the other side of the bureau plat, drinking brandy with Asa, were on pause. He gathered his hat, clapped it on, and left, and she jumped as the front door slammed.

"I wonder what could be the matter." She frowned at her stitches.

"Well." Cassandra sighed and took up the quill. "A docked ship must unload, you know."

Martha did know. She had listened to enough of Mr. Gracey's prattle that some of the information had stayed, seemingly useless at the time. A docked ship must be emptied, under a deadline. She rolled her head, an ache pinching at her muscles. It was bothersome for Asa to care about tea, and it was hurtful that he wasn't locked in that office, sweating over Robert Henshaw. He never talked to her about the *Sons of Liberty,* and the secrecy began to annoy her.

The following day, in an attempt to rid herself of a headache, she pulled the rabbit fur cloak over her shoulders, tugged on her boots, and set off for the barn. Her footsteps crunched stones into the nearly frozen earth, and her breath stilled in grey gusts. She tacked the little paint mare she'd ridden, (what seemed years ago, on her first visit to the Estate) and swung into the saddle astride. A chill ran to her bones, but the nice sort of chill—exhilaration, freedom.

She set off for Griffin's with the idea that she might be able to see the ships, at the very least gather some idea of what was so damn important. Once there, she strained her eyes, peering through the ocean mist. Typically, when the ships made berth, the men on the waterfront swarmed, heaving rowboats, tossing cargo to the sodden wood of the docks.

But it was not like that. She didn't dare come close; all along the harbor, grim figures paced, muskets shouldered, forming a barrier between the ships and the dock. The vessels loomed like castles in the water, clung with haze, and an eerie stillness hung low in the air. The *Dartmouth* was mammoth—only a time or two, in her strolls down Long Wharf, had she seen a ship of that size. She only stayed a few moments (irrationally worried that Asa might "catch" her) before turning the horse with a grimace.

Back at Wyeth House, she was hurt by what she'd seen. She hated her ignorance, and wished, with an annoying awareness of her ineptitude, that Asa would talk to her the way Mr. Gracey had. William would've told her everything, with maddening desperation. But Asa was tight-lipped, and she hated it, too. She realized, chin on her knees, trying not to cry, that she no longer found the same solace in indifference.

She was jealous of the strength that fed Asa every day. She wanted to be dragged to her feet, too. Even when she was tired, or drunk, or hungry. She wanted to swing fists, and break glass.

❋

It wasn't just that Elijah Standish had shot dead a British ensign at Whitehall that clearly ground Asa down over the passing days. The hours not spent locked with Kit Beck in the office were invested in grueling travel back and forth to Boston, on, as he muttered, "wharf business." The tea ships were still moored, uniform, bursting with cargo. A petition to return them to London was flatly denied. Asa was listless, and he hadn't wanted to fuck, which was unusual for a man typically so eager.

She tried not to let it hurt her feelings.

Drafts curled under doors and through the cracks of windows. A damp cold, as if the inevitable frost and ice were still attempting to choke the life out of the veins of autumn. She couldn't sleep. His bags were packed, stacked, breaking the floorboards the longer she stared. Tomorrow, he'd leave. Just like that. Months and months of pining, then kissing, then endless nights of making love, desperately attempting to heal the ills of the world in his arms–just like that, it'd stop.

But only for a few weeks, he'd promised. A handful of days for travel. A week in court. A week or two to button up Elijah's affairs in New York. He said it exactly like that, as if it were the only way it would go. She sat at the dressing table, pulling a brush through her hair, over and over until it shone copper in the firelight. He was pacing back and forth in front of the grate, one arm wrapped around his middle, curled fingers on his chin, clutching a lump of papers. A time or two she caught him glancing at her hair, spilling over the back of the chair, but he was stoic.

She threw the brush down.

"What are you reading?"

"Stuff and nonsense." He frowned. "Never mind. I've got a speech to make at the South Church tomorrow. *Hem*–how does this sound: march your asses in a straight line to the wharf, you pack of useless cunts."

He tossed the papers on the bed.

"Oh. I-I don't know. I suppose it depends–"

The frown darkened, and folded his arms, regarding her warily. He didn't speak, so she cleared her throat.

"It sounds as if you're a proper politician."

"Aye." He reached over her to pour a brandy. Her gut clenched naturally, a reaction to proximity and scent. "Not all politicians are lawyers," he stated, leaning at the hips against the dressing table. "But every lawyer is a politician, you see. Every tradesman is, too."

"That's a lot of things to keep track of."

"Not really." He shook his head. "No. It's all the same body. Tradesmen are the heart of port cities like Boston. Politicians are the spleen–the–the anger. A fellow needs spite like that, to get things done." He nodded, more to himself; his eyes flickered, skipping floorboards, bright and consumed.

She turned, her chin on her palm. "What are you doing at the wharf tomorrow, Asa?"

"I told you, I'm making a speech." He leaned, kissing her hard. "I like it when you call me Asa. Keep doing it."

"I beg your pardon, but you know what I mean." She flushed. "You're secretive. I know the ships aren't going back to London, so what are you doing?"

He studied her for a moment. Then he put back the brandy and began to pace again, hands on his hips. "I had a thought," he said. In the shadows, she noted the rise and fall of his shoulders. "Just a thought, mind you."

She bit her tongue, eyes on the floor. A strategy she'd learned, the only one that would ever loosen his lips. *Don't look him in the eye.*

"Martha. I have enemies at the ports."

"Competitors, sir."

"No, no—not competitors. Enemies. You know, the sorts of merchants who rap a common fellow on the back of his knees, and tread on his frock while he's down. You know the sort." He smiled, nodding as if he were carefully curating his words. "The ones who stay in textiles for the sake of loyalty. And anyone who feeds from the Dutch hand, well, heaven forbid. Heaven forbid you should feed at all, unless you're cutting your teeth on silk and needles."

She watched. The fire in the hearth hissed, the only sound in the following silence. "You feed from the Dutch hand," she reminded him quietly.

"Aye." He paused in his pacing. "I do. But I think—well, I've been feeling rather full lately. Do you know what I mean, darling?"

She didn't reply. A chill curled her toes. In two strides he was behind her, hands gently turning her head, holding her face to the mirror. She pressed her fingers between her knees, clamping down tremors.

"Look at you." He pushed his nose into her hair, warm breath tickling her ear. "You're so goddamn beautiful. I can't ask for anything else."

"That's sweet, thank you," she muttered.

"Is it? I'm pushing back my plate, Martha."

"You're speaking in riddles." She squirmed inwardly, not only embarrassment. Nothing bothered her more than unnecessary dramatics. Yet, something told her that though he was bantering to a degree, his tongue wasn't in his cheek.

He rested his chin on her head. "I realized something."

"What's that?"

"I own the port of Boston." He traced her chin, tipping her face. "Don't look away, darling. Look in the mirror, look at me."

She blinked, meeting her reflection. Sky blue stars, wet, bright. Then his eyes, burning bronze over sunset red. He was certainly bantering. She shivered as the lightest touch ran the curve of her jaw, fingers working into her hair at her temples.

"Let me tell you what happens."

"Yes—" Suddenly, her breath betrayed her, and her chest sank. "Yes," she whispered. "What happens?"

"When the partisans and princes tie their sloops to my wharves. What happens when they start pulling pistols on *my* men."

She jerked, gasping. Her jaw pinched, rudely gripped, forcing her face to the mirror, locking her reflection centered. She couldn't move, couldn't bat off his hand as she might've done in the throes of a lively fuck; she was frozen, her heart jumping to a rhythm far beyond comfort.

He smiled at her in the glass. "I opened the doors. I shut them. Hell, I might even get a bit frisky, and toss the key in the harbor. Look at my face," he reminded her, his grip tightening on her jaw. "My eyes."

But it was innate embarrassment that dropped her eyes. To the candle sconces, yellow halos beside the mantel. To the grate, licking flames up a black throat chimney. Anything, not to face the real fire, burning out the russet, trapping her in a window of glass. His hand left her jaw, and he gripped her by the shoulders and dragged her roughly to her feet, pushing the chair away with the heel of his boot. Her body lagged before she found her footing, rooting into the floor.

She inhaled sharply. Cold air rushed and raced up the back of her legs.

"Asa, what are you doing? What on earth–" Her head lurched, bent at the back of the neck. Heat shot from the pulled tendons, racing to her groin; one hand wrapped the length of her hair, once, twice, tugging her scalp, locking her head into place.

In the mirror, she met his eyes. "Asa!"

"Martha, when I tell you to look at me, you look at me."

In the glass, she was wide-eyed. Wet lips parted, pupils throbbing. Her veins pulsed and emptied and pulsed–a fight or flight. Disobedience or–what? Eager subservience. She didn't break, watching his reflection unfasten his breeches. Pushing her down. Elbows smarting on burr walnut, her lungs lost, rushing, pushed into cold air. Still, she didn't look away; he was everything, so much more than she. She was too little, in that moment. Skin, bones, crushable, pathetic; too stupid to understand riddles, and he–he was everything they'd written on paper.

It wasn't silliness. It was true.

"I want you to watch. Watch while I fuck you, Martha." His voice came low beside her ear, thrumming to her belly, racing to her sex. "Open your mouth."

A finger fit between her teeth. Another. Another–in the glass, it was natural. She opened wider, pulling her tongue to the back of her throat. The intrusion sent a rush of saliva pooling around her gums, and she fought the urge to gag. He pulled away, dragging skin over teeth, and cupped his hand under her mouth.

"Spit."

"Asa, that's disgusting!"

"Spit, unless you want me to fuck you raw."

She spat, audibly. In the mirror, still locked by his hand strangling her hair, she watched him wetting himself. Her thighs smarted against the front of the dressing table, her palms dug into nothing–and pain tore through her hips. One thrust; she wasn't ready. Another, knocking her off her elbows, only to be dragged back up, facing herself in the glass. Thrust after ramming thrust, and she watched like she was watching someone else.

The girl in the glass should've been frightened. Begging him to stop, telling him the truth; that the knob of a dressing table drawer ground into her thigh, and her elbows were scraping up splinters. That she wasn't primed, and he burned inside her, stretching delicate tissues too wide, hitting too hard at the front of her womb. But all she could do was watch. His eyes, his face. Never leaving. Sweat breaking at the roots of his hair. Every movement; some she felt, some she didn't.

Her scalp went numb.

"That hurts, doesn't it, darling?"

Slamming, hard–her breath surged.

"Yes, sir, it hurts!"

"But you like it, don't you?"

Harder. God, what was his intention, to break through her body? Now, she was wet. She could feel it, seeping down her legs, priming her inner thighs. She could hear it in the empty room, mingling with the hissing and popping of the grate. Abruptly, she was broken from the glass, and her temple smarted, her cheek pinned hard against the dressing table, his fingers deep in her hair. Harder, harder, harder–she ground her lip, tasting blood, tasting tears.

"You like it, Martha," his voice hissed in her ear. "Tell me you like it, don't lie to me!"

"I like it, sir!"

"Good woman, you are." Hot breath misted her neck, his chin pressing painfully into the base of her skull. "God, yes, pain starts to feel so damn good. You're a little whore for it, aren't you? Tell me again how much you like it!"

"I like it," she gasped. "I love it–I want it!"

"You'll get it, you will. Just wait," he breathed, fisting her hair harder, pushing her deeper. "Wait till it feels so good, you don't know what to do when it's gone."

His palm hit the dressing table, breaking her vision. Her body lurched, the top of her head hitting the frame of the mirror. His breath flooded. Hot, heavy, labored. For a moment, his forehead rested on her temple, and the relentless movement paused. He was swollen inside of her; she knew the feeling. In a minute, he'd be done. In a minute, he'd pull out, and paint her backside with pearl blood.

And she'd be hollow.

"Now tell me something, darling."

"Yes–yes," she mumbled. Her words were nearly slurred; she was hazy, weak, drunk on fucking. Her head lurched, her temples burning. Strand after strand of hair, tested, punished–

"Tell me this," he demanded. "Don't you dare lie for my feelings." His voice was low, guttural in her ear, words thick through clenched teeth.

"Tell me this, darling," he repeated. "Am I fucking you hard enough?"

Her throat smarted. Her head lifted, meeting her eyes in the mirror once more. A woman in the mirror. Not a girl. Her lip swollen from biting. Eyes wide, pupils pinpricks in blue fire. Flushed skin, adrenaline rushing through her veins like ocean surges. She dug her nails into the dressing table, pulling her pelvis over the hard edge. Pleasure smarted, rushing through her limbs, tightening her muscles around him.

She locked his eyes in the mirror.

"No, sir." She swallowed, hard. She dared to raise a brow at his reflection.

"No. You are *not* fucking me hard enough!"

Her body lolled and slammed into wood and wrought iron handles. Again, again, again, and she watched. She watched him sweat. She watched his parted mouth, his eyes, gazing at her as if she were a queen, venerated by fucking. Laid out on an altar, splinters in her fingertips, only satisfied by the sacrifice of her own body. He was right; pain felt so good, after a while, so good, that she forgot it even hurt. Just another feeling, like stepping into a warm bath. Walking barefoot in the summer.

Running through the rain.

A sweet, good feeling. Too good. Meant to be cut short by reminders that it hurt, to warn her that she needed to stop. That she needed to drink the port and taste her tears and hate the pinch of her heart. That he had to kiss the poppy, night after night, because it loved him, and craved his attention.

She didn't finish, but she watched him finish. His eyes never left hers as she took it in, every flinch of his body. The tightening in his jaw. Every flicker of sweat on muscle as the swelling burst, and he dropped over her, gasping, palms pinning her hands. She gripped, aching, absorbing every last pulse deep inside her body. Emptying himself, where he was meant to be emptied.

She closed her eyes, a soft laugh falling from her mouth. It was sweet victory, making a man finish like that! Feeling him shudder and beat. God, now she knew what she'd missed! She tugged her hands loose and circled the back of his neck, sighing, running her fingers through curls damp with sweat.

"Asa!"

"Darling," he murmured, "are you all right?"

"Oh, yes, sir. I'm all right."

326

She hated it when he left her. A rush trickled down her legs, then another. God, yes, it was gratifying! She stretched, fingers flexing like a purring cat. Gently, he lifted her at the waist, and turned her around, pulling her hair over her shoulder.

"Sweetheart," he breathed, "you're going to have bruises tomorrow."

"That's what you wanted, wasn't it?"

He nodded, dazed, pulling her close, wrapping his arms around her, nearly as if he were sorry, but his heart slammed against her ear, wild with exertion. Now was the time for tenderness; it always went that way, and she surrendered to his movements like a dance. Turning when he pushed the house dress from her shoulders, falling to the floor like an unveiled bride. Loosening the bones of her back when he lifted her from the floor, and carried her to the bed, giving in to the cloud softness of bedding and warm candlelight. To wound on purpose, so he could mend in turn; cold cloth on her face, her belly, between her legs, healing kisses from her temples to her toes.

Then she followed his shadow, and listened to the thrum of his voice, politely calling Sam to draw a bath.

She sank in soapy water, the firelight licking her skin golden. He sat on the floor, leaning on the copper tub, papers in his lap, spectacles deliberate on the end of his nose. Certainly not the man who'd fucked her raw an hour before. One hand floated in the water, toying with her hair.

"Martha." He frowned, gathering the papers and squaring them at the edges.

"Yes?"

"I've had a thought." He turned, removing the spectacles. For a moment he regarded her in silence, biting at the end of the temple piece. Then he dipped his head. "When I come back—*hem*. I've had a thought."

"What's that, sir?"

"Marry me, Martha."

She stared at him. "W-what?"

His eyes didn't break. "Marry me."

She rose, hands on the edge of the tub. Something shifted, tangible; her heart slowed—she held her breath, taking it in. She'd forgotten, since what seemed like years ago, he was going to court her, and go to William, and do everything right. So many summer nights had been spent, stealing kisses, drunk on grief and brandy, spun up in aching midnights, that she'd forgotten.

"Asa—I—"

"Marry me," he repeated. He settled, crossing his legs, and regarded her squarely. "I love you. You're a powder-keg of a woman, Martha Ann Gracey. If I consider it, even for a moment—" He paused, and reached, cradling her cheek. "The thought of waking up without you, however many mornings I've got left—well, it drives me mad. So say yes, darling. Marry me."

The word was off her lips before it had even formed as a thought. It didn't warrant consideration; she knew it, the moment she spoke it, and her heart swelled, bursting with the strangest thing, the one thing she'd forgotten how to feel.

"Yes!"

Happiness. Right there, in his eyes. In his smile, breaking his face, like a storm cloud split in two.

"Yes—yes!"

She'd never been more sure that something was right. And to see him happy was addictive. His poppy, her port. She spun her fingers through his hair, crying, and kissed him, over and over.

"Now." He drew back, touching the end of her nose. "I want a proper wedding. I won't be stuffy, I promise."

"A proper wedding! What's a proper wedding to you? You don't like parties!"

"That's right. But *you* deserve a bloody coronation. I can sulk in the corner, don't worry about me. I'm thinking a magistrate from the city, in the spring. Open the windows and the doors, round up some guests, and let Cassie decorate. She'll hang me, you know, if she can't decorate."

"Don't you think we should be married in a church?"

"The church can suck my cock, honestly." He grimaced. "Men of the law do the same things just as well. A judge can damn you or save you, certainly. A good lawyer can make you see God. Say his sacred name, at the very least."

"You're a heathen!"

"That I am." He frowned, then flicked his spectacles open and placed them on his nose. "All right, how about you help me with this speech? Seems like something a wife would do."

A wife. But she didn't help him with the speech. Not two lines in, she was lifted from the tub, gripped by the buttocks, and carried to the bed. The December drafts weren't felt. He made soft, eager love to her for hours, bringing her over the edge more than once, no matter how her sore body grated in protest. Bleary, drunk on a vibrant, bursting infatuation–more than love, something more potent, she tossed and turned, drifting in dreams blank and bright. He fell asleep, head resting on her belly, her fingers playing with his hair.

She brushed the wound, hazy. He didn't stir. She realized, watching the rise and fall of passive breath, that he'd paced. He'd fucked. He'd made love, he'd exhausted himself.

But he hadn't touched the laudanum.

Her fingertips found a heartbeat, thumping softly over damaged bone, and she leaned and pressed a kiss into the center of the diamond.

21

on the ROAD to NEW YORK

A damp, grey dawn coaxed her eyes open. Asa's warm body was no longer in the bed; she sat up, rubbing her eyes. The room was pungent with sex and tobacco and rose water, hailing her sore body and the copper tub. The folding panel was tucked open, and a yellow light flickered cozily over the book boxes. Black coffee spiced the air. She rose, stretching like a cat, and fumbled for her dressing gown.

There was nothing more satisfying, he'd expertly taught her, than waking so deliciously sore, and she was raw. She smiled, wrapping her dressing gown tight, and slipped around the folding panel.

"Oh God–Sam!"

Sam stood by the window, arms folded. His eyes snapped to the wall; she'd never seen a man blush such an alarming shade of red. Asa was lost in a haze of pipe smoke, record book open, lounging low in the chair.

"Martha. Good, you're awake," he said pleasantly. "Have a seat. Christ, Sam, this isn't a Puritan meetinghouse. Stop staring at the bloody wall."

"Yes, sir." Sam stared at the floor instead.

Martha flushed and sat, tugging the gown tighter over her breasts.

Asa tapped his pipe out and leaned forward. "Sam and I were going through the reports, Miss Martha, and I noticed something I'd like to talk you about."

She eyed him sideways. What was this, after a night of glorious fucking, she was being pressed? "Yes? What's going on?"

"Hmm, well." He frowned, checking the record book. "About a week ago, Sam noted a bridle was missing from the tack-room wall. Do you know anything about that?"

For a moment, she was genuinely confused. Why would he be quizzing her about a missing bridle? It wasn't as if she ever left...*Oh.* That useless, listless trip to Griffin's, barely more than four hours out of the house. She'd probably taken the bridle off and tossed it in a corner somewhere, miffed. She hadn't supposed Sam to be elected as the hawk-eyed watch of Wyeth Estate.

"I don't know." She smiled sweetly. "I'm not sure what you're talking about."

"Sam?" Asa bent back in the chair. "Do you know what I'm talking about?"

"Yes, sir, I do," said Sam.

"Then why don't you tell Miss Martha how a bridle came to be missing from my tack-room wall."

"Yes, sir." Sam cleared his throat against his fist, then stated, flatly: "Mid-morning on December the eighth, I was rounding the gardens when I saw Miss Gracey headed towards the barn, dressed for travel in her cloak and boots. A few minutes later, she emerged from the barn with a tacked horse, the paint Arab mare, Agnes. I watched her ride away from the

332

house, down the drive. Thinking it unsafe for a lady, I followed her on horseback at a comfortable distance. She traveled through the city, stopping only at Griffin's for a short time, and then returned safely to the house. She untacked the horse and put her away, but left the bridle on a barrel. I didn't see it at first, and noted it missing." He cleared his throat again. "Miss Gracey did rub her horse down. Properly." He shifted. "Sir."

"Thank you, Sam," said Asa. "Now–" He rounded. "Darling, would you care to explain why you thought it was appropriate to ride to Griffin's, alone?"

"Appropriate?" She stared at him. "I'm sorry, I didn't realize I had to ask permission to ride."

"This isn't an issue of asking permission." His eyes flickered, bright over his spectacles. "This is a matter of something that never should've occurred in the first place. And I have to say, I'm concerned, being as I distinctly told you–twice now–not to ride on the road alone."

Warmth swelled in her chest. Indignation, at the worst; she was still weak from the antics of the night before, but the tone of his voice was grounding.

"Asa, I beg your pardon." She doubled down. "But you can't exactly just…*tell* me where I can't go."

"Really." He leaned forward, pressing his knuckles. "Because I have a piece of paper in my secretary that would state otherwise. You are a ward of the Estate for three more months. It's written into law that I can tell you *exactly* what to do." He poured a cup of coffee, arrogant. "And what not to do. Including riding by yourself, eight and a half miles into the middle of a rioting city, crawling with lobsterbacks and all manner of Tory fiends!"

A sterling silver coffee pot dropped with a decisive bang.

"I didn't see any soldiers." She shoulders rose by instinct. "No one was rioting, the city was peaceful. I just needed some fresh air."

"Fresh air? You can open the door, and walk outside into acres of gardens and pretty things to look at. There're a million and one things you could be doing in the house, yet all I see is you sulking behind Cassie!"

"Sulking!" She bristled. "Sir, that was uncalled for!"

"Well, it's true. You got lucky. Boston is a hellish mess. I want you to focus on the house, all right?" He leaned back, clapping a hand on the bureau plat. "You're not to go riding to the city again. Or the fields. In fact, you're not to go riding at all."

"What! That isn't fair, there's nothing to do in the house!"

"There are plenty of things to do," he snapped. She jumped, startled by a rise in octave. "Sew a pretty dress. Learn how to make a bloody meat pie or something. Not every moment is for fun. Besides, you're not a trophy wife. I'm marrying her," he added to Sam, who nodded hastily. "I have a house to run. I don't expect you to tiptoe around in an apron and mobcap, but you can't just do whatever you please. Furthermore." He nearly ripped the spectacles off, pointing them at her for emphasis. "Redcoats rape little girls like you."

"What on earth. That is dramatic!"

"Bollocks, it's not. They might look pretty in their wigs and jackets, but there's nothing a redcoat fancies more than a riotous rape. So *stay* at the Estate. Don't go outside of the gardens." He slammed the record book shut, opened a drawer, and tossed it down with a thud.

Pure indignation drove her to her feet. He was audacious! Certainly, he'd told her "what to do" a time or two, but it'd always been drowned out by longing, a recognition that she wasn't his quite yet. *Well.* She balled her fists, fighting a flaring in her nostrils.

Brown eyes held steady, brow cocked. "What, why are you looking at me like that? You think I don't mean it?"

"I understand what you mean, Mr. Wyeth."

"Case in point, that's not what I meant." He rose, crossing his arms. "Sam, get the fuck out of here."

Once Sam was gone, Martha bunched her skirt and moved to the folding panel. Abruptly, she wanted nothing more than for the conversation to stop. Deflection was the easiest course of action, the past had taught her, when men acted so silly; an easily employed tactic with Mr. Gracey, who was never there for a fight. Don't say *yes* and definitely don't explicitly say *no;* not that she had reason to fear the wrath of a man crossed in his opinion, but something told her that Asa didn't fight pretty.

"Are you really walking away from me, young lady?" His voice boomed, probably more than he'd meant it to. She whirled, gripping her dressing gown hard.

"Young…lady? I beg your pardon, but that is bold!"

"It isn't. Get back in my office now, and sit down. I'm not done talking to you."

"How–how dare you, I'm sorry! But you can't tell me what to do!"

"Sit your pert little ass down, Martha Ann Wyeth! That's right, I'll remind you, you agreed to marry me last night." His eyes blazed. "Reconsidering, aye?"

She stared at him, breathing hard. He was most certainly angry. And it *was* bold, uncomfortably so, when she had, in fact, agreed to marry him. Not that she would ever take it back; even as startled as she was, it was hard not to drop her affront and hurdle herself into his arms. To agree to things she'd never agreed to, for a man—not even Robert.

Yet, a womanly instinct flared in the pit of her gut. A rising guard, perhaps, even when she knew it wasn't necessary.

"So what?" She fought a trembling lip. "I'm to sit in the house, with my hands in my lap, while you do whatever you please in New York?"

"I'll do whatever I please with two flintlocks strapped to my waist. Can you tuck a flintlock in your bodice? Furthermore, if you somehow managed to pull the trigger, you'd be blown into the next county. Jesus Christ."

"So you *will* do whatever you please." Her brain raced, searching for something—a sideways blow, if not a low one, something he'd have to answer for. "I know what you're going to do," she accused shakily. "You're going to be in New York for weeks, and there's whorehouses everywhere. Cassie told me. That's right, I know you sleep with whores, I read it in Papa's diary!"

Cassandra had told her no such thing, but it didn't matter. He blinked, staring at her in a sort of stoic disbelief. *Yes, I said it—so what!* It wasn't that she even cared. The retort had, seemingly, dealt the grounding punch he deserved; he sat, crossing a boot over his knee. Just staring at her, jaw working.

Finally, "You're concerned about me sleeping with whores in New York."

"Well, you do sleep with them!"

"Hmm." He nodded thoughtfully, curling a finger under his chin. "That's right, I have slept with whores. I've kept myself a bachelor precisely because I love whores so much. A fellow can't enjoy his strumpets, you see, with a nagging wife."

"I beg your pardon!"

"When I was in New York, Jesus. Just a fellow with a hole in my head, aimlessly fucking my way around the Holy Ground. Before that, aye, London. Oh God, the London whores–"

"Stop, you're taunting me!"

"Say what I will about the British," he mused with a sigh, "but an English hussy after a bottle of gin knows her way around a pecker."

"Asa!"

"You realize how ridiculous you sound." He picked up his spectacles, opened them with a flick of his wrist, and placed them complacently on the bridge of his nose. "I'm thirty-nine years old. My life didn't begin the moment I met you, what, not even a year ago? So don't ask me to forgo my dignity for silly promises you know aren't necessary. Besides." He settled in the chair. "We both know this isn't about my propensity for prostitutes. So what is it?"

Of course, he was right, and the dry way in which he pointed it out only irritated her further. What worked on Asa Wyeth? Nothing, that she'd tried. Flirting could be ignored. Threats were hollow; he simply turned his ears off. Even her body was moot, if his mood were ornery enough.

She crossed her arms. "You never talk to me," she said, fighting tears.

"I'm not much of a talker."

"Oh, that is not even a little true!" She stamped her foot. "You talk ears off all day in the courtroom! And–and you're making a speech at the South Church. I saw your papers, it's twenty pages long. Everyone will fall asleep in the pews!"

He snorted–a suppressed laugh–which only sent her flying.

"And I just sit here and guess. I don't dare ask, because you won't tell! Oh–stop laughing at me!"

He watched her for so long that her belly squirmed, then took out his pipe and began coolly packing the bowl. "Sit down," he said levelly. "Tell me exactly what you want to know. Go on, I've got to be on the road in an hour, and I still have to wipe Cassie's tears."

She sat, pouting on the outside, wary on the inside. It certainly looked like a cracked door; his eyes weren't teasing. The worst result would be embarrassment, and that was already distinct, flushing her cheeks. She drew a deep breath, twisting her fingers in her lap.

"I want to know what's going on with Robert." She raised her chin. "And I want to know what you're doing at the wharf."

"I already told you what I'm doing at the wharf."

"You spoke in riddles, and I can't stand it!"

"Martha. Really?" He blinked, nearly an eye roll, and she smoothed a prickle up her spine. "Do I need to spell it out for you? Or is your confidence in me just that feeble?"

"No, it's just that—"

"Darling, tradesmen are politicians. We make the rules, and we change them as we see need. I've been in this dirty business long enough, it isn't the first rug I've pulled." He blew a billow of smoke. "I understand it's new to you, so I'll talk. Then please, just let me work."

"Yes." Her fingers trembled, but she clamped them down. "Sir." *God, you sound like Sam. What're you going to do, lick his boots?*

"I'm going to light a fire under some asses." He shrugged. "I'm good at lighting fires under asses. A relatively harmless call to action and the ports will close."

"You're…closing the ports?"

"Hmm, yes. Give it a few months, the affront needs time to travel to London. In the meantime, whatever sloops I've got

338

loose in the water will be stripped, and sent to Rhode Island. Does that make sense?"

"Yes, it makes sense," she muttered, "but why would you want to close the ports?"

"I told you, I'm a politician."

As if that answered the question.

"How are you going to close the ports, exactly?" she asked, innocently.

"That," he answered decidedly, "I will not discuss. Any rate, you'll read about it in the papers in a day or two. Which I noticed you've been reading. Good for you."

Good for you. He'd meant it as a compliment, but why did it grate her nerves so? As if it were a surprise that she was clever enough to read the papers. If only he knew the way Mr. Gracey had raised her! Bored over record books, because she already knew how to do all the sums. Rolling her eyes over tricks of trade, because she already knew all the loopholes. "Good for you" certainly did not have the same glowing ring to it as "good woman, Martha—oh *God,* yes—"

She clenched her sore thighs.

"Now on the matter of Mr. Henshaw," he said stiffly, "I'm not permitted to speak, and it's only hurting you to ask."

"You're not permitted? You talk about Mr. Standish's case!"

His eyes flickered. "Mr. Henshaw is not a 'case'. He's a fugitive."

"But he *will* be a case. Can't you at least tell me what the bounty hunters found?"

"I can't. I'm sorry. This is a private, delicate, legal matter, and it must be handled as such. When Robert Henshaw stands in a courtroom, I'll put you up in the gallery box like a bloody opera, and you can spit on him from there. In the meantime, as I've said, you have to trust me." He sat forward, clearly irritated. "Mr. Henshaw's case isn't my case."

"It isn't your case?" She stared, heat bubbling at the bottom of her belly—not lust, but definite anger. "What do you mean? You've invested hours into Mr. Standish, and Robert just isn't your case?"

A drawer slammed. She jumped, pressing her knuckles to her mouth.

"First of all." His tone was ice. "Standish has been on the run since December of last year. I've been working this case longer than I've known you, Miss Gracey." Her name was spoken with such chill, a glance had her surprised his lips weren't blue. "Would you demote the importance of another man's life—an innocent man, by the very solid case that I've built—because it doesn't fit your idea of how time should turn? And no, Robert's case is not my case. Robert's case is Wyeth Enterprises against the House of Henshaw, and it's been entrusted to the very capable Mr. Isiah Cooper, of Cooper and Sons Practices of Law." He huffed a cloud of smoke. "But something tells me that *you* already know that."

Tears rolled—she couldn't help it.

"Bloody great." He bit the end of his pipe. "Now you're crying." He rose, running a hand through his hair. "Martha, for the love of Christ, please don't do this. I had a wonderful night with you last night. I love you. Please, don't pitch my head. I have to bring Elijah home, it's imperative." There was a trace of desperation in his eyes. "It's imperative," he repeated. "All right?"

She watched his Adam's apple move as he swallowed. Her nose ran, and she scrubbed a sleeve under. Of course, he wasn't wearing a cravat. His hair was still mussed from making love all night. He always looked so beautiful, like he belonged in the

340

predawn, as if the cogs and pulleys of the world wouldn't run unless he dragged himself out of bed first, and muttered and paced and set things in order.

As if he knew everything.

"Martha, please don't cry." He reached and tipped her chin. "Trust me. That's all I ask. Now, why don't you go back to bed? Sit and talk to me, I have a few more things to pack. I'll ring for tea. Please."

Twice, he'd said that word, in the same breath. She glanced at him, vision bleary. He was soft, earnest nearly. Her challenges were an inconvenience, and they must be tidied up—and fast—because he was leaving. And leaving a sniffling woman (who'd just agreed to be his wife) on poor terms—well, that was unfinished business, and it wouldn't do. And to a blemished man, it was dangerous.

She nodded. She pressed her cheek to his chest when he pulled her into his arms. She relished the warmth of his breath, brushing her hair, when he kissed the top of her head.

But his relief pinched her heart with the slightest unease.

Mr. Gracey's affection had been demonstrated in desperate oversharing. It made no sense that a man (especially a man like Asa, a career bachelor) could expect to tangle himself with a woman without telling her things. Without sharing, even things he didn't want to share. The brief hurt (as she watched him tuck things into his bags, rearranging and fussing), dissipated into the unfamiliar annoyance. She hid it well, smiling over bites of biscuit and gulps of rank Dutch tea.

But it was still there, smarting startlingly like lust.

Everything was ready. Boxes and bags were packed tight in a post-chaise carriage, waiting at the bottom of the portico steps. Jed was tacked, head low, ears flicking off a misty rain. In the hall, voices echoed. Cassandra crying and clinging, Asa making promises. Bennet, self-important, blew in and out. Both Sam and Kit Beck were traveling to New York; Kit for his testimonial, Sam as Asa's unshakeable shadow, and Bennet (heady, with two pistols strapped to his waist) had been elected man of the house.

Saying goodbye to Asa was not easy. The more he walked around the room, spinning her head, the more he looked like an angel, and the easier it was to forget that she'd made a fool of herself. The easier it was, to convince herself she had no right to be angry. Besides, she didn't want him to leave on a bad note. She put aside her tea and biscuits, turned off her head, and invested herself in kisses, in assurances, in promises. For good measure, she knelt in front of the red leather chair, until he was white-knuckled and wide-eyed. The power mended some of his superiority, tripping signals in her brain, and when he sighed himself empty in the back of her throat, she swallowed without choking. He praised her service, but in the back of her mind, something told her it put her in a place. He'd never said she was only for making pies and sucking cock, but in light of that morning's conversation, his gratitude was a little too reassuring.

Besides, she wasn't about to let him finish inside of her again. The night before had been a passionate mistake, one that she'd hastily attempted to correct when he'd stepped out to fetch Sam for the bath. Squatting over the chamber pot to relieve herself had pushed out some of the semen, and under rose-scented water, she'd flushed, expelling as much as she could. She wasn't sure where his head was on the matter, but the hours after, tangled in sweat-damp bedding, ended in him finishing twice into a towel.

It made sense. The pearl fluid was the rise or fall of a woman, the enchanted life-giving elixir; and even though she'd spoken

342

the word "yes," the thought of being pregnant–even as beautiful as Cassandra was–terrified her. The idea had crossed to ask Cassandra for an herb or a potion of some sort to put her mind at ease, but she abandoned the idea when Asa drew her aside to the tea room.

"Watch Cassie," he said grimly. "I think she's laboring, though she won't admit it. Put her to bed as soon as I leave. Maybe if you talk to her, she'll behave herself. She's already had I don't know how many losses. She needs this baby."

Martha's heart pinched. She hadn't realized how precious, how mindfully protected the child was. And Cassandra had wanted an army of boys. She nodded fast. "Yes, I'll see her to bed. I'll-I'll read to her."

"Thank you. Adeline knows what to do, and have Judith stand by if she needs help. If anything happens, I've arranged for a surgeon-apothecary to come from the city."

"Yes, sir."

"Thank you, darling. You be good. I love you. Martha–" He touched her nose. "*No* riding on the roads."

She watched him leave from the portico, shivering in the damp air. She'd said her goodbyes. She'd given as many kisses as she could, without bursting into tears. Cassandra, pale, temples drawn, clung to his neck, kissing his cheek in a rare show of affection.

"You'll bring him back, or I'll sever your bollocks, I will," she hissed into his cravat.

"Branded like a market pig," he assured her, kissing the top of her head. He leaned to kiss her swollen belly, too, and Martha dropped her eyes. There was something too tender about the gesture. Something that didn't make sense with wild fucking, thrashing heads, and closing ports. Cassandra had nearly wet herself with excitement when Asa had told her the happy news, and for a time, lost in questions and exclamations of delight, Martha had forgotten the gravity of her promise. What flowers would spin around the banister in the hall, what drinks would be served, or what color the wedding gown would be took precedence over the fact that at the heart of it all, Asa was a buck in the rut, and she was a wild-eyed doe, tripping over her own unsteady legs.

It had been an easy promise to make, and it wasn't as if she took it back. Of course not. So they'd had a little fight, and he'd mended it well enough, as a considerate fellow. It was still early in the day, so she followed Cassandra into the kitchens, and even tentatively asked if she could help knead dough. Her head cleared as she busied her hands, muscles aching pleasantly as she worked.

It wasn't that Cassandra needed to be in the kitchen. She chose to be, and it was a quality that Asa seemed to admire in women. Homemakers, not idle gentry, languid with nothing to do but pine in silk and stare out of windows. He'd never say it explicitly, but when she wore simple homespun and let her hair down, he may as well have snorted like a bull and chased her through Wyeth House. She smiled to herself, patting her hands on her apron, puffs of flour settling on the floor. Cassandra, mashing aggressively with a mortar, winced and leaned into the counter.

Martha glanced. "Are you in labor, Cassie?"

Cassandra grunted. "Maybe. It's hard to tell. The buggers like to pull tricks, at the end. Get my hopes up."

"Mr. Wyeth said you were in labor. He said you should go to bed."

"What the hell does he know," Cassandra muttered, mashing once more. "I'll go to bed once my feet can't hold me up anymore. Gah–Jesus, little heathen!" She grimaced again, biting her lip.

Martha watched warily, her heart pacing uncomfortably fast. After a moment: "Cassie. What–what does it feel like?"

"What does it feel like?" Cassandra snorted, straightening. "Well. A bit like being gutted on the inside, honestly. Like your womb's been shredded to ribbons, and the little ghoul is in there, just laughing and pulling on 'em." She shook out her apron. "But when you hear the cry you've been waiting for, for so many months, well, you just sort of forget the pain."

"What does it feel like..." She hesitated, flushing. "Being...you know..."

Cassandra cocked a brow. "Pregnant? Why, are you?"

"No! Of course not. I've been careful."

"Well." The apron was tossed to the side, and Cassandra stretched through her spine, hands behind her head. "My brother's going to want babies out of you, I can tell you that. God, you should've seen him with little Elijah. I hardly needed a nursemaid, he brooded over that baby like a mother hen." She chuckled. "He'd tuck him in the front of his frock and do up the buttons so he didn't fall out. They paced all over the house in New York, reading law books. Elijah and I actually got to sleep, and Emory got my boy through the worst of the colic."

Martha smiled weakly, her brain ordering her to pass over what Cassandra had said.

"At first," Cassandra sighed. "I was ill, and very tired. And then, when your belly starts to push out, you feel it. Like a glow. A warmth, right there where the baby grows."

"Can you feel it... move?"

"Oh yes. Not at first, but a few months in. Wriggling like a fish. And you feel like a queen–like you rule your house. Like you'd bite the head off anyone who dared cross you. And when you look at your man…" She sighed again, smiling distantly. "You love him ten times more, and you're bound to him ten times tighter. Just knowing you're carrying a part of him, from a part of him, you know? It's damn heady."

The fire in the hearth crackled, and a draft whistled under the door. Martha watched the flames, eyes dry. A punch landed in the middle of her heart, the part that was always sore. The part that never seemed to scab over.

Cassandra's happiness wasn't hitting her in quite the way she'd wanted. Suddenly, she *did* feel bound–trapped. How easy it had been to say yes, when she was limp and hazy and thoroughly loved…she'd handed over everything, with one word. Her thoughts. Her body. Her idle time.

Her freedom. And her desires–*Robert*–brushed to the side.

She fumbled, pulling off her apron. Cassandra's eyes screwed shut, a hand pressing into her belly.

"It wouldn't hurt to lay down, for a little," said Martha, forcing herself to sound bright. "Just to rest. Here." She threaded her arm through Cassandra's, who grunted in gratitude. "Let me help you."

She kept her word, poker-straight by Cassandra's side, mouthing passages from a crumpled copy of *A Midsummer Night's Dream*. Puck's assertion, "I'll put a girdle round about the earth in forty minutes," brought heavy snores from the pile of blankets, and Martha stood, her knees cracking. Her toes were cold, her fingers cramped. Adeline and Judith drifted in and out, bringing towels, soaps, and basins. Two chairs were arranged in front of the grate, facing one another.

Martha glanced at Cassandra. Her expression was close to peaceful, if not slightly strained; otherwise, the labor was only betrayed by an occasional wince.

She left, her heart heavy, and paced in her room, where she hadn't spent a night in weeks. She tried not to think, but her brain was too full, too tangled. Her fists clenched and unclenched. Time passed–how much, she did not know. A glass of Madeira, and another. Another. The world outside roiled grey, the only light cast by carnation cinders in the fireplace.

Out of nowhere, Robert's eyes ate holes through her heart. Perhaps it was the suffering caused by her "no," but there was something else that bothered her. As easy as it was to be with Asa–to make love to him, to laugh with him over a brandy–he had a definite hold on her that Robert never had. Robert had been dismissible. His opinions, though noted as far as were necessary to gain his favor, were inwardly disregarded.

But not Asa Wyeth.

Asa was going to be her husband. Furthermore, he was currently her warden. An easy truth to forget, when wardens didn't typically have their wards begging for more cock. By that fact, on paper, she "had" to listen to him; it was a heavy realization, for a girl who'd never been disobedient in her life. No one had ever given her a substantial rule to break. Robert had courted her in a manner that only inconvenienced her when she was with him, and sweet Mr. Gracey had never said *don't do this* or *don't do that.*

Must wives really be subservient to a man, forever? Cassandra certainly didn't seem like the bending and breaking sort. She told Asa "what to do" all the time, whether he listened or not. But what was she like with Elijah Standish? To love a man who'd been merely accused of murder seemed blind and unforgivable. Yet, Cassandra clearly loved her man more than anything in the world, despite the turmoil born from his actions.

But to obey a man who saved a murderer? If she were being honest, Asa's subconscious mistakes were the only thing that successfully snuffed her lust. Her point of contention. He turned papers over when she entered the room. He'd moved the hairpin from the bedside table. He still read *Love In Excess*. He never talked to her about things, other than in clipped euphemisms. As if he didn't trust her enough to let her in on the secret; as if she weren't delicate enough to handle the embarrassingly tender bruises on his heart.

She found herself in bed, the midnight hour closing. An uncomfortable sleep came, broken often by the settling of the house. Shadows danced behind dry lids, the sound of muffled cries breaking mindless dreams. It wrecked her with guilt, but a time or two she pulled the pillow over her head to block the sound.

In the torrid center of a dream, she awoke with a jolt. The room was black. The fire had died, and her toes and fingertips were numb. Outside wafting curtains, the moon was high in an ink sky blown with gold-dust stars; the rain had cleared. Her head was oddly sharp, despite the multiple glasses of Madeira.

The cries from the hall were calm.

And the image of the *Dartmouth* was mammoth, eating at both sides of her brain.

In that stillness, the damage was already done. The curtains had dropped on whatever "relatively harmless call to action" would ruin the city of Boston, and Asa was long gone, post-chaise rolling under the moon. She could see him, legs crossed, hat on his knee, beautiful head resting on the wall of the carriage. Angel-brown eyes closed. A book slipping on his lap.

Her heart swelled and broke.

She stumbled to the wardrobe, where she pulled on a shift and a petticoat and a heavy wool gown. Wool stockings clipped with leather garters, a satchel around her waist, the rabbit fur cloak around her shoulders. One of many gifts—rose-cut diamonds. Flowers. Desperate kisses. The best bolts of cloth, the ones she'd ached for, in the days when the gentry passed by on the other side of a foggy window.

Gifts that said–all too clearly, no matter how he attempted to hide it–*Martha, please. Please, don't leave me.*

She never would. Which was why the ties must be broken, and they must be broken–now.

She opened the top dressing table drawer and took out the folding knife, that so long ago had been a whisper. Etched with his name, an aching promise of beautiful things. Once, twice, a trembling thumb ran over the words: *Asahel Emory Wyeth | 1735.*

Then, without a second thought, she tucked it into the satchel at her waist and slipped noiselessly out of the room.

22

ANN STREET

Carrying her boots by the laces, she made her way noiselessly through the corridor. The moon was at its peak; she guessed it to be the early hours of the morning, confirmed by the languidly ticking grandfather clock in the library.

Just past three o'clock.

Asa's room was eerily silent. She'd brought it to life with him for weeks, much to his chagrin. Leaving the bed unmade, a dress balled in the corner, the fireplace roaring at all hours. Now, it was cold, December drafts spinning low. The bed was made, the hearth dead. The folding panel was firmly closed; she pried it open with trembling fingers and slipped through.

His scent permeated the floorboards, absorbed in burr walnut and red leather, immediately awakening the reflex lust. *Stop it, Martha—really.* A picture flashed. A torturous memory, riding him like a lean horse on the chair, gasping, her fingers tangled in his hair. He'd begged her to look in his eyes, but all she wanted was to fuck, to grind her feelings into nothing. To forget, to think about the pleasure and the pleasure only.

She stared at the chair, fighting a twinge of guilt. It passed swiftly when she noticed *Love In Excess* was back on the bookshelf, tucked between *Milton* and *Dryden*.

Of course, she crossed the room and plucked it out, irritation bristling. She read the note in the front again, once, twice. *Forever, G.* Heat pooled in her belly, her toes curling cold. If that girl were here today, she'd slap the daylights out of her! Perhaps a ringing slap would've saved Asa the heartbreak, and she the doubt. Still, it wasn't just Grace that peeved her. Asa should've burned that book, the morning he'd taken her virginity–no, the day he'd first kissed her. Instead, he kept reading it and reading it. She flipped through the pages, the worn paper blue under the moonlight. It was unmarked other than the note in the front, and she was about to return it to its begrudged place, when she caught sight of curved black script–a note, on the inside back cover.

Asa's handwriting. She moved to the window, a sick feeling stealing in. What now, more blows to the heart, another reason to doubt herself? She strained to make out the words.

Angel, I'm sorry.

I'm sorry that I shut the door. I'm sorry that I didn't say goodbye. I'm sorry I didn't always say the right things. Forgive me. Please, let me go. I'm so goddamn tired. I'm tired of going to sleep and waking up, I'm tired of finding things to push you out of my head. I want to purge you. I hate you. Take the shackles off, angel, please, pull the trigger. Whatever it takes for you to stay in Salem. It's where you belong, you goddamn witch, I would dig you from the grave just to fuck your bones, I would burn you at the stake.

I would scatter your ashes on the grounds of Henshaw House, where you belong. I'd piss on them. You've raped me. You've ruined me.

I'm sorry, I'm sorry, I'm sorry–please, angel, forgive me! I love you.

351

She snapped the cover shut and pushed the book back in its place, her mouth full of cold spit. She swallowed hard, forcing it down. For a few minutes she simply stood, knuckles to her lips, shaking against raw sobs, but no tears came; her eyes were dusty and painful. The brandy decanter glittered on the bureau plat, and she lurched, popped the stopper, and drank. Fire spat through her veins. Her heart reared, and she raced, fumbling through drawers, not caring what was displaced, not caring if he knew.

Real anger. True, to her core, and she'd never been angry at Asa like that. Who knows when those words had been written; it could've been yesterday–or seven years ago. It didn't matter. It stung, harsher than if he'd slapped her across the face. Cutting with the same connotation, but worse.

Worse because it wasn't his fault, and it was her misunderstanding that drove the knife so excruciatingly. Furthermore, he was right. His life hadn't begun the moment he'd met her, and neither had hers.

And it didn't end, the moment she loved him.

She ransacked his office. She opened every drawer, flung open every door, tossing things back in their places. In the back of a drawer in the secretary she found a few rolling musket balls and a small box of twisted powder paper, but whatever weapons he kept stashed in the suite had evidently been entrusted to Bennet. Damn–*damn it!* She stood in the middle of the room, her head frighteningly clear. *Think, think, Martha!* Reeling, she reached for the decanter again, took a breath, and poured herself a proper glass.

God, she'd never been this angry. This alert, this nightmarishly unhuman. Perhaps that was how he got things done–rage. She put back the liquid fire, and then, in a flash of red, ears pulsing with heartbeat, she flung the glass across the room. It smattered against the mantel, glittering diamonds raining over the floor.

Jesus, what is wrong with you, you've woken the house! She waited like stone but heard nothing, nothing but her heart, assaulting her ears. Skittering glass, powder on the floorboards…

Of course. Of course!

She hitched her skirts and darted back to the office, where she stuffed her satchel with the loose powder papers. Then she gathered her boots and slipped out, closing the door noiselessly behind her.

In the parlor, Papa Wyeth was caged behind a new pane of glass, his eyes–Asa's–watching her innocently. God, as if he'd never done anything wrong in his life! The portrait beside him didn't look like Asa anymore. Too young, too innocent, certainly no one she'd ever known, certainly not a man she'd ever loved so much it hurt. Or been so angry with, she could've punched herself.

She dragged a chair, climbed it, and stood on her tiptoes. For a moment, she simply stared at the pistol. A reverent shrine, an offering to all the ghosts that moaned down the corridors. Then, hands shaking, she reached for it; it balanced delicately on two brass hooks, much heavier than she'd expected. She wrestled for a moment until it broke free, pulling her wrist to her side. Breathless, she stepped down and stood shivering in the middle of the room.

Polished bone, with a slick brass barrel and lock. The steel side plates were decorated in curling, scripted adornments, clinging to ivory like grasping fingers. The butt was capped with rich metal; she turned it, heart in her throat. Diamond-shaped. The center rose in a delicate peak, discolored as if it had spent

353

many years grating on a man's thigh. In tiny letters, pressed into the walnut stock, was a name: *Asahel Moses Wyeth*.

Such a small thing, yet it carried so much weight. She turned it upwards, making out a wad of paper deep in the bottom of the barrel. All this time, it'd been loaded. Watching over smiles and laughter, tea and conversations; evenings playing cards, reading papers, emptying bottles. She struggled with the cock for a moment, her thumb cracking, and finally locked it into place.

A time or two, eyes stinging with cold, she'd stood by his side on the backside of the barn, watching him tousle with the drilling militiamen. He'd looked like a god, pulling the trigger. Blowing an innocent corncob to bits off the fencerow, as if it were the center of a man's heart. Dropping a ball and paper down the barrel, ramrod held in his perfect teeth, forehead bunched in a concentrated frown. She could've ripped his britches off right then and rode him against the back of the barn.

"You don't want to load with cloth wadding," he'd stated, sure of himself. "Takes too much bloody time, you see." He'd gone on to explain how he only used paper capsules, mindfully pre-measured with powder. Half in the plate, half down the barrel. "Just drop the ball, and wad it with the paper," he enlightened her, as if she cared. She smiled, barely listening–thinking about *his* cock rather than the cock of the silly pistol. Nevertheless, some of the information remained, emerging with a yawn from a cob-webbed corner of her brain. She put the pistol in the satchel and padded back through the hall.

She slid out the front door with all the furtiveness of a cat. On the front steps, she laced her boots; the sodden ground kicked up droplets as she made her way to the barn. Thank God that she'd been brought up a cottage girl, unbound by the pomp of girls like the Dunaways. They wouldn't have been able to slip the bridle over the horse's head in the darkness the way she did. Her disordered freedom had offered her both sides of the coin, and for Asa to tell her she couldn't ride was insulting.

Daring, even.

William Gracey had never cared. It had even made him chuckle.

The ride from the Estate to the city was unsettling in its ease. She cried, most of the way.

The road was clear and easy to navigate with the foliage dead. The rain that day had been a mere mist, and the earth was still firm, taking hoofbeats without troublesome give. Eight and a half miles: she'd taken it in healthy trot last time, mindful to slow to a walk a time or two and let the horse rest, and cleared the time in a little over an hour. Her impatience–and an uncomfortable fear, fluttering in her chest like a caged bird– drove her heels, and she rode at a jolting trot, then coaxed the horse into a canter. Earth flew, and her nose ran, eyes tearing in the wind. A low branch lashed her cheek, but she barely felt it.

For a moment she forgot what she was doing, and simply rode, falling into a primal rhythm with the horse. There was no one on the road. It was nearly eerie, high moonlight throwing cracked black shadows over the path. No soldiers. No vagabonds or gypsies or anything that would've spurred her into a gallop.

Not that those things had ever kept her off the roads.

She pulled to a stop on the first hill over the city. The road entered just south of the Common; slate towers and steeples sprawled black, save for a few pinpricks of lantern light. Fiercely, she wiped her eyes on the back of her hand, squinting into the dimness. One hand in the satchel, one clutching the reins, she gripped the folding knife rather than the pistol. She'd filled the powder pan in the barn, but still—would it really blow her into the next county? Had she put too much powder in, or not enough? Was that really all she needed to do, just cock, and fire? Besides, there was nearly no one on the streets. Only an occasional ghost of a figure, lost in cloaked eclipses. Even the taverns had been cleared at that hour.

Nothing to skirt. Nothing to fear. Everything was bathed in moonlit blue, still like a painting. She passed the Old South Church—shuttered. Had he really made a speech in front of five thousand people? How many of them had fallen asleep in the pews? Had he taunted the spleen of slighted men, with the image of her burning his brain?

He probably had. He'd probably done it with a hard cock hidden behind the pulpit.

Passing through the protection of buildings and breaking into the ocean air, a peculiar, familiar smell prickled her nose. She peered down Long Wharf. The water was black, only a lantern or two offering any light. With a grimace, she turned down Kilby Street, picking through the shops and houses, winding her way to Griffin's. The wharf was unusually empty. Fisherman, sailors, tradesmen, shouting, swearing, making it the bedlam that it was during the day, were nowhere in sight.

She slid out of the saddle, her hand moving from the knife to the pistol, and led the horse closer to the water. A waft of ocean wind blew low to the ground, bringing with it a gust of leaves. *Leaves, on the wharf… how odd.* She stooped and picked one up, grinding it between thumb and forefinger, and inhaled it under her nose.

Bohea. English tea.

God, it was a full memory! Brought to a tangible thing, in one whiff. She wiped her hands on her skirts, swallowing a feeling of dread. It was everywhere. Turning and twisting in the placid wind, blanketing the sodden wood. She wasn't entirely alone; a figure wandered here or there, head down, and the feeling in the air was strangely shameful. A lone man with a broom hurriedly swept leaves over the docks into the water. No one spoke. No one shouted. Only hushed whispers lost in gusts.

She stepped closer, her eyes adjusting to the glare of the moon on the water. And the water—it churned, a brown barnyard muck of a color. All around the docks, clinging to thick wooden posts, lapping the boats in the water, were more leaves. Thousands, millions, slowing the ocean to sluggish churn.

Bohea, steeping in the world's cup.

Bohea! Parties and fake laughter, spinning drunk with Robert in the ballroom. Hannah Dunaway, giggling like a bird. Frances, head down, white gloves motioning to follow. Those simple days of paying levies, and drinking tea, the finest tea—sodden in the sea, crimping with salt, the water strewn with splintered crates, bobbing in a moonlit dance.

March your asses in a straight line to the wharf, you pack of useless cunts.

She gasped and dropped the reins, rushing to edge of the dock. Should she care…was this senseless, or was it admirable, a flawless political stunt? Brown eyes flickered, ironic, behind the carnage. Boots beating a war song.

So this was Asa Wyeth, pushing back his plate.

This was what happened when the partisans and princes tied their sloops to his wharves. This was what happened when they started pulling pistols on his men. Real English tea, enough to fill every caddy in New England. The last thing to remind her of the days when tea didn't matter, the days when she sat, a sweet, smoky cup singeing her fingers, erasing the headache from last night's port.

Perhaps it was the cold, pushing at her eyes and sealing her nose, but she began to cry again. Silently, and then to sob, pitching her shoulders.

She dropped to her knees, grasping at the leaves, fumbling to fill the satchel. She stuffed her sleeves, down the front of her habit, not caring that the men, gathering in muttering groups, stared at her. By the time she'd filled the satchel, the moon had rounded the sky, and the docks were beginning to fill, curious faces straining to the carnage in the water.

If anything, once the sting of the slap faded, she should be proud. He'd probably been the only cool-headed one in that room of five thousand. She would've bet none of them had thought about the ports closing. Or why Asa Wyeth would want to close the ports in the first place. Or why he hated some of them, just as much as he hated his Tory rivals.

The Bohea stung her senses, clinging to the walls of her nostrils. A little bit of Hyson, too, if she breathed deep enough. Mr. Gracey's favorite. She'd sort the leaves back at Wyeth House, rinse them, dry them by the fire, and then, she would drink them. In her room, not Asa's. In the tea room, where Bohea belonged, where he still batted off Robert's spirit, where she didn't remember.

She grimaced. Was he shooting his own foot? Not that it mattered—he could twist his tongue, talk himself out of it. Sloops to Rhode Island. Just another secret, that she'd never be privy to the ins and outs of. Well, she was done waiting for him to speak! She was done, waiting for him to offer some sort of balm of assurance to heal the hissing pain of her heartbreak.

She shifted, turning to memorize the picture of the docks, tea churning brown in cupped harbor hands. All the eyes, watching, as if they couldn't believe it were true; too fantastic a tale, that so many men could have the same affront at the same time. That they could all channel it so gracefully, so spitefully. The ships, quiet in the misted darkness, looked new. Faces stripped of years of suffering and hardship, as if the tea were a burden, dragging anchors to the bottom of the ocean.

Turn around now, go back to London, the cold seemed to whisper.

Lifted. Forgiven. *Forgive me. Please. Let me go. I'm so goddamn tired.*

The leaves scratched against her skin, snapping her into awareness. She pulled the rabbit fur up over the bottom of her face and coaxed the horse into a trot, moving down the wharf and back into the blackness of Kilby Street.

And turned on King Street. Who was this Isiah Cooper, the faceless man entrusted with Mr. Gracey's justice? Her vision blurred, the leaves working more and more uncomfortably under her habit. It was too dark to make out signs; only a rare few lanterns were lit, a rare few hems brushing damp brick. The horse's hooves grated in her ears, and her heart, despite rambling justifications, beat uncomfortably fast, tangled with doubts. Second thoughts.

No. No, Asa, you can't just write that—you can't read that. You can't keep that!

What sort of man wrote something like that? *I would dig you from the grave just to fuck your bones—*

A man who should never be allowed to grip her that hard. Secrets for secrets. If that was the way he wanted things, it hurt, like a fist curling around her heart. A flick of his finger, tipping her equilibrium. Her head, aching with unshed tears, shielded her from beautiful memories. The way he made love to her as if she fed his very being. The way just looking at her made his eyes go soft; the quiet reverence, as if he couldn't believe she were real. Was she the sort of girl whose bones he would dig up? *God— stop it, Martha!* She rounded the corner onto Union Street.

And Ann Street. The stones that had held her feet as she grew up. Her happiness, right there, staring back at her in shop windows, in creaking *The Sign Of's*, swaying in the ocean drafts. She stopped the horse and stared, eyes burning. A hunched figure in a cloak lit a lantern; a wagon rolled by, reins slack. For so long, she couldn't look away. It hurt too hard, the tears were too sharp. She hung her head, then at last, she pushed back her hood.

General Store, William D. Gracey, Proprietor.

Swinging at an angle, like a broken arm. The front window (the big glass pane, once the pride of William's heart) was cracked like ice. Not shattered, but split, from corner to corner at a diagonal, meeting in a crystal mess of barely held shards. As if a rock had been thrown, or a fist punched. The discomfort of the tea leaves forgotten, she dismounted and tethered the horse quickly. She'd never feared anything on Ann Street before, but nevertheless, her hand closed around the folding knife, prying it open with her thumb. She held it at her side beneath the cloak and hurried across the moon-bathed brick.

The wrought iron latch that held the door hung loose, worked halfway off the hinges. And the lock…it was punched out. How long? She found it hard to believe that the last time Asa had been there had been time he'd barred the doors. He was at the *Dragon* all the time, and it was a mere turn of a street in distance. Gripping the knife, she pushed at the door with the toe of her boot.

It yawned into blackness.

In a few moments, her eyes adjusted to the dim. The shelves were nearly empty, papers purged from the cubbies behind the counter. The stools were flipped. Stacked where the counter met the wall was a tower of empty snifters, one knocked on its side. The wind gusting through the open door rocked it, and it rolled down the length of the counter and fell to the floor with a smash. She jumped, palms sweating, nails biting her skin.

She waited.

Nothing. Then—a squeak, and a rat flew over the floor, missing her foot by an inch, and hurdled itself into the darkness. Her heart pounded. *Just a rat, just a rat.* The swollen, frantic feeling of fear was one unfamiliar; she'd never been chased, never been hunted, never faced a threat that she couldn't comprehend head-on. Even Robert, lunging at her in the tea room, hadn't elicited the fight or flight, the urge to just run, and never look back.

But she held steady. Still, nothing—it was a tomb. The state of the door might have indicated vandalism, but oddly, the shop was mainly orderly. She breathed deep, taking it in, her senses flaring. A few items were still on the shelves, pushed into cobwebbed corners. Tins, that had once been filled with Dutch teas, coffee, nuts, or millet. Moldy rolls of burlap and crusty twine. In the center of the room, the bins that had once held bolts of cloth, lace, and spools of thread, were empty. Stepping over an overturned barrel, she wove through the shelves until she found a small tin, crouched, and emptied the Bohea from her sleeves and the satchel, packing it tight. Then she tucked it, placing the pistol carefully beside it. The folding knife she kept clutched in a hidden hand.

The door to the counting room was ajar. Unlike the shop floor, it was still mostly the way William had left it, the deep smell of myrrh oil still potent in the cold air. The bureau plat still stood against the wall to the left, tucked underneath the window. Caroline Gracey still surveyed the room from her shelf, like a complacent hawk on a mountain. The moonlight afforded enough light that she could see it had been cleared; the sloppy stacks of books and haphazard paper had been gathered, surely tucked in a cabinet somewhere at Wyeth House. His port decanter was there, empty, with the stopper beside it.

Her eyes circled the room, and gathering nothing, she crossed to the bureau plat and pulled open one of the stacked drawers.

Nothing, other than the ink stains spotting the wood. Part of a broken quill pen. She shut it and went on to the next. Nothing there either, besides a drifting ball of dust. In the bottom drawer, a little brown bottle, half-empty, amber poison licking the sides: laudanum. So Asa had been there. She grimaced, dropped the bottle, and pulled open the middle drawer.

The dictionary. She ran her fingertips over the crisp leather cover. It'd been reverently placed in the middle of the drawer, padded by a piece of red velvet, a neatly trimmed quill to one side, and a short, stoppered inkwell to the other. A shrine. Mindful not to knock it out of place, she opened the front cover, and a tiny gust from the movement blew askew a slip of thin paper. She picked it up, scanning it, her curiosity piqued. How odd, arranged with lines and numbers, like an invoice. And a name…

A name.

Henshaw.

Her heart stopped. Henshaw, on an invoice? She tipped the paper to the moonlight, her heart in her throat, eyes frantically muddling words. *Remit payment…to Wyeth Enterprises…balance due…outstanding balance…*She shook her head, clearing her vision, and drew a shuddering breath.

Deposited to: Merchant's Bank - Wyeth Enterprises - Q1, 1773
For account: H.E. Dunaway — House of Henshaw | Description of payments and outstanding balances
January 3rd, 1773 ———————— £95

February 7th, 1773 ———————————— *£125*
March ——————————————— *No payment remitted*
Sum: £220
Outstanding Balance: £7,536

A debt extension has been made to the closure of Q4, 1773. At the peril of property confiscation, please remit payment in full by December 31st, 1773.

She tossed it in the drawer, taking a step back. Cassandra's voice, grim, tickled the back of her brain. *He had a bad debt once, think it scared him for life.* Life, love, and now money. Where, where had her judgement lapsed, that she'd never questioned these things, that she'd never read between the lines, or just considered for a moment—what sort of man Robert Henshaw might be!

Asa *had* been here. Abruptly, his scent flooded her nostrils, stinging her throat—whether it was real or conjured, she tucked the invoice back into the dictionary and closed it.

She'd trapped herself, somewhere between her own treachery and Asa's infuriating silence.

No questions asked, no lies told. So this was forever, then? Holding back questions behind tight smiles and deflections? Fucking out their differences, at the end of the day?

She froze, knuckles white around the knife. Another rat raced through a beam of blue, tail whipping behind the refuge of the bureau plat. A weight pressed on the back of her neck. She batted down fine hairs, swallowing—again, again, in a feeble attempt to push her heart back down. A presence sucked the air through the floor. A shuffle, a shift. *Just a rat, Martha. Just another rat. Just your heartbeat. Not boots. Not pacing.* Asa's boots, back and forth, back and forth, the unbreakable war beat—

A scrape. A sigh. A groan of hot breath, pushing putrid air—sleep, time, fear—*rum*.

She whirled. Split by the shadow and moonlight, sallow eyes glinting, a man stood in the far corner. Hair hung in gray strings, caked with grease; cracked lips protruded over teeth far too large for his mouth. From one limp hand dangled a bottle, nearly empty, the source of the sour-sweet smell of blackstrap rum. A red coat, straining at the seams, barely covered his chest—so broad she couldn't have closed her arms around it.

A red coat. *A redcoat.*

Redcoats rape little girls like you.

He swayed, pitching with drunkenness. *Run, Martha—run!* But she couldn't move. Her feet grew roots. She hadn't felt the motion or signaled it to her head, but her fist raised, level with her temple, clutching the open folding knife.

"What's this?" His voice was stone on stone, stifled by a Cockney accent so thick he may've had a cloth wadded in his mouth. Wet eyes, grey in the moonlight, glittered. "Lil' girl, what're you doing out so early? No need for knives, darlin'."

Move. Move! What was wrong with her fear? Her head knew she needed to run! She could outrun him in a second, he was so drunk, yet it was fight or flight, and her body was telling her the wrong thing. Too much freedom. Too many close calls she hadn't even realized were close, and now, her bones locked, and the only thing she could do was stare.

"What's your name, lil' girl?" The soldier swayed. "You shouldn't be out alone, not in the dark. You lost?" He took another step, passing out of a beam of moonlight. A sword hung from his belt, loose, the tip just scraping the floor.

She gripped the knife.

"Are you a bad girl?" He grinned, teeth splitting half his face. "Only a bad girl would be out at an hour like this, all by herself. C'mon, now, lovely, what's your name?"

"This–this–" Her tongue was dust. She swallowed, three, four, five times–*run, please!* "This i-is my father's–my father's shop. Please–get out. Sir."

"Get out." He gaped, bottle swinging his arm low. Then he chuckled, wiping a hand over his lips. "God Almighty, what's a lowly servant of the king got to do in this hellhole of a city for some respect? Can't even get a good whore. Knocked under the chin by a girl at a bawdy house, I was. Imagine that. They was shinin' my boots in London, they was. They was lickin' them." He cocked his head. "Do you lick boots, lil' girl?"

"I-I don't *lick* boots." A heat flared, then died, chilled by rigid fear. "This is my father's building, and–and you've vandalized it, s-sir!"

"I wouldn't dream." He spread his hands. "A palace like this? The door was open, I thought I'd have a nip out the cold. We take what we can get, poor infantrymen. Rats of the army we are, in this bloody city. Officers and cap'ins up at the high houses, and us footmen–well, the gutter'll do. A barn, if I'm lucky. 'Aven't you a heart, lil' girl?" Another step ate the distance. His legs were slightly bowed, the heels of his boots hitting the floor with an off-kilter *clack*.

Her nails sank into the bureau plat. *Run. Move. Please!*

The soldier paused. Took a rooting swig from the blackstrap.

"You color that hair, girl?"

"I-I beg your pardon–"

"Only a bawdy girl'd 'ave hair like that."

"I-I'm *not* a bawdy girl!" Heat surged again, and her fingers tingled with blood. "Please, leave! This is my father's b-building. I'll have the locks changed–"

"Your father. Who's your father, girl?"

"G-Gracey. William Gracey!"

"I don't bloody know who that it is." He spat over his shoulder, ran a hand over his mouth. "I don't keep mind of shopkeepers an' common street folk, 'less a willing bawdy girl walks by. 'An you look an awful lot like a bawdy girl. Look at that hair."

"A girl can have red hair!"

Her gut tightened, sucked into the bottom of her ribs. He took a step closer, swaying, *clacking,* dragging. Bottle swinging.

Run.

She bolted. Her hand, now in the satchel, fumbling for the pistol, was seized, caught in a grip so tight her skin sunk to the bone. She twisted, lurching, fighting to keep her fist clutching the knife free—but it was useless. The rum bottle fell with a thud; her backside hit the lip of the bureau plat, sending a ripple of pain up her spine. Both wrists were trapped high in the air, veins smarting, cut off by massive fingers. A cloud of rancid rum and decaying teeth blasted her nose, rushing bile to her throat.

She shrieked, twisting, kicking—

"Let me *go*—let me go! I am *not* a bad woman!"

"Where you come from, lil' girl?" The heat of his body, elevated with drink, rushed through her clothes. "Aye, where you come from? Where's your man, lil' girl?"

Her mouth watered from the smell. She spat, lurching forward, nearly clipping his chin with her forehead.

He leered, the iron-grip hands tightening. "Bloody whore! Bloody whore, spit in an officer's face, aye. No man's gonna come running when you scream, lil' girl. I'll clog your throat with my pecker—"

"You're not an officer, you're an infantryman! Oh, fuck you, sir!" She spat again. Twisting—battering with her boots, wrangling arms and legs wildly in a frantic dance–"I'm Mrs. Wyeth! I'm Mrs. Wyeth–he'll come running, you'd better believe it, with an army! Let go–let me *go!*"

But she was trapped. One leg planted, a boot caging her in–one hand, the one not sweating with the knife, was released, and she clawed and punched. From the spinning sides of her vision, she caught big fingers, wrestling with a black leather belt. Sallow white skin, thighs as big as barrels, bollocks tight–grunting, heaving breath–the folding knife was flung through the doorway. One hand clapped over her mouth, a finger pushing into the empty space at the very back of her gums.

She couldn't scream.

Bile rushed. She choked; her head snapped, her spine cracking against cherry wood, vision pulsing, black to blue moonlight, spinning with rutting grunts and clogged screeching. Her heart wasn't beating anymore, as if her body signaled that it didn't need to. The ceiling rolled. Oak beams. Spiderwebs, ash dust, falling from the joists. A blunt cock, white, half-limp, fondled by a frantic hand, jerking, sweating–bollocks slapping–both her wrists pinned over her head.

Redcoats rape little girls like you.

Her knees locked. Ripped apart. Locked again, convulsing–strings of gray hair, salt sweat stinging her eyes. She tried to kick. Knock his bollocks with her boot–something. Claws. Spit. The glittering whites of eyes…choking on her own tongue… numbness to submission and then, to nothing but blackness.

And then–she was free.

A fist, swinging from the blackness, clipped the soldier at the temple. He stumbled off, one hand to the wall, one on a bent knee, gasping.

"What the hell, can't a fella have a lil' fun with a bawdy girl!"

She scrambled, struggling to stand on legs she could no longer feel. Another figure backed into the beam of blue. Tall. Broad shoulders. A soldier's white britches and red coat. Hair, long, gold, tight in a queue. Muscled hands loose at his sides, blue eyes ice in the dim light.

"Leave off, Brandon," the soldier said easily. "Too early in the day for strumpets."

That voice.

That beautiful face. Those eyes.

Anywhere, anytime, in all her dreams. All her anger, her anguish.

Her port, her doubt, her fear.

Robert Henshaw.

23

TURN OUT YOUR POCKETS

Robert Henshaw.
Not the same Robert Henshaw. The brawniness that had once held a room in command was gone, swallowed by the red soldier's coat. A man who had once had the freedom for fencing, boxing, hunting, was gone, traded for a ghost in sheer muscle, clinging to big bones, the ruddiness lost in cracked lips and dazed blue eyes.

Was it really him? *No, your head is playing tricks!* But then, he opened his mouth to speak again.

"Martha. Martha Gracey. What are you doing here?"

He took a step forward at the same moment her head broke the trance. Her feet planted. Her fingers, with no direction from her head, flipped open the satchel and plucked out the pistol. She leveled it, the smell of black powder tickling her nose.

"Martha!"

"Stop! Don't you dare!"

"Martha." Another step. His boots were bare, no spurs. A musket was strapped over one shoulder with a leather tie, and he fumbled, picking at the buckle.

"Stop!" she hissed. Her thumb slipped on the plate. Her kneecaps shifted, buckling under a surge and sigh of adrenaline. She drew a sharp breath, nostrils aching, fine hairs on the back of her neck erect like a bristled dog's.

"Don't move. Don't move, Mr. Henshaw!"

He held out his hands.

A groan elicited from the crumpled figure slumped against the wall, and the soldier rubbed his eyes, bobbing with rum drunkenness. "Aye, Henshaw," he slurred, "can't an honest soldier enjoy a bawdy girl?"

"Leave off, Brandon." Robert kicked him squarely in the side of the haunch. Stumbling with a hand to the wall, the soldier flopped into the shop room, and with a quantity of clatter and banging, the front door swung shut. The grind of metal on metal shrieked, and the iron bolt settled into stillness.

That man had almost raped her. Much closer to success than Robert had come. Yet now that he was gone, it was as if the strings—tying her to the floor, looped around her hands, holding up the pistol—pulled through the crack of the door with him, disintegrating in the predawn. And she was alone. Alone with Robert Henshaw, in a vandalized building.

On a day of reckoning in Boston.

Asa's treachery screamed, saturating the color of Robert's coat.

Lobsterbacks, redcoats.

Redcoats rape little girls like you.

Her belly roiled, but she swallowed, eyes on the pistol cock.

Robert stooped, tugging the musket strap free and placing his weapon on the floor. It was a display of submission, yet, she'd spent too many hours with Asa—an ever-ready crow with a flickering side-eye, prepared for the worst and expecting it, too.

She straightened the barrel. "Turn out y-your pockets." Louder– "Turn out your pockets!"

"Martha, I won't hurt you. I'm level, I've not been drinking."

"Turn them *out.*" Her voice was a high-pitched shriek, and he complied, turning out his pockets. A sterling cigar case, and a pocket tinderbox. A small pot of dubbin. He opened the red coat, revealing nothing. He took off his boots and shook them out and put them back on. His movements were hurried with foreign obedience, something she'd never known of Robert Henshaw.

Then he stood, hands at his sides. He was right, she could tell; his eyes were clear, unhindered by the churn of alcohol. Without the ruddiness to his countenance, he was nearly common. Just another soldier, starving in a broken building.

Her throat opened.

He shifted. "I won't hurt you."

Everything screamed for her to lay the pistol down. Yet, her heart was at the end of her finger, hovering over the trigger. *You could shoot. You should shoot.* What did the depositions mean, what was the esquire's promise? The statements, the deputies, the loopholes. *Manslaughter.*

Elijah Standish.

"You shouldn't be out at this hour." Robert nodded at the door. "The vulgar ones are out. The ones that sleep all day." He pushed the musket with his boot; it spun and stopped in front of the bureau plat. "The ones they won't let in the disorderly houses."

"What–what are you doing out at this hour?" She fought the urge to blink. "W-why are you wearing a red coat?"

"It doesn't matter. Put the pistol down, for God's sake." He shook his head. "You're here, this isn't an accident."

"Where were you? There were bloodhounds, bounty hunters—"

"That isn't important."

"You killed Papa!" Her voice rang in the stillness, pinging from joist to joist. The moonlight was fading, the room now gray in the predawn. A shadow flickered past the window, breaking her vision. A bird, or a passing figure. Her horse—would the drunken soldier take her horse? What evils would a man commit, in the protection of dimness? Rape, certainly. Plunder.

She lurched, frantic thoughts broken by a flash of red and white. Robert pitched forward, circling the pistol's barrel with a burly fist, and with a turn of his wrist, it came free. She gasped, stumbling, hands on her knees.

He crossed the room and placed the weapon on the shelf beside Caroline Gracey—too high for her to reach.

"Talk to me, Martha."

Just like that. All her bravery and driving anger—her instincts—were stripped from her hands like a toy taken from a child. She flew, bolting for the back door, but he moved like a watchdog, his body blocking her escape.

"Don't!" he shouted. "I swear to God, I won't hurt you!"

"Then don't trap me here!"

Run. But to be stopped, dragged from her horse by the ankles, if she were lucky enough the mare was still waiting? She stared at him, cold air chafing her throat. *The knife. The knife, where is the knife?* Under a shelf, caught under a floorboard.

She was helpless.

She turned. "Are you going to rape me?"

"Rape you?" His expression was genuinely perplexed. "I would never do such a thing."

"Oh—you—you wouldn't!"

"That was not my intent. You misread me."

"You can't take back a rape. You ruined me that day!"

"I was in a desperate state of mind," said Robert hoarsely. "I won't step near you, I promise."

"Did you make a mistake at the Tuckers, then? At a party," she gasped. "We were at a party! Why–why–I can't think of a reason to justify it!"

"You don't know everything." His tone went cold.

"Apparently not! If I hurt you even a little, I can't be sorry for it, after what you did to me at Wyeth House!" Trapped like a dog, her instincts were to act like one. "What, were you drunk that day? Had you taken some sort of drug?"

A flicker of familiar haughtiness passed. "I wasn't. I was frightened if you must know."

"Frightened!"

"Yes. You know it's true. I had everything going against me that day. You." His mouth tightened. "Frances. My cousin. I was witless, through no fault of mine."

"So you thought if you raped me, I'd have to marry you." She turned to the side, hands clutching her skirts, and spat–once, twice. "Tell me the truth, Mr. Henshaw!"

"That is not what I thought."

"It is, though!" she shrieked. "Why, why do you care? All you wanted was nice things and parties–that wasn't me, and you knew that! You had all that already, so what was I, What–" She flung open the top drawer, fumbling for the invoice. "What is this?" She thrust it forward. "Do you have a debt to Mr. Wyeth?"

"Don't talk of my cousin."

"Does the House of Henshaw have a debt to Asa Wyeth? Answer me, now!" She balled the paper, flinging it across the room. It tumbled, stopping at the tip of his boot. "I need reasons–I need something–"

"Don't say his name!"

"Don't you *dare* tell me what I can and cannot say!"

The more her words tumbled, the more the fear dissipated. *Redcoats rape little girls like you.* Well, she hadn't been raped. The world was something bigger, with more give, more take—no, this wasn't an accident! An answer to an aching question, that Asa would never find on the pages of a law book. That he would never pen, that he'd never read.

But she didn't need reasons. She'd cried enough tears, searching for the why. She strung herself weary, waiting for it to manifest on Asa's lips.

So, what now? Turn Robert in?

It wasn't possible.

The pistol was gone. If she'd felt the way she felt now, in hindsight, she might've tripped the trigger. Now, Robert was marked in his distance, hands in plain sight. His chest heaving, face pale, but he was still.

"Does it?" she repeated. "Does the House of Henshaw have a debt?"

His nostrils flared, and he shifted, eyes hard, lips parted, but still he didn't reply.

"Is this what this is for?" she insisted. "Money? You didn't love me, I was nothing, I was an ear to talk into, so why, Robert?"

A wild, primal anger overtook her, and she shot forward, swinging, claws sinking, ripping at the ridiculous red coat, tearing at sallow skin. All the while, he didn't move. Hands at his sides, not even attempting to bat her off. God, he was a different man! Dry, like a corpse. And the look in his eyes wasn't regret. It wasn't remorse. It wasn't pity. It was nothing, even as she kicked with the frozen blocks of her boots.

Finally, he took a step back, raising one hand to his cheek to shield the assault. She reeled, bent at the waist, and vomited into the corner.

While she retched brandy, he watched her in silence. Shaking, she stumbled, and ran her knuckles over her mouth. The air reeked of vomit, but the fear was erased, too weak to matter. *Asa will know. Maybe he'll find me here. Dead.* Yet somehow she knew that if she leveled with Robert–demanded that he step aside and let her free–he would do it. No apologies. No lies.

In an irregular movement, he ran a hand over his hair. "I'm leaving Boston," he said stiffly.

"He had bloodhounds," she whispered. "Deputies. Bounty hunters. Where *were* you?"

"It doesn't matter."

"You left. You left that night, didn't you?"

He nodded.

"Why did you?"

He stared at his boots.

"Why did you shoot? Tell me, give me something, for the love of God. I can't turn you in. You know that!"

"Martha–" He squared his shoulders–"This is a misunderstanding."

"A misunderstanding!"

"You can believe whatever you want." A faint irritation hissed, though he clearly fought it, scuffing the toe of his boot. "Wyeth leveraged me too harshly. He struck a blow at the wrong time, in the wrong place. His behavior that night was sickening, and you know it. Whatever it means to you, I meant what I said."

"What on earth!"

"I meant what I said!" She jumped. His fists balled, his breath shallow, eyes suddenly reddening. "I loved you, Martha! Did you think I was for show? I could've built a life with you if he'd stayed in New York!"

"You owe him debts!"

"You know nothing about debts. Those are not my debts."

"Your name is on his accounts!"

"That is a flyaway receipt! Those debts do not bear the name of Henshaw! I am paying for the mistakes of my mother!"

"So what was *I*, then?" She threw up her hands. "Was I money? Because you knew Mr. Wyeth partnered with Papa. You knew, didn't you? So what was I, an open door? To save you?"

"Save me." His upper lip twitched in a barely perceivable sneer. "I don't need saving now, nor then, from anyone, especially not Wyeth. This is an incredible conversation. I told you the truth. I loved you. I still love you, if I'm being open. But you see how it's ruined." His temples were impossibly tight. "Ruined. You see? You were mine then. And he turned you, just like that. It was easy, wasn't it?"

She pulled the chair from the bureau plat and sat, her knees so numb, her belly so empty, she couldn't support herself. Though he was still, his anger was so palpable, that she wondered if he might swing. But no; he might rape, but a gentleman would never dare raise his hand.

"I know why," he said. "I've watched it. He puts questions into a girl's head. Oh, what a fellow! Why is he like that? He's so goddamn rude, it's endearing after a while, isn't it? And you start to wonder why you didn't fancy him in the first place."

She was about to open her mouth, but something–a barely perceptible awareness, of something–paused her tongue.

She hung her head, eyes on the bureau plat.

"Where are you now, Martha? At the cottage?"

"I'm not at the cottage." She paused, working through the numbness. Then–"I'm living at the Estate."

"With him?"

"I'm living at the Estate," she said stiffly, "because I'm a ward of the Estate."

"You're a ward of the Estate." Abruptly, he circled, crossing his arms, and leaned against the wall by the doorway. A few moments of silence followed, aching in a room gray with impending sunrise. For a moment, her thoughts snapped, dissociating. Had Cassandra had the baby? Was she all right? Would anyone notice when—if—she came home at such a ridiculous hour, with war-torn eyes? Pockets and satchel and sleeves dusty with dictatorial tea.

If she came home. *Home.*

Wyeth House. It was home. All of her desires ached to be there, and nowhere else. Safe, in the big bedroom that was too empty, too clean, with Asa's arms holding her tight. Now that she was here, in the opposite world, her body screamed for it. Her soul ached for it. She belonged there.

Why had she been so angry at Asa for demanding she stay? Such a silly thing! He was more than right. It was his brashness that raised the bristles up her spine, the very thing Robert was claiming so easily charmed. She'd been too wild to be charmed. Robert had failed. Asa had succeeded, but only because she'd wanted him to—sweet Asa. God, he needed saving, more than he knew. A clumsy prince, raised by sailors, cradled at night by the benches of public houses. Wild and ridiculous, a part of Jed. His crown always lopsided, no matter how many times he grumbled and pushed it straight.

She glanced through her fingers. Was this a gift, or a lesson? She straightened her spine. "Yes, it was in the will. It's not Papa's fault. He thought he was doing the right thing."

"Martha." He shifted against the wall. "Are you safe?"

Silence.

"You look thin."

She stared at the cherry.

"Martha." His voice was cold. "What are you doing there."
Movement—she held her breath, counting footsteps. A smell
rose, not the musk-soaked Robert she knew; he now smelled of
work. A man who'd worn the same coat for too long without
washing it. Old earth and dried sweat.

She exhaled, madly recalling smoke and salt. Castile soap.
Honeysuckle tickling a windowsill, vanilla, coffee–

"Please, Mr. Henshaw," she breathed. "Don't come near
me."

He obediently paused, then circled to the corner, positioning
himself in her line of sight.

"You need to at least tell me you're safe," he said. "Be
truthful. I can send someone. It doesn't have to be me. Hannah
is with the Tuckers now, you can stay there. Your face." He
grimaced. "Were you hit?"

Her fingers flew to the place where the branch had stung her
cheek.

"Martha, I know his moods. He's not all there, in the head.
If he's hurting you, you must tell me. I promise, but I can get
you somewhere safe."

He's not all there in the head. It would've been laughable if the
situation were different. "He has moods," she alluded. "He can
be angry." She paused. "Sometimes."

"Did he do this to you—your face?"

She didn't reply.

He exhaled sharply, chin out, eyes tight. "Did he hit you? Tell
the truth, Martha."

With no room for thought, she nodded fast.

He began to pace, boots scuffing dust clouds in the air. "I
can help you." Pacing, pacing; her belly turned. "I have to leave

the city, but I can help you. You can go, you can stay with Hannah, or Mama and Frances. The house has been ransacked, they won't be bothering you–the deputies." He paused. Close. Too close, enough that the smell hit her again. Turned earth, open air. A heavy, cold-chapped hand dropped briefly on her hunched shoulder.

She begged herself to keep her composure. Not to vomit again. Not to cry.

"Martha," he whispered, "I can help you out of Boston."

"Robert. Robert, you killed my father. In front of a crowd– of Tories. Mr. Wyeth's enemies. So you can say kind things to me, but it doesn't change that. That bullet." She hunched, refusing to meet his eyes. Too much was dangerous; not enough was hopeless. "Who was that bullet meant for?"

For too long, he stared, eyes cold, unreadable. Then, his hand still on her shoulder, "William was innocent. Do you really think I would've done something so terrible, out of spite?"

Asa was right.

"I'm not that wretched of a man. It doesn't surprise me that Wyeth hits you. Now he's got you trapped in a wardship, so you'll stay. You'll stay." His voice rose a pitch. "Because he's an attorney, with the nose of a bloodhound. God, you have no idea how harrowing these months have been for me. No idea! You don't know that man, you don't know the peril he's put me in."

She raised her face, forcing softness into her eyes.

"I'd rather go hungry in a red coat than live the rest of my life meddling with these merchants. These goddamn rat-nosed lawyers! I only came back to Boston to turn over the accounts. And then I'm gone–I swear, I'll die on the field if this nonsense comes to a head. I'll be glad to die. Wyeth destroyed me over an agreement that I didn't even make. And what's more, he took you. And now look at you. Beaten. Starved. What else?" He spat. "He's violated you, hasn't he?"

She froze. Was anger more to her benefit, or affront, or fear? Knowing Robert, as he stood before her now, she landed on the decision easily. She nodded.

"He has," she said clearly. "Once Mr. Gracey's assets were settled. About a month after the funeral. He takes me whenever he wants." She kept her tone dull.

"Jesus! Against your will?"

"I don't really have much of a choice," she muttered. "He owns the roof over my head and the meals on my plate. I was– I was attracted to him, at first, but it was strange…and–" She frowned at her fingers. "Fast. I didn't know what sort of man he was. Then I was his. I know Papa would've objected, and once he was gone–"

"I'm sorry, Martha, God–I'm so sorry! I can help you, I give you somewhere to stay!"

"I'm marrying him." She stared into nothing. "I agreed to marry him. What am I supposed to do? I'm a woman with no relatives, and no prospects, all of my assets owned by the Enterprise. Nothing is mine. I have nowhere to go." Her eyes burned. "So I…I said yes."

"You're marrying him." A pass of the old Robert showed. A lift in the shoulders, a straightening in the spine, as if he couldn't believe she'd do something so foolish. Yet something else, too… she fought the urge to narrow her eyes.

She cleared her throat, raw after so much screaming. "I ran tonight, but I have to go back."

Scurrying feet. She jerked her head to the side, catching another rat disappearing around the counting room door.

"Why do you have to go back?"

"He owns me."

"He doesn't own you! You can leave," he said bitterly. "You can run. I will happily offer you safety! If he owns you, why on earth are you here?"

"He's on the road now, for Standish's case. He never lets me out of the house. I escaped. Just for a moment, but I have to go back."

I have to go back. The gravity of her words was a warning shrill, dulled in rushes and ebbs of punishing arousal. How she maintained her poise was nearly laughable. The idea had entered fast, in a wild moment of fitting pieces and searching for reasons; and to say "Standish" only sealed what was surely providence. The answer to an aching prayer, that she'd cried out too many nights. The throbbing behind conversations and smiles and love, the tainting poison at the bottom of every cup, that forever failed to kill her misery. And Asa.

She realized then how much she really loved Asa Wyeth. Here, this was fate; this was love. She could be his answer. His vindication. His pistol, his sword, when he was too addled to know that was what he really needed to wield. Not pens, not books.

Steel, gunpowder; hissing lead. Elijah Standish had been brave enough, and where was he now? A day closer to freedom, with only a word to ever haunt him.

"He won't find me in Boston. However much you want me dead," he said stiffly, "I'm not a scent dog's treat anymore. I know who to stay with. I know where to go."

"You know I can't turn you in." She ran a hand under her nose. "You've taken my pistol. What am I supposed to do, take you to the deputies? It's not as if you'd go."

"Martha—"

Suddenly, the careful avoidance shattered. He closed the distance and dropped to his knees. His hands on her hands, weathered by winter, rough like they'd never been in the idle days of courtship. Too much like Asa's, lean-boned, callouses built into the fingertips, hardened by years of gripping the sides of sloops—no—*no*—

"Don't touch me, Mr. Henshaw!"

"Martha, listen to me." He gripped her fingers, stacked and pinched. "I was in a ruined state of mind, that's how much I loved you! I was broken, you understand! Never, I would never hurt you like that. It was anger, it was protection, because I knew—I know, and you've proven it to me."

He touched the bruise on her cheek, and she squeezed her eyes shut. A gust of breath hit her nostrils, carrying a muddy smell, faintly spiced with cinnamon. *Snuff.* God, Robert Henshaw, rubbing snuff? He never would've done something that unseemly then. He could've made a habit of sneering at the vices of other men, when he was so far above needing any of his own.

"I've proven what, Mr. Henshaw?" She fought to keep her voice steady, but her words grated.

"That he is a monster." He traced the bruise, following the line of her jaw, curling under her chin, turning her face. Her eyes snapped open, meeting his, far too earnest to belong to a man who'd ended an innocent life. A sob caught in her throat, but she stared, dancing from blue pool to blue pool.

"And you don't have to stay." He pitched his voice low. "I have places you can go. I have people I trust. You don't have to marry him, Martha."

"I—I am a ward. Of the Estate. I have to stay."

"You don't have to marry him! If he's hit you once, he'll hit you again." He rudely turned her face from side to side. "This is not the first time he's struck you, am I right?"

She clenched her teeth.

"Is it?"

"It–it is–it is not the first time he's struck me."

Vindication lit in his eyes. It was vile; beyond that, it was evil. Justifying himself with her lie, spoken for a completely different reason. But Asa wouldn't know, it wouldn't go so far! This was all that mattered. For months she'd suffered and he'd suffered, and wasted his time, and told her he had it all figured out, when Robert had slipped through his fingers, again and again.

Slipped through his fingers into a red coat. A shield, a suit of armor. An open door, to his freedom. Yet, here he was–not in front of Asa's court, but in front of Martha Gracey's.

"Martha, you can go. Now. Tonight."

"I–I need to think." She pulled back. It was instinctual, but nevertheless the correct reaction. "He's not in the city," she whispered. "I'm safe, for now. Mrs. Standish has been kind to me. She doesn't know, but she's–she's a friend to me. She needs me right now."

"When will he return?"

"I–I don't know. He said a month, or more. But–" Bile stung sour in her throat. "Robert. Would you–would you wait? You know how much you've hurt me. But if you can help me, if you really made a mistake–" She shifted in the chair, facing his stooped figure. It took everything, grating her bones, fighting her instincts. "When are you leaving Boston?"

"I'd rather not say. I need to be mindful, you understand."

"Before he comes back?" She kept her eyes down, daring and frantic. "I'm not running away with you, Robert. But if you can find me a way out of this–this mess! I don't–I don't want to marry him. I–I'd rather die!"

It was the easiest thing in the world to cry, and her tears triggered the wanted response. He stood and held out a hand. It took her teeth sunk into her lip to accept it, but she did, and he pulled her to her feet.

"Can I write you?" she whispered. "Where?"

He said nothing, only turned, dropped her hand, and crossed the room, where he lifted the pistol off the shelf and placed it in her open hands. She blinked, staring at the weight in her palms.

"Write to me at Nehemiah's," he said hoarsely. "I won't be there, so keep the bloodhounds off. Hannah is Mrs. Tucker now, she will know where to direct your letters."

She pushed the pistol into the satchel, and he stepped aside and gestured through the door. She moved to bolt, but her shoulders were snatched hard, and a cold, simple kiss was ground into her forehead. She gasped, her head screaming with pictures. The silver tea service, rattling. The pink rivers on her skin, high ceilings, spinning with port, unbearable summer...

"I have to go!" she gasped. Stumbling, she pulled her skirts around her knees and ran, hurdling her numb body into a gust of December air. Like the cracking of ice in pure silence, she heard, breaking in mad nothingness–

"Martha! Come back to me."

24

a CUP *of* TEA

The city flew by in a rattle of hoofbeats on brick. A taunting song, manslaughter, *manslaughter*, over and over. She held a canter, slipping in and out of hidden streets, dodging startled figures. Everyone turned to Griffin's like aimless ghosts, called to a churchyard where Asa Wyeth's sins rose from the dead with the coming dawn. Perhaps they, like she, were starved of knowledge, lured by the smell of Bohea, so long aching for such a good thing that even being Boston–the rebel of the world–was not enough. Now, Bohea was nothing but a reminder of the gravest error, or the most horrifying stroke of luck.

Boston faded into black headstones. The path was relatively empty (only a wagon, and a man on foot) and she rode the horse to a froth, eyes locked. The only thing in the world that mattered was Wyeth House. Old rain, sitting on the surface of the earth, made a crust of ice, splintering with each hoofbeat. The animal heaved. She rode at a gallop until miles gone, she reined to a walk, fell over the pommel, and burst into tears. The high shattered, rushing down her arms, loose over the horse's neck.

Even her bones trembled. Sobs wrenched, rattling her head to toe, feet hanging like flopping clubs, dangling from the stirrups.

The horse wheezed, head down, and plodded.

Her sobs died in silent air. She laid still, cheeks smarting from settled tears. The sky was cerulean with daylight when the horse rounded the drive; she scanned but saw no one. Lurking Sam was at least gone, and Bennet's duty was within the walls of Wyeth House. No one could know. If Asa found out, never would he set foot in that shop, no matter how earnestly she begged. The lie was simply too great.

She skirted the yard, rounding the barn from the backside. If she were seen, a ride to the fields was a lesser crime than a ride to the city. In the barn, she performed all the proper things as if Asa were breathing down her neck. Saddle and bridle to the tack-room wall. Blanket hung. She rubbed down the horse, even flipping her hooves and prying loose stones and mud, and brushed her, ripping twigs and balls of earth from her tail. Big brown eyes followed her every move, and in a panic, she checked her steps.

Stumbling down the path from the barn, she detoured towards the kitchen and snatched a basket from the henhouse wall. Batting broody chickens aside, she filled the basket, then dipped back into the yard and slipped in through the kitchen. A few of the house girls worked over the prepping tables. The hearth roared, and the abrupt change in temperature nearly broke her. She dropped the basket, pulling her face into the rabbit fur, and darted up the stairs. It was enough–it had to be– the thought of human eyes on her made her sick. She hurdled through the empty dining room, and on the other side of Asa's room, she barred the door, ripped off the cloak and satchel, and dropped, back to the wall.

She must've sat like that for an hour. The grate was dead, the bed made crisply. Like awakening after a nightmare and understanding that it wasn't real. Something to remember in breaks and flashes. Something that if she didn't dwell on, if she didn't cry about for too long, she would forget the worst parts of. The soldier, pinning her wrists in the air–the memory was fading, fast. It didn't matter, because here she was, on the other side. Heart beating. Small fears surged and died in frantic reasoning. The crumpled invoice. The folding knife, somewhere hidden in the shadows.

And Robert. *No!* No, he was faceless, he was no threat. Encountering him was providence. Not a mistake, driven to life by her flippancy, her disregard. This supposed disregard, by Asa's standards, was righteous indignation. It had brought her here, with a promise.

She rose stiffly. In the mirror, she was a wraith, eyes punched with black circles, hair tangled, skin white. Even without the fire, the room felt warm compared to the damp chill of the ocean wind. Trembling, she slipped out of the habit and ran a brush through her hair, freeing it of knots. After so many nights spent wrapped in Asa's arms, her dressing things had made it to his table, haphazardly tossed in the top drawer. What would hide hollow eyes? Would anything mask fear? Finally, the girl regarding her might be excused as one who'd simply had a poor night's rest. The bruise was not nearly as dramatic as Robert had made it out to be, and a dot of blanc paint was enough to cover it.

Naked, she slipped under the blankets and laid still, eyes to the ceiling. She listened, but the house was silent. Perhaps Cassandra had already given birth. For a moment, she closed her eyes, but like lightning, blue flashed. She rolled her head to the side, staring at the table where she'd placed the satchel.

Her eyes went dry. The light under the door finally broke with scurrying feet, and distantly, a wail faded and swelled. Cassandra was still laboring. Another promise broken, another betrayal. What sort of friend was she, what sort of wife, what sort of woman? Shaken by the horrors of rape now twice, and her head still couldn't understand the gravity. Merely a "thing" that had occurred, an inconvenience, like any small happening in any day. She could barely remember it now, only in scented memories of blackstrap and rotting gums. Nothing to be afraid of.

Not when she held justice so close.

She'd cried all her tears on the way home. Staring at the pistol, she tried desperately to make them come again because they should. But Robert was only segments of a tall, lean body, a different man. And he'd saved her, like Asa had saved her. A blow to the head. *How fucking ironic,* she thought bitterly. A frantic shout rang through the door, not Cassandra, but Judith. Hurried, desperate voices... she closed her eyes. The sunlight faded and swelled through the curtains.

Sleep. Please sleep.

A scream broke the erratic nature of her thoughts. Cassandra. *You have to go to her. You promised.* She rolled, her feet hitting the floor with a painful thud. How much time had passed, how long the cries had interrupted her sick thoughts, was hard to say. The sun was midmorning high, glaring with a nauseating brilliance. *Asa, I'm sorry. I'm sorry, I'm so sorry!* It was too much, to lay in his scent, in his room, among his demons and her broken promises. Something must mend it.

If she'd broken one promise, she'd make good one another. If she must to tell one lie, she'd do everything else with the deepest truth. That had to be enough.

On the other side of the door, the hall was too wide, too tall, too cold. She ate the distance with numb strides and passed into the opposite corridor. Cassandra's room was just down the hall from her own, barely inhabited since Asa had taken her virginity. For a moment, she hesitated. The screams were consistent and wild, but her fear was used up. She shook her head and turned the knob.

The scene on the other side was oddly contained, despite the noise. Judith poked at the grate. Adeline was at the head of the bed, patting Cassandra's brow with a cloth. The woman lay pale as a ghost, her hands knotted. Sweat beaded visibly on her forehead. Her eyes were wild, filled with too much white, the way Asa looked when he had the worst of headaches.

Adeline turned, wringing the cloth. "Miss Gracey, thank God. She's been calling for you!"

"I–I'm sorry," Martha mumbled. "I don't know what happened. I was up so late. How–how is she?" She shut the door firmly and crossed the room to the head of the bed. Cassandra's eyes snapped to her face.

"Martha–Martha!"

"Cassie–" She reached for her hand; it was slick with sweat.

"Emory's in New York, isn't he? He did go? Oh, Jesus!" Her spine arched, pushing her head into the pillows. "He promised he would go, I'll lop his bollocks off if he's still at the wharf!"

"He's not–I mean, I'm sure he's well on the road." Hastily, Martha pulled up a chair and sat. A near-manic awareness pierced the fog of lost sleep, and strangely, her heart slowed. She glanced around the room, breathing in a brazen smell. A rusty tang, a dampness, like new earth. She turned to Judith, who, content with the position of the logs on the grate, was now wringing a towel over a metal bucket.

"Is she bleeding?"

Judith huffed. "A little. Her waters broke."

"What does that mean?"

"Oh, don't talk about me as if I'm not here!" snapped Cassandra, attempting to sit, only to collapse. "I'll lop Elijah's bollocks off, too, if he makes it back to Boston."

"When," interrupted Martha, smiling tightly. "You can lop them off *when* he gets back. Judith," she pressed, "How much longer?"

"Hard to say," Judith grunted. "Hours. It takes a long time, to have a baby."

It was easy to forget that nearly two decades ago, Judith had busied her hands over a different tub under a different roof. A different woman, Caroline Gracey, pushed a dead baby girl into the world, and slipped out of it, as if she'd completed the last task on her list and could finally rest. Martha glanced at Cassandra and tried to smile. Her head tumbled, pinging with memories and voices–Robert's, deep and smooth. The rattling rum-drunk soldier. Whispers of leaves, tickling the docks. The *swish-swish* of an old man with a broom, pushing Bohea into the ocean like dust in a bin, not the precious gold that it was.

She shook her head. "Cassie, have you thought about a name? For the baby?"

Cassandra's eyes settled into a haze. A trickle of sweat ran from her forehead to her temple, and Martha snatched a nearby towel, dabbing it dry. "Yes…yes. I was thinking Benjamin, at first. But it's too common."

"It's a strong name." Martha kept her tone light.

"Yes, but everyone is a Benjamin these days. Elijah got his Elijah." Cassandra smiled, but it was broken by a wracking tremor, seizing her torso; her swollen belly pinched, contorting to a peak, and she yelped.

Martha watched uneasily.

"So." She fought the urge to cover her ears. "What name?"

"I thought Hosea," Cassandra huffed. "But it's so very biblical. Elijah is just as much of a heathen as Em, I don't think he'd care for it. What do you think of Alexander?"

"Alexander Standish. That's a very noble name."

"Noble." Cassandra smiled, distant, eyes on the ceiling. "Yes, it is noble, isn't it? I could call him Alex, for short."

"You suppose it's a boy?"

"Yes, yes. I'm sure it's a boy. After all this, I want to give my Elijah a big strong boy. Standish and Sons…" She breathed, her voice dropping to a whisper. "Standish and Sons Practices of Law. Oh no–Wyeth-Standish and Sons." She smiled dreamily, seeming to forget that Asa had a broom waiting for Elijah at the warehouse. "You're going to give me some nieces and nephews, aren't you, dear? They can play together. Our babies."

Martha corrected herself, shaking her hand free. Her knuckles had gone white, squeezing Cassandra's fingers. "I'm sorry. Yes. Yes, I'm sure, one day." She wrung out her wrist, grimacing. The very thought soured all the aching, beautiful memories. Not as a bad thing–no, having Asa's babies was a matter-of-time fact. But not something she wanted to think about, weak from dying panic, unhealed by necessary sleep and time.

"Cassie." She stood quickly. "Would you like some coffee? Or–" Her mind raced. "Tea. Tea, yes–I have nice tea. Good tea."

Without waiting for a reply, she dropped the towel and turned, darting from the room. From Asa's room, she took the satchel, removed the tin and the pistol, and with the weapon tucked under the folds of her house dress, she tiptoed back into the hall. She paused at the parlor. The grate was alive, the floors spotless, the chair she'd misplaced the night before righted. Hastily, she pulled it back out, climbed on the tips of her toes, and placed the pistol back on the iron hooks. It landed with almost a relieved sigh. Back where it belonged.

Back to haunting the house in silence.

In Cassandra's room, ears pricked with preliminary annoyance, she pushed the tin into Adeline's arms and returned to her seat, gathering Cassandra's sweat-slippery hand. "Prepare that, Adeline, brew it strong," she ordered, ignoring Adeline's horrified expression.

"What is it?" Cassandra struggled to sit. "I smell it…It smells like New York."

"It's Bohea," said Martha stiffly. "I had it, leftover from before Mr. Gracey purged the shop."

"Mr. Wyeth–oh!" protested Adeline. "Mr. Wyeth will turn me out of the house. I can't brew this!"

"Just brew it!" Martha swatted at the hairs on the back of her neck. "Mr. Wyeth isn't here, so there'll be no offense. I won't tell him. Oh, for God's sake," she snapped, broken by Adeline's sincere hesitation. Couldn't these people think for themselves? "It's a cup of tea, just fucking brew it!"

Adeline scampered. The tea was brewed, steeped, and gulped. Three cups gone, and Cassandra didn't say a word in protest. Midway through the fourth, she sat and wearily swung her legs over the bed.

"Adeline," she murmured. "Bring the pot, please, m'dear. I need to use the pot."

"Chairs," snapped Judith, pointing. "Get her to the chairs."

For that time, she forgot about Robert. Cassandra's problems were removed, separate from the demons of Ann Street. Besides, her body was too weary to do anything but follow orders. Blood, sweat, tears were the only things left. Moments turned to half a turn of the clock, then another. Hours.

The room swam in a milky color, like a sky hiding the sun in an endless cloud. Her hands moved, but she didn't feel them, wringing rags and pushing blood in circles on sweating skin. She kept her eyes on the corner. That place, where she was safe. The madness of the world did not affect her when she couldn't touch it.

She talked. She told Cassandra that Asa had said the case was as good as won, and that Elijah would be in the chaise on the way to Boston in a week. She lied, batting off visions of blue eyes. She whispered words that meant nothing. Lies that didn't matter. Her arms ached, wrapped around Cassandra's middle, her bones sinking into the hard chair, bearing down as if the pains were her own. Whatever it took, to say she was sorry. For scoffing, for thoughtless indignation. When he was right, and he'd only said it to make sure she was safe.

What healed that sort of betrayal? Splitting her body in two, starting at the place he loved her the most–her cunt, her love, her pleasure, ripped in two by the bulbous head and twisted shoulders of the largest, lankiest baby, tangled in blood and tissues, screaming to the ceiling.

She waited. The day went dark, and still, she waited, hunched in a chair by the side of the bed. Cassandra lay limp, lips blue, bleeding relentlessly. The baby–a girl–sprawled peacefully over her swollen breasts. The surgeon-apothecary came, muttered over his spectacles, stitched with his head bobbing, and packed up his bag, giving pointed instructions to have her drink the juice of a squeezed orange. Adeline, frantic, tore apart the kitchen from top to bottom, but no oranges could be found. Martha, having spent so many listless afternoons, watching over Cassandra's herbs and potions, recalled little things, maybe useful, maybe not. A time or two, when a headache raged, she'd seen Cassandra drop a heaping spoon of sugar into Asa's tea, claiming it helped "calm the tremors and flush out the pallor." So Adeline made Bohea thick with sugar and fruit tincture.

The bleeding stopped, but the iron smell clung to every particle of dust. Still, she stayed, hunger roaring through her belly to her ears, spinning her head. One moment, and she laid down her head. Another, and she felt Cassandra's fingers, slipping into hers. She closed her eyes. Blearily, she turned her head—was it Cassandra, or Caroline? No, the baby cooed and rustled, and Cassandra smiled.

She laid her head down, eyes locked on the wall, leaking tears that were barely felt. A soft hand brushed her hair, lingering, pushing back the tears.

She clung to that hand.

"Cassandra," she whispered. "Cassandra, are you well?"

"I'm well. Go to sleep, Martha. You've done enough."

25

MY WOMAN, MY REBEL, MY WIFE

Cassandra healed slowly as Christmas passed, with half-hearted celebration. One week, gone. Then another. Young Elijah Standish grew irritable, trapped in the house with his baby sister's warbling cries, and took to the gardens, where he smacked the snow off low-hanging branches or swiped the feet out of unsuspecting chickens. The baby, who Cassandra claimed she still "could not believe" was a girl, was Amy Prudence, or "whatever Elijah wanted, later." The infant now opened her eyes to the chuckles and coos of "Amy Prue."

The baby was sweet, but it was difficult for Martha to understand where Cassandra was coming from. Doubly so, when the child looked disturbingly like her mother, by proxy like Asa. Whomever Elijah Standish was, his pedigree clearly held nothing over the blood of Wyeth, manifested in wispy chestnut curls, the most ridiculously sized brown eyes, and the soft bends at the corners of her little mouth. A beautiful baby. Something deep in her gut ached, a primal twinge that scraped the walls of her womb.

She did everything for Cassandra, as days faded into brutally cold nights. Anything to take her mind away from the words itching at her fingertips. She bathed the woman, massaging her scalp with oils; she rubbed her legs, still swollen from birth. She fixed her Bohea, and Cassandra didn't ask questions. They sat together on the bed, whispering, while Amy Prue slept in the middle, and snow slapped at the windows.

The more time passed, the more what had occurred in the shop faded into a nightmare, something her sleep-tripped brain had conjured. And even though it had happened, it was less threatening when considered in the enveloping arms of Wyeth House. She didn't sleep well, unless she dozed off next to Cassandra, breathing in smoky Bohea, but she could finally just think. The disordered thoughts shook dust and stood straight.

First, it was a pure panic. What had she done? *God—I've ruined everything—I should've gone to the deputies!* Then, flushed with Asa's brandy, she reasoned with herself, staring down *Love In Excess*. No. This was it, the one thing that was better and smarter and more foolproof than manslaughter. Than Benefit of Clergy. Than a silly branded letter. If Asa could do it, other esquires could do it, and just like that, Robert Henshaw could walk free. It was inevitable, after all, that Elijah would come to Boston; she'd spent so much time assuring Cassandra that any other outcome was impossible, she'd started to believe it herself. And Asa's confidence in himself as a lawyer was the one area of his expertise untouched by Robert, unscathed by Papa Wyeth.

Something his, and his alone.

A few days for travel.

She sat behind the bureau plat over a blank paper, spinning with port. Still the words didn't come, and she fell asleep on Asa's side of the bed, sucking ink off her fingertips.

A week for the trial.

She wrote the note, then balled it and tossed it into the fire. She wrote it again. Why did it seem so childish on paper? A Martha and Robert game. Whispers and sly smiles….She grimaced at herself in the mirror.

A week or two, to button up Elijah's affairs in New York.

She was sitting in the parlor, sewing on the settee with Cassandra, when the letter came. Amy Prue cooed at the ceiling in front of the grate, and Elijah the Young scowled at white sunlight. The paper was crumpled, stained with melted snow, delivered in Bennet's gloved hand. Cassandra nearly ripped it, fumbling to break the seal. New York, a dreamland, an impossible place where the damned went to be saved. In a courtroom gallery, on the stand, in chains on the middle of the floor. Cassandra shrieked, bouncing to her feet, never mind that Dr. Warren had sewn her back together a mere three weeks before.

"He's done it, the bastard!" She clapped a hand over her mouth. "Martha, Elijah is coming home!"

Martha took the letter tentatively. The sight of Asa's handwriting sent her heart flying, the tone of his voice hitting her immediately.

Cass,

Elijah's shaken the cuffs. Expect the wagons before we arrive in Boston. Sent them off this morning. You've got too many bloody things, you'd better sort it before it goes through my doors. I won't have you cluttering my house with this bosh.

Edmund was to check the mailbag at Cromwell's Head twice a day. If this is late, his servitude is in shaky standing, and I give you leave to rap his shins when I get back.

Very good,

E

Just knowing his hand had touched that paper, his head had thought those words! The ached rushed, burning for his hands. His mouth. His eyes. Any day, he'd be home; the letter was dated five days prior. She'd be back in his arms, back to being tangled all night, covered in kisses, blushing from his words. Back to fucking like animals until she lost sense of time, as if none of the terrible things had happened. The tea had stayed on the ships and she hadn't gone to Ann Street, back to when she still couldn't quite remember what Robert Henshaw looked like because it'd been so long since she'd seen his face.

For two days, she trailed Cassandra, dusting, changing bedding, rearranging. One morning she awoke to the crunch of gravel in the drive. She scrambled, shaking loose the blankets, and peered out of the window. A line of wagons, piled high with boxes, trunks, and barrels, circled the drive, pulling to a halt in front of the portico.

"You're not going back to New York?" she asked Cassandra, staring at the mess in the hall. She bit her thumb, frowning. Bosh, indeed. Most of it was, taking up a quarter of the hall, stacked so high it brushed the bottom of the buffalo hide. Cassandra squealed with delight, tearing open boxes, and sighing over tacky candelabras and brilliant paintings.

"We'll find a place in the country," she said brightly, brushing dust from a rusty tea service. "Emory will get Elijah back on his feet, I know he will."

Martha's brain pinched, thinking of Asa's off-the-cuff threat—*he'll be sweeping the floors of my warehouses*—yet, her heart swelled with a settled kind of happiness. She hadn't felt it for months. Thank God, Cassandra wasn't leaving! Even roused several times a night by Amy Prue's cries, she would rather sleep by Cassandra's side than alone.

That feeling followed her through the day. Perhaps because her hands were busy, discovering treasures in boxes, giggling with Cassandra over the prospect of Asa's horror. When dinner was cleared, she padded down the corridor, slipped into her room, and shut the door noiselessly.

She poured herself a glass of port and sat, once more facing the blank sheet of paper. She counted out three weeks. Asa's record books were one of the few things not shrouded in secret, often left open to the day. He'd taken the current one to New York–a day would never be missed–but his routine was generally followed. One evening she'd studied the latest, marveling over the detail. A story unfolded, albeit quite boring, of a man busy enough to send heads spinning, on paper more of a mathematical formula than flesh and blood. If he went here, he went there directly after, without deviation. Typically, it was court, the Common if the case was a day and resulted in a lashing, then the wharf, then the *Dragon,* then back to Wyeth House. Days without court were a little more difficult to pinpoint, but one thing was always consistent: he'd ride to Boston in the morning.

Bringing him to Boston wasn't the problem. The problem was bringing him to Ann Street.

She picked up a quill, dipped it, and scribbled a date. Then– *the counting room. He will be in New York until the end of the month.* She paused, biting her knuckle. *I want to discuss now that I've had time to think. Things are getting worse. I'm frightened.*

She shook her head, the complete absurdity of having a pleasant day with Cassandra souring in an instant. How could anything be pleasant with this taunting body, swaying over her like a corpse at the gallows? She read what she'd written, once, twice, until it started to sound like nonsense. She poured another glass, and another, pacing, reading, spinning on her heels, until in a surge of port-driven madness, she plucked the quill back up, scribbled the address, and closed it, using a brass button as a seal rather than the scripted crest of Wyeth Enterprises. Then she padded from the room and through the corridor, where the floor was cold as ice under her feet. Through the dining room and the service door, into the kitchen, where a lone maidservant swept the floor.

The mailbag hung by the door. She smiled tightly, slipping past the swinging broom, and tucked the letter into the depths, shielded by a dozen others. It would be gone by the morning. Head down, she turned away. Then paused, turning back. The maidservant eyed her quizzically but did not comment. Finally, she rounded the door, stumbling with port, and fled.

Curled in a ball on Asa's bed, she cried her eyes raw.

✻

She awoke, her nose sealed. The sun was high, glaring over a blanket of fresh snow. God–no, no, *no*–she scrambled for her dressing gown, but it was too late. The mailbag was empty before dawn. It must be empty before Asa left in the morning, and no one under Wyeth servitude would deviate from routine simply because he was gone for a month. Shadows flickered from the window, breaking the sunlight. Voices reached her port-muddled ears. A *crunch-crunch* of shifting horse's hooves in the drive. Her heart lodged in her throat; she swung numb feet to the floor and pulled aside the curtain.

Long black boots, greatcoat swaying. There he was, hand on Jed's nose, certainly not as if he'd never left. His hair fell tousled over his ears, in need of a trim. A few day's beard speckled his jaw. She stared, her heart thundering. He was wild–vindicated. A frontiersman. The letter was forgotten, and she scrambled, splashed her face with cold water, and braided her hair over her shoulder with trembling fingers. Her body ached, pulling to him, sparking at the fissions–the separation lines, her lips, her breasts, even her feet, so tenderly adored.

She threw a quick glance around the room. The pistol was back where it belonged, the Bohea tucked well behind the other caddies in the kitchen, safe from a man who rarely drank tea. She'd long since polished off his brandy, but he wouldn't mind. *Love In Excess*…she hadn't touched it, since the fateful day of his departure.

She had to see him, to run. She bolted through the hall, out the front door, and down the portico steps, snow burning her bare feet.

She wasn't Grace. She'd stayed. She'd waited.

"Asa!" she shrieked. "Asa!"

"Darling, for Christ's sake, where are your shoes–"

She ran, hurling herself into his arms. The warmth was immediate, the feeling of instant comfort and protection. Figures blurred in her peripheral; voices rose, and laughter rang in dead winter air. She pulled back, searching for his mouth, sealing lips to lips. The bad memories crumbled. She opened her mouth, aching tongue to tongue; he'd been drinking coffee in the chaise–she could taste it–and suddenly, everything she'd done in the stabbing, fear-driven days he'd been gone, made more sense.

"All right," he muttered, pulling away. "Don't make me lose my britches before I get in the house. You're thin," he added, predictably.

"And you have a beard!" she laughed, running her fingers along the line of his jaw. "I like it, you should wear it!"

"Ridiculous. Politicians can't have beards. Now get your skinny ass inside, before you catch a cold." Yet even as he said it, his arms tightened, lifting her from the ground, seeking more kisses. She was breathless by the time he let her down, blushing hot. From the door of the chaise, pretending not to notice, a tall figure rummaged through a bag. About a head shorter than Asa, but broad, and thick-muscled, he turned, and *manslaughter* had a face.

Elijah Standish smiled a craggy smile, plucking a tattered wool cap from his head and bowing dramatically low. Yet, it was not condescending.

"You must be Miss Martha," he said pleasantly. His accent was New York, but he clearly hadn't spent as much time as Asa soaking up the dialect of sailors and ragamuffins. Silver hair hung in thick folds like an owl's wing, brushing to the middle of his back. The structure of his bones was thick, with high cheekbones, deep-set blue eyes, and a charmingly crooked nose. He stooped, and she smiled quickly and extended her hand, which he kissed.

"Hem," said Asa irritably, and Martha dropped her hand, flushing. She was about to open her mouth to respond when the air was shattered by a piercing shriek. Cassandra, hair flying, covered in flour up to her elbows, hurdled from the house, tripped down the steps, and flung herself into Elijah's arms.

The sight sunk her heart. Hastily, she turned back to Asa, threading her arm through his.

"Sir, I can't believe you did it!"

"Not a thing, really," he said, with a frown.

The parlor came alive. The blinds were rolled up, coffee was served, gusts of cold air burst and faded as trunks were brought to join the towering mess in the hall. Elijah the Young, in the first display of emotion Martha had witnessed, took one look at his father, hid a crumpled face in the crook of his elbow, and burst into tears. Asa rapped him on the shoulder, and Elijah Standish pounded his back.

Amy Prue was roused and brought out for display.

"A girl," observed Elijah with a chuckle. The baby fit exactly in the crook of his elbow. "Well done, my dear, well done–" turning to kiss Cassandra for the hundredth time. Martha, curled on Asa's lap, dropped her eyes. A certain unease pitched the perfection of the image, in a flash of red, singed and healed flesh–impossible to ignore. The letter M, branded on the flat pad of Elijah's right thumb. It could've been nothing if she hadn't known to look for it. A simple slip of a pocketknife, a finger slammed in a door.

She narrowed her eyes. Elijah Standish certainly did not seem like the sort of man who would kill without justice. He was soft-spoken, steady, exuding fatherliness–nearly as if sweet William Douglas lived in the body of a frontiersman, minus Mr. Gracey's hazy innocence and tittering self-doubt.

"You'd better hand that baby over to Emory before he has a fit." Cassandra interjected a tale of Asa's crowning success to pluck the infant from Elijah's arms.

"Never mind," muttered Asa, but he tapped out his pipe and accepted the bundle. Martha shifted on his lap. The baby was drowsy, and nestled her head below Asa's chin, cheeks smushed, breathing through her bud of a mouth. It was an oddly natural scene, as if he had obtained something he'd been searching for for years.

"You'll get yours, don't be jealous," said Cassandra drily, increasing Martha's discomfort. "You should've seen Martha. She's a veritable midwife. Marry her quick, Emory, or I'll find a way to marry her myself!"

403

"You're bloody sweet." Asa turned, and she met his mouth by instinct in a hasty kiss.

"Well, she is," Cassandra went on. "She was by my side through the worst of it, and I do say I'm miffed I've to make room for this brute in the bed," she added, rapping Elijah on the back of the head. "She's been up with the baby, she's bathed my sorry ass, she's fed me off a spoon. An angel, Emory, an angel…"

Martha burned. Cassandra had missed the connotation, but Asa had not. He was studying her, eyes blazing; not just love, but adoration, a glowing orb in a cold room. Cassandra's praise was a gift to him.

Martha had never seen him look as happy as he did right then. A baby nestled on his chest, his woman on his knee. A sculptor could've chiseled the scene and called it something like *Victory*.

Laughter and glaring sunlight bled into high afternoon. The letter bag was empty; she'd checked on a trip to the kitchen with Cassandra, clinging to an impossible hope. Deep breaths took her from one moment to another, unease ebbing and flowing where there should've been happiness. Just another feeling, another change, that would come and pass and integrate. *Nothing to worry about.* Maybe Robert wouldn't come. The possibility of failure was a desperate attempt to calm herself, and it mainly worked; her plan, after all, had been hasty and ill-considered.

It was still early afternoon, but she could sense Asa's weariness. There was a calmness to his eyes, nearly foreign; he'd climbed the mountain, and on the other side, he could rest. She stood, watching him strip his clothes, unable to calm the thundering of her heart. Seeing his body was a drug, a first sip of port after the worst day. He sank into the copper tub, and she

404

circled and washed his shoulders, his back, lathering castile soap. Steam rose, spiced with balsam and olive oil. She washed his hair, weaving fingers through tangled curls, massaging his temples and the back of his neck.

"How is your head?" she asked.

"All right." He hooked her neck and pulled her down for a kiss. She sank, gripping the edge of the tub. Over and over, a gentle, eating kiss, as if he wanted to be sure she was still the same girl, as if he couldn't understand why she was still there.

The guilt lashed like a whip.

"Martha, you're an angel. What you've done for Cassie–"

"She would've done the same for me." She flushed. "You need a haircut. Do you trust me? Let me shave you if you don't want to wear a beard."

She held out a towel, wrapping and tucking it around his middle, blushing at the sight of him already thick with arousal. *No, no!* She'd fucked her way through so many feelings, but nothing like this. Taking him now would open a wound too deep. She must take care of him first; if she were an angel, her hands must prove it.

She positioned him at the dressing table. From the top drawer she took a set of shears she occasionally used to cut the cracked ends off her own hair, and went to work. He watched her in the mirror as she snipped, chestnut curls falling like noiseless petals. She found his shaving things from the mound of travel bags, and lathered soap in a dish.

"Lean back." Her fingers trembled, and she slipped by his ear–he was touching her, already, she could sense it before his fingers ever met her flesh. She drew back with a gasp. Without opening his eyes, he found the arm of her dressing gown and pushed it down her shoulder. Then the knot slipped, and the gown fell to the floor in a heap; cold air rushed, at war with guilt and aching proximity.

Naked, shaking, she continued to shave, scraping off silver hairs and wiping the blade clean on a kerchief.

"Martha."

"Oh–yes?."

"I had–*ahem*. I had rather a time of it in New York."

"You've brought Mr. Standish home, you've done well."

"It's nothing, really." He sighed. "It wasn't a bad thing, I just got to thinking, that's all."

"Oh? What were you thinking about?"

She jolted. A fingertip, calloused from the cold, brushed over the tip of her breast, circling, skimming her collarbone, licking the curve of her side. *Asa, stop!* How could she do this, with this shadow covering her expectations? Should she lose it in the light, and tell him what she'd done? A shudder ran through her bones; his touch met the rise of her sex, gently searching beneath the shield of her pleasure.

Then his hand dropped, palm up, in his lap. His eyes were still closed; still, he seemed weary.

"Myself." He shrugged. "What I want, really. Thinking about what I read about Griffin's."

"It was a proper plan," she assured him. Her hands shook, but she shaved, mindfully, around the curve of his jaw, fighting to ignore the pungent smell of washed man.

"I was ill in New York, one evening." He opened his eyes, staring at the ceiling. "Rather thought I wasn't going to make it to court the next day. Bloody headache. I knew I had a bottle in my bag, but–I don't know, darling, I just couldn't do it. I couldn't tip it."

"The laudanum?"

"Hmm. I don't know what it was, exactly, I just didn't want the feeling. I'd rather feel the eye of a goddamn headache. So I did. Probably slept an hour that night, and I went to court looking like death. Standish said it was my best day." He smiled briefly. "I don't remember what I said, only that I went back to the house and ate like a damn pig."

She paused. "You didn't tip it… at all?"

He shrugged again. "No."

"Asa." For a moment the guilt faded. She cupped his jaw, turning his face. "That's very good, I–I'm proud of you!"

"I'd like to keep it that way. If you can help me." He met her eyes, drowsy. "I need you to help me. That's not easy for a fellow to admit, all right, so don't make a show of it. I think it just…well, it took me walking away for a bit to realize what I had here. Bloody little things, you know." He caught her neck, drawing her down for another kiss. "I was away from you for a month, darling," he murmured against her mouth, "and it about drove me mad."

She tightened, pressing her fingers unintentionally into the wound on the back of his head. It seemed fitting, so she didn't retract, but instead circled it gently. Her heart rate flew. His hand lingered at the crevice of her legs, seeking upwards, until she broke at the knees, opening for his touch. Sweet, slow circles, parting her mouth, increasing her breath, her heart–then he eased a finger inside of her.

"Sir," she managed through gritted teeth, "you can rest."

"I want to fuck you." He regarded her seriously. "I mean, fuck you and be done. Get my fix, aye. But you." His hand dropped back to his lap, his eyes on his finger wet with her arousal. She half expected him to put it in his mouth, as he often did, but he remained still.

"You're something to be savored." He nodded, agreeing with himself. "I realized that once I didn't have you."

"You had me, I was just waiting." She flushed, shaving the last of the silver hairs and wiping his skin clear. Jesus, it was as if he knew what she'd done! As if all of her betrayals burned in her eyes, and he was punishing her with sweetness. She turned away, battling tears, and polished the razor blade. Yet, she was swollen, aching for him. She closed her eyes, her shoulders rising. His touch followed the curvature of her back, tracing her shoulders, dropping the braided rope of her hair.

He tugged it loose.

"I missed so many things," he whispered against the small of her back. "It used to drive me mad the way you sit in my chairs. With your heels tucked up, you're wearing holes in the damask."

"Oh. I didn't notice, I'm sorry!"

"Don't be. All the chairs in New York were too bloody plump."

He turned her at the hips. A soft kiss landed on the peak of fine hair, then another, to the side, the other side, her thighs. She sighed to the ceiling, gripping his head. Then she watched, breath baited, as his mouth parted, and his tongue found that angry seed of flesh, rolling it loose, sucking it open. After so many sessions, so many patient hours spent, teasing out her cries and tears, she was useless to his tongue. Her mind went blank. Her knees buckled, but then—he drew away. Drowsy, mouth flushed, a little wet—

"Let me savor you, sweetheart." He caught her chin in thumb and forefinger and pulled her down for a kiss. A soft kiss, a bare brushing of lips, then deeper, parting her mouth. Her excitement burned, taunting her with feelings she knew she had no right to feel. Just when her mind went white and the roaring grated her ears, he drew back with a sigh.

She caught herself, palms on his shoulders.

"The way you taste, I could live off of you, you know?" He dipped his head, searching the hardened end of her right breast, teasing invisible strings to her lust, tangling ever more impossibly. She watched, lips parted, eyes wide. The sunlight magnified the smallest things. Little red lines on his knuckles, where the cold had split his skin. The pores on his nose, breath muffled against her flesh.

All at once he stood, guiding her backward, then dropped to his knees.

The towel fell to the floor. Cupping her backside, he drew her in, and buried his face deep in the crevice of her legs, eating at her pleasure. Less and less with every turn of the tongue, she bore down on his shoulders. If she could just let her mind go dark… no memories, no feelings…the pleasure could win—

"Enough!" He pressed his chin into her belly. "Darling, wait. Deny yourself, please!"

She could've cried. Pounded on his shoulder with her first. Instead, he stood, caught her hand, and pressed it against his chest, dragging her fingers down the length of his torso. The trail of hairs bubbled at the ends of her nerves. He guided her, wrapping her grip around him, hard, fully ready.

"Asa—"

"Touch me," he said softly. "Until I burn. But I'm not ready to finish, darling. Remember that."

She tightened her fingers around his girth and obediently began to work in slow, pulling strokes, grazing with her palm in kneading circles, the way he'd insisted (with no shame) that he liked it. A muscle in his thigh trembled, and his head fell forward, pressing forehead to forehead. *Until I burn.* She increased the rhythm, pushing the base of her fist into his pelvis, coaxing him free.

He flared, hard as stone, hot in her palm, and with a gasp, she let him go.

His eyes were wild, flickering with gilded fire.

"Darling," he breathed.

"Mr. Wyeth."

"Pour us a brandy, would you?"

She obeyed, his eyes following her form, swaying around the panel to the office. She poured two glasses, fighting shaking hands. It wasn't unlike Asa to play games in the bedroom, and she'd long since learned not to ask questions; the end was always worth the means, yet now, her heart ached with much more than sexual anticipation. The guilt weighed as heavy as lust, pulling her feet like lead to the floor. And already, her inability to deny herself had broken past her supposed servitude to him as her man. Her husband.

She was not like Cassandra. But if she ever could be, it was because of the way he looked at her. As if he'd kiss the ground she walked on, as if he'd crack every bone in a hand laid on her with malicious intent. He owned her, even the worst parts, never asking her to change past gently chiding her self-destructive habits. *What does he see?* She closed her eyes, hating the mess of guilt and want. God, if he could see how black she was inside, he'd hate her! So she'd have to fuck him, it didn't matter the way she felt. He wanted it, he expected it, he deserved it.

She turned back through the panel. He was perched on the bed, rummaging through his saddle bag, his breeches, hose, and shoes back on, though the clothing did little to hide his aggravated arousal. She paused, confused, but quickly crossed the room when he beckoned.

"The last day in New York," he explained, setting the brandy down, "walking Elijah's sorry ass back from the courtroom, we passed a silversmith's. Fancier than anything I've seen in

Boston." He pulled out a little black velvet bag and tipped it into his palm. A delicate gold band settled, capped with the largest diamond she'd ever seen. She stared, her heart in her throat. It was rose-cut like her earrings, the stone nearly bulbous, set in scripted gold.

She took a sip of brandy, swallowing hard. *God. Asa, please don't*–but he turned her palm, and slipped the ring onto her promise finger as if he'd held her hand when he'd bought it.

"It's beautiful," she managed. "I don't know what to say!" She turned her face to her shoulder, yet it seemed appropriate to cry. He couldn't know the reason ate at her heart like a feasting crow.

"You've spent too much," she choked. "Asa, it's really too much!"

"Nonsense." He pressed his mouth. From the saddlebag, he brought out two coils of rope and set them aside by the pillow. She hesitated, confused, but then, he took her hand and kissed her knuckles. She closed her eyes. His tongue circled the diamond, teasing her cold skin. Then, the gentlest *clinking* of bone teeth on precious stone, testing her sincerity, curling the length of her promise–her finger, deep in his mouth. She flared. God, she'd forgotten how easily he did that, with the silliest gestures! Gently, he bit at the knuckle, trying, tasting...then he dragged it out, scraping on the barest bottoms of his teeth.

"It's nonsense," he repeated. "I'll empty my coffers for you time and time again, darling. Perhaps one day it'll put a dent in your worth, though I cannot believe it."

He hooked her neck, pulling her close for another kiss. Laying her down, flat on the bed. She squirmed, holding her glass high; the diamond caught the white sun, bounding off the snow outside. Violent rings flung over the walls, catching iridescent orbs, quivering wingspans of light...and he kissed down her breasts, preying over her body. She closed her eyes, biting her lip to quell the natural response, which was to moan.

"There are parts of you I haven't touched," he whispered against the rise of her belly. "That isn't right, now is it?" Gently, he pried the brandy from her hands. The barest brush of warm breath tickled, cold when it reached her breasts. Then nothing; he'd moved away. Then a single kiss pressed into the bottom of her sternum. Then nothing, then wetness.

Cold, filling her belly, spilling down her sides. Her eyes flew open.

"Asa—"

Her belly quivered, and she glanced, fighting for control. His breath was silk, hovering over the dip of flesh—and then heat, searing in red-hot tendons, pushing brandy down her sides. He cleaned her naval first, licking it dry in slow, deep circles. Then he followed the fire trails on her skin, down her sides, pausing now and then to plant a whisper of a kiss. The only flesh on her body awake and alive had been caressed by his tongue, his lips; otherwise, she was locked, watching in a combination of terror and rushing anticipation. He drew maps with his mouth, telling tales, charting ships. Then, his head nestled between her legs, curls tickling her thighs, he went to work once more, purging her body of pent-up pleasure.

She clenched her fists, digging into the blankets. She was going to finish, while the monster ate her alive inside. And she didn't care. It had to be over—he'd started it, it must be finished—it was his beast, as much as hers!

"Martha." He stopped, his tone nearly warning. "Martha, I told you to deny yourself, didn't I?"

"Oh—Jesus God, excuse me, but this isn't fair!"

"Sit up, calm yourself." He took her by the wrists, pulling her to a seat. "Turn your hand over." She turned her hand in his palm. He pressed kisses from her wrist to the bend of her arm, then—*what on earth*—he reached for one of the coils of rope, frowning as he shook it loose. Once, twice, he wound it around her wrist at the pulse.

"These ropes." He paused, considering the knot. "I cut them, from the gallows on the Common."

She fought to control a flaring in her nostrils. Something surged past the lashing lust, a heart-racing feeling.

"Aye, I cut them," he repeated, brown eyes strangely calm. "You know how many necks have broken inside these nooses?" He gathered her other hand and bound it too, tying it in a slip knot. "Many dozens, I would say. Under my ordinances." He smiled and touched the end of her nose. "Because I said the right thing. The heft of being an esquire, aye."

"I-I don't know about this." She pulled back, but the knot tightened, and her wrist pinched. "Asa, I'm all right with games," she said defensively. "But this is plain silly—"

"I'm not playing games with you, sweetheart."

Her skin crawled under the rope. How many necks, how many lives? She glanced, her heart slamming, but he was over her now, bent at the knees, lifting her and positioning her in the center of the bed. He unwound the ropes with a concentrated frown and tossed them over the sides of the bed, where they hung like otherworldly arms. Then he lashed one rope around the bedpost, pulling it tight. Her body lurched.

Calmly, he paused, took a sip of brandy, and circled the bed to tie the other.

She was taut. Pinned, her body splayed like a sordid painting in a mahogany four-poster frame. Feet cold, toes curled, legs together at the knees. He regarded her from the end of the bed, then strode to the dressing table and poured a glass of port. For uncomfortably long, he stood, languid, one arm wrapped around his middle, taking her in. Then–

"Say the word, darling, and I'll cut you free."

It was the easiest thing she'd ever done. Shake her head no, though she was bound, mangled by the worst feelings a human could feel. Once more, his weight dipped the bed. Traces of touch followed the backs of her knees, pushing her legs apart; a rush of cold air assaulted her senses, and he bent, predatory, and in one swift movement, pushed a finger inside of her, grinding to the knuckle.

She squeezed her eyes shut, clenching her jaw. His tongue ate at her once again, and inside, the beckoning stoked wells of heat, pooling from her glands in sweat and tears and rushes. Too close, riding the crest, the harshest wave where only she existed–

But he stopped.

She dropped her shoulders, gasping to the ceiling. Without thinking, she reached to bury her fingers in his hair, but the ropes snapped, cinching her blood. She dropped back, shaking them loose; prickles of white light danced at the corners of her vision.

"Asa, you can't keep doing that," she panted. "Am I going to be tied to the bed for the rest of the day? Cassie needs me!"

"Please stop talking." He bent, kissing the top of one thigh, then the other. "Spread your legs. Wide for me, thank you. Wider." Steady fingers worked at the buttons of his breeches. "Touch me, darling. Touch my face."

It was instinctual to obey, but her hand bounced, recoiling. "I can't. I'm tied!"

"Of course. I'm sorry, darling. Let me know if you want cut, all right?" His cock was free, and his hand moved, languidly, on his knees over her, as if she were holy ground. He stroked himself slowly; she'd watched him do it more than once, angry heat balling in the pit of her gut. Jealousy, that he could pleasure himself as easily as she could, that she was not his only means to an end, coupled with a wild excitement. To indulge her eyes with his indulgence, to finish her with just a picture. Just when he was swollen, he sighed and stopped, met her eyes with a smile, and buttoned his breeches.

She followed his form, clear-cut in the sunlight, back to the dressing table. By instinct, she attempted to sit, but the ropes again angrily resisted. She dropped, staring at the ceiling, fighting back tears. He returned to the bed and sat, perched on the edge. A pocket tinderbox and match held in his hand, his pipe tucked between his teeth. He struck the flint, lit the pipe with a match, then leaned to kiss her. Her nose prickled with vanilla smoke, and she sneezed as quietly as she could.

"You don't have to tie me to the bed," she said indignantly.

His brow went up. "That so?"

"I promised you, I'm not going anywhere." Guilt dropped, leaden in her belly. It was the worst she'd ever felt. Was this punishment, or reward? Neither; it bounced, frantic, from one to the other. From the corner of her eye, she caught him setting the pipe down. Kisses trailed up her collarbone, settling on her neck; all of her wanted to bury her fingers into soap-clean curls, to breathe him in, but she couldn't. Her wrists snapped again and again, little necks at the gallows.

"Asa, please!"

"Please what, darling?" He drew back. "You want to finish. You'll finish, don't fret."

Once again she followed him with her eyes, putting a match to the smoldering tinder and lighting a candle. It was fiercely bright outside; there was no need for candlelight, but before she could wonder, her mouth was taken fiercely by another kiss. Eating, searching, dragging caresses down her jaw, her neck, her breasts—she struggled for air, arching. Down her belly, her thighs. Down her knees. Her shins, sweet, warm kisses, and his tongue, tracing the arches of her feet. Her toes curled, and she squirmed.

"Asa, you're being disgusting," she protested, fighting a pathetic break in her voice. "This really isn't necessary!"

"Darling." He settled her feet, ignoring her. "You know you like it when I strike your ass. The pain feels nice, doesn't it?"

"Well, I suppose so—oh, what a silly thing to say!"

"I gather it feels nice, the way you beg for it." He smiled. "Do you trust me, Martha?"

"I trust you. Just let me finish!"

"Sweet little hedonist." He pressed his knuckles to his mouth. "It's what I love most about you, fuck everyone else." He leaned in for another kiss. God, what had she agreed to? To the eye she was trapped, though in the back of her mind, she knew she could wriggle the ropes free and flee. Yet something made her tug them instead, tightening the knot. Whatever he wanted to do, however much it hurt, she deserved it.

He reached for the candle, snuffed it out with thumb and forefinger, and pried it free, setting the tray aside. Hand to his pocket. A letter seal caught the light, rolling through his fingers.

"I meant what I said. Back when we were happy." He regarded her seriously, though there was the faintest hint of amusement in his eyes. "This cunt." He sat, pushing her legs farther apart at the knees. "This cunt is mine. Mine to touch. Mine to pleasure. Mine to fuck raw, if it's what I want. Let your head do whatever it wants, but your cunt is mine."

And pain blazed in a circle on her flesh, right above the rise of her sex. In tandem with the pleasure, it was nearly unbearable; she thrashed, fighting for a seat, the fraying ropes spitting splinters into her skin. He tossed the candle to the bed, locking

416

her by the hipbones, and ground the letter seal into burning wax; she bucked, fighting him with her knees, only to surrender, wrapping her legs around his neck, rocking deep into the bed, tears burning her temples.

"God, yes, darling, feel it–" His voice coaxed each wracking tremor of her body, into limp surrender, into useless tears.

She was branded now, just like Elijah. Sealed like a letter, black with his thoughts; loosened with her lies, never making it to the right hands. The guilt curled like a fist in her heart. He drew back, shifting her hips, tipping her pelvis to his face. Her skin tightened under drying wax; he stroked it with his thumb, pressing kisses into her thighs; then, he settled into a forgiving pattern with his tongue. A sorry for the torture, the denial. She finished in a moment, as she knew she would, because the pain only heightened the feeling. Her body seized, and the fist broke her heart, squeezing her empty. A flash of white light wracked her from limb to limb, and she cried out, shattering the crystal-cold stillness.

And then the white light faded into twin blue flames–a smear of red, like paint–

Robert.

Her eyes flew open. Had she said that aloud? No, no! Asa was unbuttoning his breeches, a preying angel over her limp body, unassuming, consumed. He broke her fast, straining her body after so many weeks untouched, filling her emptiness, thrust after thrust. Instinctually, her hips rose, meeting the movement. She couldn't run nails down his back or grip his haunches as she always would have; she was a good, an asset, sealed under the crest of Wyeth Enterprises. A tool for his pleasure, still tender to him, grinding into her, again and again and again.

The blue dulled, now a pale sky, now nothing but blank grey, now nothing but the rising taunt of pleasure pulling her mind's eye to one place and one place only. There was nothing like that feeling, no matter how often or how efficiently he finished her with his tongue or his hands. When it happened, it was striking, frustrating; a perfect measure of time and movement, an impossibly long holding of her breath. Perhaps, he was too kind, and he'd tortured her enough, and now he was sorry. Perhaps he knew how much she needed the distraction. Whatever the case, in a matter of few short minutes, she shuddered and pulsed, driving her head into the pillow, fumbling for the ropes. Inside her he was full; she knew, even if she hadn't asked for it, he was far beyond the point of control.

"My Martha," he breathed against her throat. "My woman, my rebel, my wife—" Driving deeper, draining him empty. Then he collapsed, head nestled under her arm. The light from the diamond hit the walls, shimmering pricks of light on sweat-soaked skin.

She waited. The sunlight dimmed. The ring pushed her hand deep into the pillow, and the ropes chafed. From beside her, soft snores rose, brushing her ribcage with cool breath, and the semen draining from her body—as the hours passed—was cold and strange. He slept like a baby while she drifted, discomforts pushing her in and out of total abandonment.

When she awoke fully, the ropes were gone. She was tucked under the covers; the room had faded to a soft grey-blue, telling of dusk. From around the folding panel, vanilla smoke drifted, curling in crisp air.

Silently, she began to cry.

26

the KING *of* BOSTON

I t was pure torture, watching him over dinner. Cassandra screamed when she saw the ring, leaping up for a better look. Asa frowned and drank his port, angelic as ever at the head of the table. It took everything not to give in to tears.

All of the questions bubbled to the surface. What if Robert didn't come? And if he didn't, would it be the worst thing? Should she forget everything, and just let Asa go to Boston–to the wharves, to court, whatever took him that day. Forget about Ann Street. But Robert was in Boston! And Asa had no idea. He couldn't just go to Boston, while the man who'd once tried to end his life wandered the streets, dipping in and out of alleys and vacant buildings.

Who knows where Asa went in Boston; his boots knew the rise and pitch of every cobbled street. He was king. Boston was *his* city.

But Robert was hiding with a company of soldiers! He was protected, because no one cared about Robert Henshaw anymore. His face had long since ceased to waste the ink of the morning news. The turmoil in the city was so high, churned in the wake of the tea ship's scourge, that when a man in a red coat walked by, eyes snapped to the ground.

God, it was wretched! Goddamn wretched. She glanced across the table, flushing when he smiled at her. Her belly clenched, tender skin smarting above her naval. Fine and well, it'd been a fun session of fucking, but for a moment, he'd actually frightened her. Maybe Frances was right, he *was* out for blood. Surely, those ropes weren't really cut from the Common. A fellow couldn't just hop up on the gallows and cut the ropes down. *How silly.* She bunched her hands in her lap. Yes, maybe it was all just a bit silly, and Asa could be dramatic sometimes. Maybe it was as simple as her leading him to Robert, and Robert accepting his shackles, and wasting away in the Boston Jail. Stumbling into a courtroom, eventually, and then…what?

Elijah Standish was laughing, eyes bright like a vigilant sage. He could've held the answers to the all world's problems behind his crooked smile; he certainly handled himself as if he did. She'd spent all morning trying to hate him, but she couldn't. He was, unequivocally, the most pleasant person she'd ever met; steady, soft-spoken, oddly attentive for a man pulled in so many different directions. The only problem was the brand, flashing into view when he lifted his silverware. When he took a drink of ale. When he ran his hand through his silver hair. Small and nearly healed, it would be a white scar in a matter of weeks, yet it may as well have been blazed in his eyes, twisting every (perfectly reasonable) word that came from his mouth. Kit Beck watched him, eyes soppy; Asa laughed with him like a brother. And Cassandra clearly worshipped him.

She went to bed feeling ill.

Asa was being sweet. Intuitive to her moods, he didn't press her for what he clearly wanted; instead, he fixed her a brandy, crawled into bed behind her, and brushed her hair. The ring itched on her finger, every instinct screaming at her to take it off and fling it across the room. Maybe fight with him, a proper fight; maybe he'd say something that could justify what she'd done.

But he was horrible at properly fighting. Far too reasonable, and annoyingly composed.

She lay awake long into the hours of the night, cuddled deep in his arms. The room was so silent, she could hear his heart beating. She slipped the ring on and off, and on and off, marveling at the way it caught the moonlight through the open curtains. A thought entered.

Maybe. Just maybe, this *was* the right thing. Maybe she'd made a real decision, calculated and brave; maybe she was handing him everything he fought for day after day. Maybe for once, she could take this by the reins, without the constant need to check herself against his wisdom. He had a deep and divisive hold on the core of her, putting a pause on choices that, in the days of Robert Henshaw, would've been done without thought at all.

He didn't want her to feel that way, but she did. It was a part of love, an uncomfortable one. Evidence of sincerity and depth. Yet, if she could break it for a moment, she could be his vindication.

The thought was comforting enough that she slept. She was going to Ann Street, and Asa was going with her.

The doubts returned with the dawn.

Over breakfast, he announced to Cassandra that he'd shaken "the poppy". Clearly an issue of accountability, Elijah had to know, and Sam, Bennet, and even Kit Beck, who nodded hastily and stared at the floor. Then he ambled off to the barn, perfectly

421

happy to take a larceny case the second day home. She wondered if he wasn't telling Jed about his victory, too.

Listless, tired, and half-sick, she sat for hours in the parlor, mending from a basket of his clothes. Frocks torn at the seams, hose with holes in the heels…the man was rich, couldn't he invest in some decent things to wear? In a huff, she threw down a torn set of linen under-drawers and crossed the floor to stare over the western lawn. The sky was heavy, clouds thick with a growling snowstorm. She relented and padded out of the parlor to her room, tugged on her boots, tossed the rabbit fur cloak around her shoulders, and tucked her hands in a fox-fur muff (another desperate yet silent gift from Asa). The house was unusually quiet; she felt the need to tiptoe as she made her way to the terrace.

She felt black, standing there, fingers on the railing. A snowflake fell, spreading tiny arms as it melted under resistant stone. Without much sense of herself, she pulled her hood over her head and began to walk. She crossed through grass stiff with cold and circled to the back of the house, where she ambled aimlessly through the dead roses, trimmed back for the winter. Only Cassandra's bed of herbs, knotted and brown, disturbed the serenity of the garden. The bathing pool was covered for the season, protected by a tight shield of oiled canvas.

A shuffling of loose stone broke the still of snowfall.

"Musty, dusty, rusty, filthy, stinking old lawyer," she caught, in a humming sing-song, and Elijah Standish rounded the path.

"Mr. Standish!" She straightened. "Good day, sir."

The ratty knit cap was balanced precariously on his head, but when he saw her, he tugged it off and swooped low in bow. "M'dear. What's happening?"

"Oh—nothing much." She dropped her eyes at the sight of the purple brand. "Were you out with Mr. Wyeth?" she asked, trying to smile.

"Ah, yes. Court this morning. I sat in the gallery. He stayed at the Common to watch the whipping."

"Oh, he won? He said it was grand larceny, I think."

"I could hear the fellow bellowing halfway back to the house, so I'd reckon a win."

"I'm happy to hear it." Something gave her pause. Manslaughter, of course, the word that seemed etched on her brain forever. But she couldn't speak. She couldn't ask him to explain himself. She bent her neck, head down as he sidled by, cap swinging.

A step further into a rose graveyard, the same questions unanswered.

"Miss Gracey."

She froze.

"Miss Gracey, I understand my presence may have bit of a connotation to you."

"I don't take your meaning, sir."

In a gesture that would've been too bold from another man, he stepped forward and plucked one of her gloved hands from her muff. She jumped, a flush starting at her ears, yet, it was so akin to something Mr. Gracey would've done, she could only stand, eyes on his boots. The Martha of the days of Henshaw might have flirted with him, if she were being honest with herself. He was a craggily handsome man. But now, it was all she could do not to cry.

"You've been through enough turmoil for a girl your age, I'd say, to see you through the rest of your life." He patted her hand. "I should dearly hate to be a bad memory for you."

She frowned, her heart pinching. "Mr. Standish–Mr. Wyeth– he said you were innocent. What–what happened at Whitehall?"

"There, now." He nodded, continuing to pat. "Innocence is a concept of the courts, you see. By that fact, I hope you feel some sort of well-deserved solace. My case wasn't an easy one," he sighed, looking over the top of her head. "But Wyeth is a mad dog of a lawyer."

"But murder is murder!" She pulled her hand away, fighting the urge to wring her wrist. "I'm sorry, Mr. Standish, forgive me. It's just that–what Mr. Wyeth has given you–it's a second chance, isn't it? It might not have gone that way. Because– because the story was the same, in the end. I know Mr. Wyeth is a good lawyer–but–but–"

"You can cry, m'dear," he said softly.

"This isn't Mr. Wyeth's case." As soon as he said it, the tears gave way. Angry, she pushed them off with the side of her palm. "It's Mr. Cooper's case. And I beg your pardon, but Mr. Wyeth is not the only good lawyer in Boston!"

"Indeed, Boston is seething with beastly lawyers," he agreed. "Cooper is the one of the grossest I've laid eyes on. He apprenticed Wyeth, you know. But I understand what you're feeling, I really do." He pushed his hands deep into his pockets. "I've long considered myself ill-suited for the trade, coming to terms with the fact that I have a heart in my chest. In lawyering, you see, death is a circumstance, not a tragedy, or a grievance. And when you take the grief out of death, you see–" He paused and blew out a breath, a cloud breaking the stillness of the air.

"When you take the grief out of death, it becomes so much easier to make sense of."

Take the grief out of death.

She slipped in through the kitchen, shedding the rabbit fur. Through the library, she nearly ran into Asa, coming in through the terrace. He was carrying a Chinese porcelain vase, stuffed with a massive amount of flowers—such a large bouquet, that only his eyes were seen over the top. "G'day," he said, kicking open the office door. "Come here for a minute, darling, I want to talk to you."

Her heart picked up pace, but she bunched her skirts and followed obediently. He slammed the door behind her and went to set the flowers on the bureau plat.

"These," he said matter-of-factly, "are for you. I met a fellow after court who has a forcing garden. Grows all manner of weeds year-round, even in the cold." He took off his hat, a black wool cockade with bunched ribbon at the corners. His frock was midnight blue, embroidered at the buttonholes.

"You look well today." Her voice came weak. It was Standish's eyes that stared her down. Flushing, she crossed the room and sat. "Thank you for the flowers," she amended.

"Yes." He sat and poured a brandy. "I haven't been courting you properly, and I'm sorry for that. You deserve flowers and all sorts of trinkets."

"You give me plenty of presents, Mr. Wyeth."

He bent, rummaging in one of the drawers, and she watched the top of his head, feeling oddly trapped. Certainly, it wasn't out of character for him to extend his affection in the form of material things, but he typically would've done so with a scripted note, a neatly tied box, and a distinct absence of his physical presence. She shifted, Standish's crooked smile teasing, then, *oh God!* She snapped straight, heart catching in her throat. From the drawer, he'd brought a silver tea caddy. *Her* silver tea caddy, fit with the plaque of the British East India Trading Company.

And still dusty at the bottom with the last of the Bohea.

"Mr. Wyeth!"

"There now, don't fret." He leaned on his elbows and regarded her, eyes unreadable. "Judith gave it to me. We're friends now, you see. Enough nights snitching in, sprinkling the fireplace with the Lord's piss or whatever it is, she's purged me of the devil I think. I might start sporting a Quaker hat. D'you think it'd look fancy? Either way." He set the caddy in front of her with a decisive *clunk*. "She's gotten under my skin just enough."

"I can explain—"

"Can you? Because I can explain everything in this house, whether I did it or not." The blank expression behind his eyes twitched with suppressed anger. "And I do well know, the last time I dispatched a list to Boston with Bohea on it, was September twenty-second, seventeen-sixty-five."

"Yes, but—" She stared at her hands, frantic. How much did Judith know? No one knew she'd gone to Griffin's, of course not, no one could know that! She swallowed, attempting to calm her heart. "I dispatched it," she admitted, snatching at the first out. "I'm sorry. You were gone, and—"

"When I go, do the rules go with me? Who took the list to Boston?" He turned and coughed into his elbow, then reached for the bottom drawer of the bureau plat for the laudanum—which wasn't there.

He slammed the drawer shut. "You'd best tell me who took the list because I'll find out anyway. Save me the bloody headache."

"Sir, I don't know! I just added it to the list." She twisted her hands. Lying to Asa was not easy. Prying through his secretary was one thing, but lying to his face… even the cold, sharp dawn of Boston, cutting her skin on Ann Street, couldn't rival the discomfort.

She glanced. He glowered.

"In the kitchen," she insisted. "How am I supposed to know who takes it to the city, when Sam is gone–"

"Martha Ann Gracey!" He pushed back. "Jesus, I've half a mind to put you over my knee and spank you. But knowing you, you'd probably love it, you salacious wench! I said what I said," he added decisively. "Don't pretend to be offended. Now take your Tory caddy, and keep it out of my sight."

"This isn't fair! You never told me I couldn't have Bohea!"

"Martha." His temples tightened; she knew the expression like the back of her hand. Taut skin, eyes bloodshot, a twitch in the jaw. A headache. He cleared his throat, coughed into his elbow again, and poured himself another brandy.

"I shouldn't have to explain these things to you," he said stiffly. "You're living under the roof of a bloody Dutch pirate. Now don't cry," he added with a grimace. "Take the caddy and forget about it."

She took the caddy and flipped the lid. It was empty; even the dust had been wiped from the crevices. "What did you do with the tea?" she sniffed. "You could've at least let me finish it." His voice had softened somewhat, reverting to the Asa she knew was terrified of her tears. Hastily, she justified the lie, conjuring up the image of *Love In Excess*.

"Nonsense. I brewed it with piss in a chamber pot. For Christ's sake," he said, almost wearily, when she startled in the chair. "We'll leave it at that. No Bohea, no Hyson in the house. Understood?"

"Oh–all right." She pouted, flipping at the lid of the caddy. The indignant tears, having served their purpose, paused, but her heart was oddly heavy. She traced the plaque with her thumbs, aware that she'd successfully dented his trust. And for a man who must ride to Ann Street, it was a dangerous error.

"I'm sorry," she said sincerely. "I promise it won't happen again."

"Yes, well. That's the trouble with you. You say that, but if I never find out, it's all right. Never mind." He shook his head. "I'm going to be proper from here till the wedding, all right. You stay in your room, and I'll stay in mine. We can do other things, I want to go through the house records with you. You and Cassie will take it over, pay and servants disputes and such. I don't really have time for it anymore."

It sounded boring, but she supposed if it was time spent with him, it was something. Opportunity to regain his confidence. She rolled her shoulders, feeling better. "I'd be happy to learn."

"Good. Let me go through some books, and I'll put together a plan. In the meantime, I'm sorry I have to do this–but I've asked Judith to keep an eye on you. So if she's sulking about more than usual, that's why."

"Not Judith!" She half-rose in distress. "I said I was sorry!"

He shrugged. "She'll keep your hands out of my britches at any rate. A sharp old Puritan prude." He drained his brandy and stood. "On your feet, m'love."

"We can kiss, at least," she said despondently. Her knees felt strangely weak, and the tea caddy, hanging limp in her hand, looked ridiculous.

"Yes, darling, kissing is fine." He leaned, lifted her chin, and kissed her with disappointing chastity. "Now, where do you want these flowers?"

It was a distinct test. Judith, self-important, followed her everywhere, sniffling over her shoulder while she made meat pies with Cassandra, or poking at the hearth in the parlor while Asa drilled her over the house records. It was boring, and she felt sick, cloudy, and miserable. Three days...two days...the day before. Her head swam with anxiety, trying to focus on his voice. She still didn't know what to say, because he clearly didn't trust her. Griffin's was one thing, but if he found out she'd wandered the city, and ended up on Ann Street—God, he *would* put her over his knee.

She rubbed at the back of her neck, yawning. Asa sat, spectacles perched, scribbling out a list—prices and shorthand descriptions for the kitchens. He was merciless; on and on he went, serving her right. Stupid Sam asked for an increase in pay on September the third, seventeen-seventy-three. *Mark it as a loss in the accounts book.* Georgia, a chambermaid, opened a dispute that Button, a yard boy, had grabbed her buttocks while she emptied a pot. *Noted in the daybook.* (It was later determined that Georgia was notoriously dramatic, and she was dismissed). A barrel of husked wheat had gotten damp and grown mold. *Marked as a loss.* On December the second, mice had gotten into the salted cod, amounting in ten schillings of damage…

"Take a break," he snapped, throwing down his quill. "You're damn near snoring, woman."

"Easy." Cassandra sat pertly on the settee, sewing a sampler. "Remember, you were picking fights in the back of the public house when you were her age. I'll show her the records. We don't need your help."

"You must run Wyeth House properly. By the books, Cass." He took out his pocket tinderbox and prepared his pipe with a ferocity that further exhausted Martha.

"Well, I can attest, nobody likes the way you run it, like a damn army drill," retorted Cassandra. "Anyway, you're busy enough. Stop being such a meddler and let something go."

"Mmm. Yes." He scowled. "You're right, I'm about to be busier still. Since Standish can't show his face in a New York courtroom again, I'm rather thinking we should take the practice to Boston."

"Oh!" Cassandra leaped to her feet, as if she'd never made the suggestion, and Martha inwardly made a note, begrudging her admiration. Men, under Cassandra's thumb, seemed quite malleable.

"I'm sorry, m'love, I was going to say." Elijah lay in front of the hearth, crooked nose in a book, the heel of one shoe balanced on the toe of the other. "There are some logistics to work through–"

"Don't play me, Emory!" Cassandra cried. "He can't go into practice, he's got an M on his thumb. You said yourself, he'd be sweeping floors!"

"He's been granted full pardon and rights to property and practice," replied Asa, lighting his pipe. "The branding is a corporal farce, nothing more. He can wear a thimble or something, I don't know. Or you can hold him down, and I'll cut it off."

"I'll wear a thimble," said Elijah quickly, sitting up. Kit Beck, who was folded up in an armchair by the fire, looked sick.

"Oh–Emory!" Cassandra picked up her skirts, crossed the room, and threw her arms around her brother's neck, to which Asa grunted and pushed her off. "All right, don't make a scene," he muttered. "I'm going to crack the whip around here, aye, don't get comfortable. Elijah is liquidating the assets in New York. I want a proper practice. No more running this out of the office, I want a building in the city."

"Around King's somewhere, maybe," suggested Elijah, rising to his feet.

"No, not King's. I've got a beastly attorney on King's already."

"Something proper, though. Wyeth-Standish, there's a nice plaque for you…"

"Yes. Two stories, and secretary." Asa was clearly agitated, eyes bright through wafts of smoke. "Beck, you'd made an all right secretary. You'll never make it as a lawyer, but you've got the penmanship of a girl fresh out of ladies' school. That's useful, aye."

Kit was solemn, but his expression settled into a guilty sort of gratitude.

"This is sudden, Emory." Doubt flickered over Cassandra's face. "It's just you've got so much going on already, at the docks–"

"Yes, but I've got to cover my ass. We haven't heard anything from Parliament about Griffin's, and either some fellows are rounded up for an English trial, or we get a slap on the wrist. I rather think the ports are going to shutter, for a time."

"What! How devastating. What makes you say it?"

Martha's eyes grew heavy, and voices faded into a hum behind her thoughts. Her anxiety closed her throat, hammered at her heart, and pulled at her muscles so mercilessly that the only thing she wanted to do was go to bed, and sleep–for a long time. Until Asa wasn't mad at her anymore, until Robert was dead. He would die tomorrow, or begin to die, one way or another. But how in the world could she convince a stubborn Asa to put her on the back of a horse and take her to Ann Street?

The idea came to her like a resuscitating slap.

"Sir," she said, straightening, "if you're looking for a building in the city, what about the shop?"

"The shop?" He eyed her, dubious. "Hmm. Ann Street."

"Yes." She fought to keep her voice level. "It's not two stories, but the counting room covers a lot of space. I'm sure

some of the shelving could be converted nicely for books. And–
and Kit could sit behind the counter, like a proper clerk."

"Ann is a good location," agreed Elijah thoughtfully. "Not
far from the *Dragon*, too. Write a statement, unwind with a good
brawl–hey, all right!" Cassandra smacked him smartly on the
back of the head.

"It is a good location." Asa nodded slowly. "Good thought,
darling. I'd have to have it reconfigured a bit, but…hmm. I've a
lot of meetings at the *Dragon*. Convenient, no doubt."

"Yes, sir."

"Far enough away from the wharves…"

She watched him, her heart thundering. *I hate myself. I hate
myself. I'm going to be sick*–but she wasn't. She squared her
shoulders, smiling sweetly. "You can consider it. Go and have a
look, if you're going to the city. I-I'm sure Papa would approve."

"And you." He eyed her sideways. "Would you approve?"

She nodded quickly, fighting bile at the back of her tongue.
"Oh, yes. I certainly would."

She dragged herself to bed, her feet lead. Rising from the
chamber pot, the fatigue was at least explained–her thighs were
spotted with brown blood. *Ugh–the worst time.* She laid down, a
towel folded between her legs, and watched Judith poking at the
grate. The distant sounds of Elijah and Asa were lost in the
settling of the house; they'd popped an ancient bottle of black
rum from the cellar and were both rather tipsy by the time
Cassandra rolled her eyes and suggested she and Martha go to
bed.

Martha was more than willing. Looking at Asa made her want
to vomit. She felt like a mastermind, tapping into particular
words and ideas that spoke to his heart. Tainted, chained up like

a lie. In the dim light, the flowers he'd gotten her from the forcing garden stood proud and fresh on her dressing table.

Manslaughter. Manslaughter.

Judith's poking grated on her ears. She was about to reprimand her when the door swung open and Asa stumbled in, catching himself as he rounded. "Git out, Judith," he said, pleasantly, rolling out of his frock. "You can listen at the door, you prig. Take the poker with you, if you hear moaning, race in and bludgeon me with it, for what do I give a motherfuck."

Judith scowled and lumbered out, and Asa rounded and fell to the bed with a sigh. His arms circled beneath her breasts, drawing her close.

"If you don't mind–" She batted him off. "You reek, you're drunk!"

"Maybe I am. I just want to be with you, sweetheart."

She shifted, pulling her hips from the insistent warmth of his body. "I can't–you know, *do* anything. I-I'm on my courses."

"I see." His breath nuzzled the back of her neck, and she wanted to cry. No, scream–order him out of the room. "It's all right, darling, I'm keeping my promises. I thought you weren't feeling well. Want me to rub your back?"

Nimble fingers ran up the flesh on either side of her spine. She rolled, sighing into the bedding. Too many apple betties, or she was just that bloated! Her belly sank into the mattress. His fingers pressed the muscle at the small of her back, and she closed her eyes, feeling it for all it was worth. The calm before the storm.

"Asa," she whispered. "Are you going to Ann Street tomorrow?"

"Hmm. Should I? I think you're cunning."

"It's just—I'd love to see the shop again. Could I go with you? I just want to see it again, it's been so long." *I'm sorry, Asa. I'm so sorry—*

"All right," he sighed. "I've to go to Griffin's, and King Street anyway. Works out, I've a fellow I want you to meet on King."

His kneading touch sent her into a fitful sleep. It almost broke her, hours later, when she rolled over to watch him. One arm thrown over his head, a hand down the front of his breeches, snoring softly. All those times her innocence had wrecked her were traded. For once, she knew more than he did, and the truth was so ugly, that she had to lie.

Because Robert Henshaw couldn't go free. He couldn't lay on hearths, reading books; he couldn't sit in courtroom galleries. He wouldn't stroll through rosebush boneyards, humming silly tunes.

He would never wear a thimble on his thumb.

27

at the SIGN *of the*

GREEN DRAGON

When she awoke, it was late enough in the morning that the sun shone in garish white beams. Asa was gone. She scrambled, the towel falling from between her legs. For a moment, she forgot. She was just Martha, grieving for Mr. Gracey, yet still finding some kind of contentment in Asa's arms. Sad, but–healing. Before Griffin's. Still innocent.

Then it returned, like a punch in the gut. Her belly turned, and she stumbled to the washbasin, but nothing came up. *What if.* What if Elijah decided to come, too? What if Robert really didn't come? What if he was tired of waiting?

What if he'd never gotten the letter?

She pulled on her dressing gown, nearly in tears. On the other side of the door, Asa was rounding the corridor, fresh and clean in the sunshine. He looked sharp, in tall black boots, a blue wool cloak, and a cockaded hat, but he frowned when he saw her.

"Darling, you look ill. What's the matter?"

"Oh no, I'm not ill." She forced a smile. "I just didn't sleep very well. Are you off to the city?"

"'Bout an hour. Still want to go? You can ride in front. But if you're too tired, I can take you another day."

"No–no," she said hastily. "I still want to go. Let me get dressed."

"No hurry. I'll meet you in the barn. And darling, if you don't mind, wear something smart." His voice trailed through the hall. "The fellow I want you to meet is important."

She stood in the barn in burgundy cotton with a cream embroidered stomacher, a corset that wouldn't close, and her rabbit fur cloak. In the mirror, she'd been peaked, her eyes punched with black that no amount of icy water would wash away. Instead, she blotted powder and blended rouge and pinned her hair, anxiety souring her belly all the while. It occurred to her she hadn't done her hair up since the first night she'd spent with Asa. Always loose, or a swinging braid down her back, ready for his fingers.

She felt laughably small as he hoisted her into the saddle. Inept, as he bounced on the toe of his boot and swung up behind her. His scent, so close, (that she'd so many times craved like an addict) was too strong, and his proximity wasn't comforting. When he threaded his arms under hers and kissed her neck, her eyes burned with tears.

Over and over, she said it to herself. Manslaughter. *Manslaughter.* The rocking gate of Jed pitched her belly, and she was grateful that once out of the drive, he nudged the horse into a canter. His heartbeat sounded in her ear like a drum.

It was too bright a day for the way she felt, and it had been so long since she'd seen the city in daylight that the commotion sent her head spinning. Jed was stopped on Hannover Street; Asa helped her out of the saddle and led the horse at a walk, holding her hand, fingers threaded. The sun shone warm enough that the snow had melted off the worn bricks. She pulled back her hood tentatively, and forgot, for a moment, why she was there.

How much she'd missed Boston! How many times she'd turned the corner on Hannover Street to Ann, in and out of the shops, by herself, or with Robert. How many lazy afternoons had passed with Mr. Gracey in the counting room, how many times the salt-spiced wind had whipped her hair down Long Wharf! Here and there, she spotted a redcoat, but in the sunshine, they weren't leering. They were smart, proper. Wigs straight, hats clapped, boots gleaming with dubbin shine.

They wouldn't rape a girl. Not in the daytime. Not with this man by her side, towering, footsteps firm, holding her hand as if he owned her. She shuddered, yet, perhaps it was the fresh air, but she started to feel rather better. Closer. This would be over soon. And it could be all right. She'd felt the pistol clipped at his side, she knew he had blades under the leather of his boots.

And she was not afraid to watch Robert die.

It was strange, but she wasn't. She'd seen plenty of blood when William had died. Enough, and so precious, that the prospect of seeing it again was trivial, and expected. Asa *could* be violent. It certainly wasn't his typical state of being, but she would never forget the visceral movement, slamming Robert's head into the wall. Easy, as if he slammed heads into walls all the time. Perhaps he did—Cassandra had said he'd been a brawler in his youth. She glanced at him. He was smiling, eyes squinted in the sunshine, chestnut curls moving in the light breeze.

Turning a corner, onto Union Street.

Of course, he was smiling. Things were going his way for once. Holding his woman's hand. He'd saved Elijah's life, and now he had Wyeth-Standish–

He stopped abruptly, looping Jed's reigns around a hitching post.

"Sir, I thought–"

She turned in front of a tall red-brick building, speckled with windows and surrounded by loitering figures. Above the yawning doorway hung a sea-scathed copper statue: a dragon, tail whipped into an S, front legs tucked, as if being chased in the air. Wings to the sky, strange, almost tasteless. The *Green Dragon*. She'd passed by many times.

"What's this?" She dropped his hand. "I thought we were going to Ann."

"Ever been to a public house?" He plucked her hand back up and threaded it through his arm.

"Oh! Not inside, no."

"Politicians infest these places like rats. I've been practically living at the *Dragon* since I came back to Boston. Putting back ale, saying the right things. You might like an ale, sweetheart."

She didn't protest. It was early–not yet noon–and she'd named her time. She followed him, watching the underbelly of the dragon as she passed beneath. Inside, he led her through a hall and down a set of stairs; her interest was roused enough that Robert faded. They passed through an open door into a burst of rowdy voices and movement.

The room was dim, half under the earth. Gradually, as her eyes adjusted, she gathered it in. Loud, littered with bodies, altogether too many people to be indulging so early in the day. Almost all of the benches were occupied by men, decorum lost, hats still on, their collective voices a roar in her ears. She caught sight of a tavern girl, tray in hand, breasts nearly bursting from

438

her stays. In a dark corner, a gentleman sat with a lady on his lap, one hand around her waist, the other tucked under her skirts.

"Heavens." She tightened her grip on his arm. "I didn't suppose people were so bad in public!"

"Just stay close." Hand on the small of her back, he led her to a bench in a close corner. There was a rough-sawn bar that stretched from one wall to the other, the shelf behind it lined with tapped barrels of beer. The air was damp, smelling of too many bodies too close together, sweating sweet ciders. Everything was a shade of earthy brown; even her dress was dull in the tampered light of too few candles.

Asa ordered two beers, delivered by the busty tavern girl, who leaned her ample assets a little too close for Martha's comfort. Mr. Gracey's fondness for port had formed her taste for richer alcohols, yet there was something comforting about the density of the ale, even if it was sour. She hiccupped, and her belly felt markedly better. It was oddly appropriate to be sitting on a worn tavern bench, warm in her rabbit fur, shielded from the rabble by Asa's tall figure. He sat, elbows on the table, chin on his thumbs.

"See that fellow there." He gestured at a raggedy man with stringy hair and a toothless mouth, muttering over a tankard. With a shaky hand, he made notes in a book, a trembling quill tickling his chin. "That's Gabriel Jenkins. He writes a column for the *Massachusetts Spy,* quite riotous if you can believe it. Any fellow going after votes must be run through by Jenkins's quill first. Now that there's talk of a congress, I've thought about it."

"Oh. A congress?"

"Yes, nothing much, until we've found out how Parliament chooses to punish its miscreant children." He leaned back, running his fingers through his hair. "How'd you feel about that? A right politician's wife."

"Oh." She frowned into her beer. "I don't know. Aren't you busy enough?"

"Impossible, aye. All of these fellows are busy. All members of the Committee. Over there–" gesturing at a portly man with a skewed wig–"Mr. Young. He's a tradesman, and a man of the law, the same, but he also runs a rum distillery. Granted, he has grown sons, but still. Oh, hell–Jenkins is coming, look pretty, darling."

The withered man caught sight of Asa, paused in his muttering, and clapped his book shut, standing with a vigor that didn't match his stature. He approached in an ambling way, kicking up dust, and sat down without permission, fingers tucked protectively around his daybook.

"Wyeth," he said, in a cracking voice, "bringing a lady to a public house, in the middle of the morning? I've noted it in my book." His eyes, watery, ran over Martha's face. She tried to smile. After so many months locked in Wyeth House, studying the same challenged personalities, she'd forgotten what it was like to meet new people.

"Note away," replied Asa coolly. "It'll only make me more interesting. Martha, Mr. Jenkins–Jenkins, m'wife, Martha."

My wife. She thought to correct him, but there was something deliciously possessive about the way he said it. She wished she wasn't so out of sorts! That she looked pretty and slim, the way she used to at revels. The difference must have been amplified by a trick of the brain; Jenkins was watching her, wet eyes on her stomacher, and Asa's hand pressed into her haunch.

"I'm very pleased to meet you, sir." She cleared her throat, breaking a smile. "It's so interesting to see where Mr. Wyeth spends so much time."

Jenkins opened his daybook and took out his quill. An inkwell was produced from his pocket, and he scribbled for a time in silence. Then—"I suppose you've heard the rumors that Hutchinson is to be replaced. By the spring, I'm quite sure. Very bad news, indeed. Retaliation is close at hand."

"Yes," replied Asa, "and I think I know who it is. Bloody Thomas Gage. He'll come in balls swinging, too."

A rosy-cheeked young man slid onto the bench beside Jenkins, clearly several beers into his day. "Hallo, Wyeth," he chirped, "Who's the lady?"

"M'wife, Martha. Martha, Levi Cory, runs letters for the Committee."

"I prefer to say—" with a flourish – "*patriot courier.*"

Asa winced. Martha's head began to spin, her cheeks smarting from smiling. So many men, so many things she hadn't known he was doing! Legislators, elections, delegations. She sat, her hands curled around the beer, bewildered. He was a different Asa, one she rarely saw; smiling, laughing, arguing, his voice mingling with the surrounding din. Happy. A conversation was honed with a Nathaniel Bailey, a Weymouth legislator, and she sat back, at a loss.

It was clear he was plotting something; he never talked to important people for no reason. She knew he'd read a speech at the Old South Church to five thousand. She hadn't read that speech, even though he'd wanted her to. Her heart sank with guilt. He'd never chided her for it, either.

Yet clearly, her presence was doing something. She was a curiosity, far too sweet and innocent to sit in a tavern, but there she was, smiling prettily. Giving charming answers. *Oh, how interesting! Oh goodness, I didn't know, how dreadful!* The gentlemen were thrilled, and Asa watched her, his eyes on fire.

441

"You are a powder-keg of a woman, darling," he announced as they walked out. He kissed her, hard, and then pulled her around the side of the *Dragon*. "Wait here, I've to go around back for a piss."

"Asa, no! Someone will see you!"

He sauntered away, and she leaned against the brick, arms crossed. The balance of everything tipped, simply because he'd taken her to the *Dragon* before Ann Street. There was plenty of time; Robert should be there, and he would wait. Yet, any confidence she'd had after her conversation with Elijah was lost in a haze of sour beer. The lawyering made sense. Show up Papa Wyeth. The profiteering made sense. Show up Papa Wyeth, and the Henshaws, and the Tuckers, and all the pompous Loyalist gentry of Boston who pushed at the indentation in his skull.

But—a politician?

Perhaps, it wasn't just comeuppance. It made sense, to a certain degree, but it was almost a step too far. Hearing the drum of his boots, she rounded on him.

"Asa, are you looking to be elected?"

"Elected?" He smirked, untying Jed. "Elected for what, d'you suppose? Come along."

She threaded her arm through his. "I don't know. Are you wanting to be a legislator?"

"Hmm." He looked ahead, thoughtful. "No, I'd rather not be tied to Suffolk County. I think I've done enough damage here. But if there is a congress, I'm rather thinking I'd make a smart delegate."

"A delegate?"

"Yes. I'll have turned Boston well enough on its head by then."

"Then you'd be writing continental plans. Not—not just Massachusetts."

"That's right," he said airily, as if it wasn't a shocking thing to say. "I've got to kiss the asses of these congressmen for a bit, but I reckon it's a possibility, I've heard a fellow or two say the same." He tugged Jed's reigns, rounding the corner to Ann Street.

She stopped. A chill seeped and settled in the pit of her belly. One thing she knew about Asa Wyeth, any other doubts or darkness aside–if he wanted something, he'd get it, one way or another. He'd fight himself sick, drunk, silly with laudanum; he would spend his money, waste his time, punch his doubts through the floor until his knuckles bled.

Starve himself to prove a point.

Good God. He couldn't kill Robert Henshaw.

Robert Henshaw wasn't worth it. He was not worth ruining the name of a man who could change the world. And more terrifying than that, a prospect that hadn't crossed her mind, until then, looking at Asa, seeing his smile–almost innocent, lit with enthusiasm, happiness–

It may not be Robert Henshaw who died that day. It was just as likely it be Asa Wyeth. He may have been more than a man to her when he was making love, or commanding the house, or winning cases, or slamming heads into walls–but what was that, to the mouth of a pistol?

It was nothing.

She felt sick enough to vomit on the street. Let Robert run away. The bounty hunters would track him down, one day. Asa was a vicious lawyer; whoever this Mr. Cooper was, he could only be the same. But Asa couldn't die–he couldn't lose everything, because of a frantic, foolish choice! *Her* choice.

She dug her heels into the brick. "I-I think," she managed, "we should just go on to King's today."

He turned, frowning. "Nonsense. Come along, I want to take a look."

"I'd rather not–it's upsetting!"

"Darling." He touched her chin. The affection in his eyes was so heavy, it further spoiled the beer churning in her gut. "It's all right," he said softly. "We can make it into something better, aye. Billy would want it."

She followed, swallowing bile, but it rose again and again, eating acid at the back of her tongue. Discreetly, she turned, pretending to catch her boot, and spat on the brick. Past the hatters, *Sign of the Breeches & Gloves, the Golden Key,* too many signs, creaking out damning songs. Too many heeled shoes on hard stone. Too many voices–she stopped once more.

"Asa, I really think we should just go to King's."

But it was too late. Abruptly, he halted. There it was, back and forth, *General Store, William D. Gracey, Proprietor.* The broken window, the hanging iron latch. She stooped to tug on her laces and spat again.

He approached and looped Jed's reigns to the hitching post. "Whatever the hell," he muttered, pushing back his hat. "Bloody vandals, on Ann Street, no less." He reached under his cloak for the pistol. "Jesus. It's probably been like this for weeks."

"Asa–"

He pulled her with him, stepping forward to peer through the window. Every window, the front, the side, the windows to the counting room. She followed, her heart pounding. Nothing. Finally, he nudged open the front door with his boot, and pulling her in at the shoulders, ushered her inside, the pistol now out of his belt. She glanced down at his hand, tight on the grip. The weapon was cocked.

But the shop was still. Exactly how she'd left it. From the window by the counter, light fell in bright beams, dust dancing like snow. The same wreckage, as if the rum-drunk soldier had simply left that day, and never returned. The shelves were disarranged, but nothing was broken. A red coat was balled in the corner, dull with filth and time. Asa caught sight of it and rolled his shoulders, scowling.

"I see. Bloody redcoats. Should've known, they're so desperate for lodging."

The realization that it was simply redcoats seemed to loosen him. He knew how to handle redcoats; he could even talk to them, reasonably enough. She glanced around the room. Stillness. Clearly, nobody was there. There was no weight of presence, nothing to tickle her intuition or trigger her gut.

Robert hadn't come.

Asa, holding her hand tight, kicked open the door of the counting room. The same; not vandalized, but disarranged. Her belly roiled at the sight of the bureau plat, her body pinned by invisible hands, that short cock pressed into her thigh. White britches slack, sagging eyes, rum breath—and Robert.

Too early in the day for strumpets.

But he wasn't in the counting room either. She breathed deep, black spots irritating her vision. He hadn't gotten her letter. Or he didn't trust her, after all—she couldn't blame him. Thank Christ, thank God, they just needed to go!

"Sir, how about you and Elijah come back another time?"

But he was silent, jaw tight, a muscle working. Then he stooped and picked something from the shadow of the molding.

Her heart stopped—the folding knife.

"Martha." A pause, then— "You never returned this to me."

She dropped his arm, averting her eyes as he turned. She stared at his hand, at his thumb working over the etching of his name in bone. The truth was, she'd forgotten about the folding knife. In the pulsing excitement of the moment, all she'd known was to flee; any traces of treachery were not that, but proof that she had survived, and made the right choice. But now, seeing the betrayal sink in was like watching a hot blade cut through butter.

He tossed the knife lightly in his palm, then dropped it in his pocket. He was silent for a time, then–

"I've wasted a great deal of time," he said stiffly, "combing through my household, trying to find a serving girl stupid enough to see Bohea on a list and dispatch it anyway." He smiled tightly, but his eyes were stone. "I suppose I knew it was you, just too foolish with trust."

"Asa–"

"Oh, bloody hell! Don't *Asa* me! I *told* you not to ride to the city!" He turned, fingers working at the back of his neck. Then he brushed by her, cutting a shadow through the doorway to the shop. "Martha, what the hell am I supposed to do with you?"

She hung her head, her heart slamming. If it'd just been that– just a ride to the city–she might've unsheathed her claws for a good fight. She might've lit a fire under her doubts, boiling them to anger, and resentment–and indignation–he couldn't tell her what to do! He couldn't take away the freedoms so freely granted by herself, and never argued by William. Now, she could only drop her face, trembling, silent.

"What do I have to do to get you to *listen* to me!" he shouted. "Redcoats rape! Redcoats fuckin' rape! Was that here when you came?" He gestured at the crumpled coat in the corner. "Well, was it?"

"I made a mistake," she managed, "I wasn't thinking. I'm so tired of being locked in the house. And you–you never tell me anything–you wouldn't tell me what was happening at Griffin's–"

446

"Griffin's." He reeled. "Griffin's. Jesus Christ, it's even worse than I thought. You rode to see the tea ships, didn't you?"

"I didn't ride to Griffin's!" The counter flew before she could stop it; she clapped a hand over her mouth.

"Yes, you did!" He threw up his hands. "Admit it right now, Martha Ann, you rode to Griffin's Wharf the moment you knew I was out of the city! Jesus, I wouldn't be half as angry if you'd just spent my money on Tory shop tea!"

"Please." Her teeth sunk into her knuckle, a sob shaking her shoulders. "Please, I made a mistake, and I won't do it again!"

"And what is to convince me you've changed, aye? Because I'm here to watch you? Well, what the goddamn hell am I supposed to do, chain you to a bed? Maybe I should forget your dignity, and go back to fucking you all the time. Luck willing I'll get you pregnant and you can't leave the house!" He pushed back her hood. The anger on his face was too harsh to meet; she dropped her eyes, the fear in her belly overcoming the illness.

"But you, you would." His voice hissed in a whisper. "You're so goddamn selfish, you'd ride to the city alone, with my child growing inside of you. Wouldn't you?"

"I hadn't promised then. I mean my promise!"

"Your promises don't mean shit to me. You tell me right now, was there a redcoat in this room? Don't you dare lie to me!"

The boom of his voice only enhanced the following silence and every small sound that rose in the aftermath. A cracking of the walls, a tiny piece of bark, shedding from the joist overhead and falling to the floor with a whisper. A muffled voice, laughing, passing by outside the walls. And her lie, on the tip of her tongue, bursting like a blister to be spoken—to save her—from what? His kindness, his concern—no, she could *not* lie. Not about that.

"Yes." Her shoulders shook, tears flowing free. "There was an–an infantryman in the room, but–"

"Jesus." He pulled off his hat, running his hand over his face. "Jesus Christ, Jesus Christ…"

"I wasn't hurt, Asa!"

"Were you raped? Don't you dare lie to me!"

"I was *not* raped!" she insisted. "Let's go. Please! I want to go home!" Thank God Robert hadn't come! She could heal this, she could make this go away, if he just *didn't* come!

"I find it bloody hard to believe that a pretty girl like you could stand in a room alone with a redcoat, and not be raped. So if you were raped, I need a picture. Because whoever it was will go to slaughter in my courtroom, and I'll watch him hang by the balls at the gallows!"

"I was not raped! I promise!"

Silence. Then, "Were you touched?"

She twisted her fingers.

"Martha! Were you touched?"

"I–" The thought crossed her mind to lie again, but it was clearly futile. "I was," she choked. "A–a little."

He backed toward the shop. Paused, ran a hand through his hair, paced for a time, and then returned to the doorway. "Where?" he asked dully. "Where were you touched."

"He–he didn't touch any private part of me." She let the tears run hot trails down her nose, pathetic, and spoke, run-on, slurring. "He pressed me against the bureau plat. It didn't hurt. He was–he was drunk. He dropped his breeches around the knees and was trying to pull up my skirt, but he was stopped. That's all that happened–I swear it!"

"Did he touch you with his cock? Or did he force you to touch it in any way?"

"For–for a second, I think, I-I don't know–he was, you know…he was touching himself. But then he was stopped, that was it." *Just speak.* Give him words, truths.

"Who stopped him?"

"Another soldier."

"*Another* soldier. Another?" He threw up his hands. "Jesus, how many were there?"

"I-I don't know, it was dark–"

Pacing again, hat swinging, his figure was black against the yellow light, and the splitting of shadow made her dizzy. Her betrayal pushed momentarily to the side, he was simply the lawyer, preparing a rape case for court. Head working, jaw tight–abruptly, he stopped. Pushed his hair back, clapped his hat on. Then he faced her.

"Martha," he said. "You're right, let's go home."

"Asa, I'm *very,* very sorry. You have to believe me!"

"No." He stared at the floor. "I'm the one who should be sorry. I think you need to talk to Cassandra. A woman–I-I can hire you a governess if you think it would help."

"A governess? I'm too old for a governess!" She shook her head. "Asa, where is this coming from?"

"That's the trouble, darling. You've been hurt. And you're too damn innocent to even feel it. I'm a cad, I am, fucking you like that. Taking you to public houses–Jesus, I'm sorry." He wrung out his wrist as if to fling off the feeling. "Let's just go home, for the love of God!"

"Sir, I've always said yes to you. You've done nothing wrong!"

"You've said yes, all right." He met her eyes. "But I should've heard it differently, knowing Billy for who he was. Now take my arm. We're going back to the house."

He turned to pass into the shop, but an odd movement took hold of his body, almost as if he'd been wrung out, starting at the shoulders, and he stumbled, spurs catching the wood. Her ears rang with a cracking sound, unnatural. Then, she saw red. A flying fist caught his cheekbone, launching from the shadow on the other side of the wall.

Robert.

Asa reeled, hand to his face, and Robert darted from the dimness, catching him around the neck.

"Robert! No!" she shrieked. "Let him go–let him go, I lied! I lied!"

A gagging sound broke through the struggle. Asa's eyes pressed shut, and then, he lurched forward, arching at the waist, and kicked backward, catching Robert in the crotch with a spur. Robert stumbled, hitting one of the shelves in the shop. Breaking glass shattered the air. Asa scrambled out of his cloak, hand to the butt of his pistol–but Robert's body shot forward, a battering ram of hard muscle, catching Asa at the waist. The pistol fell to the floor with a clatter, and through the breaks of shadow, she caught the toe of Asa's boot flicking it across the room. It skittered, flying past her skirts.

"Take the pistol, Martha!" But it bounced off the wall, skimming over the floorboards, swallowed beneath the bureau plat.

She was frozen.

A wet *thud* split the air, another swinging fist catching Asa on the temple. His skin split; blood, purple in the dim light, sprayed the wall like port wine.

"Robert, please!" she screamed. "Stop–stop! I'm telling you, I lied!"

Her voice was a distraction, and Robert paused long enough to glance. His muscles bunched to barrage again, but as he darted forward, there was a sickening snap. Cartilage split. His mouth spluttered with blood, and he stumbled backward, caught in the teeth by the sharp bone of Asa's elbow. His eyes watered, and he spat.

"Wyeth—you motherfucker—you fight like a woman—ah!" He doubled at the waist, clipped in the belly with a boot.

"I'm taking you to the sheriff, Henshaw! Stand up—" Asa's fingers curled around the neck of Robert's frock, and the lolling body reeled, swinging, the blond head dashed against the wall. Over and over—glass shattered—*my beautiful glass windows*—blood ran in rivers through blond hair.

"I won't fuckin' kill you, Henshaw—"

Slam, slam, the pop of breaking skin—

"Greenleaf will never arrest me, fool, he's a friend of Dunaway!"

Robert broke free, twisting out of his frock. There was a flicker of a moment before Asa lunged again, tackling him at the waist and driving his body into a shelf. Robert flailed, throwing blind punches. In a line of light, she saw it, a silver pistol, clipped to the back of his belt. There was a scrabbling and a clattering of heels, and Robert pitched forward, gasping, a hand over his nose. Blood leaked, spurting, through his fingertips.

Asa rounded, planting a boot into the small of Robert's back, snatched the pistol from the holster, cocked it, and leveled it at the back of Robert's head.

Yes, Asa, shoot! Shoot, please—

"Henshaw, on your feet." Asa coughed. He spat.

Robert gasped, hands on the floor, leaking blood. It pooled, seeping to the black tips of her boots. His nose was broken, bent to the side, wheezing for breath.

"On your feet, man!"

"You can't take me to deputy, you fool," Robert rasped. Then again, he lunged. The movement was desperate, a wild play from a man who had evidently never brawled in his life. His forearm cracked into the bone of Asa's shins, hard enough to knock him off-balance; Asa stumbled, one palm to the earth, the other clutching the pistol to his chest. In a flash of gold and red, Robert was back on his feet, arm curled around Asa's neck, fist poised, wrist cocked. A wet thud. His index and middle finger curled, grinding over and over again into the fracture. Asa stumbled, coughing, forehead pressed to the floor, his body pitching with each blow. Far away, her voice pierced the air with screams.

Do something, do something!

She stumbled to the bureau plat, dropping to her knees. Asa's pistol was out of reach, deep in the shadows. Desperately, she clawed at the middle drawer—

"Don't move!" Robert's voice split her ears. "Don't you dare move, Martha! I will kill him, I'll kill him!"

She snatched the dictionary and hurled it blindly at his head. The corner of the spine caught his temple; the force was enough to stay his fist, and Asa rolled to his feet, hand to the wall. Blood poured from his nose. He was sickly pale, but he still held the pistol.

"You better fuckin' run, Henshaw," he said, in a mumbling slur. He coughed and spat. Finger on the trigger.

Asa, what are you doing? Shoot, just shoot—

Robert, for a frantic moment, met her eyes. Her betrayal was the deepest cut, and she couldn't look at him—she sobbed and fell to the floor, hands over her face. Robert's boots faded, and she did not look up, even as the door rattled shut behind him.

Asa dropped. One arm slack over his knee, clutching the pistol, the other, gripping the back of his head. She watched him like that, hunched until her sobs faded into silence.

He was broken. He couldn't even move. He just sat and breathed, and spat. The room settled, the sunlight on blood-licked glass throwing a peculiar pattern on the floor. Gradually she began to hear things again; horses hooves on the brick outside, footsteps, voices, and laughter. Her tears dried into numbness, a shock that locked her body. Belly churning, but unable to vomit. Her pelvis shooting with cramps, her hands curled on her lap.

Asa's boot slid and he shifted, putting a palm to the floor. Slowly. A grunt, a groan–he crouched, head in his hands. *Wait there for a minute. Two minutes. Five.* Then, hand to the wall, he stood. Rolling his neck, he moved, catching the shelves, and stumbled to the bureau plat, pulled open the drawer at the bottom, and took out the laudanum. He pulled the cork with his teeth and drank deep.

"All right." He rolled his shoulders. Brushed off his hat, and clapped it over curls damp with blood.

"On your feet, Martha," he said, turning to cough into his elbow. "I'm going to need a bloody bath."

28

CALL ME PAPA WYETH

B ack at the Estate, she stood in the barn, sobbing wildly, her body wrecked. He dismounted Jed and paced, hat in one hand, the other pressing into the back of his skull, hair matted with blood, his knuckles split–purple bruises littered his collarbone. The break beneath his eye was a river of red.

For too long he paced. Until he broke, flinging his hat. He strode to the trough in the corner of the barn and plunged his hands into the icy blackness, dashing the water over his face. A wild man, hair on end, sleeves soaked to his elbows. He pressed his face with a towel, and it blossomed through with red. Then he stood in front of her. Even with her head dipped, she could see the violent way his fingers shook.

"Martha." He lifted her chin. She fought to keep her eyes down. "I'm a tradesman, yes? Sometimes it tickles my fancy to go to court." He pushed her chin upward, her head bent to the rafters.

"Asa–"

"But I'm *not* a goddamn assassin!"

His voice boomed. Boots beat again, passing through her vision. Droplets of fresh blood spotted the floor.

"God, Martha. What the fuck am I going to do with you? What do you think, I'd just shoot him in the head? Jesus Christ! I'm a lawyer!" His fist hit the wall, and she jumped, her knuckles to her mouth. "A lawyer, a goddamn motherfucking lawyer!"

The wild high hadn't quite faded, and she found her words. "Mr. Standish walked free!" she shouted, fighting to meet the volume of his voice. "With nothing but a brand on his thumb!"

"Yes! Because my ass showed up to court every day for a week to earn that M! I fought bloody tooth and claw for that!"

"Men walk free after murdering all the time, you said it yourself! Robert is never going to hang! That bullet wasn't meant for my father, it was meant for you!"

"Self-preservation was my argument with Elijah. Jesus! Whatever the truth, that jury was sucking my cock! Elijah is goddamn lucky he was in an alley with one witness. One! How would you argue that with Robert? He was drinking a snifter at a Tory revel, thirty feet away from anyone in the courtyard!"

"If there was a shadow of a doubt, you should've pulled that trigger! You know I'm right!"

"Martha." He stared at her, grotesque; the blood on his face was nearly black, and his eyes–not flickering, nor soft, but polluted with fear. It shot past her heart, to the worst part of her soul.

"Fuck." The blood trickled to his mouth, and he ran a hand to catch it. "It's not my duty to kill for you. If he walked free, there would've been doubt. And you can't hang a man where there's doubt! But you can be goddamn sure, I've a bloodhound of a lawyer making a bulletproof case. Am I an idiot, Martha?" His eyes widened, incredulous. "Am I? Well?"

"You said they would push for manslaughter—he can walk free!"

"Oh, bloody nice. I *knew* you were going through my depositions." All at once he lurched, leaning into the wall, fingers pressing into the back of his skull. "Ah! Bloody hell, I've got a nail in my brain!"

It was instinctual for her to reach for him, but he brushed her away, stormed by, and began untacking Jed. "Funny thing, aye, that you'd think that little of me." He slipped the crown piece over the animal's ears. The bit fell with a clang into his hand. Trembling, ripping at the cinch, tossing the saddle over a stall.

She watched, cold—no, frozen—as he crouched, coughed, and vomited on the floor of the barn.

"Asa!"

"Don't you dare touch me. I swear to Jesus Christ!" He spat ribbons laced with blood. Another heave, more vomit. Jed side-stepped, ears pricked in irritation. "Have a good look, aye." He rose, running his sleeve over his mouth. "Not so dandy, is it?"

"Asa—I-I think you should go to the house—"

"Don't tell me what to do!" Chucking Jed under the chin, he led the animal away. Then he strode to where his hat had landed, brushed it off, and pushed it over wild curls. "I find it interesting, I really do. What am I to you, Martha?" He threw up a hand. "A good enough fuck? A fellow with a lot of money, who'll rot off in a few years? I don't know. But your distrust is the deepest of insults. Hours and hours of my time, how many late nights—trips to King's Street—I've got Isiah Cooper! He's a mongrel dog of an attorney, he won't beg for anyone!"

"I didn't know the extent that you'd gone. You don't speak to me about these things!" Her throat stabbed with each word. The high was dropping fast, replaced with dread, shattering the assurance that had held her head for days. Lost on Union Street, sour with beer.

"I shouldn't have to!" he insisted. "And you let him go. Just like that. Didn't you?"

She closed her eyes. The world spun. The blood, the fear, the smell of vomit, his wild disbelief; it was nearly enough to render her unconscious.

"Robert can't live," she broke. "I-I was trying to help you—I was trying to give you something!"

"You really thought I was going to shoot him, didn't you?"

"Elijah Standish shot a man!"

"Oh, Martha." He stepped near and tipping back his hat, he took her at the back of the neck and kissed her, parting her lips, pushing the taste of bile and blood from her tongue to her gums to the back of her throat. Spreading blood over the hill of her chin, in the valley beneath her nose. Her belly lurched, sickened by the iron taste.

She pulled away with a cry, hand over her mouth. "Asa, don't!"

"You go in the house, young lady," he breathed. "I will not jeopardize myself for you." He shouldered by, then paused in the doorway. "Sleep under my roof. Eat my food. As long as you want. One day, I'll come up with a fellow who can handle your selfishness." He touched the brim of his hat. "See you over the bloody dinner table."

Standing in the barn, it had taken only a moment or two before her mind snapped, and she hitched up her skirts, running after him down the slope. Gravel flew around her boots.

"Asa! Asa, wait, please!"

457

He ignored her, bursting through the kitchen, where Cassandra hummed at the prepping table. When she saw him, the knife in her hands fell with a clatter.

"Jesus! What happened to your face?"

"Brawled with a fellow at the public house," Asa grunted, brushing past her.

"Brawled with a fellow! Whatever for! Emory, you're too old to be brawling with fellows!"

"Shut the hell up, and fix me brandy with valerian. I'm getting a bath. Bring it up, straight, with twenty-five! My bloody head is going to split down the back."

Martha watched Cassandra from the corner, her hands pressing her skirts. Brandy, valerian tincture, the laudanum bottle, tapped twenty-five times... she leaned into the wall and burst into tears.

❃

Asa was not there when dinner was served.

He didn't come out of his room for three days. Head down, silent in the hall, she caught glimpses of Cassandra, hurrying, carrying bottles, muttering.

"Tavern brawls...I will tar him, I swear to Christ..."

Distantly, she caught the sounds of vomiting. The walls vibrated. Glass broke. She sat on the edge of her bed, numb. For hours and hours, she tried to make sense of it, to put together something from the fragments, some semblance of a picture that justified what she'd for so long placed so much faith in. But nothing manifested. All the things she was sure had been true didn't match up to what he'd said. Why had she done it, if she knew he'd been working with Cooper? She'd read the deposition. But the idea that she could simply hand Robert to him–no courts, no mistakes, no iron brands–had blinded her.

Just a pistol, and a feeling.

On the evening of the third day, she slipped into the corridor, sick and raw from crying, and caught Elijah strolling from the library, a smile on his face. He saw her and beckoned with a finger.

"Is he going to be all right?" She sniffed, wrapping her arms around her middle.

"Hmm. I reckon. He's talking to a bear in a skimming-dish hat, he said she looked quite pretty in the corner. It's all right, I've cut 'im off." He held up a bottle of laudanum, gave it a shake, and slipped it in his pocket.

"Should Sam go for an apothecary? I-I thought it was just twenty-five drops."

"Twenty-five drops, twenty-five times a day, to put the brute out." Elijah chuckled, then dropped his arm around her shoulders, guiding her down the corridor. "Don't worry, m'dear," he said lightly as they walked. "I reckon he'll snap out of it by morning. Ah, nothing quite blows fire through the veins of a man, better than a brawl in a public house!"

She stopped. "Mr. Standish."

Twilight cut through the windows, softening his eyes from blue to a grey. "Yes, m'dear?"

"Mr. Wyeth didn't brawl at the public house."

He smiled softly. "I know. Let's have a drink, what do you say? Cass keeps a sherry hidden in the kitchen, takes nips while she's tinkering with her herbs."

In the kitchen, it was two glasses of sherry, a fatherly pat on the back, and she was hunched on a stool, crying her eyes out.

Telling him everything. Each time he moved to pat her hand, or to straighten his spectacles, it flashed in her vision—the M, purple on his thumb. Up and down, just a hand, at the end of the arm of a kind man, holding her steady in a hopeless moment.

It made no sense. Elijah could do it for himself, but Asa couldn't. Robert could. Asa couldn't. It could've been easy; that pistol was ready, all the time, every day, burning at his hip.

"I-I wasn't trying to throw him off." She brushed at the tears, but they wouldn't stop. "I didn't know Robert knew about the pistol-whipping!"

"You're grieving," Elijah reasoned. "The mind plays tricks on us when we're most vulnerable. I don't blame you. I probably would have pulled the pistol the moment I realized he was there."

"I-I misjudged him!"

"It's not hard to do with Wyeth. He's a funny fellow." Elijah held up the sherry. "Another spot?"

There was something about the gesture that was achingly familiar. Mr. Gracey. He would've healed her ills the same way, with a soft voice, and a drink! She nodded through another rush of tears. How could she, but she felt safe, comforted by a man who had killed another man, and still sat in the kitchen, drinking sherry and making jokes. And Asa was talking to bears in skimming-dish hats—it made no sense—every last thing was so wildly different from the way she'd thought it would be.

She did not know Asa Wyeth at all.

"Wyeth's had me mad enough to throw punches if you can picture such a thing." Elijah chuckled, filling her glass. "I think it's what makes him such a canny lawyer. He plans everything to precision. The fellow doesn't get up in the morning and clean his teeth without thinking through exactly how he's going to do it. You startled him a bit, that's all. He's got something going on that you don't see, I can promise you that. He won't say it, but he does."

"Oh, that doesn't seem fair!"

"No, no it doesn't," he mused. "You've got your work cut out for you, marrying that man."

"Is that supposed to make me feel better?"

"I'm not sure." He smiled apologetically. "But forgive me for saying, Miss Gracey, I think you read him a little wrong after all. Certainly, he can brawl like a motherfucker–I've been on the receiving end. But retribution is exact, you see. If he's aiming to take down the Henshaws, he's doing it by pen, not pistol. Buying up warehouses. Spending every damn day, soaking wet on the docks, until the Tory gentry starves through the cracks. You see? A stubborn ass." He patted her hand. "The only way Robert Henshaw is going to die by Wyeth is on the end of a noose, after he's been properly run through the American courts."

"But–but Robert could go free!"

"Like me? I see your fears, my dear, and they hurt me daily. I hate to tell you this, but if Robert were set free by verdict of a jury, Asa would let him go." His eyes took on a heavy, far-away quality. "But the likelihood of that happening is little. The fellow knows how to flip a jury on its head."

It was in that moment, drunk on sherry, swollen with tears, that she realized she would never know what had happened at Whitehall. Because what had really happened was nothing to the end. Snuffed out by a judgment.

"Listen, Miss Gracey." Elijah leaned back in his chair, crossing his ankle over his knee. "Give him some time, he'll come around. But–just know."

He reached, lifting her face by the chin. She shuddered, dropping her eyes to the floor.

461

"Just know," he said softly. "There is only one man who will ever die at the end of Wyeth's pistol. Keep that in mind, all right, m'dear?"

Now she understood Asa Wyeth. Too well, too suddenly. Ensnaring Robert had been a delirious high, and she tumbled fast. It had taken all the strength left in her to smile and say goodnight to Elijah.

The idea of Robert dying at the end of Asa's pistol made sense, and it still made sense, as an action removed from Asa Wyeth. But she hadn't considered the sort of man he was. It hadn't mattered to find out. Her grief was that confusing, that sharp. No one explained it; when Asa had tried, it'd been brushed off, because all she wanted was to fuck and kiss and cry, and sit on his lap and drink his brandy. For a fleeting moment in time, those things had pretended to heal her.

She rose to a pale green dawn, stumbled to the wash basin, and vomited. Her head was swollen and aching; a bottle of Madeira had been the only thing that would put her out. She grimaced, braided her hair quickly, and tossed her dressing gown over her shoulders. She had to talk to him. To explain herself, and she would be honest! Lay bare her misconceptions, her innocence–her grief–

Asa, help me. Please.

She slipped out, turned, and froze in the corridor. He was rounding into the hall, a black willow in his greatcoat, boots, and tarpaulin hat. Pale as the moon. The split on his cheekbone had healed to a black line; his eyes were dull and shot with blood. When he saw her, he frowned and coughed into his elbow. Then, he turned on his heel with a grunt and headed for the door.

"Asa, wait! Please, sit with me for a moment–"

"Going to be late to the public house. Go back to bed, Martha, you look like hell."

She stared at him, her throat bursting. *He* was the one who looked like hell, as if he'd wrestled demons for three days in that room. Opium voices, calling from the walls.

"Sir." She drew a breath, tears blurring her vision. "You have to let me tell you that I—that I am sorry!"

There was silence. Then, he shifted and touched the brim of his hat.

"Going to be late."

"Asa, that's not fair!"

"Not fair?" A spark flickered, pulling his chin forward. "I'll tell you what's not fair." He turned and ate the distance in fierce strides. He was too tall, a tower of black, and she couldn't help it—she sobbed.

"I'll tell you what's not fair." His tone was mean, spitting. "What's not fair, is the fact that I took one look at your pert little ass walking away from me, your hand on Robert's arm, and I fell in love. Because I did, aye. I did. And it was a mistake. So how the hell do you think I feel? Writing the testimonies that may or may not justify Billy's death, when we both know it should've been me? Then off to a nice fuck with his daughter? When I owe Billy my goddamn life. Christ!" He ripped his hat off and clapped it against his thigh. "You're so—so bloody ignorant!"

"I know I've been ignorant! I know, and I'm sorry. I didn't know you felt that way about my father. I didn't know—"

"You didn't know, aye." An eyebrow rose. He composed himself, and the panic was gone; the old Asa, back on his feet. "It's a strange thing, sweetheart, how you don't know things when they're standing right in front of you. I entangled Billy in my life's work. Ever wonder why? I *know* you have. Bloody silly idea, in hindsight, wouldn't you say? Because look where we are.

Here I am, off to the public house to prove myself once again, and you—you're an orphan!"

The disgust in his expression was too much. She sobbed, clapping a hand over her mouth, but he only smiled and raised her chin with a finger. "Oh, don't worry, darling," he said cruelly. "I know the wardship ends in a month, but it's all right. I'll always take care of you. But I'm going to do it properly from now on. Not as a lover." A featherlight kiss met her forehead. "As a father. It's what you really need. I lost myself for a time, and I'm very sorry for it. It won't happen again."

"Asa—what—what are you saying?"

"There will be no magistrate, Martha." He shook his head. "Take some time to heal, as I said in the beginning. When you feel you're ready, we can work on finding you a fellow. Someone who isn't dragging so many chains. Might be nice to cut down on the clatter." He pointed at her, backing to the door. "But no fucking until there's a ring."

"This is a mistake!" She reached, balling his sleeve, but he resisted, prying her fingers loose.

"No, darling, it's not a mistake! It made sense for a minute, given the circumstances, and I acted on that reasoning. But I see it now. You're a child!"

"I-I am not! I am twenty years old, stop saying that!"

"Oh, sweetheart," he breathed. "You are always and forever proving my points. This was never about numbers."

Then he turned on his heel, boots echoing with each step; she picked up her skirts, scrambling after him.

"Asa, you stop right now! Please! You're not thinking!"

"Oh, I'm thinking, I assure you. I slept for ten hours straight, which I haven't done in years. I think I've pissed out all the laudanum. I don't have a headache. In fact." He paused, cocking his head. "I'm feeling quite good. It'll be nice, really, not to have

464

to worry about getting you off all the time. Don't fret, I'll make sure I pick you a well-hung fellow."

"You are mocking me!"

"Perhaps. Oh–you're to call me Mr. Wyeth from now on. Papa Wyeth, if you want." And he was gone, in a billow of black and the drumbeat of boots, and she dropped to the floor, sobbing into her hands.

He fought in the ugliest way. Bittersweet mockery. Telling her he knew that she knew everything, with the subtlest knifepoint, slipped under the skin of her heart, and moved–just a little. And she was sick, because he was right.

I don't know.

It had always been a cry for help, a desperate question she'd sought the answer to in all the wrong men. Robert–he had used her innocence. Mr. Gracey–poor, sweet Mr. Gracey, he had been weak in the presence of how much he loved her. Only Asa had ever asked.

What don't you know about it, darling?

She heaved herself to her feet, forced herself back to her room, and hunched over the washing basin once more.

29

MUSIC, PORT, BRANDY *and* RUM

Days. Weeks—how many, she didn't care to count. The tears dried up; she grew accustomed to his silence. Day after day she rose with her belly turning, her head bursting with thoughts, her heart sore with regret. Her twenty-first birthday came and went, and Asa said nothing. She came in from a walk in the garden to find a box on her bed, tied neatly with a chiffon ribbon. She stared at it for what seemed like forever, the lump in her throat suffocating. It was almost worse because she knew it wasn't thoughtfulness. Yet, she opened it, uncovering a stiff white stomacher, satin with metallic-threaded lace. A set of rose-colored garter ribbons. A beautifully carved wooden busk, with her name engraved on the back.

Don't wear a busk anymore, darling.

She flung it across the room, bursting into tears. They were Robert's things, things he knew she didn't want! Cassandra's assurance that he would "come around" did little to comfort when he knew how to cut so deeply. Like Elijah had said, he was calculated in his revenge. One afternoon, dreary with early spring rain, she sat stabbing with a needle in the parlor, desperately trying to forget herself. Cassandra was lost in a copy of *The Spy;* Amy Prue rolled on the floor, and Elijah the Young was tapping on the hearth with a wooden sword. Asa rounded the doorway, hand pressing the back of his neck.

"Martha," he said sharply, "I want to talk to you."

"Mr. Wyeth–"

"Well, don't just stare! I want to talk to you. Jesus, Cass, get a handle on your son!" he shouted. "He's going to knock the stones out of my hearth. Elijah! *Elijah!* Jesus Christ!"

"Fuck you, Asahel," sneered Elijah, tossing the sword to the polished floor and brushing haughtily under his uncle's arm. Asa stared at his sauntering figure in disbelief.

"Don't look so shocked," snapped Cassandra, wringing out the paper. "Where d'you suppose he learned it from? He's just playing, it's raining outside."

"Stop making excuses. Little fucker, he is," Asa countered, the case to Cassandra's point. "He'll have Wyeth House a pile of rubble! And you–" back to Martha–"this is what I want to talk to you about. I don't want you sewing in the parlor anymore. Standish nearly stuck his ass on one of your needles the other day. You're to have a sewing room. I'd better not find so much as a frayed thread on my settee!"

"Oh dear," mumbled Cassandra.

"Come on," he said, gesturing. "Come now, don't just stare at me!"

She followed him through the hall and around the turn of the stairs. Despite her misery, it was hard to quell her curiosity; the second and third floors of the house were quiet, even if she'd wandered them a time or two. Silent rooms for rare guests. He marched her down the corridor and opened a door to a quaint, well-lit room on the western side of the house. The space was arranged prettily–a chair in the corner, a settee by the window, a table with a full decanter, glassware, and a tea service. All around, bundled in baskets and crates, were bolts of cloth. Wild colors screamed at her aching eyes. Robert's colors. Rich satins, lush silk, textiles that made her feel silly for ever coveting a length of green silk.

"If there's anything else you need, I'll write an order," he said, matter-of-factly.

She faced him. "Mr. Wyeth, I *must* speak to you."

"No, you mustn't," he snapped. "You clutter up my settee with your things, it's as simple as that, and I won't have it!"

And he was gone, with a bang.

She waited until his boots faded, then circled and sat. Alone, in a prison of her own making. From the window she caught a black movement, greatcoat whipping, escaping over the western lawn. She watched, losing the will to even cry. Crying, at least, was somewhat cleansing. It was the dullness that killed her.

She poured herself a glass of port, picked through the cloths, and began to sew. For hours she sewed until the sun licked the lawn in orange tongues. She never saw Asa, skimming back, a black sentinel parting the grass. She sewed a dress for Amy Prue, then another. She stitched an apron and cut patterns for a petticoat, shears snapping, eyes dry. The house was dark by the time she poured a final glass of port; no matter how sour it set in her belly, she put it back. She'd be dead, without the haze. Noiselessly, she shut the door behind her and tiptoed through the corridor to the balcony, fingers tickled by the buffalo hide.

She paused.

The house looked different from that height. Calmer, more understandable. A pedestal above the tangled emotions, the slamming doors, the scurrying feet. Cupped hands, holding her over the roar of heartbreak. At the bottom of the stairs, she jumped, startled by a pair of glassy eyes watching her from the mouth of the passage to Asa's suite…Ham, who loped to greet her when her feet hit the floor. Poor Ham! She patted his head, stroking his satin ears with her thumbs. He could sense a quarrel in the air like he could smell the thought of roasted duck; and this, far beyond a quarrel, had him slinking against walls.

A loud sneeze betrayed Asa's presence in the suite. She straightened, and motioned for Ham to follow. He obeyed, swaying beside her through the tea room and out onto the terrace. It was beyond dusk, the world a dull blue. She skipped down the steps, feet bare despite the chill. She shivered, drawing her arms around her middle, and made her way, head down, to the bathing pool, where she paced the length of stones until she forgot where she was, but her thoughts were oddly clear. Too clear. Everything was too evident.

No more denial, no more waiting.

Three months now since she'd made a mistake. Three months now, she'd kept her silence, she'd pressed herself into walls, she'd tolerated his distant attention. Making sure she was comfortable. Mending torn seams with useless words. Trying and trying and trying to treat her like another warm body in the house, another who had a place, a service, none of which placed her at his side. In his bed. Burning under his kisses.

Maybe. She stared at the water, catching the haze from the last of a twilight sky. The cottage was hers. That life, that simplicity was hers now, forever. Maybe he'd been saving it just for her, if she needed to escape. It was possible, in a world where she'd suffered so much heartache that she'd somehow ended up under the roof of Wyeth House.

She could take Judith, and go back to the tangled fields and chipped white fence. She could fill the walls and the shelves and the turn of every corner with beautiful things. Flowers, poetry, port—everything that had given wings to Mr. Gracey's heart. She

469

could put on her gloves and take to the garden. She could grow new things. She could make promises and break them, as many times as it took for her to heal. Because it was only her.

Martha Ann Gracey.

Slowly, she twisted the ring off her promise finger. She held it in her palm for a moment, studying the contours, where his love skimmed every angle. True, torrid, beautiful—but not right.

She tossed the ring into the bathing pool. Then, she rose and walked up the terrace without a second glance.

※

An aching knot bothered her belly, following her into the next evening. She felt bloated, ugly, dull. Judith laced a blue silk gown, pulled her hair high, and clipped pearl earrings onto her lobes. It was under her own direction; the pins were in her hair, for good. Asa was the only person in the world who knew they didn't belong there, and he would never take them out again.

The knot turned her gut, but she swallowed it down, hunched over a chamber pot. Nothing came up, and the bile calmed. It was just as well; Asa wouldn't engage, past a nod as she sat at the dinner table. He was engrossed in conversation with Elijah, plate untouched, port drained. Their voices came muffled around the pounding in her ears. Quebec. Shipments from Virginia. The warehouses, pricing on the wholesale goods, the fettering of shops.

She tried to drink her port, but her stomach rose in protest.

"Martha, are you all right?" chirped Cassandra. "You look positively ill."

Asa's eyes flickered, betraying concern, but he hid it swiftly.

"Yes, I'm well." She pretended to brighten. "Just a little tired."

But she wasn't. She pressed her palms into her eyes, pushing her plate away, cold sweat beading on her forehead.

Leave.

She stumbled, rising from the table, but lost herself at the doorway. She wasn't a few steps out of the doorway when her belly pitched, and she scrambled for the closest refuge–an empty Parisian vase–and retched into the depths. Her ears rang. Distantly, she caught the scraping of a chair, and Cassandra was over her, hands on her shoulders.

"There, there–come upstairs–let me help you–"

In her room, Cassandra unbound her stays and fetched her a basin. She hunched miserably, vomiting herself dry, tears blending with sickness. The reality of herself, sitting in the darkness, succumbing to the assault, was devastating. When she was sure her belly was empty, Cassandra took the basin and laid her back, limp and damp with sweat.

"There can't be anything left in you, after all that. I'll have Judith bring you some peppermint." Cassandra moved to rise from the bed, then paused and took Martha's hand. She sat, stroking it in silence.

Martha closed her eyes. Thank God for Cassandra! And a weight had lifted, lost into the depths of the bathing pool, and she sighed, rolling her shoulders.

"Martha." Cassandra broke her momentary relief. "I know you've been sleeping with my brother."

"I'm sorry–" Despite her weariness, a hot blush rose.

"I'm not judging you, my dear." Cassandra's tone was wary. "But it would be to your benefit to be mindful. Emory's a heady man, and you're very innocent." She ran her fingers over Martha's forearms, massaging the skin. "You poor girl, you're so in love. I remember those days, in the beginning."

"I don't take your meaning–"

"I've been keeping an eye on you. You're ill, yet you've been raiding the kitchen like a starving dog." She leveled, serious. "I know you're quarreling, but when was the last time you slept with him?"

"Cassie, I don't like this conversation!"

"When, Martha?"

She stared at Cassandra, her heart pounding. The woman had, after all, wiped her body clean after the bitter loss of her virginity. "The day he came back from New York," she muttered through clenched teeth. "But not since. He said we had to be proper."

Cassandra frowned. "I see." Her fingers ran over Martha's belly, kneading gently. "But you're farther on than that."

Martha stared. The bile was rising again; her belly was lead. Yet—

"Cassandra, I bled, though." A frantic memory calmed her for a moment. "I did—since the last time he finished—inside. I just, I don't bleed very often—"

"When?"

"It was the night before he took me to Ann Street." She shuddered at the recollection. "I felt ill, I felt a little pain, my courses were starting. I'm telling you, Cassie, I don't bleed often!" She shook her head, her face burning. The memory rose, startling in hindsight. His hands on her jaw, eyes to the mirror, her hips grinding into the dressing table—

Look at me. Look at my eyes. Am I fucking you hard enough?

"Doesn't surprise me," Cassandra said testily. "You're thin as a rail and live off port wine and sugar. Well, not anymore, young lady." She stood, cracked her knuckles, and began to pace. Martha watched her feet eating the floor, her heart bursting. Dread, like two fingers, pushed deep into the back of her skull.

472

"Well, I suppose I'm off to knock some heads," Cassandra announced, after a few moments of agitated marching. "You're three months at least. Four, probably. Word to the wise, he might think he has a handle on his pecker, but keep this nugget of wisdom in your pocket, unless you want to be spitting out brats for the rest of your life. There's powder in the pan before the gun fires, and there's a lot of bloody smoke in the air after! So what–" She ground her heel, any tenderness lost–"What were you thinking!"

"Cassie, please!"

"I told you to wrap it up with a sheepskin and ribbon! Didn't I?"

"Cassandra! I–I've been eating too many apple betties, I'm just getting fat!"

"That's not an apple betty, that's a Wyeth baby!"

"Oh!" She burst into tears. "Cassie, don't shout at me!"

"Well, maybe you need to be shouted at! Jesus, I don't know if I'm angrier at you, or Emory. Certainly, I'll smack him on the head, but you could've done to close your legs every once in a while. I could hear you moaning all over this house!"

"I was just–I was looking for comfort! He was comforting me!"

"Well, that's an interesting way of putting it," Cassandra snapped. "Are you done vomiting? Because we've got to go downstairs, and you've got to tell him!"

"No! No, I can't–he hates me, Cassie! He didn't want this–he really tried–"

"Oh, certainly, would've been nearly *impossible* for him to keep his prick in his britches!" Cassandra leaned, snatched Martha's wrist, and pulled her to the edge of the bed. "I've had it with you two! Fucking around every corner. Quarreling past bedtime, when there are children! No, you're going downstairs,

473

and you're going to tell my brother you're carrying his bastard!" –dragging Martha to her feet–"And then he's going to marry you!"

"He doesn't want to marry me!"

"I don't give a horse's ass!"

She was hauled from the room, stumbling and in tears, down the corridor. The dining room was empty, save for Judith and a serving girl, taking away plates. "Of course, he's bloody hiding," Cassandra muttered, continuing her march. "He knows. Oh, he bloody knows. I swear to baby Jesus Christ I will break his shins!"

She dragged Martha through the library and beat on the office door.

"Emory!"

"Fuck off, Cass. I'm writing."

She kicked the door open with her bare foot. Asa was at the bureau plat, not writing, but drinking, hat tipped, boots up. Elijah Standish lounged in front, stockinged feet splayed, shoes in a heap. Cassandra hauled him up by the frock, pushing Martha to sit in his place. Then she reached across the bureau plat and snatched Asa's hat.

"Get that ugly thing off your head, you fucker," she barked, flinging it to the ground. "Look at that girl." She pointed at Martha. "Put on a few, hasn't she?"

Asa lowered his boots. "Whatever the hell. Get out, both of you."

"Look at her tits!" She poked, none too gently, at Martha's breasts. "Have a look at that, aye. Nice little round belly–too many ales at the public house, d'you think? Martha, been sneaking off to the public house, have you?"

Martha shook her head, choking on tears. She didn't need to see Asa, though she peered through her fingers, confirming the

474

expression she knew she'd find. Temples tight. Eyes bright. Dread, exhaustion, underlined by the fading split of blood in bruised skin. It would scar; a tattoo of her ineptitude.

"Fine work, Emory, fine work!" Cassandra railed on. "You've really done it this time. One mistake doesn't make it less of a mistake! Your bastard's been cooking in there. Months–" stamping her foot in emphasis–"God, you men are so ignorant!"

"Now, my dear," interjected Elijah, moving towards her on stockinged feet, "A child is a happy occasion, there's no need for distress–"

"A happy occasion." Cassandra reeled. "A happy occasion. Oh, Elijah Standish, I could box your ears right now! Fine, a happy occasion for a man sitting pretty on house arrest. With nothing to do but fit his thumb up his ass, waiting for his savior to roll in seasick in a chaise carriage!"

"I don't get seasick in the chaise," muttered Asa.

"Shut the hell up, you, you mongrel dog attorney!" Back to Elijah, thrusting a finger into his chest–"I'm sick of you mongrel dog attorneys, both of you! You think you're bloody untouchable. You tell me now how untouchable you are, you wouldn't last a split second in that childbed. Oh, a happy occasion, indeed! Once the blood is soaked up and months of pain and torture are forgotten! You've got the bollocks on you, Elijah Standish, now get *out* of this office!"

Once Elijah was gone, Asa shifted in his seat and poured himself a brandy. Martha dared to raise her head again. He was staring at her directly.

"You owe her an apology." Cassandra snatched the glass from her brother and downed it in a gulp. "Jesus, that's fire. All right, she's twenty-one, but she's got the head of a child, and you know it! So you do whatever you have to do to fix this! But it better be fixed!" She flew to the door, jerking it open. "There will be vows spoken in that parlor by the end of the month!"

"I'll have Sam drum up a magistrate." Asa stood abruptly, swinging his coat over his shoulders. "We'll do it tomorrow morning," he said stiffly. "I don't have court."

"No!" Cassandra shouted, so forcefully that Martha jumped in her seat. "No–" She swung around the door. "There'll be a wedding!" she shrieked. "You rat bastard, you, you don't know how long I've been itching for a proper party! You owe me this! Curtains open! Flowers all over the bloody place! Music! Port! Brandy! Rum, and enough people to suffocate you out of your insufferable box! There. Will. Be. A. *Party!*"

And she was gone, slamming the door so violently that the book boxes wobbled and one of the black push-pins sprang from the map. It skittered across the floor, settling into a hideous silence. She could nearly hear the muscle working in his jaw; she could sense his heartbeat through the floorboards to the bottoms of her feet.

"Martha."

She stared at her hands.

"Martha." He shifted. "Where is your ring?"

"I threw it," she managed in a dull whisper. "In the bathing pool."

"You threw it. In the bathing pool."

She could only nod. Her nose was sealed from too many tears, her head dull, her heart, suddenly and oddly calm in the wake of Cassandra's shrieking. She watched him put back another brandy. Then, he flung his hat on the bureau plat and twisted out of his frock. Pipe smoke blew by her hunched figure in an furious waft.

"Asa, what are you doing?"

476

He was ripping buttons on his shirtsleeves. Tugging off his boots. He flung open the door, paused, and stared at her with such a look of disbelieving fury, her belly curdled.

"I'm going for a bloody swim," he snapped, and was gone, with a bang reminiscent of Cassandra's outrage.

❀

She married Asahel Wyeth quietly on a Sunday afternoon at the end of April 1774. Golden sun landed in bright slats over the parlor floor, waxed and polished to reflect. She and Cassandra spent hours in the sewing room, fashioning the wedding gown. She chose an ivory silk, trimmed with dusty rose lace. Not quite pure enough for her to be a virgin for him again. She wanted to be. But she speckled the cloth with embroidered asters.

Every surface in the parlor was littered with spring flowers. In the dining room and the tea room, the tables were pushed against the walls, covered in decadent food. Ropes of braided leaves and flowers hung from the doorways. Shoulders touched shoulders; men from the public houses, and their wives, and shouting children. The spare pictures on the walls jumped in their frames, and poor Kit Beck stood in the corner, eating grapes off a plate.

Asa was clearly uncomfortable, in corded green silk with embroidered buttonholes and pockets. He spoke his promises without faltering, and she repeated her own. There were no flashes of white light, no pulls of desire, only a dull, strange peace. She watched him slip away while the port was poured, and when she saw him again, he had shed the pomp of the wedding attire for his favorite frock and boots.

Drinks flowed to excess under Cassandra's direction, voices bustled, laughter rolled, rising to a song-like pitch. After a time, Martha realized that her husband was gone. Through the hall, she caught him ambling down the portico with a glass of port. She followed, and found him sitting on the stone wall that circled the lower garden. He'd lit his pipe, and the smoke drifted over his head, dissipating into the sunset sky. Lifting her skirts above her ankles, she went to sit beside him.

He didn't speak, and neither did she. Instead, she found herself thinking of all the things she had wanted to be different, of all the parts of Wyeth House that were so dark, and suddenly wishing that they would never change. That she'd die a prisoner in those shining walls, all the doors locked and the windows shuttered, shackled to Asahel Wyeth for the rest of her life.

She rested her head on his shoulder. Behind the sharp-cut lines of his face, the sun burnt the crest of the garden with fiery red and lusty pink.

Evening fell, and Cassandra hummed in the parlor. Martha's eyes were heavy, and her feet ached. Her back ached. The weight in her womb was real, and her body begged for the relief of sleep. Asa had gone back inside when the pipe-bowl was empty, dutifully making exchanges with guests. Jenkins from the *Dragon* was there, making intermittent notes with his crooked quill; Asa had clearly singled him out, cornering him between Elijah Standish and the wall. He'd held his own fairly well. He laughed, his smile softening her knees. But she hadn't seen him since the guests had left and the carriages dragged off into the dusk.

He wasn't in the bedroom. Judith unlaced her and she went to bed, but she was hollow outside of his arms. The room was too large. The ceiling was too high, and her thoughts were too fast. She lay for a while, desperate to close her eyes. Finally, in exasperation, she pushed back the blankets and slipped into her house dress, and padded through the hall.

He wasn't in the parlor, where Cassandra and Adeline were sweeping the floors. If he'd not gone to the city to drown his woes at a tavern, and he wasn't in bed or in the office… She hitched her skirts, tossing her braid over her shoulder, and drifted through the tearoom and down the terrace steps. The moonlight cut prisms on the surface of the bathing pool, dancing in her vision when she looked away. She huffed and crunched through the gravel to the barn.

She followed a flicker on the walls, a dancing globe from lantern light. Asa was sitting on the floor outside Jed's stall, boots crossed at the ankles, glass in hand. She scanned the scene hurriedly, finding two empty bottles of Madeira rolling idly in the dust. Beside him was a half-spent bottle of black rum.

Anger prickled the small of her back. He was drunk! It was a rarity, seasoned as he was; he could clear a bottle of port in one sitting, and saunter down the hall without missing a beat. But the brown eyes that met hers were glassed and split with red.

She swallowed, fighting to reason with herself.

"There she is." He smiled sleepily. "My beautiful bride. Come to put me to bed?"

"I think you've had enough of that bottle."

"You think so?" He squinted, regarding the rum.

"Yes. And you can't sleep in the barn. If you don't mind, this is a bit ridiculous." She pinched her nose, flattening the flaring of her nostrils. A sudden feeling of inadequacy sank in her gut. This man was her husband. Her man, forever, by her side. And she didn't know how to care for anyone, let alone Asa. That he was a person who needed taken care of was a concept that didn't make sense.

She pushed her heels into the earth. "Stopper the bottle, let's go to bed."

"No, no." He fumbled, pouring another glass. "I'm going to finish it. Go to bed anyway, I'll be on the floor in the morning."

"You don't have to be. I–I wanted to sleep with you tonight. It's our wedding night." She couldn't help a faint defensiveness, and she hated it, because he was clearly hurt.

He scoffed. "It's not as if we'll have a nice fuck. You need to rest. Not have some bloody bull pounding away at you."

"Asa, please. I'm not ill, and Cassandra said–"

"I hope you're not talking to my sister about the way I fuck." He gestured at her with the glass. "You women wreak more bloody havoc behind your hands than I *ever* have in a courtroom."

She stared at him. Of all the days to see him break, it was the worst. He'd vowed himself to her that day–and he was clearly unhappy. Tears burned behind her eyes. "You could at least come and lay with me," she whispered.

"But I don't want to lay with you," he said. "I want to sit here, and finish this bottle, and in the morning I'll be on the damn floor. But I'll wake up, eventually. And I will still love you." His voice broke, but he cleared his throat, shaking his head. "You can be sure of that."

She turned, her heart and her stomach tangled. *Just leave him alone, let him finish his damn bottle! What's it to you?* But her sensibilities were changing. When she thought she knew someone, her doubts shouted at her.

He didn't want her to go. He needed her, even if she didn't speak.

She waited.

"Martha, I didn't marry you today out of love. I don't need to marry you to love you. I married you because you're carrying my child, and I'm a decent fellow, all right. I love you, but Jesus–I'm so–so *goddamn* angry at you!"

She fought tears. "That's–that's painful for me to hear."

"But it's true."

"I know."

He stared at the toe of his boot. "You see. Honesty is always better. It hurts, but it's better." There was a pause, and then he sighed. "I will say, darling, I didn't come back to Boston for this. But goddamn. I saw you that night, and it was over for me. I'll tell you something, I don't play. But the moment I watched you walk away, with your pretty little hand on Robert's arm–well. Bloody show me the rules."

"I'm not sure what you mean," she faltered.

"Don't pretend. I hate it." He took his pipe out of his pocket and fumbled to open the tobacco box. All at once, in a surge of curiosity–her heart pounding–she stepped forward, opened it for him, and retreated.

"*Thank* you, darling!" He smiled. "It'll be all right, in the end. You'll see. Perhaps I'm being foul right now, but you're the best woman for me. I suppose it doesn't matter how we got here. I just wish it hadn't been so excruciating." The flare of the lit tinder stung her nose, and she watched him, the chill in her fingers dropping off. "I saw you, and I wanted you. Then it was all–bloody messy. You were Billy's daughter." He grimaced. "You walked away with Robert. Martha, I really did want to hurt him. It's rotten, it is, what I did."

"You did nothing wrong. I know what he did to you."

He paused, then sighed. "That night at Midsummer's. That was on purpose. I knew he would be there, and you were begging to be touched. So I made a fine show of it. A part of me wanted him to open the door. Now look where we are, a moment of vindictive weakness, and I had to track my boots

481

through Billy's blood. I was no better than Robert–I *was* Robert." He pressed his fingers into his forehead. "An eye for an eye. Bloody interesting notion, don't you think? Now we both know that isn't how it works."

"Asa." She dropped her eyes. The lantern lit the earth a curious pink, and she scuffed her feet, stirring up dust. To see him weak was new. Almost eerily necessary, and her irritation was fading fast. She'd made many mistakes when it came to his heart, and to know he wasn't perfect–it soothed her guilt. It was selfish, she knew, but it was real.

"For what it's worth," she said with a sigh, "it wouldn't have mattered. I turned Robert away because of you."

He raised his face and watched her in silence, for uncomfortably long. She held steady, until all at once, he snatched up the tricorn from his knee, pushing it down low on his head.

"Thank you, darling." His face was hidden by the hat. "Thank you. Jesus. Don't fuckin' look at me."

All at once, her heart flared with warmth, and she stepped into the lamplight, and tugged the hat from his head. "Let's get you to bed," she insisted gently, pulling on his elbow.

He nodded. She passed her arm around his waist, and he rose, stumbling, and followed her. She wanted to cry, walking like that with him. Step by fumbling step, all the way back to Wyeth House. He fell to the bed and was asleep almost instantly, as if a weight had been lifted. But she felt it on her shoulders. A chasm had opened, and though flooded with warmth, it frightened her. The only thing she had given him was her body, and it had been enough–he was still there. But it wouldn't be enough anymore.

She was not the only one who felt grief and regret.

30

the SLOOPS WERE NEW *and* FAST

S he watched him struggle night after night in his fight
against the poppy. Sometimes he won, but most of the
time, he failed quietly, drinking in the office alone. It broke her
heart. He'd been victoriously clean until Robert's knuckles had
driven into his skull, and now, it was ten times worse. Not
because his consumption was more. It was still substantially less,
but it was a battle he'd lost in front of those he'd sworn his
victory to. At the end of each day, she went to sleep with the
guilt of it hanging in her heart.

Yet, Asa didn't chastise her. She was utterly forgiven, and
day after day, each small task completed under her fingers was
done in an aching apology. Cassandra spread out the record
books and daybooks, laid out the plans of the household, and
Martha learned, this time without grudge. Gradually the things
that had been necessary annoyances–servants' disputes, pay, lists
for the city–she took from his plate. As time passed, she found
comfort in the routine. She was mistress. A quietness settled,
calm like the gut of a forest after a rain.

But there were holes in Asa's heart, and the things that she'd learned–especially what Elijah had told her–brought a heightened awareness. It wasn't fair, and she never expressed it, but her eyes saw the pistol clipped to his hip differently. When late nights found him with his head in his hands, she brought him back to life by rubbing his shoulders or fixing him coffee. She read his speeches, instead of skimming them.

His words on paper were not the same as the ones that left his lips, much more than cries for help in paper columns. Thoughts that could've moved mountains, if brought before the correct assembly.

"I'm trying for the delegacy," he announced, sitting in bed with his spectacles perched on his nose. The window was open, gusting the scent of late spring roses. Martha sat in her customary evening seat, brushing her hair at the dressing table.

She turned. "Asa. Really?"

"Yes." He frowned at the paper on his lap. "I'm tired of Boston. I've pretty well ruined it anyway."

"So what does that mean?" She rose, crossing the room to sit at his feet.

"Well." He paused. "Travel, I suppose. I'd have to go to Philadelphia. But–I helped make the mess at the ports, you know. On purpose," he added pointedly. "But it could turn into something more interesting."

"Is there campaigning to do?"

"Not really." He tossed the paper. "I've been in it for months, getting my ass spanked at the *Dragon*. Jenkins has finally written me a pretty column. Bloody ridiculous, really," he muttered, crossing his arms with a scowl.

She took the paper, smoothing it on her thigh. "So what do you have to do? From here?"

"They'll take it to a vote in the South Church." He drained his brandy glass, then, almost sheepishly– "Sweetheart, can you fetch me the laudanum?"

She nodded quickly, pushing off the bed and padding to the office. She searched the bureau plat, coming up with the little bottle; the skull glared at her, daring her to comment. It was half-empty already. She swallowed hard, glancing around the room. Her eyes fell on the bookshelf, hating how *Love In Excess* watched at her, even after all the mistakes and forgiveness.

"Darling, you all right in there?"

"Oh. Yes!" She shook her head and snatched the laudanum and brandy. With a forced smile, she turned around the panel and crossed the room to fill his glass.

"How many drops?"

He smiled, gently prying the bottle from her hand. "Never mind." He poured it himself, an amber waterfall long enough that her fingers itched, fighting the urge to snatch it away. He topped it with brandy and put it back. Then he leveled with her, smiling, eyes bright.

"You look like a goddess," he said.

"Asa–"

"You do." He leaned forward, nudging the shoulder of her dressing gown. It fell, exposing her breasts, which, (staring at herself disgruntled in the mirror), she couldn't decide if she liked or not. Full, luscious even, driving him mad over the plunging necklines of her gowns.

"Look at me, darling. You do. Christ, I don't think you've ever been so beautiful to me."

That he could still make her blush like that! It was a gut instinct to find it silly, not in her heart–her heart ached for it–but in the cynical part of her head. She said nothing. Instead, she moved closer, slipping a hand underneath the blankets, following the length of his thigh. She worked him, leisurely, then dropped the house dress to the floor, knees planted firm on either side of his hips. She held his eyes. He didn't break; he never did.

Slowly, inch by inch, she took him, lowering herself gently, until the rise of her sex pressed into his pelvis. She was more tender than usual, and the mound of her belly brushed the muscle of his middle. He caught her hips, rising to meet her, running hands up her spine, binding her hair.

"I thought you were an angel," he whispered against her throat. "For the longest time. I'm happy to be wrong."

"I am not an angel?" She tightened, knowing it was the laudanum talking. Or perhaps it wasn't. Perhaps it let his heart speak.

"You're too real," he sighed.

❧

May faded into June, and the ports closed by royal order. Asa was markedly unperturbed; happy, even, as he pulled on his boots, frowned at his reflection in the mirror, and dropped goodbye kisses on her mouth. Her worry was not an intervention. What had happened with Robert had taught her that.

The day Sam breathlessly delivered the news, Asa placed a neat stack of letters in his eager hands and dispatched him to the city. Where those letters went exactly, she wasn't sure, but curved script and the crest of Wyeth Enterprises manifested in wagons groaning with goods. Quebec, she heard, sitting on the kitchen floor, sifting through wheat for beetles. The Carolinas. The sloops were safely moored in Rhode Island, waiting for the passing storm.

The excitement was halfway successful in blocking Robert from her thoughts. Most of the time, she had herself convinced that the beating had driven him out of the city for good. What was Asa doing? Had he gone to the deputies? Was the fight over, was Isiah Cooper paid and written off? If that was the case, it hurt–badly, but she said nothing. She didn't search the office for clues when he was gone.

But if Robert were still in the colony, Asa was a man with a death wish. Ever since Jenkin's notorious opinion piece had multiplied at the presses, *Asahel Wyeth* was a name murmured over many a cup of putrid Dutch tea. She read the piece; she cut it out and saved it. It was easy to recognize the irony and (despite his bullishness) the fact of his tongue clenched in his cheek, as he became known not as the man who shouted speeches at the pulpit; not as the man who marched "useless cunts" to the wharf. No, he'd marked his place in the history books as the man who'd insisted–absolutely *insisted*–that the decks be swept clean.

Cassandra wheezed. "You handed them brooms, not bloody muskets? Elijah, teach him to be a proper Whig!"

"A broom can a formidable weapon make," replied Elijah pleasantly. "A pen, too, I've heard tell."

"They handed over the keys without a fuss," Asa retorted. Martha patted his knee under the table, noting a reddening at the tips of his ears. "D'you think I wouldn't be in chains otherwise? A nice crime can't be committed unless you properly clean up." He huffed, turning back to his brandy.

That evening, he was off to the public house. She tied his cravat, and made no comment when he departed with the old leather letter case from the secretary tucked under his arm.

She lay awake, counting the minutes into hours, her heart beating dull and low.

She awoke, throat dry from snoring, her hands over her head and her legs tangled in blankets. The curtains were drawn, but slivers of light flickered at the edges of the window, hailing a sun long past dawn. A rapping sounded at the door. She fumbled for her house dress, raking her fingers through her hair. On the other side Cassandra stood, hands on her hips, her nostrils flared.

"Cassie. What's wrong?"

"You have a guest," said Cassandra tersely. "You don't need to dress smart."

A guest? She shook her head, frowning. "Asa isn't here, he went to the *Dragon* last night."

"Not for Emory," replied Cassandra. "It's Frances Dunaway. Come in from the path like a starved cat. I have a heart, so I put her in the parlor with some coffee and pie. If you want me to send her off, I will."

Frances Dunaway. *Frances Dunaway!* After all that had happened, after all the time passed, what on earth could she want at Wyeth House? Her brain whirred. The ports were closed, but Frances had never been groveling. But had she known the girl at all? She'd been sweet, or so the presumption had been. A dark thought entered, sparking a thrilling surge. Here she was, mistress of Wyeth House. Goddess of the Estate, with full access to Asa's jewels if she so chose to shed her apron. And Frances…what was she, without Robert?

Nothing but an ordinary Dunaway.

"Cassandra." She straightened. "I want to look pretty."

She met Frances Dunaway in the parlor, neatly tucked into one of her finest blue satin gowns, hair high, earrings clipped, and her corset notably loose, displaying the rise of her belly. She swayed as she walked through the doors, demure on the surface, her heart wild inside. Asa's ring burned on her finger, and tucked beneath the bend of her elbow was the folding knife inscribed with his name.

She was not the old Frances. Not the timid, mouse-brown and pink sigh of a girl shrinking in Hannah's shadow. She was pallid, swallowed by the folds of her cloak, the hem of which was tattered. Noticeably thinner, her skin was the wrong color, of someone who ate not nearly enough, and of all the worst things. An untouched piece of apple pie sat cooling on the table beside her; her trembling fingers clutched a cup of steaming coffee. She gulped it back when Martha entered and rose, her cloak falling. Her exposed collarbone was sunken.

She dipped in curtsy. Then, with a strange and sudden sigh, she threw her eyes up, took in the room, and burst into tears, dropping back to her seat.

Martha regarded her in silence. In her peripheral, she caught Cassandra bustling by the door with a basket of washing, surely straining her ears. Judith dusted the mantel, muttering nothing.

"Judith," she said clearly when the sniffling had died. "Go to the office, fetch Mr. Wyeth's brandy. It seems Miss Dunaway is going to need more than coffee."

The brandy was brought. One sip and Martha was relentless. The opposite of the woman who had once relied on Frances. Those days were wasted, she thought, watching the woman's sniveling figure—blurred lines of silliness and desperation. Every day since then had made her the queen who sat at Wyeth House, Asa's child in her womb, her heart four solid walls. Perhaps, it was the days spent biting her tongue, forcing her hands to do things her head told her weren't necessary. Listening to his words, as she'd never bothered to do with Mr. Gracey. Letting him change, with unspoken direction.

Frances drew a shuddering breath. "Martha. I-I'm sorry, I'm rude! I must congratulate you, Mrs. Wyeth."

The ring caught the sunlight, shattering the walls with crystals.

"Frances, I don't know why you're here."

"I'm not here for anything, other than to speak to you." Frances sighed, drying her eyes on her sleeve. "The ports have closed, Mrs. Henshaw sold everything. The servants were let go, but one girl." She drew a shuddering breath. "We are destitute. British regulars sleep on the parlor floor. Our stores are running short, and our connections have dried."

A cold fist curled around Martha's heart, at the same time a heat pooled in her belly. She straightened through her spine. "Many people are destitute."

"With Robert gone–forgive me. I don't wish to disturb you."

Martha shook her head, frowning; any sensibilities she had leftover were ironclad. "You may speak," she said coldly.

"Robert came back. For a time." Frances hunched over the empty coffee cup. "But our accounts were dissolving. Mother had no understanding of how many he had lost after Mr. Wyeth came back to Boston. We wouldn't have behaved the way we did if we had known." She hung her head. "I-I didn't know. I just lived the way I'd always lived, I didn't know what Robert contended with in silence. It doesn't make right what he did, but if he could have spoken to me–if his pride hadn't held him–"

She broke, and setting the cup aside, she began to cry again.

Frances wasn't a threat, Martha noted, the folding knife itching under her sleeve. Listening to her speak, the concealed uncertainty in her heart dissipated.

We are destitute.

She watched Frances cry. A picture formed, stark, like a lurid dream; Asa, deep in the chair at William's cherry bureau plat.

490

Shoulders to his ears, laughing. *I'd rather spend my time at the ports, carving my name under the planks.*

She shuddered. God, he was good! No one under the roof of Wyeth House wanted for anything, not even the liars or the murderers. Every letter he'd written, late nights deep in brandy and laudanum; hours in the office, hours on the road–she was fed. Not simply fed, but what she ate was good–hearty bread, rich cheese, tart apples. Rice and millet. Bottles and bottles and bottles of port. Seeing Frances, spent, ill-nourished–while she wasn't so cold not to feel a twitch of sorrow, a wild excitement tingled in her fingertips.

Frances regained herself. "I'm sorry! I don't wish to pain you with the past."

"It's all right," said Martha tightly.

"Hannah–she married Hiram Tucker."

"I'm aware," replied Martha, fighting the urge to cut her off.

Frances nodded quickly. "But Nehemiah renounced his Lordship. Three of their warehouses were burned by the rebels when they refused to purge the Bohea. It was only then he had a change of heart. Your father made the right choice; he had the foresight when we ignored the signs. It is to the detriment of the House of Henshaw!"

"The detriment? What do you mean?"

"I mean, Robert is gone." Frances picked up her fork and poked half-heartedly at the pie. "The House of Henshaw hangs by a thread."

"Frances, I'm sure you understand, I can't help you." Nothing could go with her back to that house, not even a loaf of bread. The pie was even a step too far, if Asa's opinion mattered.

"Oh! Of course." Frances set aside the fork as if she'd read Martha's thoughts. "I'm sorry I gave that impression. That's not why I came. I-I wanted to talk to you." She drew a breath. "I'm getting old, Martha. My prospects are long since dead. It's all right, really. To be honest, I've always longed for a simpler life, somewhere quiet, where I can listen to the trees. But the choices I made when I was young–oh, I cannot lie to you!"

"You told me the truth at Midsummer's." Martha twisted cold fingers. The folding knife burned.

"Part of it," Frances continued. "But not all. I lied to Hannah, and Mama and Robert. If it weren't for me–if it weren't for the way my heart felt, all the time, trying to make everyone happy, to make everything right–" Her shoulders pitched in a renewed bout of tears. "Martha, it's me. It's always been me, I've crumbled the House of Henshaw!"

"Whatever do you mean? Frances, this is silly." All at once, the tears, the riddles, the pale forlorn figure, balled on her silk settee–it was ridiculous. And it was awful, the way her heart suddenly seized and surged, battering her ribs. Whatever Frances had to say, if it had led her starving and black on a thread to Wyeth House–well then, maybe it was better left unsaid.

"Don't speak," she said, teeth gritted, "if you've nothing of importance to say."

"It isn't silly," Frances protested.

"You can leave. Nothing you say is going to change anything."

"It might change something. It might. If I can right one wrong, if I can refuse to turn my cheek for a moment! Martha, it's Grace. It's always Grace!"

Grace. Her senses flared. "What do you mean?"

"I was tied to her," Frances gulped. "By the heart. And no matter what anyone thought of her, I knew that she would do anything for me. I didn't take advantage, it wasn't my intent. The

492

thought hadn't crossed my mind at the time, that it was an–an exchange or a favor."

Martha poured another brandy and passed it to her. If the woman stopped talking, she'd shake her so hard, she'd know what silly was.

"Mr. Wyeth and I, we were not so different. He would have laid down his life for Grace. If her lips spoke a want, he'd make it real. So when I went to Grace–no, I'm ahead of myself. Mr. Dunaway–Mrs. Henshaw saw him as the savior of the House of Henshaw. He loved her, but–he'd taken on a mess."

"It was that," Frances went on. "The House was floundering when Mr. Dunaway took it over. Mr. Henshaw had sold the ships and enlisted a shipping enterprise. We were failing, hard and fast and I–I saw Robert's ineptitude. Hannah and Mrs. Henshaw only want to be comfortable. So, I started to talk to Grace, and she poured my needs out to Mr. Wyeth. I had unwittingly asked a favor that would be the end of my family. But of course, she–oh, Martha, she was an angel! If she wanted it, she knew Mr. Wyeth give it. She begged." Frances's face crumpled. "God, he made her beg! He *knew* it was a bad idea, the moment it left her lips. She tried everything. They were his family, where was his kindness and compassion–it was an investment, a proper place to put his money–and in the end, she won. She always did." She drew a breath. "Ten thousand pounds. Ten thousand pounds he lent to the House of Henshaw. But it was always with the understanding that the money would be paid back. It was *not* an investment–Mr. Wyeth made that very clear."

Martha shifted. She had to bite her tongue not to lash out with questions, but she would not forgo her newfound dignity. The image of the thin receipt, fluttering in a window draft, was batted off.

She shook her head. "And then?"

"He lent Mr. Dunaway a portion of the sum," Frances continued. "He wanted fifteen, but Mr. Wyeth talked him to ten and two sloops. The prospects for the House started to brighten; the sloops were new and fast, only two years on the water. Papa had enough to pay the crew, and fortunes started to turn. He was a fair businessman; he could've been quite successful, and I think he would've been if he had his fair chance at wet goods." She took a sip of brandy, wincing. "The House was textiles. He saw the success Wyeth Enterprises kept, and I think—maybe I'm fooling myself, but I truly believe, if it'd just been him, he and Mr. Wyeth could've got on quite well. But I started to see it, not long after the loan was secured. Grace was—well, she was—"

"She was *what*." She was what? *A cheating whore.* A witch, binding Asa in chains and spells.

"She was starting to see things differently. Some said she changed. I believe she was beginning to see the reality of her commitments. She agreed to marry Mr. Wyeth very quickly. And Robert—he had lost the possibility of a Wyeth inheritance—Martha, he was angry! Wyeth Enterprises could have been his, years before—"

"I'm aware," interrupted Martha brusquely. "Mr. Wyeth is my husband. I am aware of his injuries."

"Oh, I am sorry! I'm sure you know, I am sorry! More and more time Grace spent time with me, at Henshaw House, especially when Mr. Wyeth would go away. Robert—well, you know Robert." Frances shook her head. "He didn't exactly get his hands dirty."

"You've told me the story." The folding knife itched so excruciatingly, that Martha fought the urge to fling it from her sleeve. "Is it necessary," she said, "to tell it again?"

"I didn't tell you the whole truth. Mr. Wyeth left for the Netherlands, and as you know–Robert... acted. But what happened to Grace–"

Martha stiffened. The words Cassandra had deemed too painful to speak, the roiling ideas that had kept her awake, so many nights. Yes, Grace was dead. She was a ghost. Married to Robert Henshaw in spirit, because of what she'd done. But what had happened? What had stayed her breath? What had finally put her bones in a grave in Salem?

She waited, fingers cold on her glass.

"After Mr. Wyeth was gone, it was not a few weeks before Robert made his move. Grace leaned into him easily. She started to visit not for me, but for him. It hurt, but I bit my tongue. Months passed, and I started to notice she was ill. Not herself, for Robert or me. Then one night in tears, she told me what she feared the most." Frances paused, choking back tears. "She was– she was with child."

Martha said nothing. Her pregnant belly weighed, pressing into her thighs. A hum rose in the back of her brain, shielding her thoughts from anything but the processing of Frances's words.

"She begged me for advice," the mouse's voice pipped on. "She tried everything. She tried to rid herself of the child. More than once. I begged for her honesty. It was better for her to confess what she'd done to Mr. Wyeth, and marry Robert instead. In time, it wouldn't heal, but it would settle. Mr. Dunaway would've been more understanding, but Mrs. Henshaw–Grace was a stationer's daughter! From a family of insurrectionists. A Meriton–and a *Henshaw?* Mrs. Henshaw was furious, but Papa was–well, he was a docile man. It wasn't a few days that had him convinced the best thing for everyone was a clean start. Mr. Meriton couldn't be promised to keep his silence

495

unless his lips were sealed with money. Half of Mr. Wyeth's loan was written off, and sent to Mr. Meriton, and Grace was sent to Salem, to have the baby with relatives."

Frances paused as if she expected Martha to speak. But she did not. The whirring in her head was blaring, now white-hot anger rather than a distraction.

"Grace wrote to me," said Frances. "She begged me to speak to Mr. Wyeth. I did. I told him what happened; I owed him the truth. He went to see her. For a time I thought he could convince himself to take the child as his own. I watched him wrestle with it. It was Mrs. Standish, I think, who finally straightened his thoughts. Whatever Grace wanted, whatever she needed…it was hers for the asking, barring only his hand. He vowed the child an education. I promise you, Martha, Mr. Wyeth has shown nothing but kindness!"

"I would expect nothing less," Martha said, under her breath.

"Weeks passed, and the letters dropped away. Finally, I convinced Mr. Dunaway to take me to Salem. But when we arrived, the house was silent, and her relatives wore black. I didn't hear the cries of a baby. Grace didn't fly out to meet me. She was exiled when she brought the child to term–and the baby passed, not a day later. Grace was a little thing, not shaped for bearing children. Childbed fever took her fast. They buried her in a churchyard, to anyone but me and her family and Mr. Wyeth, an angel. I don't know the extent of what she suffered. But I went back to Boston with a truth that *must* be told. Surely, you understand that!"

Martha's teeth clenched so hard, her jaw hurt.

"I told Mr. Wyeth, and I did *not* tell Robert that I had told him. Robert never found out that Mr. Wyeth knew the truth. You can understand why he didn't treat Mr. Wyeth so differently when he came back from New York. Ignorance was his bliss, and he contended poorly with the way Mr. Wyeth treated him. But Mr. Wyeth never changed. He knew everything, and he was relentless–he was righteously cruel! The invoices for the loan were sent, not one missed. With half the money in Mr. Meriton's pocket, Papa was scrambling. He paid what he could. But when he passed, and the House of Henshaw was Robert's, the invoices never ceased. But the payments were less and less. So when I say Mr. Wyeth is out for blood, I mean he is thirsty for it. And I'm sure you know by now–as–as his…wife–he doesn't draw blood the way most men do." She blinked, eyes as big as saucers. "Martha, I didn't come to tell you stories. I didn't come to make myself feel better over ill judgment. I'm not that selfish!"

"Then why did you come? I don't need your stories."

"I know that Mr. Wyeth came across Robert in the city." Frances hung her head, shifting forward in her seat. The motion was an opening, perhaps for sympathy, and Martha recoiled.

"I'm not friendly with you, Frances," she reminded her coldly.

"I know–I know–" Frances retreated. "Hannah shielded Robert at the Tuckers for some time. Mr. Wyeth came up with the wildest reasons to put the mansion under warrant–again, and again, and again. He *knew* Robert was there. Nehemiah wouldn't reason with him. Mr. Wyeth was an enemy, so of course, he went through the deputies. You know how he does it, everything in order, according to law–but there's only so many times you can ransack a man's house. Robert was becoming quite good at hiding. I didn't know where he was, only that he sought refuge with my sister, and fled with a company of soldiers. What company, under what captain, what rank–nothing. And then, one evening, he came back to Henshaw House. Oh, Martha, he was not the same! Skin and bone. He'd shorn his hair and colored it black with hulls. He wore a cap, his clothes bare, like a beggar. His face was bruised. That picture–I'm sure you've seen it in the papers–he was nothing the same. I came to find, his time with the company had given him a place in espionage. I argued with Mrs. Henshaw, Martha, I did! I begged for him to turn himself in. But all of these months since the tea ships were scourged–"

"They weren't scourged," interrupted Martha tersely. "They swept the decks clean."

"But Mr. Wyeth's name is in the papers. Everywhere. Do you suppose Robert could ignore that? He knows, he's different, he's trained himself. And that is why I have come. If you think Mr. Wyeth is out for blood, you have no idea Robert's vindication! He will listen at the public houses, he will follow Mr. Wyeth to Philadelphia! He will–" She fell forward, her head against her arms. "He will kill Mr. Wyeth, Martha!" she cried. "Kill him! At the very least he will imprison him, a traitor to the Crown–"

Martha stared at the hunched figure. The way her bones rose through the back of her neck was unnatural to a Henshaw, a foreign growth. A terrifying image rose in her mind, of her reaching out, and pounding each bone hill back inside of her body until they were indents, caverns like the one in his skull. Aware of herself, however, she slipped her hands underneath her buttocks. "Are you saying to me," she asked carefully, "that Robert came to Henshaw House and you didn't turn him in?"

"How could I?" Frances bawled. "For what I've done, I'm thrown from his grace forever. I'm afraid of him, Martha!"

"You've come to tell me you need saving from Robert Henshaw?"

"No! No, my worry is not for myself. My worry is for Mr. Wyeth. There is a warrant on his head, don't you realize? Robert will find a way to make him pay. Please, I beg you–" her palm turned up, her fingers flexing–"I beg you, purge his name from the papers. You must tell him to go, you must tell him to leave Boston!"

"My husband's place is in the city," Martha said hoarsely. "This is *his* city. Robert will be found, and Robert will hang. Everything you've told me, I'll tell my husband."

"Telling him is the beginning, Martha–he must leave the city!"

"What is your fear? That Robert is in Boston?"

"I do not know where he is!"

"Frances, don't lie to me!"

"I am *not* lying! But I know he is never going to let Mr. Wyeth go to Philadelphia! Robert doesn't kill with pens. Robert doesn't wound with words. He's going to kill your husband! And after all this–" She lurched with a sob. "I can't–after all I've done, live with this over my head. I grew the roots of animosity when I told Grace of our desperation. I wasn't thinking about anything but my family! And look now, at the monster I've made! You can't let Mr. Wyeth die because of what I've done. It's your fight now, I've fought it for years. In vain, I kept my silence. I bowed my head while I watched him love. I broke my own heart when he looked the other way. But I don't care, I don't care–" Her fists hit her knees–"I can hurt forever, I just need to know that he is safe!"

"Frances." Martha swallowed dust. "What–what are you saying?"

"I'm baring myself to you because you deserve it," Frances sobbed. "You've won, Mr. Wyeth is yours. He was not Grace's. And he was *not* mine." She ground her eyes into her palms. "I loved him! I loved your husband, I suffered for years, watching him love somebody else. He was always there, just out of reach. And I looked the other way. When Grace was dead, I fell, I'm sorry! Oh! He was grieving, he talked to me. I was the closest thing to Grace. I failed myself, and I failed him, I misread him! He was only looking for healing, and I failed him!"

It was too much. More than a step over the line, it was a direct wound—not to Martha's heart, but to her spleen, bursting with anger. In a visceral movement, her hand, smarting with blood, pulled from beneath her leg; one moment she was there, and the next, she was towering over Frances Dunaway, palm raised. She struck her, hard, over one cheek, and then turned her jaw, and struck the other. The impact of pulsing palm to sallow bone was barely felt.

Frances' neck snapped to the side, and she closed her eyes, letting out a sigh.

"Strike me again, Martha," she breathed. "Strike me better. I'm tired of turning my cheeks!"

"No." Martha stepped back. Her fingers tingled, her wrist ached. "You'll stay away from Wyeth House," she said, her voice clear and cold. She wouldn't ask questions like the old Martha would've done. She could hear herself, curiosity and twisted jealousy, forcing the words out. *Did he kiss you? Did he fuck you? Did he break another virgin? How many times—I need to know!*

She circled the chair, her stinging hand skimming the damask. "I can't help you, Frances," she said. "I have nothing that Mr. Wyeth will give you."

"I don't want anything. I just need to know that he is safe!"

"If you'd wanted that, you should have gone to the deputies the moment Robert came to Henshaw House." Asa's parallel accusation was not lost on her; it was a lesson.

"He is protected by a company of soldiers!"

"No." She turned. "He is a fugitive, and he doesn't wear a red coat anymore, you said it yourself. You could've turned him in, Frances, but you're weak. You're meek and pathetic. If you had a quarter of my strength you could've chased my husband

and he could've been yours and none of this would've happened!"

"Martha!" Frances stood, reaching for her.

"No! Don't touch me," Martha cried. "You want to talk about turning cheeks, well, that was your moment. That was your chance to look straight ahead of you. *That* was your chance to say something. Now get out of Wyeth House—*my* house, Frances." She circled, snatched up the untouched plate of pie, and hurled it into the grate. "Not a crumb for a Henshaw from the hand of Wyeth! Don't you *dare* ever set foot on my grounds again!"

31

NOT *an* ANGEL, BUT *a* WOMAN

She paced. She paced the parlor a dozen times, then memorized the corridors with her feet. Up and down the stairs, until her pelvis ached; then she retraced to the sewing room and sat, watching the western lawn until the sun sank, setting the grass on fire. And then boots sounded on the polished floor. She waited, clutching his torn shirtsleeves, her fingers pricking with needles. An orb of blood. She placed it on her tongue; the simplest thing, capture the body, not the spirit. Capture his hands, but never his mouth. Stroke his cock, but never soothe the wounds on his heart.

Down the stairs, her fingers skimming the polished banister. Through the corridor, the library, to the office door. She stood outside, her breath oddly slow, catching little sounds: a clinking glass, the *woosh* and dull thud of a frock tossed over a chair. A man, settling down after a long day's work.

Not tonight.

She turned the knob and swung inside. He was sitting at the bureau plat, brandy in hand, spectacles perched, low in the chair. In front of him was an uncapped inkwell and a stack of paper, half black with script. When he saw her, he started a little, picked up the paper, waved it to dry the ink, and turned it over.

Turned it over. All day, she'd been level. All day, she'd reveled in the pain smarting in her fingertips, a beautiful reminder that she could strike his demons when he couldn't. All day, she stared at walls, at her own feet, eating miles of the same floor. Fighting down the panic, the wild, burgeoning feeling of holding forbidden knowledge–twisted, angry, black as hell. And he'd turned over a paper.

No. No, Asa Wyeth, you don't turn over papers for me!

She strode across the room, snatched up the paper, and darted backward, holding it high. He reacted only in a faint forward movement, and a distinct tightening in his jawline.

"You wily old bastard, you!" Her voice shook. "This is the problem! You don't trust me. You tell me nothing! I have admitted my faults, but don't you suppose if you'd spoken to me, you could've saved yourself the grief?"

He watched her, on the surface, calm–too calm. She could've shaken his shoulders, slapped the daylights out of him just like Frances. But he only shrugged and downed his brandy.

"It's just a speech," he said.

"A speech." She brandished the paper. "A speech for what? What now, are you planning on overthrowing the King? Are you going to be King of the Colonies?" All at once, the anger drove her to madness. She folded the paper and ripped it, once, twice, to shreds; pieces floated to the floor like snow.

He winced, but otherwise, the front didn't break. "It's all right," he said lightly, touching his temple. "I've got it all here."

"Got what? What? I don't want to read it on a piece of paper! I want you to tell me!"

His eyes met hers with infuriating reserve. "It's a speech for the committee. The delegacy is going before a vote tomorrow."

"Oh, it's going before a vote tomorrow? And you were going to tell me that, when? When you came home, victorious? When I happened to read it in a column, you'd admit to it, as if it were some kind of crime? God!" She brushed her fingers, the last of his speech littering the floor. "I can see it now!"

He said nothing, but his eyes followed her form. Of course, he was being decent! He had to be. She was delicate, she was young—she was a woman, and furthermore, she was largely pregnant with his child. Nothing less could be expected; impervious, impenetrable, forever and ever spinning from wall to wall, punching holes and patching them up. She stormed to the bureau plat, snatched the brandy decanter, and poured a glass. In one gulp she put it back, fire spreading fast through her veins.

"When were you going to tell me," she breathed, "that the House of Henshaw owed you a debt?"

He stared at her, unblinking.

"When, Mr. Wyeth? Because if I didn't know better, and I put all of this down on a piece of paper, I'd say it doesn't look very much like love. It looks like an invoice!"

"My darling," he replied tersely, "that is the most foolish thing I've ever heard you say. Love isn't perfect, it's about many things."

"Oh, really? Because you would've said differently about Grace. You don't love me, I'm a weapon!"

As if he knew she'd stick the barb, he held his cool. "This is nonsense," he said with a frown. "If I didn't love you, trust me, this would be much easier. I love you madly, fool that I am. Now calm yourself. Have a seat, I'll ring Judith to put you to bed."

"No! Don't you dare ring that bell! You can admit to one thing before I leave this room." Chest heaving, mouth dry, she

504

locked his eyes. With nothing in her mind but blank, white anger, the question tumbled free.

"When were you going to tell me you fucked Frances Dunaway?"

Still, nothing. Unmoving, as if she were circling him like a predatory dog.

"Because you did. You fucked Frances Dunaway!"

He leaned forward, placing both boots noiselessly on the floor. Elbows on the bureau plat, hands folded. Jaw working. After a time of aggravated silence, her heart wild, he lifted his eyes, removed his spectacles, and folded them neatly in front of him.

"You allowed a Henshaw to pass through the doors of Wyeth House." His voice could've stilled the air.

"She is a Dunaway!"

"She is a Henshaw because she lives under a Henshaw roof."

"And you fucked her!"

For a moment he was silent, chin resting in the crook of his thumb and forefinger. Then, slowly, he nodded.

"Aye. I did. I fucked Frances Dunaway."

"Is that all you have to say?" She stared at him, incredulous. "She was my friend! I followed her for years, I fell in love with you and chased you all while she watched and bit her tongue like a saint. And she was in love with you. She's still in love with you. If it were not for Frances, I may have married Robert Henshaw!"

"I sincerely hope you don't mean that." His brow rose. "I'll speak for you, I don't think you do. In fact." He gathered up the blank papers, neatly aligned them at the edges, and pushed off the bureau plat. "You're hysterical," he said matter-of-factly. Then he rose, swinging his frock over his shoulders.

"Hysterical." She gaped. "How—how dare you. You sit back down, Asahel Wyeth, I am not done talking to you!"

His palm hit the bureau plat hard. She jumped but held her ground.

"Asahel." His eyes blazed. "Really, darling, low bloody blow."

"I mean it!"

"What do you want, aye?" He threw up his hands, at last breaking from his stoicism. "Do you want me to describe it to you? Do you want me to tell you I felt love, and affection, and some sort of satisfaction? Or perhaps the truth, if it's possible for you to hear over the voices in your head. That I made a mistake. Have you ever done that? I reckon not, you *are* an angel."

"Don't you dare call me an angel! Fucking my friend, and leaving her to watch me chase you down–"

"How unconscionable. How bloody unbelievable, for a man to seek solace in a woman's arms. Think about that, before you say another word! I lost my *wife!*"

He reeled, snatching up his glass, filling it, draining it, slamming it down. She gasped. She'd broken the composure. She'd wanted to break it–her heart and her anger had begged for it. But now, she recoiled.

"Whatever you say." His tone was cold, commanding. "Whatever Cassie or Elijah says, or whatever the hell you want to think in that pretty head of yours, that woman was my wife. She was promised to me from the day I laid eyes on her and she spoke those promises to life. And that made her my wife whether she liked it or not. So yes, I fucked Frances Dunaway, I fucked her good, till she couldn't walk a straight line. I fucked her as hard as she fucked me the day she held out her hand and begged for the keys to my coffers. I came inside her, too. Pity I didn't get her pregnant. Pity she couldn't die by the same means as my wife." He sneered, brushing by her to the door. "Death by cock, what a thing to carve on a headstone."

The outburst was so out of character, so cruel, it was visceral for her to burst into tears. She did, sinking to a seat, and pressing her face with her hands. The only thing she could say, sobbing, was, "Asa! Asa...Asa..."

"I suppose you know that now, too, don't you?" He was relentless. "And you have a problem with that. But I'd suppose you to know this about me if nothing else. To err is human, to forgive divine—whatever that bloody philosopher said. But I am not a human, nor a divinity." The office door flung open, slamming against the opposite wall. "I am a goddamn lawyer, and there's nothing more depraved than that!"

And he was gone, boots shrieking on the polished floor. For a moment, she listened to the sound escaping, but then—no. No! Not like that, not again! Open the doors, rip them off the hinges. She stumbled, clutching her skirts, and ran after him. He was halfway down the corridor when she caught up, grabbing his elbow.

"Don't you dare ever walk away from me!"

"Jesus! If I shut a door, I shut a door for your sake, yet you still continue to try me!"

"If you'd talked to me I never would've gone to Griffin's. I am an asset to Robert's case, I was then and I am now!"

He flung her hand off and continued, turning in the hall, but she kept up, fury regaining with each step. How dare he—how dare he, after all that she'd seen and suffered!

"Mr. Wyeth, I've seen the same things as you! I've lost to Robert Henshaw, the same as you! For you to pretend that I need some sort of protection—I do *not!*"

He ignored her, flinging open the front door, boots beating high echoes into the drafts of the portico roof.

Down the stairs.

"Asahel Wyeth!"

He reeled, eyes huge. "Stick the knife, I don't care. I'll just numb it with a bottle of bloody laudanum later. Now leave off, I'm going to the public house."

"No you are not!" she shrieked, skipping steps, chasing him into the gravel drive. He turned in the middle of the rose garden, and something snapped. It was too much. He was too human, too ugly. Too broken. She launched at his chest, grabbing with little fists. "Stop, talk to me–right now, sir, *right* now!"

"Enough, Martha!" He grabbed her wrists, pressing them into her middle. "You're going to hurt yourself!"

"I am *not* delicate!" She shook him off. "I am not an angel! Goddamn it, I am a woman! And I will not wait for you to speak any longer, I demand it, as your wife!"

The fire stilled. He watched her in dead silence, for far too long. The roses were thick, filling her nose with sweetness, weighted with dew. Summer dusk. Peace, the sounds of harmony. Birds, crickets, the grass rustling, unknown that mere miles away a city churned with unrest, bricks black with tar, while another man ran screaming down an alley, ripping feathers from his flesh. Because of him. His part, his words, his dreams, his perfection–if anyone was an angel, it was him.

Her chin trembled. Her hands shook, but she stared him straight in the eye.

She stepped away.

"Asahel Wyeth," she breathed, "you are horribly vindictive!"

"And so what if I am?" His eyes were wild, shieldless. "So what if I am? At least I understand when someone has wronged me when it's a bloody inconvenience to you. Do you even realize how much you've been hurt? Easier to turn the other cheek than wield a sword. God, you've been nearly raped twice! Do you even remember your mother's face? The sound of her voice?"

"This is not fair!"

"Do you ever think about Billy?"

"Stop it, sir, you're hurting me!"

"Well good, then *be* hurt." His breath stung her nose, brandy sweet. "You sit here, and you look at the roses and you cry until you can't cry anymore. Rip your heart out, grind it down until it sputters, think about everyone who has put you right where you are. Hell, I don't care if I'm one of those people. Then you pick it up and put it back where it belongs! Feel the weight of it. Let it bleed down the insides of your body! And then." His shoulders pitched. "When I can see that in your eyes, I'll speak to you. Because admit it, you weren't thinking about Billy when you brought me to Ann Street. Because if you'd been thinking about Billy, I might've been more forgiving, but you were not. You were thinking about Robert, and you were thinking about me. And that is how I know you are not ready to fight. And if you're not ready to fight, then I am not ready to speak!"

He drew a breath, sharp, his shoulders dropping as if exerted. In all her time with Asa Wyeth, she had never heard him put so many words together—not in her presence—not for her ears. He had not meant to, clearly, from the distraught, confused expression in his eyes. She had broken him. For a moment, breathing hard, he watched the earth, his lips parting—pressing— parting—as if he meant to correct himself. But then, he flung his glass into the roses and was gone, disappearing up the path in a thunderstorm of swinging frock.

She lay in bed for hours staring at the wall, the baby tumbling and rolling in her womb. She watched the moon climb the star ladder of the sky until it was too bright and she rose and drew the curtains. Far past the midnight hour, she heard him come in. She listened to the creak of the folding panel, she knew the ache of the secret bottle. The bitterest, swollen heartbreak. Then his weight, dipping the bed. She didn't turn, and he didn't touch her.

She awoke just before dawn, though it didn't feel like it. It felt like a blend of the same day, the air thick with New England summer. Birdsong rang, and outside the window, the world was a placid gray-green. She watched the curtains, moving softly. The moment it was warm enough, he opened them. He'd made love to her so many times, while the moon shed light on the lines of her body. He was gone from the bed, but the orange flicker of candlelight told her where he was.

What he was doing.

She rose. From the wardrobe, she pulled out a prim green cotton gown, one of the many Cassandra had helped her sew to accommodate her growing belly. Linen stockings, ribbon garters. Plain shoes. In front of the mirror, she arranged her hair high and pinned on a summer straw hat. Then she rounded the panel.

He was curled in the chair, knees up, no shoes, chin resting on the back of his hand. Not reading. Not writing, just sitting. Her heart shifted, but she swallowed it down.

"You're going to the city for the vote today," she said clearly.

He looked up, regarding her with blank eyes. Then he nodded.

"You might not be ready to talk." She waited for her chin to tremble, her face to crumple. But it didn't. "But I'm ready to fight. And I'm doing it standing beside you, whether you like it or not. So get dressed. And—and wear something decent, not your ugly old frock!"

She swayed around the panel, pausing to look back. The hurt in his eyes was so obvious, it was hard not to hate him for it.

"I'm going with you to the South Church," she called, walking fast. "To watch you win."

❁

She sat at the back of the Old South Church, hands folded over her belly, eyes ahead. The space was mostly empty, voices bouncing from the high ceilings, the windows dull and dusty. No light to shine through, no celestial spirit to lift the sun. Asa had ridden the entire way in silence, a new lettercase on his lap— not the one that contained the lists of Robert's sins. She'd watched him from the bed, obediently dressing in clothes selected under her stony direction. Grey breeches, white hose, and black shoes. Cream linen waistcoat and storm-grey frock. Cravat tied high, hat clapped smart. In silence, she approved of the pistol clipped to his hip.

Only when the chaise stopped behind the church did he speak.

"Martha." He turned, hand on the door.

"Yes, sir."

"I want this."

He was different in that moment, years younger. The Asa in the frame beside Papa Wyeth, the Asa who still operated with some degree of hope. Without a thought, she leaned down, buried her fingers into his hair, and kissed him hard. His hat was a shield against the world, where a gathering throng shifted to and fro around the steps of the church. Waiting to see what Boston would do. Who it would send. Who were the ones who'd fought the hardest, who'd lost the most sleep, who'd written even with weary pens.

Madly, she pushed away, hands on his shoulders.

"If you want it, take it," she whispered. "But please, don't fight in silence. Don't fight alone. I'll still go back to the house with you, even if we have to try again."

Then she took his hand and stepped into the street. She walked with him through the doors, she nodded, she smiled, she put her hands into palms she didn't know. And then she sat and watched him walk to the front of the church, fading into a throng of men none of whom he was like. Their voices were a murmur, hitting the high walls and fading like an ancient chant. Surging, fading. The clearing of throats, the scratching of quills. An hour passed; she was rigid, her backside numb in the pew. The murmuring rose to laughter and loud voices. She shook her head, straining through a sudden beam of sunlight to see. He broke through the misted white, cutting shadows over the sacred walls.

"All right," he said, holding out his arm. "Come, darling, I've got a speech to finish."

"Asa—" She caught his arm. "Are you going to Philadelphia?"

He watched her, flickering from eye to eye. Then, without breaking, he clapped his hat onto his head, even though he was in a church.

"I love you," he said evenly. "And yes, I'm going to Philadelphia."

She walked with him to the front of the church. It was like a quiet wedding day, extending her hand, smiling at strangers. Only when the doors broke open did the voices rise and tumble; she shrank against his side, the gravity weighing. A crowd had gathered—a crowd! Not just for Asa, but if there was a meeting of powerful men at a church, to the wild souls of the city it only meant one step closer to the freedom that drove them mad.

A whisper at first, then a rumble.

"Wyeth. Wyeth. Wyeth!"

"Darling." He smiled tightly. "Stay here for a moment, the fellows can get a little rowdy."

She nodded and watched him through a pane of colored glass. The crowd rumbled, muffled through the walls of the church. Eager feet shook the cobbled earth, rattling the windows. She narrowed her eyes, following his broad back down the steps, watching for his signs… as expected, his eyes were tight, but he talked and gestured and smiled. The commotion was rather rowdy; someone threw millet, and it rolled in the channels of his hat. A broom was tossed in front of him; he batted it away with the toe of his shoe. A song rose, uniform, grating in common men's voices—victorious. Brutal, nearly.

"Sweep the decks! Sweep the decks!"

The sound grew, heaving like a shanty on a sloop, rising and falling in thick salt air.

"Sweep the decks, sweep the decks!"

Surging, fading…surging, fading…a boom in the air. Cargo hitting the docks, perhaps.

Her ears rang with silence. Through the glass, the world was watery red in one eye and putrid yellow in the other. In a strange moment of collective stillness, she saw him drop to his knees, and thought how odd a time it was for him to pray. Especially for a man who'd probably never whispered to God in his life. She moved to a pane of white, straining to see.

Another boom. It was not cargo dropping to the docks. He was not praying.

His body curled inward, his palm hitting the stones. Through milky glass, blood looked black—the midnight waterfall she knew like the back of her hand.

"Asa!" she screamed. "Asa!"

513

She pushed off the window, throwing herself through the doors and down the steps. That dullness was a sound she knew from the very bottom of her nightmares. Only her own cry paused it. Just before the swell and the break; just before feet started to run, and shoulders hit shoulders in panic and disbelief. From the middle of the crowd, a whirling madness rose.

And she saw him, fighting against a barrage of bodies.

She saw him, twisting against arms. She watched him, the back of his knees knocked out, his face to the stone, hands bound together with thick ropes. A knit cap, hair hanging in long strings of muddy black. A street urchin, stripped of flesh and comfort, led away by the scruff of the neck. In a break of sunlight, she caught the fevered flash of sea-glass blue, lost in madness.

Asa turned his cheek to meet the hot stones. She rushed, fighting sweating bodies, and fell beside him. Robert, captured, her heart, vindicated, suddenly meant nothing.

"Asa!" Her voice was barely real. "Asa, listen to me, Asa—don't close your eyes. Don't close your eyes!"

"It's all right, darling." He reached for her hand. Her palm slipped with blood, grasping fingers too cold for the heat of Boston summer. "Just have Sam bring the chaise round," he whispered. "I'd like to go home now."

32

the HOUNDS *of* WAR *are*
BAYING *in the* TREES

H ands she didn't know picked him up and laid him
over the seat in the chaise. Voices she didn't
recognize told her to move away, but she rooted her feet,
crouched with his hand drying blood in her hand. Forehead to
forehead, coaxing him awake with whispers. His eyes opened
and faded shut. Rivers of blood were stoppered by Sam, who
tied off the wounds with strips of ripped shirtsleeves. One, just
above the rise of his right hipbone, and the other, blown through
splinters of mangled flesh and shattered kneecap.

"Henshaw is a poor marksman," he noted. His voice faded,
his lips blue, huge pupils swallowing russet. "He never practiced.
That's the problem, you see, if you don't practice…"

"The poorest," she whispered in agreement. She couldn't
cry. Her body knew it was no time for tears. Instead, she brushed
the curls, heavy with sweat, from his eyes; she swatted flies from
open flesh. When his eyes rolled shut, she slapped his face,
nearly as hard as she'd slapped Frances Dunaway.

At the house, her hands were Cassandra's. Steady. She stripped him down to nothing but the body that had loved her. In silence, she watched, as the sick grey-green gave way to black, while Dr. Warren twisted and clamped a bullet extractor. One of the bustling bodies in the room tucked leather between his teeth, and he bit it nearly through. She held his hand. The bullet, slick with merlot blood, rolled quietly in the palm of the doctor's hand.

"His knee?" she asked.

"Completely shattered," replied the surgeon-apothecary. He polished his spectacles on his frock and took up his bag.

"Will he walk again?"

"Most likely, if we can avoid infection and fever. I don't see amputation as a necessity at this point. In the meantime," he added, gathering up a gaggle of bottles from his bag, "Keep him still and quiet." He rose, placing the bottles in Cassandra's hands. "I entrust you, Mrs. Standish," he said sincerely. "If only you'd been a man. You'd have been a formidable force against the mess of modern medicine."

"I take that as a compliment," said Cassandra stiffly, tucking the bottles into her apron. In the bed, Asa moaned, and Dr. Warren swung his bag over his shoulder and drifted out the door.

She paced, her belly fighting against the thick sweet smell of sickness blanketing the room. Asa's forehead beaded with sweat. Twice he rose and called for a bucket, and she held his shoulders while he vomited air and clear bile. Cassandra was a silent witch, leaving whispered spells with her fingertips. The wounds were redressed, soaked with vinegar, and sealed with a coating of potato starch. The bleeding stopped. He put down spoonfuls of

516

laudanum. Time passed, and she fell to her knees at the side of the bed, head in her elbow.

She slept.

She awoke at the moon's highest point to find him staring at the corner of the room. His skin was no longer pale; instead, he was flushed, the roots of his hair black with sweat. She rose and sat on the bed, palm to his forehead, and gasped. Her skin burned over his.

"Darling." He caught her hand. "You see over there, in the corner?"

"What is it, Asa?"

"You don't see? A bear, in a hat. A skimming-dish hat." He smiled, eyes impossibly bright. Not bright–no, swimming, dying–drowning.

"Doesn't she look pretty?" he murmured.

She leaned, burying her nose in wet curls, breathing in the scent of fever–it was everywhere. Black marks on the bedding. Heat, radiating from his skin, candied roses, wilting in dampness and time.

"Yes, Asa," she whispered. "Yes, I see her. She looks beautiful."

She didn't sleep anymore. Cassandra forced his jaw apart, and sprinkled his tongue with willow bark powder. He choked and swallowed and then he slept, his breathing a grating pitch in the silence of the walls. She listened, sitting at the bureau plat, eyes burning, as Elijah read to him–buckled shoes on the bed– from law books, enough of the right words to keep his eyelids moving. Dr. Warren came, flipped his arm over with a grimace, and slit the skin. Black blood pulsed into a white china bowl, and his face went ivory.

But by morning, some of the color had returned. The rasp of breathing eased, and Cassandra's willow bark, expertly forced every four hours, seemed to be doing something. His skin cooled, not as much as it should have, but enough. He slept, forced into unconsciousness by sickening dosages of laudanum.

By midday, his eyes opened, and Martha leaped to her feet.

"Water in the copper," he slurred. "Put Sam to work. And something to eat."

"No bath," snapped Cassandra, snatching for the bucket, into which he heaved nothing. "I don't care if you smell like a barnyard, the wounds stay dry. Martha, run to the kitchen, and have Adeline warm some broth. Plenty of salt."

By evening he was sitting up. Elijah perched by the bed, keeping him vigilant. She watched in silence. But she felt hollow. She wanted nothing more than to run to him, wrap her arms around his neck, kiss him silly, tell him how proud she was of him, but then—all this time, all it had taken was for him to leave her in a church, and walk out into a crowd. He took to his sickbed like he'd known for weeks he was going to be there. How was that supposed to heal the shame, the guilt, the ugliness of her grief? The laudanum would flow for the rest of his life. He would never run in the rain again; Elijah was already haggling him over what his walking stick should look like.

"An esquire must have a walking stick," Asa agreed. "Any man who walks with a limp is formidable."

She kissed him softly and he kissed her back, smoothing her hair behind her ear.

"I love you, darling."

"I love you too, Asa."

She tried to smile. But she left. She took off her shoes and walked in the garden with Ham, bare feet wet with twilight dew.

The stars, buried deep in a sleek velvet sky, wavered, ignorant of earthly heartache. Her world shrank, and she dragged herself to the edge of the bathing pool, dropped to her knees, and wept.

When she finally pulled up her skirts and made it up the terrace steps, her pelvis smarting, Cassandra found her in the tea room.

"My dear." She pulled her close, tucking her hand over her elbow. "There's a gentleman to see you in the parlor."

"A gentleman? Asa—is he all right?"

Cassandra nodded. "He's all right, he's sleeping. Best not to keep your guest waiting."

She slipped into the parlor, hand against the wall. The room was still, save for the orbs of two candles, dancing on the bottom of Papa Wyeth's chin. She pulled her skirts forward, arranging them over her bare feet; her hair, in a loose knob at the base of her neck, was unwashed, forgotten in sweat-thick hours at Asa's bedside. The muscles of her belly, tight as a drum, ached and pinched. She wandered to the mantel, fingers skimming the spotless surface, and locked eyes with Papa Wyeth.

"You're dead," she whispered. "You died of the sugar sickness."

Yet, he was alive, brown eyes glittering with oil highlights. And the longer she stared, the bluer they turned.

She startled at a rustling from the direction of the settee. A figure, barely taller than a child, rose from the shadows, pulling to his feet with the aid of a crystal-headed cane. She gasped; initially, his appearance frightened her, hunch-backed and unusual. The top of his head gleamed bald, fringed with dying strands of white hair around enormous ears. Black-rimmed spectacles stretched past the sides of his sunken cheeks. On his feet, he stood barely to Martha's shoulder.

"Ah, Mrs. Wyeth." His voice broke the air, cracked like ancient paper. "My apologies for arriving without warning. I've just had a word with your man. Cunning son of a bitch he is. Isiah Cooper," he added, extending a shaking hand. "Cooper and Sons Practices of Law."

❀

She donned a black gown and petticoat, black stockings, and boots like she was the widow at Asa's funeral. If he had died. The wild, nearly evil thought occurred to her that he still might, staring at his sleeping form from the doorway, lost in the gray shadows of early morning. Elijah had laid a walking stick across the end of the bed as a joke. The crystal head—nearly identical to the one Mr. Cooper carried—flickered when the curtains hushed, scraping the walls with barely-there fingers. He was breathing steadily, his skin wasn't flushed anymore. Sun-kissed, like always. Only the faint frown knotting his brow betrayed the pain. On the table beside the bed, the laudanum had dropped to the bottom of the bottle. Nothing but an amber crust, dried in the corners.

"What will I say?"

Of course, it was the question to ask, when a woman—young, pregnant, was asked to testify in a courtroom.

"Well, the truth, of course," replied Mr. Cooper, kneading his lip with a toothless gum. "As much of it as you wish to tell. The important parts. Where you were. What you saw. Who you were with. The things that you listened to."

The truth.

What an easy thing to tell, when given the chance unhindered, without fear of judgment. On a pedestal above opinions that held no weight; and one man, who certainly had no argument to make. It didn't matter who his lawyer was. If he even had one. She stood in the middle of the floor in a room haunted by Asa's ghost, listening to the sound of his shoes pounding on the floorboards. Catching him in the corners, legs crossed on the gallery bench, elbow leaning on a stack of books. Spectacles perched, fingers scribbling. Hat on his knee. Frown low.

Her heart groaned, but she opened her mouth. Robert's eyes, the only part of him not tangled in chains, bore holes in her belly, hating the claim that Asa had staked. The only innocence in a room soiled with guilt. Her voice bubbled, a murmuring brook, running the truth. Everything. The way he'd confused her heart the moment she'd laid eyes on him. The secrets torn open by Frances Dunaway. The way the purity went sour; the jealousy, the subtle stabs, to the white-hot anger. She took her panniers off with her voice. She laid the crook of her neck on the arm of a Spanish silk settee, and someone murmured, "Whore!"

It started to rain. Her brain split with the *boom* of a pistol, the moment it left her lips. Robert flinched, his chains grating on the damp floor. The hulls were fading from his hair; the gold fought through in strands, catching the last of the light. For a moment, she forgot why she was there.

She left the stand, hands folded at her middle, and sat. Nehemiah Tucker was next, the man who'd once sworn to toss Asa out of the mansion on his ass. A reluctant rebel, cursing the Henshaws with fierce gesticulations. Now that he knew what it felt like to starve. Now that he knew the heat of a match, spitting fire down the sides of his warehouses. A dark gratitude rose in her heart, knowing Hannah Dunaway was Hannah Tucker now; but Frances—she would die a Henshaw, forever wrinkling her nose at the stench of Mrs. Henshaw-Dunaway's rank sherry. Doomed in her desire to correct her mistakes.

Then Mr. Chestney with the stringy hair. Wild gestures, knobby fingers flying. Mr. Sander's, knees knocking, still nothing like the sort of man who would brew spirits. Voices tangled, rising high in the courtroom rafters, and her eyes no longer begged for glimpses of Robert's face. It was clear; all he had needed was the ropes, the chains, the time.

She shook her head. The room was clearing; Robert's figure disappeared through the wide-open yawn of a door. Her eyes wandered from the slope of his shoulders to the gallery seats…

Papa. He caught her eye, raising his hand, as if he was hailing a merchant at the docks. Just a dream, his bald head catching the white light of a cloud-smothered sun. A bit nervous. Trying so hard to be included. Blue eyes glassed with fresh port, locked on the sanctity of Asa's face—Asa, sweet Asa! Laughing, with his head back. Elijah Standish, owl eyes bright with mirth.

Nothing could shake that smile from Mr. Gracey's face; nothing, not war, not heartbreak, no mistake in the world, that smile that covered the hardest, cruelest thing.

Love. Tangled, despairing love.

A door slammed. She jolted, rising to her feet. She shook her head, glancing up at the gallery, but it was empty. Elijah was by her side, hand hooking her elbow.

"Chaise to the Common, Mrs. Wyeth, or would you rather go on home?"

"To the Common? What do you mean?"

"Some would say a hanging is worth their time," replied Elijah, by way of explanation. His eyes flickered, something close to mirth—but then, he sobered. "Mrs. Wyeth." He placed a hand on her shoulder. "You've suffered greatly. Your stoicism is admirable, and I mean it truly when I say, I wish you only peace and comfort. If you wish to go to the Common, I'll stand beside you. Or behind you. Or I'll fuck off, whatever you want. Lord knows you have the fortitude to do anything alone."

She dropped her eyes. From her peripheral, she watched him, big body bending and swaying as he rifled through his shoulder bag and pulled on his frock. Buttoned his sleeves. Once more, her eyes wandered to the gallery, but it was still empty. No Asa, no William. Grief played heavy tricks on the mind, Elijah had once told her.

But Elijah was real, he was firm. Robert hadn't touched him.

"Mr. Standish," she said.

He straightened.

"Mr. Standish," she repeated. "Take me to the Common."

She stood in the rain, shivering despite the clouded heat. For hours she'd waited, her thoughts on fire not with Robert, but with Asa. Had he slept? Had the fever returned? Would he really walk again? Would he go to Philadelphia, would he change the world? It was almost laughable, watching Robert tripping up the steps–steps haunted by so many final journeys. How unbelievable, that it ended with this. A ratty man with bones too big for his body, pulled sobbing before a bored audience, only there because there was nothing better to do. Not even Lord Tucker had stayed. In the back of her head, she knew Asa had probably done what he did best–"paid him off."

Elijah's eyes wandered, perhaps too jarred by what could have been his own fate.

It was an audience of one. She felt no discomfort or fear; she didn't hear the words of the hangman, muttering over a rehearsed speech. The wild blue eyes were the only thing in his body that still held life. Boring holes to the other side of her skull. Did he have final words?

"Martha," he whispered. "Martha—is he dead?"

She paused. Took him in, from the end to the beginning. The infatuation. The man he could've been if the desperation had been lost somewhere along the way. Her tongue dried, cleaving to the roof of her mouth, but through some grace, lifted by a split in the clouds, she moved.

She stepped to the edge of the gallows and extended her hand. His skin was cold as if his heart had already ceased beating. His fingers were slick with sweat, the end-of-life kind—no turning back, no second chances. She held him for a moment, face to the sky, and closed her eyes, breathing in the feeling.

Not forgiveness, but the purest vindication. In all that time she'd wasted with him, she'd never felt his hand in her hand. She'd never known the tenderness of skin to skin, nor the torrid wreckage of her own body. Now, it rumbled from her fingertips to her heart like a growing storm, tearing through the fields of her doubts and her desperations. All her mistakes, her victories, her happiness, laid flat in a torrid rain. Out in the ocean, she knew, Wyeth sloops pitched in the water; rebels ran whooping down the wharves, whipping chains of fire. Boston burned outside the perimeter of the sacred Common. Women would go hungry, their little ones clinging to their skirts; women would shoulder muskets, and men would die under the stars.

The hounds of war bayed in the trees. But through the clatter, she remembered Frances's mercy.

"Yes," she whispered, letting go of his hand. "You see? I am wearing black."

She stepped away. Barely heard through the rain, the rope lashed. His face bled purple and blue, and the House of Henshaw died in a quiet sigh.

33

NO MORE LAUDANUM

Wyeth House was dead when she returned. She stepped over the threshold, weary. Her feet ached, her heart hung like a wrecking ball.

She tugged loose her hat, dropping it to her side. Silence snaked through the hall. Not even the timid pad of Ham's paws. Hand on the back of her neck, she made her way through the corridor and slipped into the library. All of his things looked old, cracked with time–futile. All of those books he'd read, yearning for something greater than himself. She walked, running her fingers over the spines, her eyes burning with fatigue. She paused at the office, hand cradling the swell of her womb.

Behind the bureau plat, by an inch of candle, she made out the shape of Asa, forehead resting on his outstretched arm.

For a moment, her heart froze, but then, with the rise and fall of breath, she realized he was only asleep. She crossed the threshold, skirts hushing, circled behind him, and placed a steady hand on the back of his head. Warmth met her skin immediately. The window was open, the curtains flying like ghosts in the dusk. Two bottles of laudanum to the side, one empty. One half-empty. In front of him, a mess of scribbled paper, letters with broken seals.

She worked her fingers gently through his hair. He sighed and shifted, settling deeper into the crook of his arm, lost to the world.

Trembling, she reached over his head and picked up one of the letters. The wax seal was hardened and cracked with age, and when she folded back the yellowed paper, it fell loose and hit the bureau plat with a sound far too loud for the action. Her heart seized, but she struggled to focus on the words in the dying light, backing to the window.

She recognized the hand at once. She'd memorized it, every curve, every tipsy slip of the quill, every scratch of the words that hadn't come out right. Her eyes tripped, fighting not to skip for fear she would miss something.

"My dear man Wyeth,

I hope you can be convinced by now that you must return to Boston. I'll have you know, that of the seven cases of blackstrap you were so gracious to secure, I've sold all but one-half. It was a wholesale fellow by the name of Taylor who took them, a distillery man. That blackstrap will make a fine bottle of rum soon. It's sent a handful of other distilleries nipping at my heels, so I daresay, now's the time. I know Tucker and Sanders have a few distillery accounts between them. A fine bit of profit, if we can steal them like bandits. Cheap bandits we could be, you and I, if only you would return to Boston!

Besides, Boston is a right riotous place to be. Everyone is jumping ship, so to speak. Yes, I know, you can run the record books from New York. But don't forget you made me an offer, good sir. I rather think we would make a funny pair. You can scheme in the back as you like, and I will do the talking. I've been chatting with other proprietors, and I've gathered a list of every wholesale account, and pricing, some lovely names I think you'll recognize. But alas, I shall not share it with you. You've return to Boston if you wish to see it, ha!

I hope I've tempted you well enough. While I wait, I sit here and scratch my head over all the new ideas you have confused me with. It's rather torture to go out in society, but I do it for Martha. I don't know if you remember my little girl, she was the redheaded pipsqueak out in the yard, chasing the dogs that day you came by. But now she's grown up and wants to go to revels. I sigh, for it's such a contention to raise a daughter. Some fellow by the name of Robert Henshaw comes by, I suppose he has his sights set, but I find him rather a fool. Do you know the Henshaws? Are not they a relative of Wyeth? Right loyal they are. What's a fellow to do, after all, when he's raised a headstrong girl? Let it work the course, I suppose.

At any rate, you'll find enclosed Hodge's order for the tea, so if you could be spry and get that sent, I would be obliged. Happy I am to work with you, but I will say this tea is nothing to my Hyson. I will bear it, but it's quite foul. Just as you are, if you don't get return to Boston.

Very well. I am, as always, your humble and obedient incendiary,

Billy D. Gracey

February 22nd, 1773."

She folded the paper, hating the tears burning her eyes. William Gracey's love was so strong, that even with his death vindicated, it shifted walls in a haunted room.

Fighting a cry, she folded the letter and placed it back, reaching for another.

"April 10th, 1773.

Emory,

You write to me complaining of the ache in your head. I think you were probably halfway to Concord, but let me tell you something, dear brother; I will give you something to complain about if you don't watch your tone. If Papa walloped you in the head fifty times with a pistol, I'm wondering if perhaps I shouldn't make it fifty-one, to knock some sense into you. Take some bloody laudanum, and be done with it.

How about this? You're back in Boston to fill up those coffers. Take back the docks. Smile in the morning instead of being such a grouse. Maybe find a nice girl and get married. Make a baby or two. What a concept! Nothing is so bad, now is it?

If I ever hear you talk about such things again, I am coming to Boston, and you'll be sorry I did. As much of a heathen as you are, I still want you buried in a churchyard.

I love you, you insufferable fuck.
Cassie."

The desire to slap him tingled in her fingertips. Ached in her palm. Slap the sadness out of his eyes, sink her fingers into the hole in his head. Rip his skull down the seam, release the spirits that reveled like *Danse Macabre* in his brain. Tossing the letter to the floor—it was only Cassie—she reached, gripping his shoulder, ready to shake him awake and demand answers, but then, her arm flew back, her throat closing around a gasp.

Papa Wyeth's pistol. Laying innocent at an angle, it caught a bend in the candlelight, throwing gold at the ceiling. Strewn around it were torn pieces of paper, shredded into nervous pieces, black fingerprints bruising the normally spotless walnut. Ink. Just ink—she wiped with a finger, bringing it under her nose.

Black powder.

Crumpled paper, everywhere. The same words sprang, too black, at her wild eyes, again and again. *Mrs. Wyeth. My dear Mrs. Wyeth.*

My darling Mrs. Wyeth,
I am tired. I am so tired, of going to sleep and waking up. I am tired of brandy and I am tired of laudanum. Now look at me, Mrs. Wyeth—old,

528

and grumbling, you see, a hole in my head and a shattered kneecap, what good is that? A man who cannot take himself to Congress alone. No, I must travel with a walking-stick, a man-servant, a bloodletter, a shadow with a hood and a beak waiting for me to breathe in the wrong air. That's all it takes. I am weak and I am sick. My child will run strong in the rain, and I will watch from a window, stupid with drug and drink, only comforted by the knowledge that another man will one day stand where I should have stood. Swinging my little hooligan by the arms, tumbling in the grass.

Mrs. Wyeth, you deserve this happiness. So there will be no more laudanum. No more grumbling. No more headaches. No more bloody pain in my knee. No more laudanum. No more, darling, no more. I am braver now. I have no reservations. I will do what I should've done in New York. So I am sorry that Billy gifted me so with his kindness; I am sorry that he saved me. But more than anything, I am sorry, Mrs. Wyeth, that I loved you so deeply, that I could not help but ruin you.

No more laudanum, darling, no more.

Her hands pulsed with fear. Wild, cold, yet bursting like a tied vein.

There is only one man who will die at the end of Wyeth's pistol.

She backed away. *No. No, Asa, no!* Wake him, shake him, rattle his bones! It was high time another woman took over the task. Grace's days were over; her ghost had fallen with Robert Henshaw. Free, but he didn't know it yet, but he had to know it! She choked, backing to the wall.

Call Cassandra–scream, wake him, beat him senseless–

Instead, she lurched, snatching the pistol and pressing it into the swell of her belly, and bolted. Through the office, the library, flinging open doors. Let the ghosts free, let them roam, let them rush through halls and fly out the windows. Let them free–

"Sam!" she screamed into the blackness. "Sam!"

Sam rounded the parlor, silhouetted against the dying light. In one hand he held one of Asa's boots, in the other a tub of dubbin shine.

"Sam," she gasped, hand to the wall. She doubled, binding the pistol in the folds of her skirts. A sharp pain pulled at the muscles of her womb. "Sam, ready the chaise again," she panted. "I know it's late, but you must listen to me. Sam! Send Bennet to watch over Mr. Wyeth. Tell him not to leave the room—for anything, do you hear me? And then meet me at the chaise, and take me to Griffin's Wharf!"

❀

At the end of Griffin's Wharf, the wind rocked the water like a baby's cradle. The sky had cleared, pitted with stars. The thought that, mere streets away, the Common was clean of bodies and blood, elicited nothing. Robert was dead, and he was only that: dead. He wasn't a ghost. He wasn't a name she hated or loved enough to remember. He was a certificate of death; a coroner's inquest, a jury examination. An American trial.

The ocean in front of her ached with life, cradling sloops, pinprick lanterns from the decks casting crescents over the water.

It was nearly impossible to ignore the pain tearing through her pelvis. Cold sweat broke her palms, no matter how many times she wiped them dry. The pistol was an anvil on her lap, pressing into her thighs in a way so unusual that her stomach lurched in protest. She knew that it was time, but it didn't matter. When morning came, Asa would have his baby. She would not die, like Grace. She knew it, viscerally; her bones were meant to bend, her strength was honed to accept pain from a distance. In a manner, she thought, Asa had been right. Turning the other cheek was easier than wielding a sword.

She called for Sam to stop the chaise at the water's edge. Her feet hit the planks of the docks with a sound emphasized in the silence. Only a figure or two bustled, bobbing over rowboats. The pistol loose at her side, she walked stiffly to the end of the sodden wood, where the ocean pitched into blackness until the sky met the water. Another count where Asa was right: he would never run. He would never swing himself into those rowboats. He would never catch the wind-whipped ropes off the side of a sloop again.

Sam called her name from the chaise, but his voice was lost. Sea spray flecked the hem of her dress. Salt rimmed her nose and settled in the cracks of her lips, eating into her skin. Her womb curled and clenched, but she smiled and reached behind her head to pull the pin out of her hair.

She swung, and let go. Through the whipping of her hair, she didn't see where the pistol hit the water, but she felt the weight sigh into nothing. The back of her neck was wet. Her skin rose, pinpricks rippling through her body, pulling her face to the sky, eyes to the stars. Her shoulders lifted. Her bones settled, loosing from the gristle that had bound them so tight for so long. The pain was welcome.

She turned, and Sam held open the chaise door.

❁

She was mistress of Wyeth House. *Love In Excess* was taken from the armor of *Milton* and *Dryden* and duly burned, pages sinking like sand through the iron fingers of the grate. Papa Wyeth was taken to the barn, where Sam, nodding hastily, agreed that he would be pissed on and destroyed. In that space, a new

531

portrait would hang; an artist from the city would come and paint her picture, with the baby cradled in the crook of her arm. *Mrs. Martha Ann Gracey Wyeth | 1753.* Asa slept in a dream, ushered to the bed by an insistent Bennet, and Martha knocked on Cassandra's door herself. In the big airy room, away from the sweet smell of fever and drink, two chairs were arranged in front of the grate. The buckets were filled, and the towels were clean. Judith lost her prudishness, and Cassandra barked orders, her hair curling at her temples with exertion.

Lost in the sweat-slick hours of the next day, squatted on the floor, her hands bound around ropes lashed to the canopy of the bed, she gave up her remaining strength. Her body collapsed from the bottom; she tumbled and caught the baby as it entered the world, white and slick. A big baby, long and lean, wisps of red hair curling around its crumpled ears. For a terrifying moment, there was silence. Cassandra snatched the infant and rapped it smartly on the back, and the air filled with wild, desperate screams.

Somehow, the pain was gone. Sunlight threw pale beams over the carnage. And the baby. A baby boy. She lay in the bed for hours, the warm little body clinging to her breast, soft coos and cries brushing her ears. Asa was feverish again, Cassandra said, but he would be all right. He was sleeping well. She slept and woke over and over, the baby greedy with the slightest pang of hunger. Cassandra was there every time she opened her eyes. Her tea was always hot and sweet, and when morning came, the curtains were closed. The room was spotless. No blood, no tears or screams, no parts of her body, tossed hurriedly into a bucket. August roses sat on the dressing table, some heavy and a little brown, but still beautiful.

She ate salted cod and cheese and drank ale as if she sat on the bench of a public house.

Cassandra was always there. So she slept.

❁

Days blurred into nights and nights into listless mornings. Sitting up in bed, putting back hasty pudding and coffee, she read the papers, hating the headlines. *Congress* this and *Congress* that… She balled them, tossing them into the empty grate. Would Asa keep his seat? Well, he wasn't dead yet. He still had two legs, even if one of them was a mosaic of bone shards and scar tissue. Who was Robert Henshaw, and why (remind us) had he hung by the neck after a trial that lasted barely two hours? After months of mindless suffering, hoping, and regretting, was it now safe to feel happiness? The cruelty of the world. To extend anguish so long, and gift happiness in such swift and fearful breaks.

Would Asa keep his seat?

Dr. Warren declared his knee was healing well, only that it would bother him for the rest of his life. Bone would forever pierce muscle unseen. He would never run in the rain. But, with enough laudanum, he would move from the bed to the office. From the office to the library, the library to the terrace, where he would lean, filling the air with vanilla smoke.

She rose, tossing back the blankets, and snatched the baby from his bassinet.

Wyeth House had taken on a hopeful feeling in the days since the hanging–a waiting, tight sort of hope. She felt it deep in her heart. The walls were closer together now. Not so empty, no room for passing ghosts. The ceiling was not so high. The smells that wafted from the kitchen were ones that she expected:

crushed herbs, the blackest coffee, Judith's soda biscuits. Sunshine-dried cloth, sea-salt air; the tells of home.

Asa was in bed, reading listlessly from Mr. Gracey's diary. When he saw her, he tossed it in the middle of the bed and sat up.

"Darling! Cassie's been a thorn in my ass, she won't bloody let me out of this room. Jesus, you're a sight. I've not seen you so beautiful. Come here."

The sound of his voice broke her. Clutching the baby to her collarbone, she burst into tears, and in a moment she was cradled in his arms, taking in the smell of health in gasping breaths. No fever. No sweat, no sweet illness. Trembling, she passed him the baby, her heart breaking at the happiness in his eyes. That man and the one bent over the bureau plat, drunk and high, ready to finish the tunnel through his brain–perhaps, he'd forgotten that man. He didn't seem to remember. The baby rested on his bent knees, batting at the air, responding to the sound of his voice in soft coos and gargles.

"I haven't named him yet," she whispered.

"I never reckoned I'd have a boy," he mused, marveling at little fingers. "We've made a handsome one, haven't we?"

❀

The child was his healing. Hours turned into afternoons and days, blurred together in a haze of laughter and sun-warmed glass, open windows, and the thick smell of laudanum. The bassinet was moved beside the big four-poster bed, and sometimes, in hazy moments of wakefulness, she caught Asa, sitting upright, gazing at the child. Sometimes with a frown on his face, sometimes with a softness in his eyes. Over brandy and a smoke in the evenings, he wore thin the pages of William Gracey's diary.

"I *am* a merchant," he said thoughtfully, one evening. "Really. I can mutter over receipts at the bureau plat. No need for climbing sloops."

"Merchants are politicians," she reminded him. She sat, as she'd sat so many times, running a brush through her hair. It had been a good day–a successful day. With one white-knuckled hand clutching the walking stick, the other arm around her shoulders, he'd walked through the hall and into the dining room. Elijah cheered and whistled, and Cassandra stated he looked like Isiah Cooper. *A proper, musty, fusty, rusty, stinking old lawyer.* Yet, in the low light of golden flame and the softest haze of blackstrap rum, Martha's heart seized. Despite the quiet happiness weighing down her shoulders, there was a hole, obvious. The pain captured his every thought; she knew it. But something was wearily forgotten.

"Merchants are politicians," she repeated, setting the brush aside. She rose, turning to face him. The baby lay beside him, little arms thrown over his head, tiny fingers clutching a long lean one.

"Asa, look at me." Fighting a lump in her throat, she crossed and sat on the edge of the bed. It was so hard to speak when he looked like that. Like his soul was sitting in his eyes. She grabbed his hand, calloused from so many years of gripping ropes. Gathering splinters. Penning plans and folding paper. Fiercely, she pressed his palm to her lips, kissing it hard, over and over. Her tears ran down his arm.

"Darling." His voice came hoarse. "Christ, don't cry."

"Asa, this is all you need." She wiped her eyes fiercely. "Your hands–you belong in Philadelphia. That seat is yours!"

He frowned, dipping his head. "I've got plenty to do here. I want the sloops back in the ports by winter. Any fellow can take the seat, really, nothing but a farce. I belong at the docks."

"You said it yourself," she insisted. "The hounds of war are baying in the trees. You said that, the night I met you." She ran her fingers through his. "You didn't turn Boston on its head to watch it settle. This is wider than Boston now, you said that too. Continental plans. And when you've served your time, you have Wyeth-Standish. And the cottage–" She rose quickly, afraid if he kept watching her the tears wouldn't stop. "Cassie and Elijah should take the cottage! Wouldn't that be perfect? The babies could play in the fields–don't look at me like that, sir, you keep the grass too short here. Cassie would love the cottage. Think about it, I'm going for a brandy."

She turned on her heel and fled for the office. Hands trembling, she poured two glasses. The black powder had worked its way into the grain of the wood, as innocent as an ink stain to someone who didn't know. To someone whose fear wouldn't scream at the sight of everyday things. A skull-and-crossbones, grinning at her from an amber bottle. A pistol clipped to a man's hip. A length of rope; the gleam of candlelight on green silk. All of those little things were the reasons he must go.

Out of Boston. Out of Massachusetts.

Out into the world to live.

She put the brandy back and poured another. Then she slipped around the folding panel and met him with a smile.

"Well, Congressman Wyeth, what do you say?"

He watched her, but the wariness was gone. His eyes were lit, taking her in as if it were the first time he fell in love. "I think," he said quietly, "You are some kind of woman, Mrs. Wyeth."

"Thank you, sir."

"And Martha." He cleared his throat, gazing down at the baby. "I think I've rather thought of a name. D'you want to hear it?"

"Really?" Relief flooded her heart, leaving her weak. "What is it?"

"I think you'll like it." He smiled softly. She could've been mistaken, wildly searching for a break in the front, but she thought his eyes were wet. He bent over the tiny head, brushing his nose to fresh copper curls.

"A very good name," he said. "William."

❦

He would go to Philadelphia, as sure as September would come, and canvas would stretch over the bathing pool, and Cassandra would hang her herbs to dry upside down along the kitchen walls. Because September did come. Out on the Western lawn, the air potent with late summer heat, she laid out a blanket and let William bat his hands at the empty sky. Cassandra worked in the garden, turning up herbs by the roots to take to the cottage, and Elijah Standish lay in the grass, ankle over his knee, reading a book. On the steps of the terrace, Asa sat, brandy in one hand, cane across his lap.

His knee had bothered him all night and into the morning, tossing and turning in the empty room. She'd watched him in silence. The black box shadows of all the crates and packages set for Philadelphia towering in dusty light. What he would eat was served in bed, and when he did rise, it was to take up the cane and thump to the bureau plat to write. To write and drink and put back the laudanum, as if his blood were in that bottle. Now, he didn't want to take to the lawn; the unevenness of the earth bothered a shard of bone, prying further into tender muscle. He didn't speak as much, but she knew it. Instead, he was tired, (that was all), and his head was full of speeches and ideas that must be sorted before the chaise was packed.

She said nothing. Instead, she took off her shoes and buried her toes in the grass. Whether it was cruelty or not, she shook her hair loose, and turned. She raised her face to the sky, and turned again, snatching up a loose stick and tossing it for Ham. When he ran to fetch it, she chased him, laughing, even though her heart ached with sadness.

And she knew, though she didn't look back at the terrace, that Asa was watching, and hating that he could not run beside her.

Printed in Great Britain
by Amazon